'What are you?' it demanded.

'I am a man,' Kedryn said. 'I am Kedryn Caitin. I am the hef-Alador. And I would pass with my companion.'

'So,' the thing hissed slowly, 'you are the one. I know of you, and I know that you are awaited. There is one has greater claim on you than I – so I shall let you pass. You and yours. But I hunger, so you had best go swiftly.'

Kedryn nodded, unsure of the creature's meaning, but unwilling to risk questions or delay longer. If something waited for him, it would appear in time, and for now the imperative was to cross the lake and leave this thing behind. He turned to Wynett, seeing that she, too, held her talisman out towards the monster.

'Come,' he called. 'Come quickly.'

Wynett needed no further bidding and followed him as he leapt from stone to stone across the mere, not turning to see the leviathan sink slowly back beneath the surface, not seeing the smile that decorated its mouth . . .

THE SECOND BOOK OF THE KINGDOMS:
THE USURPER

Angus Wells

SPHERE BOOKS LIMITED

A Sphere Book

First published in Great Britain by Sphere Books Ltd 1989
Copyright © Angus Wells 1989

ISBN 0 7474 0262 0

Reproduced, printed and bound in Great Britain by
BPCC Hazell Books Ltd
Member of BPCC Ltd
Aylesbury, Bucks, England

Sphere Books Ltd
A Division of
Macdonald Group Ltd
66–73 Shoe Lane
London EC4P 4AB
A member of Maxwell Pergamon Publishing Corporation plc

For Nick Webb, who had faith.

Prologue

THE taste of defeat was bitter, the more so for being both unknown and unexpected. The might of the Horde he had raised was broken against the stones of the Lozin Gate, the creature he had lifted up to lead it slain by a near-beardless youth, the creature he had sent to slay that youth himself destroyed. He could not understand it, for his master had promised victory and the promise of the god Ashar was as sure as the fires of his birthing; yet it had come: the Kingdoms stood intact.

In bitterness he retreated into the forests, leaving the barbarians to their own devices, to sue for peace or flee, he no longer cared: the promises he had made them in the name of his master meant nothing, for they had failed him. And yet, even in the chagrin of his rout, he saw that a purpose still remained – the youth, the one called Kedryn Caitin, must be destroyed. He did not properly understand the significance of the young man, knowing only that Kedryn had somehow stood against the ensorcelled sword of Niloc Yarrum, had somehow escaped the berserk fury of Borsus, thus confirming the instinctive suspicion that he was, in some inexplicable way, a greater obstacle than all the armies mustered in defence of the Kingdoms. Whilst he still lived Ashar's purpose must stand in threat of thwarting, and whilst that menace should exist so must his own existence stand in danger. He must find a way to bring about his master's design.

He moved steadily deeper into the woodlands, traversing paths untrod by man, moving with a speed greater than human form might attain, the beasts of the forest scattering from his way as they would scatter from the encroaching breath of fire, sensing in him that which he was able to hide from man. Deeper and ever deeper he moved, until he came to that place where first he had known this life given him by his master, where Ashar's fires had first burned in the Beltrevan.

It was a silent, sere place devoid of birdsong or animal life. The trees were not grown back where his birthing fire had scorched the

1

ground, nor any undergrowth. Rather, it was a place that denied natural life, the earth still hidden beneath a thick layering of ash undisturbed by spoor or seeding, nubs of flame-scorched timber like rotted tooth stumps, the rock itself glass-smooth as cooled magma.

Ashar was here. He could feel the presence of the god, and he felt a chill touch of dread.

He shed the furs that had hid his frame from human sight and stood in unhuman nakedness, knowing what he must do yet fearing the wrath of his master, that fear stoking the hate he felt for Kedryn Caitin and the folk of the Kingdoms and the blue-robed followers of Ashar's enemy. He nursed the hate, letting it kindle until it burned fiercer than the dread, and then his thin lips began to move, forming words impossible for human tongue to utter. He stretched out his arms, blue flame flickering about his taloned fingers, sparking and crackling, filling the stifled air with the sharp tang of ozone. The droning of his chant grew louder, and as it did the cold fire formed in his mouth, wreathing about his mantis-features as his cratered eyes blazed red as smouldering coals. Louder and higher he chanted until the silence of the burned woodland was filled with the sound, his arms raised high, his head craned back, his frame rigid. Then, abruptly, he dropped his arms, screaming a single word: 'Ashar!'

The blue fire spurted from mouth and fingertips, converging, striking ground that exploded into flame, a great column of incandescence blazing red against a darkening sky, tongues of fire filling the blackened clearing, washing over him so that he shuddered with the ecstasy of the heat. Up and up rose the column until it seemed to link earth and heavens, seemed to burn down into the earth, a corridor to the netherworld from which he summoned his master.

And Ashar came, the knowledge of the god's presence sending him to his knees, head bowed lest he gaze upon that which even he feared to observe directly.

'You have failed me.'

The words were thunder and lightning that blasted the surrounding pines, setting them to swaying, flame dancing over their limbs.

He grovelled, prostrating himself, his mouth against the ash, his answer – his plea – spoken into the cinders.

'I did my best. I did as you bade me.'

'You say the fault is mine?'

'No, Master! Never yours; but . . .'

2

'*Excuses! Do you plead for your miserable existence? That which I have given, I can take away.*'

'I plead to continue your work, Master! Only that. I know these creatures better now. I know that Kyrie stands with them.'

'*Kyrie?*' The trees growing about the great blackened patch of forest burst into flame as the central column gouted outwards, fire roaring until it seemed all the Beltrevan must blaze. '*You affront me with that cursed name!*'

'Her power is great there.' He spoke quickly, spitting ash and hatred with each word, momentarily aware that the burning that was his god could so easily reach out to take him. 'And one there is who stands in our way – Kedryn Caitin. He withstood the magic of the sword and I believe he is favoured of her.'

'*Kedryn Caitin.*' The thunder rumbled a fraction softer, almost ruminative. '*You killed him?*'

'I tried, Master, but I could not. There is power in him; enough that three times he escaped me. He lives still.'

'*He should not,*' roared the god, '*and as he does, why should I not destroy you?*'

'I can serve you still, Master.' His clawed hands dug into the ashy soil, his malformed shape tensing in anticipation of dreadful anger. 'I know them better now and if you send me amongst them again I believe I may achieve your will – so long as I destroy this one.'

'*What is he?*' demanded Ashar, the fulguration of his voice lessened. '*A priest? Does she take men under her skirts now?*'

'A warrior. A youth. A princeling of Tamur, I believe; not a priest – she still calls women to her service. But she affords him her protection. He it was thwarted our purpose.'

'*Then he must be destroyed!*' Lightning stalked the ground about the prostrate figure. '*This time you must not fail me.*'

He drew deep, ashy breath as he recognised clemency and promised, 'No, Master. This time I shall not fail you.'

'*You have thought on this? You have a design?*'

'I have. I must go amongst them. Not the forest folk this time, but the people of the Kingdoms. Where might has failed us, subtlety may prevail. I shall seek to destroy from within, not overwhelm with swordmight but seduce.'

'*How so?*' Ashar demanded, the question a rolling peal of thunder.

'There are three kingdoms, Master,' came the answer, 'and a Lord to each. A king above them in the city they call Andurel; elected. Men are ambitious and Lords lust for kingship. Should their king die . . .'

3

'An ambitious man might be bent to my will.'

'Aye, Master. And were that man made king the youth Kedryn must obey his commands and thus fall into my hands.'

'If they know you, you are lost. I cannot protect you where that bitch holds sway.'

'I shall guise myself,' he promised, a little more confident now. 'They will not know me until it is too late. I shall bring down Kedryn Caitin and all the blue-robed whores. I swear it.'

Thunder rumbled and lightning flashed from the incandescent core of the fire, then Ashar said, *'Go, Taws, and fulfil that promise. Give me the Kingdoms.'*

He sensed the departure of the god, not daring to raise his head until the last rumblings of the thunder had long died, and then cautiously, his deep-set eyes hooded, furtive as he peered about. Flame still candled where he had created it, but now only as a fireball, no longer that column reaching into the nowhere of the otherworld. He rose, more confident now, and stalked to the centre of that flame, basking in it, renewing his strength and his hope in the aftermath of Ashar's presence.

Through the final waning of the light and all the hours of darkness he remained there, until the sun rose again, shedding brightness over the looming shadows of the deep timber. Then he gestured and the flame died. He clad himself again in the furs that hid his frame and went once more from that place, about Ashar's business.

In time, as he moved steadily southwards towards the Kingdoms, he encountered barbarians, scattered groups mostly, the first to flee the scene of battle, their bearded features sullen in defeat. He avoided them, unsure of the reception he might receive and unwilling to expend energy on defence, knowing that he would need all his strength for what lay ahead. Only when he had come close to the pass through the Lozins where the two forts stood did he reveal himself.

There was a solitary Caroc separated, he presumed, by dint of wounds from his tribesmen. The warrior limped, leaning heavily on the shaft of his broken spear, stained bandages about one leg, his beard blood-crusted from a savage cut across his cheek. Shield and axe were slung on his back and in his eyes was the disillusion of a belief gone down in ruin. Taws stepped from the shelter of the trees to confront him and the tribesman mouthed a curse, shaping his left hand in the three-fingered gesture of warding even as he levelled the broken spear.

4

'You know me,' Taws said, his voice soft as a serpent's hiss.
'Taws the sorcerer!' The Caroc spat the words like a curse. 'Taws the betrayer!' Where did you run, mage? Where were you when the *hef-Ulan* fell? When Balandir died? Where are your promises now, mage?'

'With Ashar my master,' Taws responded. 'Where ever they were.'
'Ashar has deserted us,' said the warrior bluntly. 'Now stand aside or test your magic against my blade.'

Taws' eyes burned red at this sally, glowing as might coals set in the pit of a furnace. He made a small gesture and the Caroc's spear shaft burst into flame, eliciting a cry of alarm from the man, who threw the burning wood from him and reached awkwardly for the axe shaft jutting above his right shoulder.

His hand froze upon the leather bindings as Taws' gaze transfixed him, and he stood, rooted in the moment, his lips slackening as the mage drew closer. Taws set narrow hands upon the brawny shoulders and stared deep into the warrior's eyes. 'What happened?' he demanded. 'After Niloc Yarrum fell and Ymrath died, what happened then?'

'Balandir led us,' murmured the Caroc, his voice dreamy, 'but the Horde was divided. The Drott and the Yath resented him and the Vistral went back to the forest with Ymrath's death. Tamur, Kesh and Ust-Galich came against us and they were too many, for we argued too long amongst ourselves. Had you been there to announce Balandir hef-Ulan we might have prevailed, but you were not and the armies of the Kingdoms rode out from High Fort to defeat us. Balandir was slain and we were lost. The Kingdoms offered peace and Vran of the Yath spoke for that. He persuaded the rest. We were allowed to remove our dead and return to the Beltrevan.'

Taws nodded. 'And now?'

'Now the Kingdoms celebrate their victory and rebuild their fort. I know no more than that.'

'It is enough,' Taws murmured.

And drew the warrior close, bending to drop his head, ash-white lips descending upon the man's as the ruby eyes sparked an unholy fire. Panic flared for an instant in the warrior's eyes, then faded as the orbs dulled and the limbs fell slack. Taws released his grip and the corpse slumped to the ground, drained of more than life. The mage sighed his satisfaction and commenced his southwards journey.

Within a matter of days he came in sight of High Fort. The walls stood jagged where the catapults of the Horde had battered the

5

stone and the rumble of the Idre was augmented by the hammers of stonemasons as they carved fresh blocks from the Lozin walls. The wreckage of the catapults was gone, though the memory of the Horde remained in the devastation of the timber and the scorched grass of a myriad cookfires. There were soldiers present, escorting the civilian masons, Tamurin archers and Galichian pikemen, patrols of mounted Keshi forcing the mage to hide as he awaited the opportunity he sought with growing impatience.

It came with the first snow of the encroaching winter. All day Taws had hidden within a circle of rocks close to the Beltrevan road, his furs drawn close about his angular frame as he awaited his opportunity. He watched the masons carve their blocks and manhandle them on to carts that rumbled ponderously towards the fort; the archers and pikemen huddle under winter cloaks, the bowmen holding their weapons close against them for fear the snow might slacken strings; the horsemen canter past on the treacherous surface. Dusk approached, deceptive behind the steady curtaining of snow. He saw the masons stow their tools and start back under the watchful eyes of the guards, and heard before he saw the clatter of a returning Keshi patrol.

The riders were swathed in snow-dusted black, each cape emblazoned with the horsehead emblem of their kingdom, sabres on their belts and lances upright in their hands. They appeared less concerned with the danger of barbarian treaty-breakers than with a swift return the warmth of High Fort, where food and a measure of *evshan* would stave off the growing chill. He did not know whether it was sheer good fortune or the will of his master, still strong here in the last reaches of the Beltrevan, that afforded him his chance, but when it came he took it with alacrity.

A shod hoof slipped on the churned roadway and a horse went down with a scream of alarm. The rider sprang nimbly from the saddle, tossing his lance to a companion as he urged his mount to its feet, then cursed as the animal raised a sprained foreleg. Taws could not yet understand the language of the Keshi cavalrymen, but the conversation explained itself as the troop moved off into the dusk, leaving their comrade to walk his horse in.

Taws came out from his hiding place then, the snow that clung to his furs rendering him near-invisible until he was almost on the Keshi. The horse snickered nervously and the man turned, a hand dropping to his sword hilt as he saw the tall, white-maned figure approaching. His mouth opened to shout a warning that failed to

6

materialise because Taws' hand fastened about his wrist and the mage's eyes burned redly into his, quelling the cry stillborn. The horse shrilled and tore free of the slack-fingered grip, running as best its injury allowed into the the shrouding snow. Taws loomed above the bow-legged rider, his rubescent gaze probing deep into the fear-filled eyes. For long moments he stood facing the man, then nodded, murmuring a name: 'Hattim Sethiyan.' Then, as he had done with the wounded Caroc, he stooped to kiss the Keshi, that awful caress draining the light from the man's eyes, the tension from his limbs, so that when the mage released him he crumpled slack to the ground, his body seeming deflated, emptied.

Taws licked his fleshless lips and bent to lift the man, raising the corpse as easily as he might a child. He strode across the roadway and through the rocks beyond to the bank of the Idre. The Keshi's body splashed as it struck the surface of the river, turned twice as the current caught it, and then was gone. Taws stood for a moment, staring at the water, then turned about and strode towards the fort, towards the Three Kingdoms.

The snow that had begun to mantle the forests of the Beltrevan had not yet found footing south of the Lozins, though winter sent chill feelers probing over the hills of Tamur and the northern plains of Kesh, frosting the grasslands and crusting pools with shining ice. To the west it remained a threat, the vast bowl formed by the sweep of the Lozin range and the Gadrizels protected by the encircling peaks. In time the wolf-weather would come, but as yet the fertile lands surrounding the sacred city of Estrevan remained untouched. The harvest was gathered in and thanks given to Kyrie for her bounty, the granaries of the city stocked against the isolation of the cold time, larders hung with cured meat and thick winter quilts brought out to air. The days still held a hint of mellow autumn, but the nights grew chill, and on this particular night a wind had got up, blowing out of the north to buffet the walls and tall towers of the city, prompting the inhabitants to draw shutters against its onslaught and light fires in their hearths.

At the centre of the city stood the halls of the Sisters of Kyrie, spreading from the single tower raised by the founders just as the buildings of the lay population had spread about that place of worship until the site chosen for its isolation had become a bustling community. The styles of the buildings were varied, for all who sought sanctuary in Estrevan were welcomed and the populace came from all of the Kingdoms, bringing their own architectural patterns to create a diffusion of fashions that somehow succeeded in blending together to form a homogenous whole.

The central tower was a plain column of bluish stone, set with windows and balconies, the apex flat and circled by a wall from which the Paramount Sister might look out over the city and the fertile lands beyond. At the topmost level of that tower a group of Sisters was gathered in a small chamber.

Thick candles set within columns of glass filled the room with mellow light. Shutters of dark wood were drawn over the windows, their gloss reflecting the gleam of the candles, contrasting pleasantly with the simplicity of the plain, rough-plastered walls. In one corner, a hearth of hewn stone held a crackling fire that from time to time sent flickering tongues of flame into the room as the wind blowing from the north gusted and turned to penetrate the chimney. The blue-robed women seated about the circular table at the room's centre ignored the sparking of the logs, their attention focused on the woman seated in a low-backed chair close to the blaze. She was a woman in her middle years, older than some of the listeners, younger than others, unremarkable in appearance save for the intensity of her eyes, which, like her voice, was compelling.

'You have all studied Alaria's Text,' she said, 'and you have all heard the news from the Lozin Gate. Now I would hear your thoughts.'

There was a pause, a hesitation marked by the soft rustling of gowns and an almost nervous clearing of throats, then an old woman, her kindly features lined, her hair silver, said, 'The Text is vague, Gerat, but I do not believe the danger is ended yet.'

'Surely it is,' a younger woman objected, 'and Alaria's prophecy fulfilled – Kedryn Caitin is of Tamur on his father's side and of the Blood on his mother's; he slew Niloc Yarrum to win the day for the Kingdoms; the Horde is defeated. Does that not fulfil the prophecy?'

'But Ashar's Messenger was not found, Porelle,' murmured the first speaker, 'and consequently the danger still exists.'

'The Horde is broken,' argued Porelle, 'the forest folk scattered. I think you fear shadows, Jara.'

Jara smiled fondly, shaking her head. 'I think my greater years endow me with greater patience, little Sister. As I read it, the Text tells us the Messenger must be destroyed, not merely defeated.'

'He will rise again,' announced the woman to Jara's left, opening

8

the thin, leather-bound book she held, 'Listen: *And that poison shall sour the fruit that it shall taste bitter on the tongue and ferment to bring forth pestilence.* What else can it mean?'

. 'Was the Horde not a pestilence, Lavia?' Porelle demanded.

'Indeed it was,' Lavia agreed, ducking a grey-streaked head, 'but the poison that formed it exists still.'

'Can we be sure of that?' asked the other. 'Our seekers find no trace of the Messenger and Darr's *mehdri* tell us the barbarians spoke of his disappearance. Perhaps his master called him back.'

'Perhaps,' said Lavia dubiously, 'but I do not think so. Save to foment some other design.'

'The Beltrevan is Ashar's domain,' offered a fresh speaker, the youngest there, 'and surely the defeat of the Horde must lessen his power. Kyrie bound him with the Lozin wall and without the Horde how can he broach that confinement?'

'He created the Messenger for that purpose,' said Lavia, 'and Ashar is not one to accept defeat easily.'

'There is a passage in the Text,' Jara said, 'a few lines after that talk of poisoned fruit . . . Lavia, your eyes are better than mine.'

'*Fire shall consume the tree*, is that the one?' Lavia asked, and when Jara nodded: '*Yet the roots that lay beneath shall remain and the ash of that burning shall cloud the vision of men that they see not what is, nor hear what shall be.* Shall I go on?'

'No, thank you.' Jara shook her head, 'I believe that makes Lavia's point, Reena – Ashar is, indeed, held beyond the Lozin wall. He cannot, himself, cross that barrier without the support of his worshippers, but that does not prevent him from sending his Messenger.' She paused as Lavia murmured agreement, then continued, 'I believe the roots to which Alaria referred are the many faces of Ashar, and the ash of the burning the defeat of the Horde, which even now prompts a false belief in safety.'

Reena looked to Porelle, who smiled and shrugged, saying, 'I do not think my belief is false, Jara. How could the Messenger prosper within the boundaries of the Kingdoms? Tamur, Kesh, Ust-Galich, all hold to Kyrie. Not even the Sandurkan follow Ashar. So what power might the Messenger wield outside his master's domain?'

'He needs only a foothold, and few are pure,' answered the older woman, 'From a tiny spark a fire may grow.'

'Do you say that Ashar might find worshippers within the Kingdoms?' Reena's plain features registered a mixture of disgust and shock. 'Surely not!'

'Not necessarily worshippers,' Jara responded evenly, 'but let us look beyond the immediacy of the deities; let us consider them as concepts.'

Reena appeared more shocked at this and Jara reached out to pat her hand reassuringly. 'I intend no blasphemy, Sister, but I am of less fundamental a bent than you. I mean that Ashar may not require conscious worship to work his fell designs, but a turn of mind suitable to his purpose. What, after all, does he represent?'

'Evil,' said Reena promptly. 'Lust; avarice.'

'Disorder, ambition, chaos,' added Porelle.

'Indeed,' murmured Jara, 'and are there not ambitious men in the Kingdoms? Does greed not exist there? Do some men not lust after power?'

'You suggest the Messenger may seek out such men?' asked Lavia, seeing Jara's point.

'I do,' confirmed the silver-haired woman. 'It is my belief the Messenger lives still, and that Ashar will send him south to suborn to his foul cause. That is my interpretation of the Text.'

'Who would accept him?' demanded Reena, outrage curling her somewhat fleshy lips.

'He would be recognised,' said Porelle, 'and slain.'

Jara bowed her head in partial acknowledgment. 'Perhaps,' she said to Porelle, 'though I am not certain. As a concept Ashar has many faces – might not his minion enjoy the same art of subterfuge? I have no doubt he can disguise himself to confuse the eyes of men, and his power may be such that if he foregoes the use of overt sorcery he may even deceive our Sisters. Most of those within the Kingdoms are, after all, possessed of practical talents. As for your doubt, Reena, I repeat that there are some who might be tempted by his promises.'

'We cannot overlook that possibility,' murmured Gerat. 'For the sake of the Kingdoms and our Lady we must not.'

Silence fell with the ending of the sentence, broken for a while only by the soft thud of wind-battered shutters and the crepitation of the fire. It seemed the wintry chill that gripped the plain surrounding Estrevan had entered the room. Reena shivered, folding her arms across her breast. Porelle stared at Jara as though unable to believe the older Sister's words. Lavia sighed, stroking the covers of the book she held as if seeking reassurance there. Gerat studied their faces, her own calm despite the unease that had grown since first Darr's messengers had brought her word. Finally she spoke, 'You are the finest scholars in the Sacred City – that is why I asked that each of you study Alaria's Text – and I had hoped we might finally unravel its complexities. But it appears that is not to be, so let me add my own thoughts.

'We know that Alaria was gifted with a vision sent by our Lady that we might prepare defences against Ashar. To that end the Paramount Sister Galina asked the acolyte Yrla to consider quitting her studies here and contemplate marriage. No more than that, for – as you know – it is not the way of the Lady to force decisions, but Yrla chose of her own free will and left Estrevan after studying the Text, which convinced her of the path she must take. She was wed to Bedyr Caitin of Tamur and their child, Kedryn, has proven to be the one Alaria foretold. *From western stone and river's core shall come that one who may oppose the fire.* As Porelle has pointed out, Kedryn Caitin *did* turn back the Horde when he slew Niloc Yarrum. Our Sister, Wynette, sent word with Darr's messengers that Kedryn was marked by Ashar's minion; that when Grania dispelled the glamour the Messenger brought against High Fort there was a joining of minds that would appear to have imbued Kedryn with a power I do not pretend to comprehend. Suffice it to say that the Lady blessed him, that he was able to defeat the leader of the Horde. And that a warrior, ensorcelled by the Messenger, came against Kedryn and blinded him before he was dispatched.

'I believe that Kedryn Caitin is the Chosen One foretold in the Text and that only he – though he may not know it – has the answer to the questions the Text raises.

'I side with Jara and Lavia in the interpretation of the Text. I believe that the Messenger lives still, and that Ashar will seek to send him against the Kingdoms again.

'His strength will be lessened south of the Lozin wall, but it will remain potent. How he will go about his master's work I do not know, but I believe we must warn our Sisters in the Kingdoms of this, and ourselves stand ready.

'I ask you to continue your studies of the Text, for in time Kedryn Caitin will journey here, seeking to regain his sight. I do not know if we shall able to restore vision to him, but I *am* convinced that he is the only one capable of ending Ashar's threat and I hope that we may furnish him with the answers he will doubtless seek.'

'*In darkness shall he see, though blindness swathe him.*' Lavia murmured, a finger tracing the line. 'I had wondered about that.'

'I do not understand it,' said Porelle, 'though I bow to the wisdom of the Paramount Sister.'

'Are we then agreed?' asked Gerat gently, looking from face to face. 'Our studies must continue whilst we await Kedryn's coming?'

'And warn our Sisters in the east,' nodded Jara.

'The mehdri will carry word,' Gerat promised. 'Sisters?'

'It is all we can do,' said Lavia.

'I am in accord,' Reena murmured.

'And I,' said Porelle, though a trifle dubiously.

'Thank you,' said Gerat. 'Now it is late and I have kept you from the dining hall long enough. Let me delay you no further.'

'Do you not join?' asked Reena. 'I should like to discuss those lines concerning his blindness.'

'In a little while,' promised Gerat with a gentle smile. 'For the moment I should like to be alone to think on everything you have said.'

Reena nodded and rose with the others, leaving the soft-lit room where the Paramount Sister sat, her features composed.

Only when she was alone did Gerat allow some measure of her own doubts to show. She stood, crossing to a carved oak door that opened on to a narrow spiral stairway winding steeply up to the roof of the tower. She shivered as she stepped out into the night and the wind struck her, sending her long hair in a streaming pennant behind her as she faced into it, setting her hands on the chilled stone of the surrounding wall to stare out across the rooftops of Estrevan. She dismissed the cold, instinctively adjusting her mind so that her body refused to recognise its bite, letting her gaze wander from the star-scattered panoply above to the kaleidoscope of twinkling lights that shone serene as grounded stars from the streets of the Sacred City.

If only, she thought, the Text were clearer. I have read it and re-read it, and I have studied every word Galina wrote, yet still I can only guess. If only I was sure. Can I guide properly when so much of my advice is based on surmise? Or is that what Kyrie intended? To advise without shaping our decisions for us. If so, I pray that what I do is right.

She sighed and turned from her contemplation of the City, returning to the warmth of the room, where she banked the fire before making her way to the dining hall and the questions she knew would await her there.

Chapter One

'ME? Why me? What do I know of such things?'

Kedryn's voice was tinged with alarm, and a hint of bitterness. Bedyr studied him, pain in his brown eyes as he saw the bandage that encircled his son's face, knowing that within the dark world the young man now inhabited fear must be a constant companion: so far neither the blue-robed Sister Hospitaller seated beside Kedryn nor those of King Darr's entourage had found a cure for his blindness, and in that, at least, Ashar's Messenger had won a victory. He glanced at Wynett, seeing his own pain reflected in her blue eyes, wondering if the latest potions with which the young Sister had steeped the bandage might prove effective, not sure whether to go on or leave Kedryn to his brooding. He frowned a question and Wynett ducked the wheaten glory of her hair in agreement, urging him to continue.

'Because you slew their leader,' he said gently, 'and it appears that only the man who defeated their *hef-Ulan* may be accepted as spokesman for the Kingdoms.'

'Spokesman!' Kedryn spat the word, his hands clenching into fists around the stem of the goblet he clutched as though he sought to crush the receptacle. 'I suppose I am good for little else.'

'There is much for which you are good,' Wynett said softly. 'Is this not an opportunity?'

'How so?' Kedryn's head turned as he spoke, as though the absence of vision imparted by the ensorcelled sword affected his hearing too. 'They will laugh at a blind man. And what can I say to them? I am – *was*,' he corrected bitterly, '– a warrior, not a diplomat.'

'You are the warrior who slew Niloc Yarrum,' Wynett responded, her voice even, devoid of hurtful pity, 'and they know that. They respect you for it, no matter the wounds you sustained, and they will listen to you. You have an opportunity to do much good.'

Kedryn grunted doubtfully and swung his sightless head in Bedyr's direction.

13

'How say you, father?'

'Wynett is right,' said the Lord of Tamur. 'We have a unique opportunity to forge a lasting peace with the forest folk, and I believe that chance hinges on you.'

'The prophecy again?' Kedryn murmured.

'Perhaps,' Bedyr nodded. 'At the very least, surely the Lady must look with favour on the one who brings peace betwixt the Kingdoms and the Beltrevan.'

'And shall there be another price to pay?' his son demanded. 'Shall I give up some other part of myself to secure another victory?'

Bedyr opened his mouth to speak, but Wynett raised a hand, urging him to silence. 'Look into your soul, Kedryn,' she advised. 'You will find the answers there.'

'I need an answer to this damnable affliction,' he retorted. 'Let the Lady restore my sight and I'll gladly serve her.'

'She will give you back your eyes,' Wynett promised with complete confidence, 'I have no doubt of that. Mayhap you must travel to Estrevan, but there *will* be a cure.'

Kedryn let go the goblet and raised his hands to his head, sinking fingers into long brown hair as he sighed, his mouth down-turned.

'Forgive me, Wynett; father. This cursed darkness renders me irritable. Let me think on it. Leave me alone for a while.'

'Very well.' Bedyr rose, tall and broad-shouldered, his sternly handsome features creased with a pity he knew his son would not welcome. In that, as in appearance, they were alike: Tamurin were proud; their suffering was done in silence, privately.

Wynett came with him as he quit the chamber, stepping out into the stone-flagged corridor that tunnelled through the depths of High Fort, sighing as the door closed.

'There will be a cure,' she said fiercely. 'There must be. I cannot believe the Lady intends him to remain blind.'

Bedyr studied her lovely face, hearing in her voice more than he thought she was prepared to acknowledge. He had watched them since the fighting ended with growing concern, for he could see his son falling in love with the youthful Sister; and see in Wynett's responses a reciprocated affection that she could not admit for her vows of celibacy. It was more than a dependancy on the Sister, even though her ministrations had inevitably thrown them closer together than would have been possible had Kedryn soldierly duties to attend; and on Wynett's part he could see in her eyes, hear in her voice, a burgeoning feeling that must eventually conflict with her promises to the Sisterhood. She was a dedicated hospitaller, sworn since she had chosen to forego her rank as King Darr's daughter to the way of the Lady; yet to maintain that promise she must remain celibate, or lose her healing talent. He was uncertain how it all might end, and afraid that his son might suffer a hurt as great as blindness in result.

'Once matters here are settled he must go to Estrevan,' he said, not voicing the certainty that Kedryn would want her to accompany him.

'Aye,' Wynett nodded. 'In Estrevan they must surely find a cure.'

'I pray so,' Bedyr murmured.

While they spoke Kedryn sat in silence and darkness, fighting the fear that was never far from the surface. Save, perhaps, when Wynett was with him and he could feel her hands in his or smell the sun-scent of her hair. He would not admit it to anyone, but it was always there like some lurking beast prowling about the edges of his consciousness, seeking to rend his mind and drive it into the escape of madness. He hardly dared admit it to himself, for to do so would be to acknowledge that he was blind forever, and so he forced himself to cope as best he could. To do as much as he was able alone, without assistance. But this – how could he face the warlords of the defeated Horde and argue terms? A blind man?

'Lady,' he moaned, 'how much more do you ask of me?'

He stretched out a hand until he found the table beside him, then spidered his fingers across the smoothly polished surface until they touched the wine jug. Lifting it carefully, he filled his goblet, cursing as the beverage overflowed, wetting his hand. He brought the vintage to his lips and drank, and as he did so a random thought flitted across his mind. Sister Grania had enjoyed this wine and Grania had given her life to the defeating of Ashar. She had used her power to speed the *Vashti* north up to the Idre and then, even though she knew that disruption of the natural order had weakened her greatly, she had pitted herself against the glamour of the Messenger. And died as the price of victory. She had done that unquestioningly, and in the moment of her dying he had heard her voice speak inside his head. Now it seemed she spoke again, not in words he might transcribe or repeat, but in emotions, in certainties, and he knew suddenly what he must do.

He raised the goblet in a toast and set it aside, his leather breeks rustling as he rose and walked warily across the room, halting when his outthrust hands touched the cool stone of the wall. He moved sideways until he found the door. Opened it and stepped into the corridor.

'Prince Kedryn!'

The guard stationed there came close, a hand cupping Kedryn's elbow.

'Take me to my father,' he commanded, and allowed the man to lead him slowly along the echoing corridor, once again doing his best to memorise the route.

Bedyr was found in the chamber Rycol, Chatelain of High Fort, had set aside for the planning of strategy. It was a wide, low-ceilinged room, heated against the mounting chill by a great hearth, the fire there augmenting the flambeaux that burned along the walls. Ancient weapons decorated the stones and at the centre was a long, oaken table surrounded by high-backed chairs of carved, dark wood. King Darr sat at the head, his pale, thinning hair bound by a simple coronet, his kindly features lined with sympathy as Kedryn entered. To his left, the shield position a mark of deference to his status as commander of the fort, sat the hawk-faced Rycol, to his right, Bedyr. Jarl, Lord of Kesh, occupied the seat to Bedyr's right, his oiled black hair and hooked nose a contrast to the softly-handsome features of the golden-haired Lord of Ust-Galich, Hattim Sethiyan, who faced him across the table. It was Jarl who rose bow-legged to drag back a seat and murmer, 'Here, Kedryn, at my side.'

'Thank you, my Lord,' Kedryn responded, easing himself down. 'Are all assembled?'

'We are,' confirmed the king, 'and we thank you for your presence, Prince of Tamur.'

'Brannoc?' Kedryn asked. 'Is he here?'

'The outlaw? What need have we of him?' demanded Hattim.

Kedryn held his temper in check with some difficulty as he heard the insolence in the Galichian's voice. There was no love lost between them since Kedryn had defeated Hattim in the duel that had forced the ruler of the southernmost kingdom to commit to the expedition against the Horde, and whilst he was prepared to forget the affair, Hattim was ever mindful of his embarrassment.

'He knows the forest folk better than any present,' Kedryn said.

'And proved himself a most valuable ally in the siege,' added Rycol, his own initial animosity towards the halfbreed wolfshead long forgotten.

'Send for him,' Darr ordered the soldier who had escorted Kedryn.

'Knowing the forest folk seems to me of little moment,' Hattim

16

grunted, his tone piqued. 'We know we have beaten them. What further knowledge do we require?'

'If I am to discuss peace terms with them, my Lord, I must understand them,' Kedryn answered evenly.

'Discuss? Peace terms?' Hattim laughed. 'We are the victors – we dictate and they accede. Or we ride into the Beltrevan and wipe them out.'

'To what end?' asked Kedryn, carefully modulating his tone. 'We should lose men in such a venture and have no hope of destroying them all. That way would build nothing but resentment that would fester until some new chieftain should rise to form the Confederation afresh. Sooner than commit the Kingdoms to endless war, I would argue for peace.'

'There speaks the voice of reason,' King Darr remarked admiringly.

'Will they listen?' asked Jarl, his own voice dubious.

'Brannoc can best advise us on that,' Kedryn pointed out.

'Enough lives have been lost already,' said Bedyr. 'If Kedryn sees a way to bring a lasting peace, I say we listen.'

'Tamur has two voices, the one echoing the other.' Rancour put an edge to Hattim's words. 'I say we strike while we have our full force in the one place and end the threat of the Beltrevan forever.'

'How long do you think such a campaign might last, Hattim?' Bedyr demanded. 'Corwyn built the forts to hold the woodlanders out because that was the only way he saw to end the conflict. We have seen the danger of that bottling – had Kedryn not slain the hef-Ulan the Horde would likely have overrun us. If we go into the Beltrevan we can count on years of warfare. And I, for one, would like to see my home again: I say we listen to my son's proposals.'

'Our Lord of Tamur speaks with reason,' agreed Darr. 'I would not see the Kingdoms in jeopardy, but I would mightily like to see Andurel again.'

Hattim snorted, but before he was able to bring forth a fresh argument Jarl said, 'For all Lord Rycol's hospitality I cannot say I enjoy these northern climes, and the horses of Kesh will soon stand in need of winter forage. I am not sure we *can* sustain a prolonged campaign in the Beltrevan.'

'Winters are harsh here,' murmured Rycol, 'and long. If Prince Kedryn has a way to bring about some acceptable and binding peace, I say we hear him out.'

'That has my vote,' nodded Jarl. 'Providing the terms *are* binding.'

17

'It would appear I am outvoted,' snapped Hattim. 'Very well, let us listen to what the Prince of Tamur has to say. Perhaps he sees something here that escapes my vision.'

Bedyr's face grew bleak at the deliberate emphasis the Lord of Ust-Galich set on those references to sight and his hand dropped to the hilt of the long-bladed Tamurin dirk sheathed on his belt. Kedryn felt a flash of anger that he stilled, confident in the correctitude of his plan and, since that moment of insight, strangely calm. It was as though Hattim's provocation could touch him only momentarily, the Galichian's spiteful intent too petty to consider.

'An unworthy sally,' Darr said, his voice cold with reproach. 'Kedryn has served us too well for that.'

'Forgive me,' Hattim murmured with transparent insincerity, 'Prince Kedryn's eloquence led me to overlook his affliction.'

'I may find myself unable to overlook yours,' Bedyr warned, menace in his voice.

Hattim glowered at the Tamurin, then affected a smile, shrugging as he said, 'I ask the forgiveness of both the Lord and Prince of Tamur. I will henceforth watch my tongue.'

'Do so,' Bedyr snapped.

Kedryn could not see the dismissive gesture the Lord of Ust-Galich made, but he heard the snort that accompanied it and knew that Hattim remained an enemy. It was unimportant: the ruler of the southern kingdom was outnumbered by those willing to listen to his suggestions, and almost certainly as anxious to return to his homeland as the others. His bellicose objections were at variance with his original unwillingness to act in concert with his peers and based, Kedryn was certain, on nothing more than a desire to oppose any measures suggested by Tamur. If he could convince these lords – and the barbarian chieftains – of the sense of his scheme, then Hattim would doubtless fall into agreement. He leant back in his chair, listening to the sputtering of the fire and the whistle of the wind that blew down the long canyon of the Idre, aware that the others waited on him to speak, to outline his suggestions, but unwilling to voice them until Brannoc was present and able to advise him of the woodlanders' likely reactions.

How long a time passed he found it difficult to assess, for time elongated in his dark world. The absence of visual stimuli robbed him of the small diversions that occupied so much of a sighted man's perceptions. He could hear the wind, but only guess at the aspect of the sky. He could not see the glass he knew filled the embrasures of the chamber, but through it he could hear the masons working on the walls, though not study their progress. His world had become largely internalised, and the spaces of his mind were staggeringly vast. He heard Jarl shift beside him, the Keshi's robe – black, he guessed, and marked with the horsehead of the plains kingdom – rustling. He could hear fingers drumming softly on the tabletop, knowing that was Hattim from the clinking of the bracelets the Galichian favoured. The distinctive creak of leather came from his father or Rycol, he could not be sure which.

Then he heard the door swing open and felt cool air brush his cheek. Boots padded on flagstones and Brannoc's voice said, 'My Lords, Kedryn, how goes it?'

'Well enough, friend,' he answered, smiling as Brannoc's hand settled firm on his shoulder, wondering how Hattim took the appearance of the one-time outlaw.

Brannoc might easily pass for a woodlander, being of mixed parentage, of which one half was forest-born. He was dark as any Caroc, with hair black as a Keshi's, usually worn in braids that he decorated barbarically with shells and feathers. He favoured motley leather – Kedryn could smell it as Brannoc took a seat beside him – and there would be two daggers on his person even here amongst friends, one openly displayed at his waist, the other strapped to his left forearm. He had won the respect of most in the room, but Hattim, to judge by the grunt Kedryn heard, took it ill that he must bow to the superior knowledge of a man he considered distinctly inferio..

King Darr said, 'Brannoc, Prince Kedryn has a notion he may effect a lasting peace betwixt Kingdoms and Beltrevan and desires your advice concerning the forest folk.'

'He shall have it,' promised Brannoc, his tone suggesting he was quite undaunted by the illustrious company. 'Ask away, Kedryn.'

'My father tells me the woodlanders will speak only with me.' Kedryn said. 'Why? Surely the king must represent the Three Kingdoms in any parley.'

'Normally – if such a term applies in these circumstances – they would treat with Darr,' Brannoc answered. 'But you slew Niloc Yarrum, hef-Ulan of the Horde, and that puts you in a unique position. You must understand the nature of the forest folk, my Lords. They do not customarily act in unity: each tribe has its own territory, which is considered inviolate. They fight amongst themselves for hunting grounds, slaves, booty. Consequently they seldom pose any real threat to the Kingdoms, being far too occupied with their own internal struggling. But Niloc Yarrum – like Drul before him – overcame those differences to band all the tribes in the Confederation, to raise the Horde.'

'The Messenger,' interposed Darr, 'did he not have something to do with that?'

'Indeed,' Brannoc confirmed. 'Ashar's minion raised Niloc Yarrum to become hef-Ulan through sorcery. I have spoken with Drott prisoners and they all tell the same story – how the Messenger came amongst them and bestowed power on Yarrum. That is the exact reason Kedryn is now so important to them – by defeating Yarrum he also defeated the Messenger. He stood against Ashar's elected and prevailed where no other could. Were he of the forest, they would proclaim *him* hef-Ulan and he could command them by swordright. Because he is of the Kingdoms, however, they find themselves in a predicament. They cannot accept Kedryn as their overlord, but they view him as their conqueror. Perhaps we should say he is, to them, the champion of the Kingdoms.'

'And so he speaks on our behalf,' suggested Darr.

'You have it,' agreed Brannoc with cheerful disrespect. 'They know the terms must come from you, but they will only hear them spoken by Kedryn.'

'Why speak terms at all?' asked Hattim. 'Will they not disperse now? Scatter back to their barbaric ways?'

'Mayhap,' Brannoc allowed, 'but mayhap not. Niloc Yarrum was Ulan of the Drott and his death has left that tribe leaderless for the moment. Likewise, Balandir of the Caroc and Ymrath of the Vistral died, and there are ambitious men in all three tribes. Vran of the Yath is the most senior Ulan now, and he has a taste for power. The Messenger has disappeared, but the memory of the Horde remains and some might well seek to raise it again whilst the tribes are still congregated.

'If Kedryn has a way to diffuse that situation, it will likely save you a long and bloody campaign should Vran or any of the erstwhile ulans succeed in uniting the remnants of the Horde.'

'We withstood the siege,' said Rycol, 'and repairs are underway, but High Fort was sore hurt by the conflict. Should a determined attack be mounted now, I cannot be sure my walls will stand.'

'We have all our armies here,' said Hattim. 'Sufficient men to trounce them soundly.'

20

'Sufficient to withstand a siege, perhaps,' said Brannoc. 'But a winter campaign in the Beltrevan?'

'The forests are no cavalry field,' said Jarl. 'The Beltrevan in winter is no place for my horses.'

'We can wait for spring,' said Hattim.

'We can end it now,' said Kedryn.

'I am loath to hold the armies here throughout the winter,' Darr murmured. 'Already much of our harvest has been lost, and men will be needed for the spring planting.'

'What do you propose?' Bedyr asked.

Kedryn cocked his head in Brannoc's direction and said, 'What might guarantee their dispersal, Brannoc? How might we persuade them of our desire for peace – and guarantee their agreement?'

There was a pause as Brannoc thought, then he said, 'It is customary for each tribe to bury its dead within the boundaries of its own territory. One reason they are prepared to parley is to arrange that. If they were allowed to gather up their dead they might well disperse.

'Then, as the conqueror of Niloc Yarrum, you are in a position to demand binding promises from the ulans.

'Further, if the chieftains see at first hand the full might of the Kingdoms, they might think twice about reneging.'

'They outnumber us,' said Rycol. 'Can we impress them with a display of strength?'

'Whilst the taste of defeat is fresh, yes,' answered Brannoc. 'The forest folk are not accustomed to such organised warfare as the Kingdoms mount.'

'Then that is it,' Kedryn announced before any objections might be raised. 'I must extract from each chieftain the promise that he will lead his tribe back into the forests with their dead. We must summon them to a parley where they may see all our forces and give them our terms. How say you, my Lords?'

'I say we cannot trust them,' snapped Hattim. 'If we are to discuss terms, let us take hostages.'

'Surely that would provide further reason for resentment,' Kedryn suggested.

'Save for Vran, and Darien of the Grymard, you would find it difficult to select hostages,' said Brannoc. 'They have been too busy fighting us to battle amongst themselves for the ulans' torques.'

Kedryn heard Darr laugh then. 'It appears that such resounding victory leaves us in a quandary, my Lord Hattim,' said the king. 'The

21

Drott and Caroc are by far the greatest of the tribes, and if we cannot secure hostages from them, what good to take but two ulans?'

It successfully defused the Galichian's argument, and Kedryn knew that Darr stood with him. He waited for Jarl and Bedyr to respond.

'I do not see that we have anything to lose,' he heard his father say, 'save a long and bloody campaign.'

'Can we trust their word?' asked Jarl.

'Given to Kedryn,' Brannoc confirmed. 'It would be tantamount to swearing allegiance to the hef-Ulan.'

'But who would give it?' Hattim asked, his voice petulant. 'You say only Vran and Darien remain.'

'As ulans,' came the answer. 'There are still ala-Ulans who will vie for the torques. Extract a promise from each and they are bound.'

'Does it not make sense?' Kedryn demanded. 'We allow them to return to the Beltrevan with their dead, without harassment. In return, they undertake to mount no further attacks on either fort.' He paused, knowledge coming unbidden to his mind, the words forming as though of their own accord. 'And there is a further consideration – it was Ashar's minion fuelled this conflict. Should the forest folk return in hatred and resentment Ashar's power must surely be increased. Let them return in peace assured of our good will, and that power must be weakened.'

'It has my support,' said Bedyr, respect in his voice.

'And mine,' added Rycol.

'Aye,' Jarl said slowly, 'it makes sense. You carry a wise head, Kedryn.'

'My Lord of Ust-Galich?' Darr prompted. 'How say you?'

Hattim paused before speaking, then: 'It appears I am outnumbered, so what matter what I say? However – aye, I am in accord.'

'And I,' Darr announced. 'I had thought to see a costly campaign and I am delighted the Prince of Tamur has succeeded in showing us a way to avoid such bloodshed. I thank you, Kedryn.'

Kedryn bowed his head in acknowledgement, surprised at himself. He had entered the chamber with little more than the conviction that it was better to end the conflict than press the initial victory, and only a vague idea of how he might achieve that end. Yet when he had begun to speak he had felt himself possessed of a calm certainty that what he did was right, not only for the sake of the men whose lives would be lost in the fighting, but also for the unity of the Kingdoms, and that had gifted him with eloquence and determination. He had grown, he thought, from the battle-hungry youth who had first gone warlike into the forests in search of glory. Or perhaps that joining of minds against the Messenger's darkness had endowed him with some part of Grania's intellect, for it had been a talent of hers to predicate futures from the facts of the present and the assurance he felt was unfamiliar.

'Let us then send word,' he heard Darr say, 'and prepare for the meeting. Will you each ready your men, my Lords? And Brannoc – perhaps you are best suited to carry our suggestions to the forest folk.'

There was a murmur of agreement and a scraping of chairs as they rose. Kedryn came to his feet, aware of Brannoc standing close by, then felt a hand upon his shoulder as his father asked, 'Shall I escort you to your chamber?'

'I would speak with Wynett,' he answered.

'She tends the wounded,' Bedyr said. 'Will you await her in the garden?'

Kedryn nodded and allowed his father to steer him from the room, listening to Bedyr's murmured warnings as they descended stairs and made their way through the yards of High Fort to the small garden surrounded by the walls of the hospital. Bedyr settled a cloak about his shoulders and left him there, promising to return once he had informed the Tamurin of the anticipated parley.

Kedryn sat, feeling a breeze rustle his shoulder-length hair, chill with the first taste of winter. He could smell the dampness of the Idre on the draught and wondered how long it would be before snow fell. Over the pounding of the masons' hammers and the muted sounds of soldiery going about their duties he heard birds singing and he smelled the soil where flower beds and herb gardens had been turned against the advent of the cold months. Absence of sight appeared to be heightening his sense of smell and his powers of hearing and he concentrated on identifying the stimuli that would have gone unremarked had he had been able to see. He knew that Wynett approached from the soft sound of her footfalls and the scent of her as she drew close, turning to greet her before she spoke.

'Bedyr told me of your proposal,' she said, admiration in her voice, 'and I am glad.'

Kedryn reached out unthinking and found her hands, holding them in both of his as she settled herself beside him.

'I remembered what Grania had done,' he said slowly, not sure how to put it, 'and that persuaded me to speak. It was as though she communicated with me in some way. Does that sound foolish? I cannot explain it better.'

He felt Wynett's grip tighten and sensed excitement even though her response was measured.

'It does not sound foolish, but tell me more – tell me exactly how you felt the communication.'

He shrugged, pursing his lips as he sought the inadequate words that might describe an essentially emotional experience.

'I remembered how she gave her life, and when I did it seemed so . . . petty of me to sit bemoaning my fate. Then it came to me that I should seek a treaty of some kind. Persuade the Kingdoms to deal gently with the woodlanders, for I knew – though I cannot say how – that that was the best way for all of us. It was not a thing of words: I did not hear her voice, but it seemed that perhaps some part of her was with me.'

'It may be,' Wynett said gently. 'Perhaps a part of her remained with you after the joining.'

'But you were part of that,' he frowned, 'and you have not said anything.'

'I have not felt it,' she answered. 'At least, not in the same way. Grania was a Sister, and through that vocation she shared her being with me, so perhaps I cannot notice what has always been with me. For you it would be different because you have never known the ways of Estrevan. We are attuned to one another through our training and our talents, and we accept that just as you accept the weight of a sword on your belt without noticing it hangs there.'

'Why do I not feel you in the same way?' he demanded.

He could not see the blush that suffused Wynett's cheeks then, or the way her blue eyes studied his face, but he heard the slight intake of her breath and felt the tension in her fingers.

'We . . .' she paused. 'Our relationship is different, Kedryn. Grania's feelings for you were . . . those of an elder Sister. Her concern was solely for the Kingdoms, for the general good. Mine . . .'

She broke off and he heard the rustle of her hair as she shook her head, the scent of it intoxicating to his nostrils. She moved to withdraw her hands but he tightened his grip, refusing to release her.

'Yours are?' he pressed.

'I nursed you back to health when you were wounded.' He thought it sounded like an excuse. 'That creates a bond.'

'You have nursed others,' he said, cursing the blindness that denied him sight of her face; knowing at the same time that were he not blind she would likely not be saying these things.

'But not like you,' she said quickly. 'There is a difference to you. Are you not the one the Text foretold?'

'It is more than that,' he insisted.

'Kedryn, I am a Sister. I am vowed to celibacy.'

Her voice was a curious mixture of determination and something he dared to hope was regret. He said, 'And if you were not?'

'Then it would be different. But I *am* of Estrevan.'

'My mother was of Estrevan, yet she chose to wed my father.'

'The Text foretold it. Besides, Yrla had not taken her final vows.'

'Is there no dispensation?'

Wynett sighed and said, 'Of course. But I do not wish to forsake my vows.'

Kedryn was tempted then to open his heart, to reveal the conviction that had been growing within and beg her to relinquish her promises to the Sorority, but he was afraid of her reaction, afraid that so open a declaration might drive her from him. Besides, he was blind and a poor match for any woman. So he remained silent.

'Do you understand?' she asked him, her voice gentle.

'Aye,' he murmured.

'Thank you.'

He felt her lean close, her breath sweet, her lips soft as they brushed his cheek. Then, as he turned his head, she pulled back, extricating her hands, setting an indefinable distance between them. He straightened his back, leaning against the cool, rough stone of the wall behind.

'After,' he said, 'When the parley is done, I will travel to Estrevan.'

'And my Sisters there will find a way to regain your sight,' she promised.

'Will you accompany me?'

The question seemed to take her by surprise. 'I do not think . . . I have duties here,' she said. 'I have done all I can.'

'Consider it,' he urged. 'It would be a great comfort to me. And I am, after all,' this with exaggerated melancholy, 'a poor, blind warrior in great need of Sisterly care.'

Wynett laughed at that, and he was pleased to have lightened the moment for her, though nonetheless determined to persuade her. Or, at least, continue trying. She cared for him, he knew; that was obvious from her kiss, from the time she spent with him, and he felt certain that were she not of the Sisterhood his advances would be welcomed. But, as she had reminded him, she was dedicated to Kyrie's service and he must therefore tread a most delicate path. Were he to press his suit with the full weight of the emotion he could feel growing within him he was afraid he might scare her into refusing all contact, and he dreaded that. Frustrating as it was to find himself so close to the woman he had come to desire above all others whilst not daring to touch her or speak out, to have no contact at all would be infinitely worse. He lived in hope that something might occur to change the situation, forcing himself meanwhile to rest content with what he had.

'I shall consider it,' she promised, 'and attend my duties now. Come, let me see what effect my latest efforts have had.'

He heard her rise and climbed to his feet, grateful for the hand she gave him as he paced the flagged pathway of the little garden into the hospital.

There she took him to the chamber where the artifacts of her talent were stored, seating him as she prepared to remove the bandage from his damaged eyes. He sat listening to the sounds of her preparations, sniffing the medicinal odours of the place until she murmured a warning and he felt her closeness. Her fingers were cool as they touched his temples and he felt a pressure as she slid a blade beneath the cloth that encircled his head. There was the faint rasping sound of steel against silk and he felt his eyelids lift automatically. His eyes were opened but saw nothing save the darkness that had clouded them since the ensorcelled blade struck him. He blinked, but it made no difference.

'What do you see?' she asked.

'Nothing,' he replied as he felt the heat of the candle she raised before his face. 'I can feel the flame. I see only blackness.'

Wynett made a little tutting noise and the heat went away from his face.

'Tilt your head,' she ordered, 'and keep your eyes open.'

He did as she bade him and felt her hand smooth and soft upon his cheek, then the moist impact of liquid. He fought the impulse to blink, feeling the drops she applied filling his lids to spill over on to his cheeks, like tears. Both of Wynett's hands held his head back, resting against his temples and cheeks, her thumbs gently massaging the area directly behind his eyes.

He gasped, unable to resist jerking his head forwards as the blurred image of a window imposed itself on the darkness. There was an absence of colour to the image, grey where he knew white

26

plaster stood, the glass that filled the embrasure like winter ice, beyond it a darker greyness, as though he peered into a mist.

'What is it?' she demanded, excitement in her voice, moving from behind him.

As she moved, as the contact with her hands ceased, the image abruptly disappeared and he sighed.

'I thought I saw the window.' He shook his head, laughing bitterly. 'But perhaps I looked at a memory.'

'Describe it,' she urged.

He did so and she said, 'The sky *is* dark. Mayhap your sight returns.'

Kedryn grunted, cynical, afraid to permit himself too much hope even as he wished with a fervency so fierce it was almost painful that she was right.

'Try again,' Wynett suggested.

He did and there was nothing.

'Wait,' she said, and moved behind him again, setting her hands to his temples once more, commencing the gentle massage, 'Is there anything now?'

He stared into the darkness, willing it to fade, constructing the image of the window in his mind. He saw it clearly in his imagination, but not with his eyes and after a while he sighed and said, 'There is nothing.'

'There is hope,' Wynett countered.

'Blind hope,' he responded.

'You must not give up.' She removed her hands and he heard her bustling about the room. 'It may be these preparations of mine are taking effect.'

He shrugged, his spirits sinking again in the aftermath of that moment of optimism, gloom overcoming him. He sat silently as she settled pads of cotton over his eyes, the unguent in which they were soaked tingling, then wound a fresh bandage about his head, smoothing his hair into place.

'We shall try again,' she promised. 'And we shall continue trying until your sight is restored.'

Kedryn nodded dolefully, consoling himself with the thought that he would, at least, be guaranteed her company.

'You must not give up hope,' she repeated. 'If I cannot effect a cure, then Estrevan will find a way. You *must* believe that.'

He nodded again, though he wondered how long he must wait, resenting his helplessness, knowing that if Estrevan should prove

27

his only hope he faced a journey of several months duration, and that only after matters here were settled. The calm that had filled him was departed now and only his will kept him from shouting his anguish. He felt close to weeping for all of Wynett's assurances, and fought the impulse to reach for her, seeking comfort in her closeness, to hold her and sob out his frustration.

But he was Tamurin so he nodded and said, 'Aye.'

Wynett heard the pain in his stoic reply and struggled with her own impulse to comfort him. There was a great temptation to cross the small distance that separated them and put her arms about his shoulders, draw his head to her bosom and murmur words of comfort. For an instant she wondered what it would feel like to stand inside his embrace, his lean body hard against hers, to give herself up to the caresses she knew he would welcome. Then she forced such thoughts away, reminding herself of her vows, that she was of Estrevan and sworn to the service of Kyrie, her talents needed – and lost should she forego the celibacy that was their price. She was grateful for Bedyr's entrance.

The Lord of Tamur stood in the doorway with a question in his eyes. He looked the warrior his son might now never be, clad in leathern breeks and high ridings boots, a simple jerkin with the clenched fist of his kingdom emblazoned on the left breast laced loose over a plain shirt. A longsword hung at his side, matched by the long dirk his people favoured on his right hip. His thick brown hair was gathered off his face by a strand of leather, and in his physique and stance and gravely handsome features, Wynett saw what his son would one day become. Unless the glamour of the Messenger prevailed and Kedryn remained blind, for Bedyr's eyes were clear and hazel; and greatly troubled.

'Is there progress?' he asked.

Before Wynett could reply, Kedryn said. 'No,' and rose to his feet, moving awkwardly around the chair to grope his way to the door. He halted as he encountered Bedyr's outthrust hand, turning slightly to bow and say, 'I thank you, Sister Wynett. Please forgive my surliness.'

There were tears in Wynett's eyes as she watched Bedyr lead him away. No one could see the tears that oozed from Kedryn's because they were hidden by his bandage.

Bedyr sensed his son's mood and forewent the questions he wanted to ask, explaining instead that he had passed word to Tepshen Lahl to prepare the Tamurin army for the parley, while

Brannoc was even now leaving the fortress to bring word to the barbarian chieftains.

'Your suggestions showed sound judgement,' he complimented as they crossed a courtyard, measuring his paces to Kedryn's less confident steps. 'You surprised us all, I think.'

'I was guided,' Kedryn murmured.

'Guided?' Bedyr glanced at his son. 'By what?'

'I am not sure.' Kedryn reiterated what he had told Wynett. 'It seemed the words came to me.'

Bedyr grunted thoughtfully. 'Your mother would understand it better than I, but did Wynett not have some explanation?'

'She did,' said Kedryn, 'She suggested that some part of Grania lives on in me. So I embarrassed her by asking why we do not share the same rapport.'

'She is a Sister,' Bedyr said, understanding his son; sharing his pain. 'Do you know what the Sandurkan call them?'

'No.' Kedryn cursed as he stumbled against an uneven flagstone, clutching at his father's shoulder for support.

'Untouchables,' said Bedyr. 'They have their own gods, but they respect the work the Sisters do and consequently leave them alone.'

'Do you give me a lesson?' Kedryn asked, mouth curving in a bitter smile.

'Do you need a lesson?' countered Bedyr.

'I need my sight!' Kedryn could not prevent the anger that tainted his response.

'And patience until it returns,' his father advised.

'For a moment,' Kedryn broke off as Bedyr warned him of a step, and they entered the corridor that led to the great hall, 'I thought I could see. Wynett put something in my eyes and massaged my temples and I thought I saw the window of her chamber. But it passed and I suppose it was merely my imagination.'

'Was that Wynett's opinion?' asked Bedyr.

'She was not sure. She hopes her ministrations have an effect, but she did not see what I saw. Or imagined I saw.'

'Mayhap they do. You must not give up hope.'

Kedryn snorted. 'So everyone tells me.'

'Or become bitter,' Bedyr admonished gently. 'Even if Wynett is unable to restore your sight, once our business here is done we shall travel to Estrevan. Meanwhile, however, you are proving a most effective diplomat.'

'I had thought to be a warrior,' Kedryn grunted, pausing as a door was opened, the guard there murmuring a respectful greeting that he answered with a curt nod.

'You have proven yourself in battle,' Bedyr told him, 'and as you will some day be Lord of Tamur, a measure of diplomacy is no bad thing to have.'

'A blind Lord?' required the younger man doubtfully. 'How should a blind man rule Tamur?'

'With justice and wisdom,' answered Bedyr. 'Both of which you possess, as you demonstrated today.'

'I think I should rather be a sighted warrior than a blind lord,' Kedryn murmured.

'For now be a diplomat again,' Bedyr said. 'We enter the hall, and Hattim may well seek some opportunity to belittle you.'

'Does he resent me so much?' Kedryn wondered. 'Surely he can no longer consider me either threat or rival.'

'He remembers that you bested him with the *kabah*,' warned Bedyr, 'and doubtless that Ashrivelle looked on you with favour.'

In the months intervening between his encounter with the king's daughter and the ending of the siege, Kedryn had almost forgotten the princess Ashrivelle. It was strange, he thought, as Bedyr led him towards the high table, that when first he had come to Andurel and seen her, he had considered Ashrivelle the loveliest woman imaginable. Then, in the heady confidence of his youth, he had allowed himself to imagine finding favour in her eyes; and – as Bedyr said – seen it there. Now he thought only of Wynett, whose beauty lay as much in her character as in her visage. Now he doubted that Ashrivelle would find much to please her in a blind man, and it seemed Wynett was, as the Sandurkan had it, untouchable. He was, he thought bitterly, denied everything he wanted.

'The duel is behind us,' he said quietly, 'and Hattim's way to Ashrivelle is clear. She would hardly consider me a suitable husband now.'

'Are you so experienced then?' Bedyr chided. 'Do you know the ways of women so well?'

'Would she accept a blind husband?' Kedryn grunted irritably. 'Besides, I love . . .'

He broke off: it was best not to admit it, even to himself.

Bedyr surprised him by saying, 'I know. We must talk of it later.'

Kedryn gasped his surprise, for he had not suspected his feelings were so transparent that any but Wynett herself might have sensed

30

them. He had said nothing to his father, and Bedyr had spent relatively little time with him of late, being so much concerned with the aftermath of battle, but it appeared he was more obvious than he had thought.

'I should welcome that,' he murmured.

'It is time, I think,' Bedyr said. 'And it is oft helpful to discuss a problem with a friend.'

He squeezed his son's shoulder as he spoke, and Kedryn took comfort from the pressure, his gloomy mood lightening a fraction.

It darkened again as they entered the hall and he heard the buzz of conversation falter, guessing that those present saw him and turned in his direction, not needing eyes to see the expressions of sympathy on their faces for he could hear it in the greetings that came his way as Bedyr guided him to the table set at the head of the long room.

'Here,' his father instructed, easing a chair back. 'There is a cup to your right and a jug ready. Darr sits to your left in conversation with Jarl. The others are not yet come.'

'My lords,' Kedryn said, easing into the chair.

'Kedryn,' responded the king, 'I thank you again for the wisdom you brought to our proceedings.'

'Aye, you spoke well.' Jarl's voice was gruff with unspoken compassion.

'Thank you,' he answered, grateful that they had the tact not to refer to his predicament. 'I am pleased I was able to offer something.'

'You offered much,' said Darr. 'A lasting peace with the Beltrevan can be nothing but beneficial to us all.'

Kedryn smiled, putting his hands on the surface of the table and reaching carefully for the cup, lifting it that the waiting servant might fill it. He brought it to his lips and felt pleased with himself that he managed that, and the replacement, without spilling the rich, Galichian wine.

'Hattim comes,' Bedyr warned.

'The peacock lord,' muttered Jarl, disapproval in his voice. 'What finery! How he struts!'

'Lord Jarl,' Darr chided, 'are we not allies? Let us at least retain a semblance of friendship.'

'That alliance was forced on him by Kedryn's victory in the *trajea*,' the Keshi grunted, 'and you know it, Darr. Had the lad not bested him, Hattim would have found excuses to leave the fighting to us and likely have settled himself in Andurel.'

'Jarl, Jarl,' Darr murmured, 'you cannot be sure of that.'

31

'He lusts for the throne,' retorted the swarthy lord. 'And that I *can* be sure of.'

'He is ambitious,' the king admitted, 'but whilst you and our Lord of Tamur oppose him, he can entertain no hope of gaining that seat.'

'Not rightfully,' Jarl responded, 'but the likes of Hattim do not always do what is right.'

'Do you suspect treason, Jarl?' asked Bedyr.

Kedryn heard the Keshi's robe shift as his shoulders hunched in a shrug. 'No,' he admitted, 'but I do not trust Hattim.'

'He fought with us,' said Darr. 'Let us remember that and forget our differences.'

Kedryn heard Jarl snort, but any reply he might have given was cut short by the arrival of the Lord of Ust-Galich.

'King Darr, my Lords, Prince Kedryn.' His greeting was bland enough. 'I find you well?'

From the scraping of wood on stone Kedryn guessed that Hattim took a chair to Jarl's left. He could imagine the contrast between them, Hattim in the opulent gold and green he seemed to favour, that taste extending even to his armour, his hair so blond as to shine yellow, carefully arranged to expose the earring suspended from his right lobe, his wrists spanned by intricate bracelets, whilst Jarl would be wearing his customary black, his dark hair braided in the Keshi fashion, his only jewellery the rings on left thumb and two fingers. Darr, he guessed, would wear the plain grey robe that appeared his customary attire on any but formal occasions, his sole mark of status the medallion about his neck, the tripartite crown of Andurel raised in bas-relief from the silver disc. He and Bedyr both wore leather, practical and comfortable. A stranger entering the hall might well assume that Hattim Sethiyan was the most elevated there, at least until they spoke, for Darr had an air of quiet authority whilst Hattim exuded a sense of petulant dissatisfaction.

He appeared now, however, to be doing his best to maintain some semblance of unity with his fellow lords. His conversation was polite and he took pains to avoid any reference to Kedryn's blindness, seemingly convinced – against his earlier objections – of the sense of treating with the forest folk.

Kedryn listened to the talk without taking much part. It was mostly to do with the readying of their forces for the parley, and his own attention was largely occupied with the difficulty of eating food he could not see. His nose told him that roasted pork sat on his platter, and he knew it was already cut for him, but he had still to spear the pieces and bring them to his mouth, not knowing whether fat dribbled on to his shirt, and only able to guess at what vegetable he lifted to his lips. It was embarrassing, and he had so far avoided eating so publicly as much as he was able, but Bedyr had given him no chance this time and he guessed that his father sought to prove a point to Hattim, or even to his son. Consequently he ate largely in silence, speaking only when a remark was addressed directly to him and thankful when the meal ended and he was able to excuse himself.

Bedyr brought him to his chamber, set high in one of the turrets overlooking the canyon of the Idre. Heat from the fire blazing in the hearth struck his face as he entered and he crossed the room with a greater confidence than he showed beyond its now-familiar confines to throw open the shutters and allow in a cooling draught of wintry air. He had determined early that he would not be cosseted, and earned sundry bruises as he paced about the stone-walled room acquainting himself with its distances and angles and furniture until he was able to move with a degree of surety. Now he leant upon the embrasure, feeling the wind on his face, hearing the steady dinning of the great river as he pictured the remembered view in his mind. Behind him he heard Bedyr settle in a chair and fill two glasses. He drew the shutters closed and turned, walking to the empty chair and lowering himself into it with a feeling of pride that was sullied by the knowledge that a sighted man would undertake so simple an action automatically, thinking nothing of it.

'Evshan,' his father said, pushing a goblet towards him. 'And time to talk, I think.'

Kedryn felt instantly apprehensive, swallowing a generous measure of the fiery liquor. He was not sure he wanted to discuss his feelings, but Bedyr gave him no choice.

'Do you love Wynett?'

Kedryn knew that his father was not a man to prevaricate, but the bluntness of the question still took him by surprise. He grunted, seeking to hide momentary confusion behind a second swallow of evshan.

'She is a Sister,' he answered, 'sworn to celibacy. As you pointed out – untouchable.'

'I know what she is,' Bedyr murmured, 'and I did not ask you that. Do you love her?'

'I . . .' Kedryn began, then gulped and said, 'Yes! Lady help me, but I cannot prevent myself. I love her.'

It was in the open now, spoken, and he felt curiously better for it. 'Does she reciprocate?' asked Bedyr.

That was far harder to answer for he could not be sure. Indeed, he had to admit that he did not know. There was a bond, of that he was certain, but whether she shared his feelings remained so far unguessable.

He told Bedyr as much and his father said, 'It is often the case that a hurt man comes to think he loves the one who heals him. Or the one who seeks to heal him, simply because they share that commonality of purpose. They spend much time together, and the care bestowed by the one may be mistranslated.'

'It is not that,' Kedryn retorted. 'I am sure it is not. What I saw in Ashrivelle is magnified in Wynett – and I did see her. Before I was blinded I saw her and felt that were she not a Sister . . .'

'But she *is* a Sister,' Bedyr finished for him.

'As she reminds me,' Kedryn nodded, 'but I cannot help my feelings. And I do not think they are the result of her ministrations. I think I began to feel this when first she tended me; when all I suffered was the arrow wound.'

Bedyr grunted then and there was the sound of the jar gurgling to tip more evshan into their goblets. 'Would you have her relinquish her vows?' he asked.

'Do you ask me what I wish for? Or whether I would force her to such a thing? If I could, which I cannot!'

He could not see his father's sad smile, but he felt the hand that grasped his shoulder, squeezing, then retreating. He smiled thinly and continued, 'If Wynett should choose to relinquish her vows – of her own free will – because she loves me, then I should be mightily happy. Had I my eyes, I think I should ask her. But sightless, I am afraid.'

'To ask?' Bedyr queried gently. 'Or of the answer?'

Kedryn chuckled, more than a little sourly. 'Of both. I feel . . . I am not sure, but sometimes I think she *does* reciprocate. But her duty to the Lady stands between us.'

'There is dispensation,' Bedyr said slowly. 'Devotion to the Lady is based on free will, and there have been Sisters who have chosen to give up their talents. It must be a terrible decision – the lives of the Sisters are based upon the notion of general care, of loving no individuals above another. Wynett gave up much to become a Sister – as Darr's daughter, she had much to give up – and to foresake that which she has pursued so faithfully would be a heartbreaking choice.'

'Do you say I should seek to forget her?' Kedryn demanded.

'Could you?' countered his father. 'You are young and there will be other women.'

'Not like Wynett!' he answered fiercely. 'I saw Ashrivelle and thought I wanted her, but now – even though I am blind – she pales in comparison with Wynett. I can remember how she looks, Father. How both of them look, but there is so much more to Wynett!'

'Mayhap you have merely known her longer,' Bedyr suggested.

'Mayhap,' said Kedryn, 'but I do not believe it is that.'

'You appear convinced,' Bedyr said.

'I am,' Kedryn agreed. 'And I do not know what to do! I am afraid to speak my mind for fear I shall alienate her; and afraid to lose her if I do not.'

'Were she not of the Sisterhood I should council speaking out,' said Bedyr. 'But as she is, I advise patience. And perhaps resignation. I think that if you express your feelings now you will lose any chance you may have. Of course, you may have none, and that is something you must accept. For now, however, I advise you to wait. Let matters take their natural course and accept the outcome whatever it may be.'

'But before long we depart for Caitin Hold,' Kedryn objected. 'And thence to Estrevan. And if Wynett remains here I shall have no chance at all.'

'Perhaps Wynett will not remain,' Bedyr said carefully. 'Mayhap she will accompany you to the Sacred City.'

'I asked her that and she prevaricated,' Kedryn murmured.

'But she did not refuse outright?' asked Bedyr.

'No.'

'Then wait until it is time,' Bedyr said. 'A woman – even a Sister – will often surprise you with her choice.'

Chapter Two

DESPITE the wind that blew knife-cold between the great rock walls bounding the Idre the sky remained a sullen grey, the upper reaches of the Lozin peaks lost in the overcast as though stone and sky fused together. The battered ramparts of the fort towered dark and forbidding above the wind-lashed water of the river, and the town that sat below the fort seemed to huddle against the buffeting of the wind, shutters drawn closed, the smoke that rose from the chimneys tattered by the gusts and sent streaming southwards. The Idre herself matched the shading of the heavens, canescent as ash, the surface swelling and surging to send spume lashing high against the moles that sheltered the river craft bobbing on the waves. It was a time for firesides and mulled wine; for story telling as leatherwork was mended or harness repaired; a time for readying against the long days of wolf-weather promised by the ominous firmament.

Tepshen Lahl wished that he was warm behind closed shutters, sat by a fireside with a goblet of spiced and heated wine at his elbow and his hands busy with the repair of his war gear. In all the years he had spent in Tamur, the easterner had yet to grow accustomed to the severity of her winters, and each year, as he felt the approach of the white months, he could not resist the painful return of memories of his foresaken homeland.

It had been so long ago that he had fled, a refugee with only a slaughtered family and a price on his head behind him, that he was now as much Tamurin as Bundakai, but still, as the cold came down to chill his bones, he thought of his home. It was a milder place than the mountainous country that had offered him sanctuary and friendship, where the differentiation between the seasons was less marked, more subtle than the dramatic changes of Tamur's hills and valleys, and while he was in every other way acclimatised, he still found the winters unpleasant.

It was not, however, his way to show that. He was *kyo* – a swordmaster – and as such bound by disciplines instilled from so early a date as to be now a way of life, so he kept the grimace of displeasure from his sallow features and screwed his almond-shaped eyes to tighter slits against the bite of the cold as he drew his fur-lined cloak about him and surveyed the warriors paraded on the plain before him. They stood in silent ranks, archers and swordsmen, halbadiers and cavalry, stoic in the chill, awaiting his orders. They trusted him – there could be no doubting that, for when Bedyr had sent word to raise the men of Tamur to the defence of the Kingdoms they had come unquestioning, accepting him as lieutenant of their lord. He was proud of that, and if there was any regret at all attached to his appreciation of their loyalty, it was that he had seen too little of the fighting, arriving after Kedryn had slain the leader of the barbarian Horde. It was a small regret, vastly outweighed by his relief at finding both Kedryn and Bedyr safe, if not unscathed, but – kyo and bundakai that he was – he would have liked a little more real combat rather than the harrying of an essentially defeated army.

He grunted, reaching up to smooth his oiled queue beneath the high collar of his cloak, and gestured, dismissing the waiting warriors.

They broke formation with practised efficiency, wheeling in ordered ranks to march back to the tents that covered the plain like vari-coloured mushrooms. Smoother, he thought, than the Keshi horsemen who thundered noisily over the sere ground, and more threatening than the Galichians, who lacked the discipline to ignore the cold and complained bitterly of the northern climes. He did not like the Galichians much, considering them soft, though he had a fondness for the hot-headed equestrians of Kesh. All, though, would do. They had defeated the Horde and now they would impress its leaders with their order and magnanimity, just as Kedryn had suggested. An almost imperceptible smile curved his lips at the thought: at the difference between this manner of cementing a peace and that of the Bundakai. In his homeland there would have been no talk of mercy or parleys. A renegotiation of alliances, perhaps; but that only between clans of equal status, not with hairy barbarians. The Bundakai would have ended the conflict with the ritual execution of the defeated leaders, their sons included, and the threat of mass extermination should any object. That he could accept the wisdom of Kedryn's suggestion was indication of how deeply he had absorbed the ways of the Kingdoms.

That thought prompted another as he turned his horse and heeled the stallion to a canter towards the gates of High Fort. Kedryn's blindness troubled him. Indeed, it knifed a sadness into his soul, for Kedryn was as a son to him and it pained the kyo to witness the young man's suffering and the seeming inability of the Sisters to restore his sight.

Tepshen Lahl was not a follower of Kyrie. For all his adoption of Tamurin ways, he could still not accept the pre-eminence of a female, and whilst he recognised the value of the Sisterhood in such material manifestations as healing and far-sight, he did not subscribe to their faith in the Lady. If Estrevan could find a cure for Kedryn's loss of sight it would be through skill with medicaments or the surgeon's tools, not through prayer. And meanwhile the affliction was creating a problem of its own. Kedryn had served well – had proven himself a warrior – and deserved his due reward. That meed, had Kedryn his way, would be the hand of the Sister Wynett; yet that was denied him by the – foolish, to the easterner's mind – vows of celibacy taken by the Sorority. Wynett was suitable: she was attractive, if pale gold hair and round blue eyes were a man's taste, and her bloodline was indisputable; she was of an age to bear children; and Tepshen Lahl had seen the looks she cast in Kedryn's direction when she thought herself unobserved, whilst Kedryn's own feelings were transparent. That so small a thing as a misguided adherence to some foolish notion of purity should deny them both what they clearly desired was, to the kyo's mind, madness. Yet it remained, a barrier, and Tepshen Lahl could see the problem becoming as great an affliction as the sightlessness. Were these the lands of the Bundakai, King Darr would have absolved the vow and given Wynett to Kedryn, and the woman – dutifully – would have accepted with gratitude.

But these were not the lands of the Bundakai, and so Kedryn went frustrated by more than his blindness whilst Wynett was clearly torn between duty and desire. Better for Kedryn to quit High Fort, the easterner thought, and seek the ministrations of Estrevan, leaving the woman behind. Or console himself with one of the fort's doxies. At least put Wynett from his mind. Yet he would not, or could not, and now his plan for the parley meant a longer sojourn and more time in the Sister's company that must inevitably result in a harder parting when such time came.

'Dream of the unattainable,' the kyo recited to the wind, 'but do not live in dreams.'

Then he set such musings aside as the stallion's hooves clattered on the glacis fronting the fort and he slowed to a walk as the guards saluted, ushering him through the great gates.

He crossed the courtyard and rode down the long tunnel leading to the stables, dismounting as a groom came out to take the reins. He loosened his cloak, grateful for the lessening of the wind within the confines of the fort, and set an habitual hand to the scabbard of the long, straightedged sword that was now his only material link with his home as he proceeded to negotiate the yards and walkways leading to Bedyr's chambers.

The place was busy with the work of reconstruction, tilers repairing roofs holed by barbarian missiles, squads levelling pitted yards, laying fresh flags cut from the Lozin walls, carpenters lading the crisp air with the pleasant odour of cut wood, while on the ramparts he could hear the creaking of the winches that hauled up the massive slabs that would rebuild the ravaged buttresses. It was none too soon, for winter would render such activities dangerous as ice and wind settled in, and a damaged fort was like a wounded swordsman – open to attack. That was another sound reason for Kedryn's suggestion, and the kyo smiled his admiration of the young man's new-found wisdom.

'You seem pleased,' Bedyr remarked as Tepshen entered the room.

The easterner nodded, shedding his cloak and crossing to the fire as he said, 'The repairs go well. And the men are ready.'

He slipped the fastenings of his scabbard loose and set his sheathed blade against a chair, holding out his hands to the welcoming blaze.

'Brannoc is not yet returned,' Bedyr told him, 'so no time is yet agreed.'

'Best soon,' murmured Tepshen, turning to present his back to the fire as he eased the latchings of his jerkin loose. 'An idle army finds itself work.'

'An eastern proverb?' queried Bedyr, smiling.

'A general observation.' The easterner shrugged and settled himself in a chair, turning it to face across to where the Lord of Tamur sat at a table covered with papers. 'The town is too small to accommodate them all and soon they will grow restless.'

'Jarl is already anxious to return home,' Bedyr nodded, 'and I'd lief see Yrla again. No doubt the men feel much the same way.'

'They will do their duty,' Tepshen said, reaching out to secure a mug that he filled from the copper jug warming by the hearth, 'but the sooner they can, and be gone, the better.'

'Aye.' Bedyr pushed the papers aside and stretched, flexing his shoulders. 'I'd take Kedryn out of here, too.'

Tepshen Lahl sipped the mulled wine, staring across the rim of the mug at his friend. 'Is there any change?'

'No.' Bedyr shook his head, his smile fading into melancholy. 'Neither in his sight or his feelings.'

'You spoke to him?'

Again Bedyr nodded. 'Aye, and he told me openly that he loves Wynett.'

Tepshen made a hissing sound, drawing in his breath, that Bedyr recognised as alarm. He said, 'And what was your response?'

'That he should consider whether his feelings are genuine or prompted by Wynett's care. He is certain they are real.'

'He knows his own mind,' grunted the kyo.

'He wants Wynett to accompany him to Estrevan,' said Bedyr.

'Will she? It might be better she did not.'

'I cannot speak for the Sister,' Bedyr answered, 'but I think I shall do my best to persuade her.'

Tepshen Lahl's inscrutable features creased in an expression Bedyr recognised as a frown. 'You do not agree?' he asked.

The kyo hissed again, thoughtfully this time, then said, 'Will that not prolong the inevitable?'

'Is it inevitable?' Bedyr heard the defensive note in his voice and wondered if he truly acted wisely, or merely out of sympathy for his blinded son. 'By the Lady, Tepshen! Has he not suffered enough? Is he not due some small compensation?'

Tepshen nodded his agreement. 'But if Wynett remains true to her vows, would a swift parting not be for the best?'

'I am not sure.' Bedyr shook his head hopelessly. 'Perhaps. Or perhaps it would fuel the darkness that pervades him. He needs hope, and if Wynett's presence will give him that, then I shall do my utmost to obtain it.'

The kyo shrugged, focusing his attention on his wine, and Bedyr saw disapproval in the motion. Tepshen would not voice his objections unless asked, for his devotion to the Caitin line was unswerving and save on those occasions when he considered contrary counsel of greater value than silence he obeyed his chosen leader with an unstinting devotion.

This, it seemed, was such a time though Bedyr, unsure of himself, was not certain but that he would prefer voiced argument. He rose from the table, pushing his chair noisily over the stone floor of the outer chamber, and crossed to the fire, helping himself to wine. He sipped the spicy brew, studying Tepshen's face as he leant against the mantel.

'Tell me why you object,' he asked: in this, as in most things, he felt the kyo's advice would be of value.

'Wynett has taken vows,' responded Tepshen, 'and she appears unwilling to foreswear them. Sooner or later Kedryn must accept that, and if she will not change her mind, then it is better he accepts it early. To bring her with us to Estrevan merely prolongs foolish hope.'

'If it is foolish,' Bedyr nodded. 'But if it is not? You have seen them together; you have seen how she looks at him.'

Tepshen nodded. 'I have, but she is still a Sister.'

'That is not irrevocable,' Bedyr pointed out.

'But unlikely to change,' Tepshen answered.

'Mayhap,' Bedyr shrugged, 'and mayhap I shall not be able to persuade her to go, but I think I must try.'

'You are his father: if you think it best, then so be it.'

Bedyr smiled ruefully. 'It may be that in this instance a father's wishes are not for the best.'

'But,' said Tepshen, 'you believe they are.'

'I do,' said Bedyr. 'At the very least, Wynett – if she agrees to accompany him – will have a chance to continue her ministrations, and they may have some effect. Even if not, he will have her company – and I think that without that his mood will become bleak. I would avoid that if I can.'

'Then persuade her,' said Tepshen.

Bedyr nodded again, his smile becoming warmer as he heard the acceptance in his friend's voice. 'Until this parley is done, however, we are bound to High Fort.'

'Aye,' the easterner grunted, then turned as a knocking echoed against the door. Unthinking, he set a hand to his scabbard as Bedyr crossed the room, shifting the lacquered case to his knees as he set down his mug.

Bedyr swung the door open to reveal a soldier in messenger's livery, his face alight with excitement.

'My lord,' he announced, 'Brannoc has returned with word from the barbarians and the king requests your presence in the Council Chamber.'

41

Bedyr thanked him and beckoned for Tepshen Lahl to follow him as he strode towards Kedryn's quarters.

'Lord Bedyr,' the messenger called after them, 'Prince Kedryn is already summoned. He was with Sister Wynett.'

'Where else?' Bedyr murmured, exchanging glances with Tepshen.

Darr was conversing with Brannoc when they reached the chamber, the outlaw lounging at ease as though speaking with kings was an everyday occurrence, his casual attitude eliciting a disapproving frown from Rycol, who sat, stiff-spined, across the table. Jarl and Hattim joined them moments later, and then Kedryn, led by a liveried warrior. Bedyr saw his son seated and waited eagerly for the monarch to speak.

'I believe,' Darr announced, 'that it is Brannoc's words you would hear rather than mine. So. . .'

He gestured for the wolfshead to proceed and Brannoc beamed, setting elbows to the table as he studied the expectant faces turned in his direction.

'I have spoken with the ulans,' he began, 'and they are agreed on a parley. Vran speaks for the Yath; Darien for the Grymard. There are three contenders for Yarrum's torque – Threnol, Farlan and Cord – who had best be present if the Drott are to be bound by the terms. The Caroc have already decided the ascendancy and will be represented by Remyd. Ostral and Gryth speak for the Vistral.

'They will enter High Fort only on Kedryn's word, however. And that they will not hear unless he goes to them. I suggest that on the morrow Kedryn ride out to meet them – they will be waiting on the Beltrevan road.'

'In ambush?' demanded Hattim. 'Ready to seize the Prince of Tamur?'

'Alone,' countered Brannoc cheerfully, 'I have their word on it.'

'The promise of barbarians?' sneered the Lord of Ust-Galich, his tone prompting Kedryn to wonder if he spoke out of genuine concern or merely a desire to oppose.

'The blood promise of ulans and ala-Ulans,' Brannoc answered, making little attempt to conceal the contempt in his voice. 'The equivalent, in the Beltrevan, of you, my lord.'

Hattim gasped at the insult, but before he was able to protest, Kedryn asked, 'Do you trust them, Brannoc?'

'Aye,' the outlaw told him. 'In this, I do.'

'Then I place my trust in them,' said Kedryn.

42

'With an escort,' Bedyr said cautiously.

'I would suggest Tepshen and myself,' Brannoc advised. 'And ten good men. More would indicate a lack of faith.'

'I shall ride with you,' Bedyr declared. 'In case.'

'Bedyr,' Darr murmured, 'would you place all Tamur's eggs in the one basket? I understand your concern, but should this prove the ambush our lord of Ust-Galich suggests then your presence can make little difference – save to deprive your kingdom of lord and prince together.'

'The king speaks wisely, father,' Kedryn added. 'And I trust Brannoc's judgement in this matter. Let us demonstrate faith – and show we are not afraid.'

'Again, wisdom,' Jarl complimented. 'Listen to your son, Bedyr.'

Bedyr nodded, unhappy with the arrangement but willing to accept the terms. Darr said, 'I would ask my Lord Kesh to have four squadrons of his swiftest horsemen standing ready. In case.'

'So long as they do not show themselves,' said Brannoc.

'They will be ready,' Jarl promised, 'And I shall be at their head.'

'You will assure them safe conduct,' Brannoc continued, addressing Kedryn. 'For themselves and their *gehrim.*'

'Their bodyguards?' Hattim snorted. 'They dare ask that *body-guards* accompany them?'

'It is their custom,' said Brannoc. 'Twelve warriors from each tribe. Sixty men are small threat to the armies of the Kingdoms.'

'It is a matter of protocol,' Hattim argued. 'They are the defeated ones, yet they dictate terms.'

'I am not sure there *is* a protocol to cover this,' Darr murmured gently, 'and as Brannoc points out – there is scant threat to us.'

Hattim's face blackened at this further reverse, but once again Kedryn pre-empted his objections by suggesting a vote. All save Hattim voiced their acceptance, and the lord of Ust-Galich was once more forced to acquiesce.

'After I have given them my word,' Kedryn asked, 'what then?'

'With safe conduct guaranteed you need only arrange a time,' said Brannoc. 'Perhaps the following day?'

'The armies are ready?' Darr asked, and when he had that confirmed said, 'Then – if Kedryn is agreeable – let us set the time for noon.'

It was agreed and they set to discussing the exact form of the parley. It was decided that pavilions should be raised below the fort, through which the barbarian chieftains would proceed, emerging from the southern gates, the first woodlanders to set foot in the Three Kingdoms. Escorted by a guard of honour, they would meet Darr and the lords of Tamur, Kesh and Ust-Galich in full sight of the massed warriors. In return for their promises of peace they would be allowed to retrieve their fallen and return to the Beltrevan. Then Brannoc, much to Kedryn's amusement for he suspected an ulterior motive, suggested that the time was ripe for opening stronger trade links with the forest folk.

'There is much they cannot obtain in the forests,' the wolfshead pointed out, his voice earnest, 'and the goods of the Kingdoms are highly prized. What small degree of trade has taken place has been – let us say, unofficial. Scarcely sufficient to satisfy the demand.'

Kedryn heard Rycol's splutter, midway between merriment and vexation, and wished that he could see the chatelain's visage as Brannoc outlined a plan that made excellent sense – and would undoubtedly provide the outlaw with a far greater profit than his previous clandestine activities as a smuggler.

'Let them but acquire a taste for the goods of the Kingdoms and they will likely be loath to forego such luxuries,' he continued, ignoring Rycol's grunt, 'and consequently less likely to sever the links by act of war.'

'You would have some experience of such transactions,' Rycol remarked drily.

'I have some small personal interest,' Brannoc responded in an innocent voice, 'but my purpose now is to cement the peace.'

'There is another advantage beyond the commercial,' Darr interjected. 'Should we regularise trade, we should afford ourselves excellent opportunity to maintain a degree of surveillance within the Beltrevan. Perhaps we should suggest seasonal fairs.'

'My lord,' Brannoc announced admiringly, 'you have the foresight of a freebooter.'

Darr laughed and said, 'How say you, my lords?'

'Who would organise such junkets?' asked Rycol. 'And where? For all the parleys in the world, I'd not be overjoyed to see barbarian tents encamped below my walls.'

'Within the forest,' Brannoc said quickly, confirming Kedryn's suspicion that this was something the outlaw had dreamed up with an eye to turning a personal profit, 'a day's ride from either fort. A pack horse's ride – less for cavalry.'

'I could accept that,' Rycol allowed.

'It would also provide an opportunity to renew peace promises,'

Darr added, 'though organisation would be necessary, and my lords Rycol and Fengrif are doubtless busy enough tending their forts, so we should need a trustworthy administrator.'

'One familiar with the forest folk,' Kedryn said, no longer able to contain himself. 'A man who speaks their language and knows their ways. One they trust and who can be trusted by us. Is there such a man?'

Brannoc cleared his throat.

'Who else?' asked Bedyr, understanding his son's drift.

'Who do you suggest?' wondered Jarl.

Kedryn heard Rycol bark laughter and say, 'I nominate Brannoc.'

'I?' responded the wolfshead with transparent surprise.

'You,' Rycol chuckled, echoed by Bedyr. 'You have, after all, the advantage of familiarity with such dealings.'

'Do you agree?' Darr asked, and Kedryn heard the lords voice their assent.

'And you, my friend?' the king queried. 'Would you undertake such an appointment?'

'I am honoured by your trust,' Brannoc said modestly. 'It would behove me ill to refuse.'

'We had best give you a suitable title then,' the king decided, his own voice betraying laughter. 'One to match so elevated a position.'

'Warden of the Forest?' suggested Kedryn.

'Excellent!' Darr applauded. 'Brannoc, from henceforth you are our Warden of the Forest. I shall have my scribes draw up official documents, and we shall announce your appointment at the parley.'

'I am overwhelmed,' the newly-appointed Warden declared. 'Though such responsibility weighs heavy I shall administer my duties loyally. Whatever they may be.'

'You will, of course, keep the commanders of both High and Low Forts informed of your activities,' the king decided, 'though I am sure you will receive every assistance.'

'I look forward to working closely with my Lord Rycol,' Brannoc said solemnly, and Kedryn wondered what expression that produced on the chatelain's stern features, for it had not been so long ago that he had advocated hanging Brannoc for the very activities now rendered legal. It was strange, he thought, how the world turned.

'Am I to provide funding for this?' asked Rycol in a carefully controlled voice.

'I feel we may safely leave our new Warden with that task,' Darr said. 'Some tithe on the merchants perhaps?'

'A true freebooter,' Brannoc murmured.

'There is much of that in the duties of a king,' Darr retorted, chuckling. 'And now may we assume these matters settled?'

There was general agreement, followed by a scraping of chairs as the assembly rose. Bedyr turned to Kedryn saying, 'I would speak with the king, shall I see you in your chambers?' and Kedryn nodded, feeling Tepshen Lahl's hand upon his arm as he stood up.

He realised that Brannoc stood close by from the woodsmoke odour of the wolfshead's leathers and murmured, 'Your purse will doubtless gain weight from this, Warden.'

Brannoc laughed cheerfully. 'But with honest gold, now, my friend.'

Kedryn heard Tepshen Lahl snort laughter and began to chuckle himself.

'Will you accompany us? I'd enjoy friendly company.'

'Of course,' Brannoc agreed, taking his elbow to assist him in the negotiation of the corridors. 'You have something to drink in your chamber? This diplomacy has dried my throat.'

Bedyr watched them depart, thankful that his son had two such good friends, though when he turned towards Darr his face was sombre.

'Come,' the king motioned for Bedyr to follow him out of the Council Chamber to the rooms set aside for his use. They were as regal as High Fort could offer, being a military bastion rather than a palace, though Darr seemed perfectly at ease within the stone-walled chambers, the floor of the outer room strewn with rushes, a fire burning in a simple hearth before which stood two plain chairs, a low table between them carrying a flask of carved crystal and matching goblets.

'My bones begin to feel the chill,' Darr smiled, filling the goblets with rich Galichian wine. 'Or is it age?'

'You are scarce older than I,' Bedyr replied. 'Mayhap kingship puts the chill there.'

'Mayhap,' Darr agreed. 'It is no easy task guiding this realm of ours, though Kedryn has proven mightily useful in that matter of late. He grows apace, my friend.'

'He has matured,' Bedyr nodded, stretching his booted feet towards the fire, 'and it is his future I'd discuss.'

Darr indicated that he should continue, sipping the fruity vintage as he listened to Bedyr outline his earlier conversation with Kedryn, his face growing troubled as he heard of the young man's

46

declaration and Bedyr's desire that Wynett should accompany him to Estrevan.

'What would you have me do?' he asked when Bedyr was finished. 'I cannot command Wynett as a father, for such ties were set aside when she chose to follow Kyrie. And I do not think it a good idea to speak as a king. If she does accompany you, better it be of her own free will.'

'Of course,' Bedyr agreed, 'I would not have it any other way. But as both king and father, might you not *suggest?*'

'Is that the wisest course?' Darr asked. 'By the Lady, old friend, I'd do everything in my power to see Kedryn happy. Kyrie knows, we owe him enough; but I am uncertain that you see this clearly. I feel the ties of blood may cloud your vision.'

'Tepshen Lahl said much the same,' Bedyr admitted, 'but I see Kedryn's mood shift like the striker of a bell, each movement wringing his soul. If he continues in this matter, I fear for his sanity. I fear that if Wynett remains here he may sink into a darkness of the soul to match his blindness. At least if she went with him to Estrevan he would have that consolation along the way.'

'But when he reached the Sacred City?' Darr wondered. 'What then?'

'Then the chance of his regaining his sight becomes more probable,' Bedyr said. 'And if he does not – and if Wynett should then opt to return here – there would at least be the counsels of the city to shore him up.'

'You have a point,' the king allowed, his voice thoughtful. 'I shall discuss it with the Sisters of Andurel, and if they deem it best that Wynett go with you I shall ask her to consider the possibility. I cannot do more than that, my friend – you know as well as I the limitations of my authority.'

'I accept that and I thank you,' Bedyr nodded.

'It is little enough,' Darr murmured, stroking at his thinning hair, his eyes fixed thoughtfully on the fire, as if the flames might provide answers to the doubts Bedyr read on his face. 'And while we talk of Kedryn, what thought have you given to his part in Alaria's prophecy?'

Now Bedyr turned towards the flames, his features grave, the corners of his mouth tugging down as he contemplated the question. 'I am not so conversant with the Text that I feel able to give valid • answer,' he said at last, 'but I believe we must accept that my son is the one foretold, and that alone persuades me I am right to seek your

47

aid in persuading Wynett to accompany him. If the Messenger still lives then Kedryn must eventually face him, and he will be better equipped for that struggle if his mind is at peace.'

Darr grunted his assent and asked, 'Do you think Wynett's resolve might weaken in his company?'

Bedyr smiled briefly, admiring his friend's perspicacity. 'You see through me, Darr – Aye, I believe it might.'

'Were Ashrivelle to find favour with him . . .' the king said softly.

'I had thought of that,' Bedyr said, 'and tried to put the notion in his mind. But he is fixated on Wynett.'

'It would be so much easier,' Darr went on, almost to himself. 'I'd be happy to see my younger daughter wed to the blood of Tamur. And it would resolve the problem of Hattim Sethiyan.'

'He presses his suit?' asked Bedyr, recognising the concern in Darr's tone.

'He does,' the king nodded refilling his goblet, 'and he finds favour in her eyes. There was an exchange of tokens on our departure.'

'He has the right,' Bedyr said, studying Darr's features.

'And so I can do little to prevent the courtship,' the king said, a mixture of sadness and irritation in his voice, 'even though I do not believe he loves her so much for herself as for what she represents.'

'He still harbours that ambition?' Bedyr asked.

'He would be king,' Darr confirmed, 'and even though marriage to my daughter cannot guarantee that elevation, it would mightily enhance his claim.'

'You are not so old.' Bedyr set a hand to his friend's arm, thinking even as he did so that Darr *had* aged greatly during his years as sovereign. 'You will rule us long yet.'

'But not forever,' smiled Darr, his grey eyes weary. 'The time must come when the Kingdoms choose a new ruler. And Hattim Sethiyan looks to that time.'

'He would not have my support,' Bedyr grunted, reaching for the wine flask. 'Nor Jarl's.'

'To whom would you lend your voice?' Darr asked, taking the Lord of Tamur by surprise. 'The time must come to face the question of succession and I have but the two daughters. Let us assume for the moment that Wynett remains dedicated to the Lady, that leaves only Ashrivelle heir to the High Throne. Whoever marries her claims by all our customs first right to Andurel.'

'I had not thought much on it.' Bedyr shrugged, frowning. 'I had assumed a nomination of candidates and a selection in the customary manner. The Sisterhood would have their usual say, and I doubt they would support a Sethiyan claimant.'

'Who, then?' asked Darr. 'Jarl might well nominate his son.'

'Kemm?' Bedyr shook his head. 'Kemm is no ruler. An excellent tender of horses – and I mean no disrespect – but not a king. He will ward Kesh well enough when Jarl dies, but I do not believe he could govern the Three Kingdoms.'

'Jarl might disagree,' Darr said.

'I wonder,' Bedyr shrugged. 'Jarl left Kemm behird to tend the herds. Had he looked to put a crown on the lad's head, he would surely have brought him north with the armies.'

'And Ashrivelle would not, I suspect, favour such an alliance,' Darr nodded. 'It is a problem, my friend.'

'But one that we need not face for some time,' said Bedyr. 'There are years in you yet, and who knows what the future holds?'

'Estrevan might afford us some guidance when the mehdri I sent return,' said Darr. 'Meanwhile, I have no doubt that when Hattim marches south he will pursue Ashrivelle, and if she accepts as I believe she will, I shall have little alternative save to agree.'

'But marriage alone does not ensure his ascendancy,' Bedyr repeated. 'He would still require the agreement of myself and Jarl.'

'And you would withhold it,' Darr said, not asking a question.

'Hattim Sethiyan is not the man to take your place,' confirmed Bedyr.

'So we come full circle.' Darr smiled wanly, staring at his goblet. 'Who is to succeed me? Were Kedryn to claim my daughter's hand I should most happily announce him my heir. But if he loves Wynett, and is anyway gone to Estrevan . . . Mayhap I should declare a regency.'

The suggestion took Bedyr by surprise and so for a moment he stared at his royal friend nonplussed. He had not known Darr so melancholy: it was as if the onslaught of winter set a pessimism on the king that turned his mind to gloomy thoughts. He saw Darr staring at him and shook his head vigorously. 'Not I. Tamur is my domain and I'd not leave her for Andurel.'

'Jarl would support you.' Darr's voice was soft. 'And Kemm would not object, I think.'

'But Hattim undoubtedly would,' Bedyr said quickly, not liking the direction the conversation had taken. He had sought the king's help in persuading Wynett to accompany Kedryn to Estrevan and not thought beyond that, but now he suddenly found himself caught up in the politics of the Kingdoms with Darr seemingly measuring his head for the crown. Devoid of such ambition, he found the prospect alarming.

'As would the Sisterhood,' continued Darr with what appeared to Bedyr a ruthless insistance.

'Darr,' he argued, 'I am a warrior. I defend my borders and do what I can to govern my Tamurin wisely. I lack your foresight; your skills in handling people. I am not the stuff of which kings are made.'

'Nor is Hattim Sethiyan,' Darr countered.

'He cannot claim the White Palace without the support of Kesh and Tamur,' retorted Bedyr.

'But wed to Ashrivelle he strengthens the claim,' murmured the king. 'And should no other contender offer himself . . .'

'Marriage alone is not enough,' Bedyr insisted.

'But the throne must be filled,' Darr said. 'And I have no son, so the crown must descend through the female line. Without a ruler in the White Palace, the Kingdoms will devolve back into disunity. Would you see chaos again?'

'No,' Bedyr said helplessly, 'but . . .'

'Think on it,' urged Darr. 'You would have my support.'

'And I thank you for that,' smiled Bedyr, 'but I maintain that I am no king.'

'You may, though, have raised one,' Darr said softly. 'Think on that, also.'

'Kedryn?' Bedyr frowned doubtfully. 'He is too young.'

'As we agreed, he matures apace,' Darr rejoined. 'And he demonstrates fine judgement. His victory over Niloc Yarrum has earned him the respect of all – and I do not speak of the morrow, but some years hence.'

'Many years hence, I hope,' Bedyr remarked loyally.

'Consider it.' Darr touched the medallion hung about his neck, turning it so that firelight glinted from the shining surface. 'In time the succession will become vital to our hard-won unity, and when that time arrives Kedryn may well prove the one to take my place. I ask only that you think on it – and say nothing of this conversation. Save, perhaps, to your wife. But not to Kedryn or any other.'

'Kedryn has sufficient to think on,' nodded Bedyr. 'Too much.'

'Indeed,' Darr agreed. 'And were others to learn of my feelings there might well be the danger of assassination.'

'Hattim would not dare,' rasped Bedyr. 'And Jarl would not stoop so low.'

'Mayhap not,' shrugged the king, 'but silence remains the safest course, and I must ask your word that this remains our secret, shared only with Yrla.'

Bedyr stared at the man who was both his friend and his king, seeking in the calm grey eyes some indication as to whether Darr spoke from natural caution or suspicion. Darr's gaze remained, however, unfathomable, and the set of his careworn features suggested he did not wish to discuss the matter further.

'You have it,' Bedyr promised.

'Thank you,' smiled the monarch.

As his possible future was discussed, Kedryn sat drinking with Tepshen Lahl and Brannoc, the enthusiasm he had felt in the Council Chamber somewhat abated now that he had time to consider the implications of the task ahead.

'How shall I go to them?' he wondered. 'Led by the hand? They will see a helpless blind man.'

'On horseback,' said Brannoc as if there was no debating it. 'Horses are prized in the Beltrevan – few ride save the greatest of the ulans – and you will come to them as a conqueror.'

'But. . .' Kedryn began, interrupted by Tepshen Lahl.

'Brannoc is right. And you *can* ride a horse.'

'Blind?' he demanded, dubiously.

'The horse has eyes,' said the kyo, 'and you have ridden at night. We shall not be charging into battle, so the pace will be easy. You can do it.'

'Tepshen and I will flank you,' added Brannoc. 'A word from either one of us will be sufficient to guide you.'

'And when I dismount?' Kedryn asked.

'Do as I bid you,' said the outlaw.

'They will still see that I cannot.' Kedryn touched fingers to the cloth encircling his skull.

'They will see the warrior who slew Niloc Yarrum,' countered Brannoc. 'The *hef-Alador* – the conqueror of the greatest. Did I tell you that is what they call you?'

'No,' Kedryn shook his head.

'I must have forgotten in my desire to arrange more binding ties,' Brannoc chuckled, prompting laughter from the younger man. 'No matter – you have their respect and it will not diminish because you wear a bandage over your eyes.'

Kedryn shrugged. 'I have little choice, do I?'

'None,' said Tepshen Lahl succincly. 'You began this thing and you must carry it through.'

'So be it,' Kedryn sighed, hoping that he could.

The cloud that had hung low about the Lozins for the past days broke up as Kedryn left High Fort, the overcast swirling and shifting into great banks of storm-threatening grey through which a wintry sun shed fleeting light on the escort of ten Tamurin riding behind their prince. They were dressed in battle gear, breast plates and mail glinting proudly, the blue peace pennants of their lances snapping and fluttering in the wind that still blew fierce down the canyon of the Idre. Kedryn rode at their head, brown hair streaming from the dark blue bandage covering his eyes. He had allowed Bedyr, advised by Brannoc, to choose his clothing, foregoing his familiar outfit of unadorned brown leather in favour of gear more suitable to so auspicious an occasion. Black breeks of soft hide overlaid with mesh mail clad the legs he used to steer his war horse, a massive but reassuringly docile stallion offered by Jarl, and a matching jerkin sat light upon his chest, surmounted by a tunic of silver-grey bearing the fist of Tamur within a circle of pure white. His dirk was belted to his waist and his sword slung on his saddle, a ribbon of blue about the hilt, indicating his peaceful intent.

Tepshen Lahl rode on his left and Brannoc to his right, both close enough they could guide the Keshi stallion should such assistance prove necessary. The kyo wore light armour, a breast-plate, vambraces and grieves, over breeks and jerkin of grey hide, the Tamurin fist inlaid on the metal that protected his chest, a half-helm covering his oiled hair, its cheek pieces emphasising the slant of his yellow eyes. His sword was slung in battle position on his back, but like Kedryn's the hilt was adorned with a blue peace ribbon. Brannoc had retained his customary garb of motley leather, the tunic a patchwork of browns and greens reminiscent of the forest in summer bloom. His hair was freshly dressed, the shells woven into his braids tinkling softly beneath the battering of the wind, joined on this day by small clusters of the red and white feathers that were a mark of peaceful intent in the Beltrevan. A similar cluster fluttered from the hilt of the Keshi sabre jutting above his left shoulder, and a larger bunching from the pole he carried upright in his right hand.

Kedryn rode in silence, listening to the thunder of the river and the clatter of shod hooves on the hard stone of the road, thinking that the last time he had taken this trail it had been in the opposite direction, at a desperate gallop, with the pain of an ensorcelled arrow throbbing like fire in his left shoulder. He had seen little of it then, being largely lost in the fever of the wound and its concomitant magic, and he wondered if he would ever again have sight of the trail that reached into the vastness of the forest country. He gritted his teeth, pushing such melancholy from his mind as he voiced a silent prayer to the Lady for guidance and eloquence, wondering even as he did so if she heard him.

He had hoped for a recurrence of that enlightenment that had gripped him before, revealing the way he should take and seeming to form his words unbidden, but it had not come, and he had embarked from High Fort burdened by doubt that he could accomplish his self-chosen task successfully. It was, however, as Tepshen Lahl had said: a thing begun that must be finished, and he was determined to dispense his duty as best he was able. It would, at very least, free him for the journey to Estrevan, and he still clung to the hope that Wynett would accompany him.

She had been there at the gate to see him off, taking his hand after Bedyr and Darr had wished him well, Jarl assuring him that the Keshi squadrons stood ready to come to his aid should such prove needed. Even Hattim had grunted an insincere farewell. But it was Wynett's adieu that he valued most, for he had heard concern and trust in her voice as she called on the Lady to bless his going and ensure his safe return, and when he had squeezed her hand he had felt the pressure returned. It was a small enough gesture, but it gave him the hope he needed to stave off the darkness that threatened to invest his soul.

'They are there!'

Brannoc's voice interrupted his musing, and he straightened in his saddle, assuming what he hoped was a suitable expression for a – what had the outlaw said they called him? – hef-Alador.

'Slowly,' he heard Tepshen Lahl advise softly. 'Walk. Halt.'

He reined in, hearing Brannoc call out in the language of the forest, unfamiliar with the gutteral tongue, recognising only his barbarian title and his own name. Strange voices replied and then Brannoc said, 'Dismount.'

He heard the creak of leather and the faint chinking of mail as his companions climbed from their horses and swung down himself, allowing someone to take his reins as Tepshen Lahl murmured, 'Walk straight ahead. Yes. Stop. There is a chair.'

53

He let the kyo steer him, feeling the seat behind his knees, lowering himself into it cautiously as his heart thudded beneath his ribs so loud, it seemed, that the forest folk must hear it.

'There are eight of them,' Tepshen Lahl murmured. 'Seated facing you.'

'They bid you welcome,' Brannoc said, 'and hail you as the conqueror of Niloc Yarrum.'

'Tell them I thank them for their welcome,' Kedryn responded, 'and that I welcome the trust they demonstrate by this meeting. Tell them the time for fighting is ended and I would discuss peace between us.'

He waited as Brannoc translated, feeling a strange calm, a certainty akin to that which had gripped him when he faced the leader of these barbarian warriors. Perhaps the Lady was with him, after all.

'They say they are ready to talk peace,' Brannoc announced after the gutteral replies had faded to silence, 'and if you will outline your terms they will consider them.'

A barely audible intake of Tepshen Lahl's breath indicated the kyo's opinion of such presumption, but Kedryn ignored it, knowing what it must cost the proud woodlanders to sue for terms. He nodded, marshalling his thoughts, forgetting all the carefully prepared speeches he had sat up most of the night devising.

'We have fought,' he said at last, pausing every so often that Brannoc might translate his words, 'and brave warriors have died on both sides. Niloc Yarrum was favoured of Ashar – raised by the Messenger – but not even he could bring down the Three Kingdoms. Not even the god of the Beltrevan was able to overcome the strength which flows from the Lady.

'Does this not indicate that the Lady is greater than Ashar?

'Greater and more merciful, for it is not her way to grind the neck of a defeated foe in the dust, but rather to offer her hand in friendship that foes may become allies, that war between the Beltrevan and the Kingdoms might end.

'This is what I offer, as the conqueror of Niloc Yarrum and the spokesman of the Kingdoms: on the morrow the chieftains of the tribes shall enter the gates of High Fort in peace, that promises may be exchanged between the Beltrevan and the Kingdoms, ensuring that we fight no more. The dead of the Beltrevan shall be gathered and returned to their people for burial in their own fashion. We shall open our gates to trade between us and agree on times when there shall be gatherings for such exchange. The bounty of the Kingdoms

54

may thus be had honestly, without bloodshed, and our peoples talk in peace and amity.

'This is what I offer. How say they?'

He waited, listening to the babble of gutteral words that followed. Then Brannoc said, 'They ask what is the alternative?'

'War,' Kedryn replied tersely.

Again there was that stirring, the sound of voices and armoured bodies shifting position. The wind was cold on his face, chilling the sweat that he abruptly realised beaded his forehead, and he clenched his teeth, cursing the fell magic that had robbed him of his sight that he was unable to study the features of the woodlanders and judge their mood. He heard Tepshen Lahl's chair creak slightly, wondering if the kyo tensed in readiness for swordplay. If the horn sounded, summoning Jarl's Keshi riders to the rescue, he decided he would draw his dirk and sell his life as dear as he was able.

Then Brannoc said, 'They say they understand war, it is peace they find hard to comprehend.'

Kedryn forced a smile and said, 'War against the Kingdoms is futile. Have they not seen that?'

'They follow Ashar, not the Lady,' Brannoc translated when the response came, 'and Ashar is a god of war.'

'Who could not bring them victory,' Kedryn retorted. 'Even though he sent his Messenger to aid them.'

There was a silence after the outlaw interpreted his words, then a grunting, and what Kedryn thought was a laugh. Finally, the answer: 'The hef-Alador speaks true, and as he defeated the Messenger's chosen leader, he must know these things.'

'I do,' he nodded, hoping he sounded convincing, 'and I say the time for war is ended, the time for peace come. Tell them the Kingdoms can be generous in peace – and fierce in battle.'

'They have seen the one,' Brannoc told him after a lengthy reply, 'and they would know the other. They say they will come into High Fort on the morrow and make the agreements suggested.'

'Excellent,' Kedryn nodded, feeling the tension ease from him.

There was a further exchange and Brannoc chuckled, saying, 'They want to know if horses are to be part of our trading.'

Kedryn paused, wondering if it was wise to allow these fierce tribesman the advantage of Keshi mounts. Then he smiled and said, 'There will be a horse for each ulan. Whomsoever shall lay final claim to the chieftains' torque of the Drott and Vistral shall also claim the horse.'

'That should keep them busy fighting amongst themselves,' Brannoc murmured before translating the promise.

'They will breed from them,' warned Tepshen Lahl.

'Not from geldings,' Kedryn whispered, eliciting a snort of approval from the easterner.

'They will present themselves at the gates at noon,' Brannoc announced. 'Until then they bid you farewell.'

'Until then,' Kedryn answered, standing.

He heard Tepshen Lahl clear his throat softly and stepped towards the sound, not sure why no reference had been made to his blindness and seeking to impress the woodlanders with his agility. 'Turn,' he heard the kyo murmur almost inaudibly. 'Now walk ahead.'

He obeyed, feeling Tepshen fall into step beside him, slowing when he heard the chink of a bridle and the whoof of air from a horse's nostrils.

'Your reins with your left hand,' Tepshen hissed, and he put out his hand to feel the leathers placed in his arms, moving automatically to the mounting position. It was easier than he had anticipated, his right hand finding the stirrup and turning it to accommodate his left foot with the dexterity of long practice. He swung up, settling into the saddle unaided, then eased the stallion's head around, confident that his companions were with him, and touched heels to flanks, lifting the Keshi charger to an easy canter as relief washed over him.

'That was well done,' Tepshen Lahl complimented.

'Especially the offer of the horses,' added Brannoc. 'I must look into that aspect of trade. In my capacity as Warden, of course.'

Kedryn threw back his head and laughed aloud.

Behind them, the ulans and ala-Ulans watched their departure, then turned to gesture at the surrounding rocks, waving the Gehrim concealed there down. The shaven-headed bodyguards removed the arrows from their bows and set the shafts in the quivers, descending to the trail where they stood in silence as the chieftains voiced their individual opinions of the meeting.

'There is much to be gained,' Vran opined.

'We could not take their Ashar-damned fort,' nodded Darien. 'Mayhap the hef-Alador is right – their Lady *is* mightier than Ashar.'

Remyd of the Caroc made the three-fingered warding gesture, glancing about as though he feared the god might hear his blasphemy and strike them down.

'A woman?' grunted Cord scornfully, his contempt shared by his fellow Drott.

'The Messenger deserted us,' Vran pointed out.

'Perhaps Ashar tests us,' suggested Gryth of the Vistral.

'I will test you,' grunted Ostral. 'For the horse.'

Gryth's hand fell to his sword hilt, his bearded features twisting in a snarl.

'This is not the time!' warned Vran. 'You fight for the torque in the circle. Before your tribe, where all can see.'

'Aye,' Darien agreed. 'And let us first see what we may obtain from the Kingdoms without bloodshed.'

'Mayhap horses for all,' said Farlan hopefully.

Cord and Threnol grunted laughter, thinking that it would be the man who took the torque and became ulan of the Drott who would decide to which hogan the animals went.

'Let us return,' Darien advised, 'and tell our people what we have decided.'

The others nodded their assent and the chieftains walked to where their stocky forest ponies stood waiting, mounting and riding away as the warriors of the Gehrim broke into a run about them.

When they were gone from sight a soot-black crow that had perched all the while upon the winter-denuded limb of a wind-lashed tree flapped its wings and soared over the empty roadway. It spiralled, riding the air currents high enough that it could see both groups depart the scene before it adjusted the set of its pin feathers and began to descend. It landed heavily, talons scraping on the stone where the men had sat, and stood for a moment, turning its great-beaked head this way and that, studying the rocks through eyes that glowed red as molten lava. Then it cawed once and the air about it shimmered, wan winter sunlight seeming to focus upon a point that became incandescent, the cold momentarily driven back by the flash of sulphurous fire that exploded around it. When the fulgency waned, Taws stood there, his lipless mouth curved in a smile.

'So,' he murmured to the empty air, his voice a sussuration menacing as a serpent's hiss, 'they go into the Kingdoms. Master, I see the way.'

Chapter Three

THE shapeshifting was arduous, depleting his stored energy to far greater extent than external manifestation of his powers, and for long moments he stood in silence, white-maned head bowed and cratered eyes shut as he sucked in great gasps of the cold, river-moist air, his body adjusting to its more familiar configuration. At last he raised his head, stretching to his full height, staring southwards in the direction of the Kingdoms. He was tempted to await the arrival of the masons, to lure one in amongst the rocks and replenish his strength with the sweet essence of humankind, but deemed that too risky a venture, choosing instead to slink back to his hiding place and succour himself with rest. He was too close to the attainment of his first goal to jeopardise the venture for want of sustenance – and the death of another Kingdomer might alert the blue-robed enemy to his presence.

He could feel the strength of their cursed goddess here, this close to the walls of High Fort, now that he was no longer sustained by the mass-mind of the Horde, and he knew that he must employ cunning to breach the defences she had established. Swept through on the headlong tide of barbarian invasion he would have encountered no difficulty, but the forest folk had deserted him and he was alone, huddled in a niche of protective rock as he dreamed of revenge and domination. It had been only with an effort of will that he had held back from blasting the Ashar-damned princeling with searing fire as the mewling boy mouthed his platitudes and seduced the chieftains with his promises, but he had known that the act, sweet as it would have been, could not serve his master's purpose, for Kedryn's death was but a part of that design, and to kill the boy then would have betrayed his presence. Better to wait and relish the sapor of anticipated vengeance enhanced by the knowledge that it was Kedryn himself who opened the way.

Without that opening – without the *invitation* to cross the thaumatological barriers that denied his master access to the

58

Kingdoms – he doubted he could have found a way to the one he sought. Now, however, it was clear: he needed only bide his time and attach himself to the woodlanders bade welcome to the fort.

There would be danger, of course, and it would weaken him, for he would require all his puissance to ward himself with concealing magic, establishing a barrier about himself that the blue-robed women might remain unaware of his coming. But most would be occupied with the arrival of the forest folk and once inside the fort he believed he could find refuge until the time might come to seek out the one he had selected as the instrument of his vengeance and his master's awful design. Until that time he would rest, harbouring his strength.

He crouched beneath the shadow of great boulders, drawing his furs close about him as the high altitude winds harlequined the sky with cloud patterns, sunlight and darkness patchworking the ground. The Idre hissed and rumbled beyond the Beltrevan trail and after a while he became aware of the sharper clatter of the masons' hammers, the sound of voices drifting on the wind that skirled the edges of the forest. The proximity of the men edged his hunger and he fought the temptation to seek them out, promising himself a feasting once he had achieved his objective. He thought of Kedryn, wondering why the princeling hid his eyes behind a bandage; presumably because of some wound received during the fighting, though how, or at whose hand, he did not know, for Borsus had failed to return after he had sent the warrior, berserk, in search of the boy. It was of no great consequence and in time he would find out, perhaps even restore vison so that Kedryn might look upon his face as he sucked out the boy's life. That was a pleasant thought, and he warmed himself with it as he waited for the day to wane and night to fall that he might go about his master's business.

He was ready when the sun appeared over the rimrock of the Lozins, spilling wan light between the canyon walls. The sky was a sulphurous grey, drifting the thin threat of snow over the barren nudity of the rock-strewn terrain, a skein of geese arrowing south as he studied the heavens, invoking Ashar's help as he prepared for the transmogrification that would carry hi n into the Kingdoms. The cantrip was completed before the column of barbarians appeared and he had time to position himself close to where they must pass. He saw them coming, Vran, Darien and Remyd abreast as befitted the most senior, riding the small, thick-coated horses of the Beltrevan, the three Drott ala-Ulans behind, the two Vistral at the rear, all clad in their finest gear, luxuriant cloaks of bear and wolf and otter draping their shoulders. Around them in a protective semi-circle marched the sixty Gehrim, each bearing a spear from which fluttered the red and white clusters of the peace feathers. The Gehrim were clad in leather and link mail, concealing helms obscuring their features, and he dismissed them as potential carriers, bracing his hindmost legs as he saw that Remyd would pass closest to his position.

As they drew level he sprang out, marvelling at the strength of the form he had selected, landing easily on the Caroc ulan's mount.

The animal snorted as it sensed his presence, switching its tail and skittering across the trail. Remyd mouthed a curse and heeled the pony into line as the enhancement of the glamour took effect and the beast lost its awareness of Taws' inhabitation of its hide, continuing its steady plodding as the transformed mage began to work his way forwards from the hindquarters through the bristling forest of hair. He found the cantle of Remyd's saddle and vaulted upwards, all six of his legs making easy purchase in the thickness of the wolfskin cloak, up which he scuttled to the shoulder. Remyd's skull was covered with a round helm of cured bullhide banded with rings of metal, cheek flaps covering the sides of his red-bearded face. Taws leapt from the Caroc's shoulder to the profusion of greasy hair that hid his neck, working his way down into the grumous mass. So close to the man's skin he could no longer contain his hunger and drove the labrum of his chosen form down through the tissue to pierce a blood vessel. Remyd grunted, reaching his free hand up to scratch at his neck, but he was accustomed to fleas and after that initial exploration paid Taws no further attention.

The mage drank his fill, the blood sustaining his tiny form, strengthening him so that after a while he withdrew the needle of his mouth parts and rode the mane of the Caroc's hair as he drew steadily closer to High Fort.

The gates stood open, lined on either side by warriors, and the barbarian chieftains slowed their advance, peering warily at the armed men as the surrounding Gehrim clutched their spears, ready to fight. Then, from the shadows of the arch, Kedryn stepped into view, flanked by the one called Brannoc. The latter called a greeting that to Taws' changed senses was a mere booming of sound, a vibration of the air akin to the background rumble of the river, and he adjusted the cantrip governing his state that he might understand what they said. He knew it would be the last time he could interfere directly, for the woodlanders moved forwards on the shout and he drew himself in, focusing all his powers on concealment as they approached the entrance.

The strength of the Lady was almost palpable here, pressing down upon him so that for a moment he feared discovery or destruction, but then Kedryn himself called a welcome and from behind him stepped King Darr, regal in tunic of royal blue, the crown of the Kingdoms glinting about his temples, his own voice raised in greeting. There were others, too, the lords of Tamur and Kesh and Ust-Galich, he guessed, and the chatelains of High and Low Forts, their faces solemn as they bowed the invitation to enter.

It was enough: he was of the party bade welcome to the fortress – *invited* into the Kingdoms – and it allowed him access, countering the defensive magicks. Had he then possessed lungs, he would have sighed his relief, for the pressure eased as they crossed the portal and the chieftains dismounted in the stone-walled courtyard, staring about them at the nobles and warriors who stared back, all thinking that not very long ago they had been bent on destroying one another. Introductions were effected and he learnt that the tall, broad-shouldered man so much like Kedryn was, in fact, the boy's father, Bedyr Caitin of Tamur; that the beak nosed lord in robes of black silk was Jarl of Kesh; and that the dandified figure in gold and green was Hattim Sethiyan of Ust-Galich. The rest he dismissed for they were not important: he now had the information he required, and needed only bide his time, awaiting the propitious moment.

A warrior not of the Kingdoms to judge by the luteous shading of his skin moved to Kedryn's side, guiding the youth as he asked the forest folk to follow him and proceeded into the bowels of the fort, accompanied by the others. They passed Sisters in their blue robes as they traversed the corridors and courtyards, but none appeared aware of Taws' presence and he emerged from the southern gates riding Remyd's hair with a savage satisfaction thrilling his insectile frame.

The wind blew less fierce here, breaking on the barrier of the mountain wall and the ramparts of the fort, but it was still strong enough to stream the pennants fluttering from the myriad lance heads and tents that covered the plain beyond the town. Folk from the settlement were clustered at the foot of the glacis, their features suspicious as they eyed the party moving slowly past them, seeming less ready to forgive past threat than the warriors who had fought their battle. Taws paid them scant attention, for his senses were fixed on the army spread before him. From the elevation of the glacis he could

61

see that all the warriors of the Kingdoms were drawn up in ranks before a baldachin erected above a dais of polished wood. The columns supporting the canopy stood proud with the banners of the Kingdoms, the tripartite crown of Andurel standing golden against the white background of the pennant, the fist of Tamur within a circle of pale blue, the black horse head of Kesh ringed with silver, and the brilliant sunburst of Ust-Galich set against a green that matched the hue of Hattim's robes. The warriors surrounded the pavilion, Keshi horsemen standing their mounts between phalanxes of Tamurin archers and Galichian spearmen, cuirassed halbadiers and lightly-armoured swordsmen rubbing shoulders with axe-bearers and irregulars, as though every able-bodied man in the Kingdoms had answered the call to war. There was a power of purpose in them, a faith and a determination that dinned against the mage's senses as the ranks parted to afford the barbarians and their hosts passage through to the dais. He was grateful when Remyd mounted the steps and took the seat offered by Darr, setting a little distance between him and the watching army.

Food and wine were brought, and the woodlanders set to eating with gusto, drinking deep of the vintages as negotiations proceeded. They observed a demonstration of Keshi equestrian skills and Tamurin bowmanship; five superb horses were paraded before them, eliciting grunts of admiration and covetous glances; five wagons laden with wine kegs were shown; and the forest folk agreed to all the terms outlined by Darr.

It was of no moment to Taws, for the woodlanders were no longer useful to him, save Remyd who served as his carrier, and that for not much longer. He listened to them betray his master with promises of peace and the bribes of trade, hearing the one called Brannoc announced Warden of the Forest. He watched as each man drew a blade across his palm, spilling red blood into a goblet of chased silver, vowing that should he foreswear his oath his lifeblood should flow in full measure, the goblet then scoured with cleansing fire – in mockery, to Taws' mind, of Ashar.

And then his time came.

The sun lowered towards the western horizon and the chieftains grew restless, unwilling for all their declarations of friendship to spend the night behind the walls of High Fort. They rose, unsteady from the wine and evshan they had consumed, and swore a final oath, clasping hands with each lord in turn. As Remyd's bloodied palm touched Hattim's the mage propelled himself out from the barbarian's hair on to the arm. He bunched his hindlegs and sprang, arcing outwards to land upon the silken sleeve of the Galichian's robe. Rapidly he leapt again, hurling himself to Hattim's shoulder and burrowing into the soft fur that adorned the collar of the tunic. Hattim, his handsome features contorted in barely disguised disgust as he wiped his smeared palm with a square of silk, did not see the flea.

He did not see it as he sat at supper, nor after as he disrobed prepatory to retirement, and Taws found himself ensconced within a wardrobe as the lord of Ust-Galich donned night attire and climbed beneath the thick bearskin covering his bed.

While Hattim slept the mage emerged from his place of conceal-ment, launching his altered frame across the floor to spring on to the bed. The bearskin was a forest that he negotiated to emerge overlooking Hattim's exposed throat, his compound eyes fixed on the pulse that throbbed above the Galichian's carotid artery. He hopped delicately on to the soft skin, the lobes of his labium touching the flesh as the needle-like stylets pierced the surface to allow the blood-sucking labrum access to the rich life-essence. He drank deep, slaking hunger, and sprang away as Hattim stirred, returning to the safety of the wardrobe. It was too early yet – and too dangerous – to risk exposing his presence, and he contented himself with the feast and the knowledge he had gleaned. Soon, he knew, Hattim would quit the fort to return to his kingdom and then, when he judged the moment right, the mage would reveal himself and begin his work.

'Those filthy barbarians have filled the place with fleas!'

Hattim stretched in the heated waters of High Fort's bath-house, dabbing irritably at the bites on his neck.

'I have not suffered.' Kedryn wished that he had chosen another time to avail himself of the facilities, but he had been unaware of Hattim's presence until Tepshen Lahl murmured a warning, and by then it was too late, courtesy preventing his departure. 'Is it not late in the year for such attacks?'

'Mayhap, but I am still bitten. Look.'

There was a splashing as the Galichian shifted position, then a grunt and, 'Forgive me – I forget.'

The apology did not sound sincere, but still Kedryn smiled his dismissal as Hattim added, 'Take my word for it. I am plagued with the accursed things.'

'You depart on the morrow, my Lord. Mayhap they will quit you then.'

'I trust they will,' Hattim retorted. 'I trust they will remain in these Lady-forsaken climes.'

The insulting reference to Tamur brought a hiss of disapproval from Tepshen Lahl and Kedryn gestured, indicating the kyo should ignore the Galichian's rudeness. He had come to the baths to cleanse himself and think in peace, not seeking argument or company, for there was much on his mind and he had hoped that solitude and the soothing water might help him assemble his thoughts in some sensible manner.

Mostly they were concerned with Wynett and his own imminent departure.

He had attended the hospital regularly since the parley, dutifully submittingly himself to the ministrations of the Sister Hospitaller, although with increasingly less hope of her curing his blindness than from a desire to spend as much time as possible in her presence. Neither she nor the Sisters who had accompanied King Darr north had succeeded in undoing the glamour that stole his sight and it was generally accepted that only in Estrevan might he find Sisters possessed of the necessary talents to lift the gramarye. Now, with the treaties agreed, there was no further reason to linger in the north and Bedyr had voiced the opinion that departure for Caitin Hold, and thence to Estrevan, was his wisest course of action. He had spoken again to Wynett of her accompanying him, but she had proven evasive, refusing to commit herself one way or the other. Sensing that this was a dilemma for her, born of what he hoped was growing affection, he had exercised self-discipline and refrained from pressing her on the matter, even though he longed to hold her and beg her to come with him. Now it could be only a matter of days before he left, the Tamurin army already broken up and the warriors marching back to homes and families they longed to see again, only a token force remaining to escort their Lord and Prince home to Caitin Hold. He found himself torn between the desire to revisit the familiar surroundings of his own home, to hear his mother's voice and then journey on to the Sacred City in hope of regaining his sight and the painful ache of likely parting – perhaps for ever – with Wynett.

Already the bulk of Jarl's Keshi were transferred across the Idre, and on the morrow the king took ship with Galen Sadreth on the *Vashti* for distant Andurel. Hattim had announced that he would follow the river down too, leaving his army to travel overland, and only Bedyr had so far failed to set a date for the return journey. Kedryn was unsure of his father's reasons, for Bedyr had, uncharacteristically, proven as evasive as Wynett when questioned in the matter. He sensed that his father had some plan afoot, but what it was he had no idea, Bedyr merely advising him when he pressed the matter to bide his time.

He felt that he had done all he could in the matter of his love, short of openly declaring it to the Sister – which was, he felt certain, the one thing that would guarantee her refusal to accompany him – and he found himself in a quandary. He had come to the bath-house seeking the peace of mind that might aid him in resolving the problem, and instead found Hattim Sethiyan complaining of fleas.

He lay back, letting the heated water flow over him, blocking out the Galichian's voice as he pondered his dilemma. His departure could not be much longer delayed and he might be forced to bid Wynett farewell. He could think of no means he had not already tried to persuade her to come with him and he was forced to contemplate the future without her. It frightened him: he had found happiness in her presence and he did not like the thought of leaving her behind. Perhaps, whatever the Sisters of Estrevan might accomplish, of never seeing her again. The calm he had hoped to find faded, replaced with a black despair, through which Hattim's words came as no more than the gurgling of the water in the pipes that fed the massive tub.

'I said your father delays your departure.'

'No doubt he has his reasons.'

Hattim's tone was petulant and Kedryn answered in kind, shortly, uninterested in the Galichian's observations. It was curious enough that the southern lord should make conversation at all for he mostly ignored Kedryn, and on those occasions he found himself forced to speak with the younger man it was briefly and less than courteously. Kedryn, in turn, did his best to avoid Hattim, which had been relatively easy, the Galichian spending much time of late in his chambers whilst Kedryn, when not able to commandeer Wynett's company, passed the hours exercising with Tepshen Lahl, who refused to accept blindness as a reason for sloth.

'No doubt,' Hattim snapped back, 'but why? I had thought you anxious to make your pilgrimage.'

'We shall depart in time,' Kedryn replied tersely.

'For Caitin Hold and thence to Estrevan?'

'Aye.' Kedryn wondered why Hattim needed ask the question, common knowledge that it was.

'And Sister Wynett will go with you?'

Kedryn's jaw dropped and then clenched at the arrogant presumption of the query, intruding as it did on his inmost thoughts.

'I do not know, my lord,' he responded formally. 'It will be her decision.'

'She makes a prettier nurse than your bondsman.'

Kedryn heard Tepshen Lahl shift position at this insult, water lapping against his chest as the easterner tensed. Quickly he said, 'Tepshen is not a bondsman, Lord Hattim. He is a freeman who chooses to grace Tamur with his loyalty.'

'My apologies,' Hattim offered negligently. 'Boredom renders me forgetful.'

'Then you must be pleased at the imminence of your departure,' Kedryn retorted.

'I am,' Hattim agreed, an indefinable undercurrent in his voice, 'I am mightily pleased.'

Kedryn wondered what it was he heard in the Galichian's tone, or if he merely imagined it, his blindness denying him the ability to read the expression on the man's face. Perhaps Hattim was simply anxious to depart the rude hospitality of High Fort, anxious to return to the softer climes of Ust-Galich. Or was there something else?

He heard water slap against the tiled confines of the bath as Hattim rose, the sucking sounds of a body lifting.

'We shall meet again,' the lord of Ust-Galich declared. 'Until then, farewell.'

Kedryn listened to bare feet pad moistly across the floor and heard a door swing softly closed. 'Has he gone?' he asked quietly.

'Aye,' Tepshen Lahl confirmed. 'Not before time.'

'He lacks manners,' Kedryn observed.

Tepshen grunted, the sound expressing his opinion of Hattim Sethiyan effectively as any words.

'But we shall not suffer his company much longer,' Kedryn murmured.

'No,' said Tepshen, something in his response prompting a fresh wave of curiosity.

'What is it?' Kedryn asked. 'What did you see?'

'Did you not hear it?' countered the easterner.

'He sounded . . .' Kedryn paused, trying to pin down exactly what it was he had heard in Sethiyan's tone, '. . . different.'

'There was hate in his eyes,' Tepshen declared. 'He tried to hide it, but it was there.'

'Of me?' Kedryn shrugged, sending wavelets across the pool. 'The trajea is long behind us.'

'Perhaps there is something else,' the kyo suggested. 'Envy? I am not sure, but that man is your enemy and you had best beware.'

'What threat can he offer?' asked Kedryn. 'He departs on the morrow for the south, and we shall soon return to Caitin Hold. After that there will be the Gadrizels and all the Kormish Waste between us.'

'Even so,' murmured Tepshen, leaving the sentence unfinished.

'Even so,' Kedryn said firmly, fighting the melancholy the statement induced, 'I shall forget Hattim Sethiyan. Now will you help me from this tub? I have soaked long enough.'

He rose, feeling Tepshen's sinewy arm descend about his shoulders, steering him towards the steps emerging from the pool. They climbed out and stood gasping beneath the cascade of icy water channelled from the same spring as fed the tub, its invigorating chill tingling almost painfully on skin heated by the bath. Shivering, Kedryn took the towel the kyo passed him and set to rubbing warmth back into his body. Then, refreshed, he dressed and went looking for Wynett.

He could not find her, however, for the Sister was then seated in King Darr's private chambers, her face troubled as she heard out Bedyr Caitin, eyes the hue of cornflowers in high summer shifting from the serious, almost supplicatory visage of the Lord of Tamur to the gentle features of her royal father and on to meet the calm gaze of Bethany, paramount of the Andurel Sisters now that Grania was dead.

'I ask you to consider it for Kedryn's sake,' Bedyr urged.

'Do you ask me to place my vows in jeopardy?' she countered, a blush suffusing her tanned face as she wrung her hands.

'How should that be?' asked Bethany, softly.

'I find him attractive!' Wynett said, the admission deepening the roseate glow decorating her cheeks. 'And he has all but declared his love for me. It is hopeless, Sister! I am sworn to the Lady – and I *will not* break my vows.'

'It is your will alone that defends your promise,' Bethany said. 'I cannot believe that Kedryn would presume to force himself upon you, so there can be no question of your reneging on your fealty unless you choose it.'

'But the temptation will be there,' Wynett retorted. 'And what pain might I cause Kedryn? I would not inflict further suffering on him.'

'He will suffer if he must leave you behind,' Bedyr said.

'A brief pain,' answered Wynett. 'To accompany him to Estrevan can only protract his anguish.'

'Your presence would be a comfort, not an anguish,' Bedyr declared. 'His blindness brings him to the brink of despair, and your company lifts him. I would not impose upon you, but I ask you to consider that in deciding.'

'There is another consideration,' Bethany interjected. 'Kedryn is the one foretold in Alaria's Text.'

'I know that,' Wynett acknowledged, 'But how does that affect my decision?'

'He is the one – likely the only one – able to defeat Ashar's purpose,' the elder Sister said slowly. 'We are agreed the Messenger lives still – by all accounts he fled back into his master's domain when he saw the Horde defeated, but he was not destroyed – and while he lives, the Kingdoms stand in danger. How he might next threaten us I do not know, but the Text clearly indicates that only Kedryn may stand against him in the final battle. Kedryn, however, stands in danger of sinking into despair. We had not foreseen the glamour that robs him of sight, and that is presently a mighty aid to Ashar, for loss of sight – as Bedyr says – robs Kedryn of hope.'

'I cannot restore his sight,' Wynett interrupted. 'I have tried! I have done everything in my power, but my talent is not strong enough.'

'Perhaps not,' continued Bethany calmly, 'but you do offer him hope.'

'I will not offer him false hope,' Wynett said quickly. 'I cannot believe the Lady would ask that of me, and I would not insult Kedryn with duplicity.'

'I do not ask that you should,' Bethany informed the younger woman firmly. 'I state a fact: in his present mood Kedryn is weakened. Despair breeds doubt and he is vulnerable to whatever machinations Ashar's minion might bring against him. Your presence alone uplifts him, and therefore I ask that you consider Bedyr's request.

'It is your decision, Sister, and should you choose to remain here none will lay blame at your door.'

'But he must know his hopes are futile.' Wynett's voice was plaintive. 'I could not offer him what he wants; nor allow him to believe falsely.'

'No,' Bethany agreed, 'were you to decide it best to accompany him you should make clear your feelings. Let Kedryn know that you go

68

with him as Kyrie's acolyte, companion to the Chosen One, and for that reason alone if that is truly the diktat of your heart.'

'Would that not be to fuel hope where none exists?' asked Wynett, her frown dubious.

'You can do no more than tell him the truth,' Bethany advised. 'What he believes then is of his choosing.'

'So his hopes would be dashed when we reached Estrevan,' Wynett said. 'Is that kind?'

'He would have hope until then,' countered the older woman, 'and be consequently warded against despair.'

Wynett shook her head helplessly, unsure which way to turn. In Bedyr's eyes she saw a mute plea that she should help his son, the desire of a fond father to aid his child in whatever way he might; Bethany's gaze was calm and unreadable, forcing upon her the prime consideration of the Lady's teachings: that self-determination, free choice, was all. She looked to Darr, who smiled and shrugged, speaking for the first time.

'I do not speak as your father,' he declared, 'nor do I wish to influence you with royal desires. I speak as one to whom the governance of these Kingdoms has been entrusted, and as a friend to Kedryn. What Bethany says is true; what Bedyr says is true: Kedryn is prey to black despair and that may – I cannot know for sure – threaten the Kingdoms. I would therefore lend my voice to the entreaties you have heard. I cannot, nor would I, command you, but I ask that you ponder on these things and decide for yourself.

'Perhaps this will aid you.' He brought a sealed packet from within his robe and Wynett gasped as she recognised the signet of the Sorority imprinted in the wax. Darr's kindly features assumed an expression of embarrassment. 'I hope you will forgive me the assumption, but it seemed to me a matter in which the advice of Estrevan may well be helpful. I do not know what it says – I sent mehdri to the Morfah Pass with a report of the situation and the senders there communicated with Estrevan. This is Gerat's reply. Best read it at your leisure, I think.'

Wynett nodded, staring at the blue-tinted parchment, her fingers touching the violet wax nervously.

'I would be alone,' she murmured, 'to think. With your permission?'

Darr smiled his agreement and she rose, inclining her head politely to Bethany and Bedyr.

In the corridor outside she halted, breathing deeply as confusion skirled through her mind random as the wind that buffetted the ramparts. The letter seemed to vibrate in her grasp and she clutched it to her bosom, disciplining herself to think calmly. She needed to be alone and she suspected that Kedryn would find her should she return to her quarters in the hospital. Just now he was the last person she wanted to see, for his presence would serve only to confuse her further and the decision she knew she must reach was too momentous to allow for such distraction. Therefore she walked away from the stairs that would carry her down to the lower regions of the fort and paced instead towards the narrow well that thrust upwards to the outer walls.

The air grew chill as she climbed, oblivious of the curious stares of the soldiery she passed, emerging on to the crenellated rampart that faced across the Idre to the east. Low Fort was a misty bulk in the overcast of late afternoon, the sky above ominously grey, livid to the north with the threat of snow. The wind streamed her blonde hair and she brushed it unthinking from her eyes, feeling her gown flatten against her body, caressed by the gusting. She found a buttress that afforded shelter from the blustering draught and leant against the cold stone as her fingers found the seal and broke it, carefully unfolding the parchment as she mouthed a prayer to the Lady for guidance and slowly tilted her head to read what was written there.

It was brief enough, a few lines only, the commencement offering greetings from her faraway sisters and the mundane hope that she was well. She did not recognise the hand that had penned the words nor the signature at the foot, but the brief sentences that offered guidance seemed to blaze from the page.

You must remember that Kedryn Caitin is the Chosen One and that you are a Sister, and therefore the Lady stands with you both. She will guide you. Look into your own heart and seek Her aid in your decision.

Wynett re-read the words, finding no further advice on the second examination, and folded the parchment. If my father hoped this would sway me, she thought, he will be disappointed, then dismissed the conceit as unworthy: Darr's concern was for the welfare of the Kingdoms, transcending pettiness and personal consideration. He had stated his case fairly and left the final decision to her. As had they all, which in a way rendered it that much the harder. Were it taken from her it would be so easy, and she might find the excuse of duty lifting the burden of choice from her shoulders. But that was clearly not to be: the decision was hers alone.

She turned, moving to the embrasure that afforded a view of the river, looking to the tumbling waters as if seeking answers in the waves that foamed the surface of the Idre. She had known it must come to this but had succeeded in driving that knowledge to the back of her mind, refusing to contemplate the inevitable until it arrived, knocking on the doors of her consciousness, indeed, upon her conscience. As much as Bedyr – as much as anyone – she had witnessed Kedryn's shifting moods. She had been aware of the fortitude with which he endured his affliction and knew that to be a barrier against the dark vampire of despair prowling the edges of his mind. She knew how much he relied on her, less now in hope of cure than of mere presence. He had not spoken his love, but it was there in his voice and his touch, and when she dared permit herself such risk as to consider it she knew that were she not a Sister she would gladly accept his affection. That was what frightened her: that the long journey to Estrevan would throw them so close together she would find herself unable to resist, forget her vows and succumb to the temptation of his embrace. And that would mean the ending of her Sisterhood, a relinquishment of everything she had sought, all she had wanted since first she felt her healing talent and secured her father's permission to depart the White Palace to take up the blue robe of the Sorority. It would, surely, render her life meaningless.

Yet she could not deny that she did love him and the thought frightened her: she had felt herself secure within her vows, content to dispense her love generally, manifesting in healing. She had not believed one man might so affect her, prompting her even to contemplate forsaking her place within the ranks of the Sisterhood.

She felt a tear course down her cheek, for she felt confronted by an insoluble problem. They were right, Darr and Bedyr – if she did not accompany Kedryn he would most likely succumb to despondency. It had not occurred to her that that chimera might render him victim to the Messenger, and Bethany's comments on that possibility served to confuse her further. Should she agree from a sense of duty? Or would that merely, as she suspected, render Kedryn prone to false hope and the consequently greater disappointment of unsatisfied anticipation? She had hoped, perhaps wrongly, perhaps unfairly, that he would depart without forcing the agony of decision upon her, but now she must face the dilemma.

'Lady,' she whispered to the wind howling along the river canyon, 'show me what I must do.'

The wind offered no more answer than the river, its shrilling only the threat of encroaching winter, the promise of snow cold as the knife of choice that turned inside her and she turned from the sheltering alcove to walk weary along the ramparts.

Below, moving solemnly along the Beltrevan road, she could see the forest folk carrying their dead back to the woodlands. There were so many lost to Ashar's design, wasted lives spent in futile hatred, driven by the blandishments of the Messenger. She had not wept for them because she had been too occupied with the task of healing, of giving life, but now her tears came, cold upon the cheeks as she observed the pitiful remnants borne on carts and litters dragged by the hulking forest hounds. She did not hear the warrior who approached her, grounding his spear as he tugged his cloak from his shoulders and held it to her.

'Sister, take this. The walls are chill.'

She turned and he saw her tears, settling the warm cloth about her with a nervous smile.

'Why do you weep, Sister?'

'For the dead,' she replied, grateful for his kindness.

'They sought it.' he said with a warrior's blunt acceptance of the bloody facts of war. 'There would have been far more had Prince Kedryn not slain the hef-Ulan. Perhaps they would have overcome us, and we should be dead. They would not mourn us, Sister.'

'Mayhap,' she allowed, 'but still they died.'

'They followed Ashar's minion.' The guard held his spear to his chest as though the stout ash pole warmed him. 'They sought to bring us down with magicks. We sought no war.'

'No,' Wynett nodded, 'we did not. But they were misled by the Messenger. He set promises before them like baubles before children, and they reached out to take what he offered.'

'He will meet his due,' the soldier grunted, shaping Kyrie's sign as though to ward off the evil even mention of the Messenger's name might provoke. 'Is Kedryn not the Chosen One? When Estrevan restores his sight he will face the Messenger and destroy him.'

'Is that what they say?' Wynett asked, wiping drying tears from her eyes.

'Aye.' The soldier appeared surprised that she should ask. 'Niloc Yarrum brought Ashar's power against him, but still the prince defeated the barbarian. I do not properly understand these things, but I know that Prince Kedryn is a hero blessed by the Lady. And I know the Messenger was not amongst the dead, so he lives still. But

Kedryn will defeat him. You are of Estrevan, Sister – you must know that.'

Wynett smiled, smoothing hair that tangled and blew about her face. 'I am a Sister Hospitaller, my friend. My talent is for healing, not foretelling.'

'It is common talk,' the warrior shrugged, confused that one of the Sorority should evince such lack of knowledge. 'Some call him the Defender and say the blood of Corwyn flows in his veins. I do not know if that is true – and good Tamurin blood is enough for me – but I know we likely owe him our lives.'

'We do,' Wynett agreed.

The soldier glanced along the windswept ramparts to where his telleman stood beside a group of masons. 'I must return to my post, Sister. Will you leave the cloak in the guard room below?'

Wynett mouthed the promise and watched the man stride away. His faith in Kedryn was simple and direct, and she knew that were she to ask his opinion he would undoubtedly tell her to go with Kedryn to Estrevan, likely tell her it was her duty.

But was it, she wondered. Was her duty not first to the Lady? And did Kedryn, albeit unwittingly, not represent a threat to that duty?

Or was this a test of her faith? Surely if that were strong enough she would find the will to resist the loving temptation within herself. To go as Bethany had suggested, strong in her faith, her resolution explained to Kedryn.

Or would that, as she believed, serve only to prolong his suffering?

There was no resolution to be found in wind or river or soldierly words, only inside her, and there she doubted her own strength. She drew the cloak tight about her, nestling her face into the high collar as though to hide, and paced along the wall to the stairwell, still undecided. All she could do, it seemed, was trust in the Lady to show her the way, and with that in mind she decided to seek out the chapel.

She was passing beneath the arched roof of a walkway when Hattim Sethiyan stepped from a shadowed chamber, blocking her path. The lord of Ust-Galich was swathed in a luxurious cloak of sable, the silver-tipped fur reflecting the light of the flambeaux that illuminated the collonaded passage, the single earring he favoured glittering. He bowed ceremoniously, an insincere smile stretching his mouth.

'Sister Wynett, you appear troubled.'

'My Lord,' she responded, hoping the formal reply would be

73

enough for him. She felt no liking for the Galichian, though she did her best to hide her antipathy.

'You doubtless ponder the merits of a visit to Estrevan.' He made no move to allow her past, seemingly intent on questioning her. 'In company with our young hero.'

'Have you become a reader of minds, my Lord?' she demanded, irritation setting an edge to her voice.

Hattim ignored it, still smiling as he pushed a hand beneath the collar of his cloak to rub at his neck. 'No, lady, not yet. I merely enquire from general interest.'

Wynett stared at him, thinking that his eyes had assumed the reddish hue of a drinker, although nothing in his manner suggested that he imbibed. Perhaps it was simply the radiance of the torches. 'I am undecided,' she said honestly.

'I see.'

There was an oddly musing quality to his voice, as though he had hoped for more definite an answer and as he brought his hand from his neck Wynett noticed a smear of blood on his fingers.

'You are hurt?' she asked.

'No!' Hattim spoke a little too swiftly, glancing at his fingers and then wiping the blood carelessly on the fur of his cape. 'Flea bites. No more than that. Our forest friends left us a gift, I think.'

'Would you have me tend them?'

Again his response was a trifle too urgent. 'No! Thank you, but they are of no great moment and will doubtless heal in time.'

'I have preparations that will ease the sting,' she offered dutifully, not liking the way he looked at her.

Hattim made a dismissive gesture, his smile oily.

'I assure you, Sister, that I am quite well. They heal of their own accord. I would not take up your time.'

'As you wish,' she allowed. 'But should you change your mind any of my Sisters will know where they are to be found.'

The Galichian essayed a deep bow that was strangely mocking. As his head ducked, the cloak fell away a little and Wynett saw a plethora of marks clustering his throat. They seemed more than a trifle to her, and Hattim Sethiyan had never struck her as one to suffer discomfort with such a casual air. He had refused her offer, however, and she chose not to comment, though it occurred to her that no one else had complained of parasites.

'Where are you bound?' he asked, adjusting the collar to conceal his neck again.

'To the chapel,' she answered, unthinking.

'To pray to your Lady, no doubt.'

Wynett nodded, wondering at the curious mode he gave the title. Was the Lady not of all the Kingdoms, so why did he choose to use the personal possessive? She said only, 'That is correct, my Lord.'

'And do you think she will give the answer you seek?'

'I believe she will answer,' Wynett replied, wishing he would let her past.

'But will it be what you want to hear?' he insisted.

'That is for the Lady to decide, not I.' She found his tone offensive.

'Quite.' Hattim nodded and at last stood back to let her go by. Wynett ducked her head briefly in recognition of his rank and moved past him, aware of his eyes following her. She quickened her step, anxious to be gone from his scrutiny for no reason she could clearly define save that she found it unpleasant, as if he stripped her with his gaze.

She made her way to the chapel, dismissing Hattim from her thoughts as she paused in the doorway, allowing the sense of tranquility that always seemed to pervade the simple room to wash over her.

It was a chamber unadorned with icons or ornaments, dark now so that torches had been set in the niches between the windows, their flames pinking the pale blue wash of the plastered walls. The floor was tiled in abstract mosaics of white and blue, reminiscent of a summer sky, that impression enhanced by the cerulean vault of the roof. Plain wooden benches were set in rows, the polished wood glowing in the torchlight. There was no one else present and Wynett sat down, staring at the far window, seeing only darkness beyond. She made the sign of the Lady and folded her hands on the lap of her robe, closing her eyes as she cleared her mind, rendering herself receptive to insight should such be granted her.

There was a quiet to the place that was found nowhere else in High Fort, a hush that was more than just absence of noise, as if the Lady touched the chamber with her presence and set it apart from the bustle of the garrison. The air, even, was different, still without hint of the mustiness, clean in her nostrils as a spring zephyr, cool without being cold. Wynett voiced a silent prayer into the stillness and waited.

Peace entered her, but when she opened her eyes and saw the

darkness beyond the window was now the black of evening she had no answer. The turmoil that had gripped her on the ramparts was faded, but no clear course of action was revealed her and she remained faced with the quandary of decision. She rose, smoothing her gown, and sighed, turning from the chapel back to the world outside.

She went to the hospital and attended those tasks that awaited her there, and then retired to her small room, busying herself with the organisation of her remedies, less from need than from a desire to be occupied.

She was measuring herbs into a sachet that would bring healing sleep to a soldier whose axe-gashed leg had festered when a knocking on her door interrupted her. The door opened and Tepshen Lahl led Kedryn into the room. The kyo inclined his pig-tailed head respectfully and murmured a greeting, settling Kedryn into the chair she indicated, then departing, closing the door behind him.

'I must speak with you,' Kedryn said swiftly, as though he needed to say the words before she stopped him or his will dissolved, 'about Estrevan. We shall be leaving soon and there are things that must be said, however difficult.'

Curiously, Wynett felt none of the apprehension she had anticipated with the arrival of this moment. It was as though the calm she had felt in the chapel still held her, and even though she guessed what he was going to say, she did not experience the dread she had expected. She said softly, 'Aye, you are right.'

Kedryn swallowed, nervously touching the bandage about his eyes, and continued in a rush, 'Within days I must go, and I cannot bear the weight of not knowing any longer. Will you accompany me? You have lightened my darkness and I am not sure I can bear it without knowing you are near. I know that you have done all you can to heal me and I do not pretend to believe you can do more, so I do not ask you to come as a healer, but simply because I quail at the prospect of the journey without you.

'I would lay no claims upon you and promise to treat you with the respect due any Sister. We should not be alone, in any event; and if we were I . . .' he paused, licking his lips nervously, his hand again fiddling with the bandage, loosening it, '. . . I would not . . . say what you do not wish to hear. I ask only that you accompany me to Estrevan and after that return here if you wish. But, Wynett, I am frightened!'

His voice broke on that and his fingers worked the bandage loose, the blue cloth drifting unnoticed to the floor. Wynett rose, moving to retrieve the cloth and Kedryn reached blindly out to find the hand she did not have the heart to remove from his grip.

'I will accept whatever you decide,' he promised, his sightless face turning towards her. 'I shall not hold it against you if you opt to remain. And I hope you will forgive me for speaking so directly.'

'Of course I forgive you. There is nothing to forgive.'

She could not resist reaching out to stroke his hair, the thick brown locks soft beneath her fingers. Kedryn groaned, turning his head and loosing her trapped hand to set his arms about her waist, his face pressing against the swell of her bosom. Wynett closed her eyes on the tears that threatened to spill and held him to her.

'I am a Sister,' she said, controlling her voice only with difficulty, 'and I am sworn to celibacy. Could you accept that?'

Kedryn began to murmur an affirmative, but then choked off the words and said, 'I must. I will.'

'I can offer you nothing,' she said gently, 'save friendship. Could you bear that?'

'Better than parting from you,' he answered.

'Kedryn, listen to me.' She eased his arms from her waist, moving a short step back to place her hands upon his cheeks and tilt his face upwards, seeing tears moist in the corners of his sightless eyes. 'I am vowed to the service of the Lady and no matter what I feel as a woman, I will not depart those vows. I cannot give you what you want and I am afraid that if I were to agree I would merely give you greater pain. If I *were* to accompany you to Estrevan, what then? Would you not wish me to stay with you there? I could not do that – I have duties here – and surely parting then would be so much the harder. For you,' she paused, her heart knocking loud within her, the calm gone now, 'and for me.'

'I,' he began, then broke off, gasping, his jaw dropping as if in shock.

'What is it?'

Fear gripped Wynett for she saw a change in his face that she could not decipher. His eyelids closed over the hazel orbs and he reached up to cover the hands she still held to his cheeks and temples with his own, the lids snapping open again, wider.

'I can see,' he said, awe in his voice.

'What?' Wynett stared at him, the thudding of her heart seeming so loud it drummed about the room, ringing in her ears so that she doubted she heard aright.

'I can see!' He looked up at her, holding her hands against his face as though afraid to break the contact. 'You have been crying. And your hair is windswept. You look as though you do not believe me.'

She shook her head and he said, 'You shake your head. Wynett! I can see!'

'Kedryn,' she took her hands from his grip and held the right towards him, folding thumb and smallest finger against her palm, 'how many fingers?'

'Three,' he said. Then moaned, anguish contorting his features as he pressed fists to his temples and cried, 'It is gone! Oh, Lady, it is gone!'

Excitement burst within Wynett and she tilted his head again, peering into his eyes. Abruptly his face calmed and in a hushed voice he said, 'It is your touch! Now I see again.'

'Look.' Wynett kept her left hand on his temple and lifted a phial from the shelf behind her. 'What is this?'

'A jar,' he said firmly. 'A small jar of dark brown glass. It has a wax-sealed stopper.'

'Now?'

She removed her hand and he bit his lip. 'It fades. It is gone.'

'And now?' She replaced her hand and he smiled.

'It returns. And your smile is like the rising sun.'

She set the phial back in its place and cupped his head. 'I asked the Lady to show me what I should do,' she told him softly. I believe she has answered my prayer.'

'Your touch restores my sight,' he murmured, touching the fingers that held his face reverently.

'The Lady restores your sight,' she corrected. 'Mayhap I am her instrument, but it is she returns vision to you.'

'Will it last?' he wondered.

'It must!' she answered fiercely. 'Perhaps not immediately, but in time . . . With the wisdom of Estrevan to aid the healing.'

He turned his face into her palm, pressing his lips to the warm flesh as Wynett smiled down at him, knowing now what she must do, knowing that the answer to her quandary was given.

'I will come with you,' she promised.

Kedryn whooped laughter, pulling her to him unthinking, rising to his full height as she came into his embrace with joy on her face to match his. Her hands were still against his cheeks, but as he bent his head and kissed her on the lips he closed his eyes, not caring now that hope was rekindled.

He felt her mouth respond and his hope soared, but then she pulled away, still touching him so that he could see her face as she said, 'I will come with you, but I am still a Sister. You must remember that. We must both remember that.'

It made no difference: he was too happy.

Chapter Four

KEDRYN'S right hand clenched on the pommel of his saddle in frustration as he listened to the warriors about him tidy their gear in preparation for triumphal entry into Caitin Hold. His mood communicated to the Keshi stallion so that the great black war-horse skittered sideways, dancing out of line to prompt a grunt of warning from Tepshen Lahl. Kedryn sighed through gritted teeth, forcing himself to relax as he unfastened his hand to reach down and pat the nervous animal, feeling the neck rise as the beast sensed the tension leave him. At the head of the column, Bedyr turned his own mount to ride back to where his son was, his face clouded as the sky above.

'I am all right,' Kedryn assured his father, though the grim set of his features told the lord of Tamur this was more façade than truth and Bedyr reached across to set a hand on the young man's shoulder.

'How many miracles can you expect?'

'One,' Kedryn answered, his voice terse.

'It will come,' Bedyr said, making his tone confident. 'Already you know the blindness may be lifted.'

'Randomly!' Kedryn's response was bitter. 'Does the Lady toy with me?'

'I do not think so.' Bedyr stared at his son's sightless eyes, watching the wind ruffle his thick brown hair. 'I think she mayhap demands patience of you, but I believe she *will* ultimately restore your sight. I do not understand these things – Estrevan will give you better answers.'

'Aye.' Kedryn nodded wearily. 'But, Father, it is so hard to bear. To see, then not! To feel a cure in sight,' he snorted cynical laughter, 'only to return to darkness.'

'Knowing now there is hope,' Bedyr said.

'I am impatient.' Kedryn shrugged, forcing a smile on to his mouth. 'I would have that hope realised.'

80

'It will come.' Bedyr's hand tightened, squeezing, and Kedryn's smile grew a fraction more genuine.

'I will bear it,' he promised.

'I know you will.'

Bedyr released his son's shoulder and reined his mount over, letting the column of Tamurin pass him until the wagon bearing Wynett and their supplies drew abreast. The Sister smiled a greeting from beneath the canopy, turning on the seat as Bedyr came alongside.

'How is he?' she asked.

'Moody,' came the reply. 'With hope in sight he longs for it the fiercer.'

Wynett nodded. 'I can only counsel patience. It is a strange thing and I do not properly understand it, though I am sure my Sisters in Estrevan will.'

'I pray so,' Bedyr said fervently. 'And I am thankful you decided to accompany us.'

'I believe the Lady wants it,' Wynett told him. 'It is her will.'

'Aye,' Bedyr acknowledged, raising a hand in brief salute before cantering back to the head of the westwards moving riders.

Wynett watched him until he reached the point where Kedryn rode the big stallion and her eyes fastened on the broad shoulders that squared as though in determination, the head resolutely up as if he looked to the distant horizon, his hair, no longer confined by the bandage, tumbling loose in the wind that gusted steadily over the plain. The wagon creaked beneath her, the prairie regular enough its passage was mostly smooth, the swaying of the vehicle almost soporific and the handler, a grizzled warrior called Dys, taciturn to the point of speechlessness. She was grateful for the quiet – it gave her time to think. And she had much to ponder now that the first stage of their journey was ending and Kedryn's home was in sight.

She had gone with him to bring the news of her agreement to Bedyr, but when she had again set her hands to Kedryn's face his vision had failed to return. His disappointment was writ large on his features and she had sent for Bethany, her own excitement turning to alarm as Kedryn cursed and ground the heels of his hands against his eyes as though he would beat sight into the orbs. Darr had appeared with the Sister and when a further demonstration was suggested, sight had briefly returned, then as quickly faded.

Bethany and the king had applauded Wynett's decision to accompany the Tamurin and urged on Kedryn a patience he clearly found hard to bear. Afterwards, Bethany had taken Wynett aside to speak privately.

'Tell me exactly what happened,' she had demanded. 'Not what you did, but how you felt.'

'Felt?' Wynett had asked. 'I felt excitement.'

'No,' Bethany had said gently, 'not when he saw, but before that. When he came to you and asked you to go with him.'

Wynett remembered clearly how her heart had fluttered at that, but although she would have preferred to remain silent, she realised the older Sister was probing for an explanation that might well help Kedryn, and so she replied with complete honesty.

'I felt pity,' she had said slowly. 'I saw his pain and I wanted to soothe it. I touched his face and I knew that it would be very hard to bid him farewell. I did not want to. I felt . . . love.'

'Which he clearly feels for you,' Bethany had murmured. 'You were both gripped by a powerful emotion.'

'I am still a Sister,' Wynett had said defensively. 'And I told him I would not break my vows.'

Bethany had made a dismissive gesture, smiling at the younger woman as she said, 'I do not suggest you would, but the emotion was there and I wonder if that bonded you. Remember you shared the joining with Grania – and that clearly has imbued Kedryn with unusual powers. Mayhap it has fused you in some way.'

'I do not understand.' Wynett had shaken her head. 'I feel the same now as then.'

Bethany had nodded thoughtfully. 'But when you sought to demonstrate to Bedyr, nothing happened. You felt disappointment? And Kedryn's anguish was obvious. You shared that pain, too, and when you tried again, his sight returned, albeit briefly.'

'Extremes,' Wynett had said softly, beginning to see an explanation.

'I think it must be that,' Bethany had agreed. 'When there is some major eruption of feeling between you a link becomes established and you are able to restore Kedryn's sight. When calm descends, the power fades. Heartfelt love, shared pain – perhaps even anger – forge a bond that enables you to give him back his sight. Is that not a sign from the Lady?'

'I took it to be so,' Wynett had nodded.

'And you must work at it,' Bethany had told her. 'It will not be easy, but you must experiment.'

'With my emotions?' Wynett had asked. 'How, Sister? I can hold my emotions in check – I must if I am to spend so much time with him! – but I cannot arouse them at will.'

'No,' Bethany had agreed, 'but while you travel there will be times enough for opportunity to arise. Use them! And when you reach Estrevan tell them everything you have learnt.'

'Very well,' Wynett had promised.

After that she had spent more time than ever in Kedryn's company and recognised that Bethany's assessment was likely correct, for when they experimented calmly nothing happened, but when Kedryn grew angry or despondent, and she felt her own emotions respond, his sight came back, sometimes for only moments, at other times for longer periods. It was hard for them both, harder since quitting High Fort, and Wynett prayed daily to the Lady for fortitude and strength of purpose that she might aid Kedryn without relinquishing her vows. She was increasingly aware of the danger, of how easily she might erase the delicate barrier that stood between them and succumb to physical expression of her emotions. And that, she felt certain, would destroy her talent and render her unable to help Kedryn at all.

He, in turn, was clearly at odds with himself. Delighted that she was with him, yet frustrated by his carefully guarded promise of respect for her status as a Sister of Kyrie. He treated her with the utmost gentility, making no allusions to his obvious feelings for her, yet unable to hide them when they spoke together, for they were expressed in his tone and his touch and did not need words. Sometimes, as the days passed, she wondered if it had not been the wiser course to remain in High Fort; yet at the same time she knew she could not have done that, for he needed her to give him hope, just as Bedyr had suggested, and for all the vagaries of his condition there *was* hope.

Darr had commended her before he left, pausing at the gangplank while the *Vashti* rocked on the winter-turbulent Idre to take her hands, his visage less regal than fatherly, his thinning grey hair fluttering in the wind.

'I thank you for what you do,' he had said softly, the words intended for her and none other, 'And I have some inkling of what it means to you. For what strength it may lend you, know that I believe you act in the best interests of the Kingdoms – that perhaps your decision is vital to our safe future. May the Lady be with you, daughter.'

He had bent and kissed her then, and she had hugged him as child to father, letting him go as Galen Sadreth shouted irreverently that wind and tides paid little heed to monarchs, prompting the king to hurry in a most unregal fashion on to the pitching barque.

Darr had stood at the stern, beside the portly boatmaster, his cloak whipped by the growing wind as the crew cast off and Galen took his craft rapidly to the flood of the river, waving until the *Vashti* was a dwindling mark against the forbidding grey of the water.

Wynett had thought on his words since then, and on Bethany's parting remark: 'Remember that you are a Sister, child, and serve the Lady. Remember, too, that her service takes many forms.'

She would have questioned the older woman as to her meaning, but Bethany had given her no time, bustling on board behind the king with her blue cloak wrapped tight about her and an expression on her face that suggested her fellow Sisters would be soon administering remedies for river sickness.

There were no such farewells from Hattim Sethiyan when the lord of Ust-Galich set sail the next day. He appeared so anxious to depart that he forgot the normal courtesies, mounting the gangplank of the vessel that would bear him south with the meanest of farewells, his adieus to Rycol and Bedyr curt to the point of rudeness, his only words to Kedryn a grunted, but somehow ominous, 'We shall doubtless meet again, Prince.' Wynett had noticed that he wore a high-collared tunic beneath his cloak, the sage green material hiding his neck, and she had wondered if he still suffered the flea bites, though only briefly for she was curiously glad to see the Galichian sail away: there was something about him that set her nerves on edge.

Jarl's departure had been far more convivial, accompanied by much slapping of shoulders and promises of friendship. He had presented Kedryn with the warhorse loaned for the first meeting with the forest folk, managing to suggest that the animal was of a nature and discipline that would serve the prince of Tamur well without making any reference to Kedryn's blindness, and in his gift, and his bluff tone, Wynett had recognised genuine fondness. He had gone on board the vessel that was to ferry him over the river accompanied by Brannoc, who explained gleefully that he was travelling to Kesh to discuss the matter of horse trading – in, of course, his newfound capacity as Warden of the Forest.

There had been a little sadness then, for – with the exception of Hattim – they had been a close company, and the sudden absence of such good friends left an emptiness.

Bedyr had filled it with preparations for their own departure, his activity suggesting that he had waited only until the armies were disbanded and the commanders safely on their way to leave himself. Wynett had attended to what few last minute arrangements were needed to satisfy her that the hospital would continue to run smoothly, and Rycol had feasted them handsomely. They set out the following day, Wynett the only woman amongst the hundred Tamurin warriors riding escort.

It was a blustery morning, robbed of brightness by the heavy banks of lowering cloud that hung above the fort. To the north snow was already falling, thicker than the earlier squalls so that the Beltrevan road was carpetted in white that churned beneath the feet of the masons to ugly slush. South of the great mountain wall the snow became rain, drifting thin and steady from the leaden sky to coat horses and cloaks with a sheen of moisture. Nonetheless, their going was cheerful, the warriors laughing at the elements and even the animals prancing with high-tossed heads and dancing hooves, as if they sensed their direction was home and welcomed that return. Wynett had wrapped herself in a thick, waterproof cloak and ignored the veiling droplets as she watched the column fall into line before and behind. Bedyr took the head, flanked by Kedryn and Tepshen Lahl, all draped in soft leather cloaks that repelled the rain, the kyo scorning to use his hood, so that his oiled hair soon ran with moisture. She had thought that on horseback it was impossible to tell Kedryn was blind, for the Keshi stallion fell into step with the two flanking animals and he sat his saddle with such casual grace that he appeared in complete control.

They had gone down through the town with the farewell cheers of the soldiery behind them and the shouts of the townsfolk ahead. The streets had been lined with people despite the inclemency of the day, many running out to touch the hem of Kedryn's cloak with an almost religious awe, parents holding children aloft that they might catch a glimpse of the young man they hailed as hero. Kedryn had seemed embarrassed by the attention, and once clear of the settlement had set heels to the stallion's flanks and lifted the warhorse to a thundering gallop that brought Wynett's heart into her mouth. Neither Tepshen Lahl or Bedyr had seemed to share her fear, for they both whooped with laughter and set off after Kedryn, who, she was sure, allowed them to catch up until they charged on either side and all three hurtled over the muddy ground where not long ago peace had been forged.

She had watched as they rode away, then wheeled, circling back to rejoin the column, and she had seen the smile on Kedryn's face as he slowed the black horse, bringing it alongside the wagon.

'Jarl was generous,' he had called to her. 'This beast is magnificent.'

'Is it wise,' she had ventured, not entirely over her fear for him, 'to gallop thus?'

'The horse has eyes to see,' was his answer, 'so all I need do is stay in the saddle.'

'But if he met a jump?' she wondered.

Kedryn had laughed, pleased at the concern he heard in her voice, and said, 'Between here and the river Sol the land is flat. Look.'

She had followed his gesturing hand and seen the plain stretching out before them, given over to grass and small farms, the only obstacles seeming to be the trees that sheltered the holdings from the wind.

It had been thus for the next three days, the land undulating somewhat but never dramatically, the gently rolling terrain the Tamurin called dumbles stretching out on all sides until they came to the river Sol.

There was a small town that spread along either bank, the two parts connected by ferryboats and a larger, flat-bottomed raft that was capable of carrying wagons or livestock, the houses built low against the ground, some even descending into the earth so that they were entered by steps that went down to warm, cellar-like rooms. The column halted there, sleeping under roofs for the first time since quitting High Fort, and Wynett was able to use the public bathhouse. They ate and rested on the east bank, and it seemed that the west must have emptied, for the ferries were in constant use, accompanied by smaller craft as the inhabitants came cheerfully to set eyes on the visitors, and the men of the settlement – who had marched with the army – gave greetings to old companions.

The next morning the rain eased off and a melancholy sun essayed a way through the clouds, painting the village – Solanul, it was named – with golden light. The river was swelling with the outspill from the Lozins, but passage over was effected without incident and they continued their westwards progress cheered afresh by the warmth of Solanul's hospitality.

By mid afternoon the dumbles gave way to a less even topography, and on the horizon bulked a plateau dark with timber. This was the Tamurin heartland, the distant swell of the massif called the Geffyn. There was, Kedryn told Wynett as they sat around the campfire

86

that evening, a town at the foot of the heights, commanding the trail that ran through the forest, and another at the crest of the rise, then only woodland until they emerged on to the central Tamurin plateau, at the heart of which stood Caitin Hold.

Mention of his home seemed to produce conflicting feelings in him, and Wynett sensed that he was torn between his desire to be reunited with his mother and his disappointment that he should return blind. She tried again to restore his sight, but the attempt proved fruitless and she soon abandoned it for fear its failure should sink him into despair.

'I hope too much,' he said morosely. 'Or for too much.'

'No,' she told him, 'you are right to hope, but you must have patience, too.'

'At least you are here.' He smiled, the expression wan in the firelight. 'And I thank the Lady for that.'

'Aye.' Wynett adjusted the folds of her cloak. 'Give thanks, for she *will* restore your sight.'

Kedryn nodded and began to speak again, but then bit off his words, shaking his head when Wynett asked what it was he said so that she knew it was to do with his feelings for her. She studied him as dispassionately as she was able, knowing how hard it was for him to leave the words unsaid and sensing how afraid he was to say them. A frown creased his brow and in the glow of the flames he looked older, shadows planing his cheeks, his hair russet in the light, and she felt a great desire to hold him, and to feel his arms about her.

She bit her lip and rose, murmuring some excuse to leave him, and crossed to where the wagon stood, setting her hands to the cold metal of the wheel rim as she murmured a prayer to the Lady.

'You are well?'

She turned, recognising Tepshen Lahl's slightly accented speech, and smiled thinly.

'Aye, thank you.'

'It is not easy for you.'

She was surprised by the easterner's comment: he had spoken little to her since leaving the fort and she knew he did not share her belief in the Lady or agree with her vows, yet concern was evident in his tone.

'No,' she said, 'but it is harder for Kedryn.'

'Whom we both love,' the kyo murmured.

'Aye,' Wynett nodded, then gasped at the admission.

Tepshen Lahl smiled, his teeth very white in the darkness. 'Love is not easy. Harder still for you. That you ride with us is an honourable thing and I thank you for it.'

'You care for him,' she said, slightly nervous, for the kyo had about him an air of controlled violence that her Estrevan-trained senses felt as palpably as she would feel the menace in a caged wolf or the green eyes of a forest cat.

'I love him,' Tepshen Lahl answered simply. 'I have no son but Kedryn. In my country I would be called his *ahn-dio* – his . . . foster father is the nearest you have. I share his pain, and because you lift that pain I share some of his feeling for you. Should you ever need a friend know that you have me.'

He bowed then, ceremoniously, as might a man on completion of a formal undertaking, and turned without further word to walk back to the fire, where he drew his sword and began to oil the blade. Wynett stood a moment longer before returning herself, better composed now, and able to engage again in conversation with less likelihood of revealing the full depth of her feelings.

The journey, for all the good she knew it did, was not easy.

The next day they traversed increasingly broken terrain and Kedryn's displays of horsemanship were curtailed, the trail dropping steeply into gulleys and crossing streams beginning to swell with the threat of seasonal flooding. Stands of timber loomed about them, winter-bare forerunners of the forest ahead, and the pace of the column slowed to allow for the wagon that rocked and groaned its way down vertiginous descents and slithered wildly on the rain-slickened gradients as they climbed, Dys' taciturnity impressive as he urged the straining horses on with little more than grunts and clicking sounds of encouragement. The rain seemed to have held off only to gain strength, for it began to lash their camp at dawn and by the time they set out it had become a downpour that masked the way ahead behind a pall of grey, driving into faces and eyes so that even Tepshen Lahl drew up his hood and rode slump-shouldered, as though driven down by the weight of liquid cascading from the sky. Wynett huddled beneath the canopy, her own cloak drawn tight about her, the hood masking her face as she clutched the bench to prevent the lurching vehicle from throwing her off. She began to think that she should forego the dignity of her blue robe and obtain riding gear and a horse, were a spare mount available.

Their camp that night was wet and less cheerful than usual, cold with the wind that clattered the bare-bones branches of the surrounding trees, threatening constantly to douse the fires as it seemed to douse conversation.

Soon after dawn they started out again, clothing clammy beneath the protective hide cloaks, the horses fretful at the ceaseless downpour and the warriors silent, save for occasional curses as water found a way into boots and cloakfronts.

They were all glad when the scouts Bedyr sent out ahead came galloping back to announce their imminent arrival in Murren, the town that marked the commencement of the trail into the Geffyn.

It was dusk by then and the lights that shone through the gloom filled them all with welcome anticipation of hot baths and wine, food and soft beds. Wynett peered out from beneath her hood as they came to the walled town, seeing lanterns bobbing through the shadows as a welcoming party came out to greet them.

It seemed composed of all the civic dignitaries, some dozen men and women, for Murren was a settlement of some size, commanding not only the approach to the Geffyn Heights, but also the crossroads that joined before the city walls, northern and southern trade routes intersecting there with the road between Caitin Hold and High Fort. There was little formality in the reception, the *alcar* merely displaying the loudest voice as he welcomed the party on behalf of his fellow councillors and urged them to take swift shelter from the rain. He would have had ostlers take in their horses, but the Tamurin warriors preferred to see the animals safely stabled themselves, allowing the eager townsfolk to take over only when they were satisfied the beasts were comfortable. Having no part to play in those arrangements, Wynett watched as Kedryn rubbed down the Keshi stallion, his movements deft with the skill of long practice and needing no eyes to govern his hands, then joined him as he walked with Bedyr and Tepshen Lahl to the inn where rooms had been reserved for them.

As in Solanul, there was not a building large enough to hold them all, and the party split into groups, each one accompanied by townsfolk intent on making them at home. The larger number, inevitably, went with Bedyr and Kedryn to the hostelry indicated by Kendar Vashan, the alcar, and the place was rapidly crowded with bodies intent on catching sight of the heroes of the recent war.

It was, fortunately, a large caravanserai, three storeys high, with balconies around the first level providing shelter from the still-teeming rain. Inside, the central room was bright with torchlight and warm with the heat emanating from the two deep hearths at either end of the low-ceilinged room. Baths were already heated, and after that luxury, their cloaks set to drying, they were offered the best Murren could offer.

Seated close to the fire at a long table decorated with dried flowers and several candelabra that looked to have been brought out of storage for the occasion, they were feasted royally. A thick vegetable soup, sufficient for a meal in itself, was followed by river trout grilled crisp, the sweet flesh succulent, then slabs of venison dressed with herbs and accompanied by numerous vegetables, finally a pudding confected of milk and sugar and eggs that led to several of the party loosening their belts and joking about the burden their hosts set upon the horses. Wines from the south and sturdier Tamurin vintages were served, and throughout the meal they were pressed with questions from those who had not taken up the call to arms and so sought firsthand accounts of the battle. Wynett noticed that everyone avoided mention of Kedryn's blindness, though all cast surreptitious glances at the prince, who was kept busy – and more than a little embarrassed – retelling the story of his duel with Niloc Yarrum.

At last, drowsy from the wines and the *rethin* – a local speciality, Vashan explained – that followed, they made their excuses and retired.

Kedryn escorted Wynett to her door, bidding her goodnight while Bedyr waited discreetly along the hall before leading his son to his own quarters. Inside, she found a small, candlelit room with a fire burning in a stone chimney and shutters drawn against the night. It was considerably more luxurious than her chambers in High Fort and the softness of the bed necessitated much turning before she was able to sleep.

She woke soon after dawn, momentarily confused at the absence of rain plopping against wet ground, and rose to use the basin set beside the bed. Dressed, she threw the shutters open and was delighted to see sunlight reflected in the puddles dotting the cobbled yard. The sky was still stormy, but bright to the east, with random shafts of brilliance lancing the cloud, hailed by the gaily-plumed cockerel that strutted proudly amongst a gaggle of hens. The promise of dry weather cheered her enormously and she went down to the hall smiling.

Kedryn and the others were already eating, serving women bringing a seemingly endless supply of steaming wheatcakes and sweetened porridge, kettles of aromatic tisane in constant motion from hearth to table. Wynett joined them, her own breakfast interrupted regularly by warriors requesting remedies for the previous night's excesses, which she dispensed from the satchel she had brought with her, thinking that she would soon need to replenish her supplies.

When they quit the inn the sun had risen, though to the north dark cloud pushed winter south across the Lozins and Kendar Vashan warned them that he expected to see snow fall before they crested the Geffyn Heights. Nonetheless it was a cheerful party that grouped in the town square and rode out through the western gate as the waving citizens gathered along the walls to see them go.

Almost immediately the road began to climb, gently at first, but then steeper, as high timber clustered ever closer on all sides until they moved along an avenue of trees. As the gradient steepened the trail began to meander, following ridges and hogbacks, traversing the rising terrain in sweeping curves, the dense woodland denying sight of the way ahead so that their journeying assumed a timeless quality, confined within the walls of the forest. Oak and ash and pine rendered the air sweet, preferable, despite the increasing chill, to the sodden odour of rain-soaked leather and damp horsehide.

'Snow comes,' Dys announced in a rare burst of eloquence. 'Tonight.'

'How do you know?' Wynett looked to the ribbon of sky visible between the treetops and saw only a bluish grey silvered by the sun.

'Smell it,' grunted the driver and lapsed back into his customary silence.

He was right, for when they halted that night, pulling off the trail into a clearing ringed by looming conifers, a soft drifting of white began to fall, lending the campsite an ethereal air, and the fires were banked high, gloves and fur-lined boots appearing from saddlebags.

'You are warm enough?' Kedryn asked as he sat beside Wynett, carefully spooning the stew that was their evening meal, courtesy of the hunters who had ranged ahead to bring down a deer and several flavoursome birds.

'Aye,' she told him, smiling. 'It is beautiful.'

'Is it?' He set his bowl aside and held out his hands, palms upwards to the flakes.

'Yes,' she said, 'it is.'

'I wish that I could see it,' he murmured, bringing a hand to his mouth to touch tongue to snow crystal. 'It seems so long since I saw snow fall on Tamur. Tell me what it looks like.'

There was such a longing in his voice that she reached out to grasp the hand, taking it in both of hers, for the ache she heard touched her, resounding in her soul.

'It is not like the snow that falls on High Fort,' she began. 'There the wind blows down the canyon and hurls snow at us like missiles. Here it falls gently, like powder from the sky. The flakes swirl above the fire, dancing in the air, and the ground whitens where they land. The tents are white with it, and the trees are frosted like the icing on a sweet cake. It dusts your hair, and . . .'

She broke off as she felt his grip tighten and saw his face turn towards her, a smile breaking on his mouth.

'I see it,' he whispered. 'Wynett, I see it! Tepshen stands there, blanketing his horse. My own is already covered. My father,' he swung his head, looking around the clearing, 'speaks with Torim. And all around us the trees stand like old men, white-haired and silent.'

'And I only hold your hand,' she said in a hushed voice.

'Yet still I see!' he answered fiercely. 'You were right – I must hope. And have faith.'

'Aye,' she said.

'Wynett,' he turned again towards her, his eyes solemn, and she felt a pang of fear for what he might now tell her, seeing it in his gaze, 'I thank you – for being here; for what you do.'

The fear faded a little and she said as calmly as she was able, 'Thank the Lady, Kedryn, for I am merely her acolyte.'

'I know.' He nodded, his gaze clouding a fraction, then blanking once more as he groaned and said, 'It is gone.'

'But it comes more frequently.'

'Because you are here.'

'And will be long yet.'

'Until Estrevan,' he murmured, his voice forlorn again.

'At least until then,' Wynett said slowly. 'And that is far away yet. Do not think so far ahead, Kedryn.'

'No.' He squeezed her hand and let it fall, extending his own towards the fire as he squared his shoulders and assumed a resolute expression.

'We shall be together a long time,' she promised.

'I hope so,' he said quietly, and then, so softly she barely heard the words, 'A lifetime, I hope.'

It was impossible for her to bear the burden of that longing and she turned her face away as though he might see the tears that filled her eyes, lifting her gaze towards the white-flecked darkness of the sky so that the droplets on her cheeks merged with the falling snow and were hidden. Lady be with me, she asked inside herself. Be with me and help me to be strong.

'I am sorry,' he murmured, his voice husky. 'I promised ... I should not have said that.'

'No matter.' She made her voice cheerful, afraid it might sound brusque. 'You still make progress.'

'Aye,' he nodded. 'In one direction, at least.'

In more than one, she thought, though I must never tell you that.

She was thankful that Bedyr came to join them then, hunkering by the fire with a skin of evshan in his hand.

'The night will be cold,' he promised, 'and tomorrow colder still.'

Wynett took the skin and allowed some of the liquor to trickle into her mouth. It warmed her body, but the chill of fear remained in her mind: this journey was by no means easy.

'Thank you,' she said, returning the skin. 'I think I will sleep now. Better for that.'

Bedyr nodded, the eyes that studied her so full of understanding she experienced a flush of embarrassment and rose quickly to her feet, crossing to where her tent had been erected and crawling inside as though to hide from that compassionate, knowledgeable gaze. She drew the flaps shut behind her and laced them tight, thankful for the protection of the screening canvas, and sat crosslegged as she used her training to impose calm upon her agitated thoughts.

After a while she felt composed again and shed her cloak, spreading it over the bedroll laid out for her, then undid her robe and removed her boots to climb, dressed only in her shift, beneath the covers. The evshan did, indeed, warm her, and made her drowsy so that sleep descended swift and soft as the snow.

She woke to the sounds of muffled movement and clambered from the bedroll to peek out through the tent flaps at a scene transformed during the night. The snow still fell and the clearing was a veiled panorama of white and grey, the pine limbs thick with the fall, the Tamurin moving knee deep through the drifts, the fires hissing and crackling as they struggled to survive beneath the soundless onslaught. The horses stood patiently, caped in whiteness, the sun, when she looked for it, a pale memory in a sky blank as Kedryn's eyes. She dressed quickly, running fingers through the tangle of her long blonde hair, and waded to the nearest fire, where kettles already steamed, the last night's stew aromatic in the crispness of the early morning.

Their going that day was slower, for they had first to dig the wagon out and then negotiate a trail heavy-laden with snow, halting often as riders attached ropes to aid the team through drifts or up the more vertiginous slopes. Around noon, however, the fall eased off and the sun poked tentatively through the overcast, then grew stronger, shining from a swordblade sky to dance brilliant light over the drifts, the white becoming an eye-watering silver over which the horsemen moved like inkblots on an unpenned page.

They made camp before sunset under the lee of a high bluff, the bare stone a dark scar against the uniformity of the snow-clad scarp of mountainside, and in the morning found that fresh snowfall hid their tracks and made their ascent harder still. Wynett had crossed Tamur only twice before, travelling to Estrevan in the spring and to High Fort in late summer and early autumn. The winters she had known in Andurel and Estrevan and High Fort had not been like this, for she had passed them warm beneath roofs, protected by walls, with heated baths readily available and hot food prepared in hotter kitchens. She had seen the land burgeon green and gold; seen it fecund beneath the summer sun; and rich with the colours of autumn, but never like this. It was magnificent and threatening at the same time, the great spread of the downslope of the Geffyn's eastern scarp spread out below her white as some vast, fresh-laundered sheet, the timber noble beneath its burden of snow; and she saw how easy it would be to die in that vastness, lost in drifts, frozen. It was little wonder the Tamurin were so hardy a folk, living in these extremes: it was a hard, proud land.

'Is all of Tamur like this?' she asked Kedryn as they ate breakfast. 'So high and rugged?'

'Most,' he answered. 'To the east – as you saw – the land is gentle, and to the south it runs down to the Ust-Idre, where it is very soft. Our best wines come from there, but the heart is up here. Beyond the Geffyn forest it flattens to the plateau, but then to north and west it is mostly mountain again.'

'And Caitin Hold?' she asked.

'Sits at the centre of the plateau. There are hills, but not like this. This is the hardest part, save perhaps for the western reaches, where Tamur meets the Gadrizels.'

'We must cross there, surely?' she wondered. 'To reach Estrevan. Will that be possible before spring?'

'I am not sure,' he said, smiling. 'Mayhap you will be forced to spend the winter in Caitin Hold.'

'Is that so bad?' she responded, her tone bantering as his, though faint alarm stirred at the back of her mind.

'I would not think so.'

He continued to smile as he said it, but his voice no longer teased and Wynett pursed her lips, reminding herself that she trod a fine line and must be careful of her words. Quickly, seeking to save him from embarrassment, she said, 'It would at least give me a chance to meet the Sister who taught you.'

'Lyassa?' Kedryn chuckled at the thought of his tutor. 'She can likely inform you better than I what geography confronts us – she spent long enough drumming it into me. That and history, and all the other things she deemed a prince of Tamur should know.'

'You are fond of her,' Wynett suggested, hearing affection in his voice.

'Of course,' he grinned. 'Lyassa was a fine tutor, though at times I believe she despaired of me. Especially when the lesson was to do with matters of the court. She set great store on dance and musical accomplishment, whilst I was more concerned with learning to use my sword and riding out to take my blooding.

'You have done that now,' Wynett responded more soberly. 'And met the king – whose high opinion of you is obvious.'

Kedryn laughed. 'Lyassa will be impressed by that. And by your royal blood.'

'My antecedents are of no importance,' Wynett told him, taking the opportunity to subtly remind him of her position, 'I am a Sister now, no longer a princess of the High Blood.'

Kedryn nodded. 'I do not forget. But still, I should not mind if we were snowbound.'

Bedyr shouted then that they should prepare to leave and any further conversation was curtailed by the preparations for departure. The tents were struck and packed on Dys' wagon and Wynett took her place beside the silent old man as Kedryn mounted the Keshi stallion and the column commenced its seemingly unending ascent of the heights.

It went on throughout that day and all of the next and they did not reach Lathan until the middle of the third day.

The town sat precarious as an Eagle's eyrie on the very edge of the escarpment, its walls seeming an extension of the rimrock, the trail disgorging on a shelf before the gates, which stood open on a large staging area flanked by wooden buildings. Their approach had been watched and as they entered the eastern plaza a welcoming committee came out to greet them, forewarned of their arrival by returning warriors.

Once again they were feasted – and beset by townsfolk anxious to hear a fresh account of the war – so that the night was old before they were able to decently excuse themselves and seek out their beds. They learned that snow had been falling for several days on the uplands, but that as best the town knew the road ahead was clear enough for safe travel, the going relatively easy after the climb. Bedyr delayed their departure for a day to rest the animals, and Wynett seized the opportunity to replenish her stocks of herbs, which had become further depleted by the pleasant excesses of their arrival.

They left Lathan with the sun rising like a disc of polished silver against a sky of sparkling pure blue, the road ahead scintillating in the brilliant light. The horses' breath plumed steam in the icy air and the hooves crunched on the packed snow, the wagon riding smooth over the harder surface. There was an air of mounting excitement as the Tamurin rode into the forest that spread dense all around, as if the hundred felt themselves to be in the heartland of their kingdom and now closer to the completion of their journey. It seemed to Wynett that these warriors belonged to the highlands, regarding the gentler eastern reaches of Tamur as soft, whilst the heights were theirs, as mountains were the natural abode of eagles. She watched them riding straight and proud, Bedyr and Kedryn and Tepshen Lahl at their head, setting a brisk pace as they drove into the great mass of trees.

For seven days they traversed the woodlands, encountering only two small villages, little more than hamlets built around inns too small to accommodate them all, but eager to provide what hospitality they might. At night they heard wolves howl, but the lupine predators stayed clear of so large a party, not yet driven by winter hunger to risk attacking the horses.

On the eighth day the forest thinned along the banks of a river sufficiently shallow they were able to ford the stream without difficulty, the timber steadily declining thereafter in both size and density until they rode across country mostly open. Low hills bulked to the north, rising into the distance to meet the Lozins, but the road they followed ran due west, scoured by the wind that began to blow once they reached the flatlands. There were occasional falls of snow, but never enough to impede their progress and they made good time, farms and villages becoming more frequent, and welcome as an escape from the bone-numbing chill of the wind. The sun shone bright for most of the way and Wynett was grateful for the charcoal stick Dys gave her to rub about her eyes as a precaution against snow blindness.

Four days from the forest they came upon a town, walled, it now seemed, as much for defence against the elements as against invasion, and found beds for the night.

Four days after that they reached Caitin Hold.

The road first descended into a broad valley, then climbed a ridge to cross a further section of flat country before climbing again to a vast mound of land at the centre of which stood the stronghold of the Lords of Tamur. Wynett gasped when she saw it, for it was far larger than High Fort, a walled town rather than a citadel. The stone that bulked from the snow-covered mountain meadow stood high as four tall men, solid and square, with towers rising higher still at each corner, the gantries of catapults jutting from their ramparts. A town surrounded the Hold on three sides, its buildings dwarfed by the mass of the fortress, a broad expanse of open ground separating the two, the area facing towards the trail devoid of buildings. Bedyr called a halt three bowshots from the walls and there was a busy fixing of gear as the warriors prepared to enter their home again. Then they remounted and went forwards, slowly at first but then lifting to a brisk canter. Dys grunted what sounded like a laugh and flicked the reins to bring the wagon team up to speed, prompting Wynett to clutch somewhat desperately for a secure hold as the vehicle trundled vigorously towards the gates.

She saw that they stood open, and that men lined the walls, whooping and waving as the column approached, but her eyes fastened on the woman who stood beneath the gate arch, for she realised this must be the Lady Yrla, Kedryn's mother.

She was tall, Wynett saw, and slender despite the fur cloak that draped her. Her hair was straight, and black as a raven's wing, bound by a simple fillet of silver from a face to inspire a balladeer. In repose it might have been serene, but now it was transformed to glowing radiance as she smiled and raised both her arms as though to embrace them all. Had that been her intent, she had no chance, for Bedyr spurred his mount to a gallop that ended scant feet from his wife as he sprang from the saddle and crossed the remaining distance at a run to sweep her into his arms, crushing

97

her against his chest as she held him and laughed and kissed him fervently.

Their embrace lasted until the riders swept in through the gates and Kedryn dismounted, moving with a careless disregard for his blindness into his mother's arms.

It was Tepshen Lahl who assisted Wynett down from the wagon into a courtyard filled with laughing, embracing warriors, their women coming to greet them with as little regard for formality as Yrla had shown. There was a warmth to the occasion that beat like the flames of a welcome hearthfire on Wynett's Estrevan-heightened senses, and for a moment she felt almost lonely amongst so happy a throng.

Then Yrla pushed Kedryn to arms length and turned grey eyes towards the Sister.

'Wynett,' she said, extricating herself from her son's hold to cross the gap between them, 'welcome to Caitin Hold.'

'My Lady.' Wynett curtsied. 'Thank you.'

'There is little formality here.' Yrla took the younger woman's elbows to raise her, smiling as she hugged the Sister. 'My name is Yrla, and I thank you for all you have done for my son.'

Mention of Kedryn painted brief distress on her features and Wynett saw that beneath her obvious joy at the reunion there was deeper-seated concern. She said, 'I have done little enough . . . Yrla. What progress he has made comes from within him. I have merely kept him company.'

'I think there is more to it than that,' Yrla responded softly, 'but we can talk of it later. For now, I am sure you would welcome hot water and rest. There are Sisters here anxious to meet you and tonight there will be a banquet to celebrate this happy day, but first let me show you to your chambers.'

She smiled, releasing Wynett as she turned to Tepshen Lahl.

'Tepshen, it is so good to have you safely returned.'

The kyo bowed, his usually impassive features creased by a smile to match hers, then put his gloved hands upon her shoulders and kissed her solemnly on both cheeks. Yrla laughed afresh and put her arms about his waist, holding him close for a moment as he said, 'It is good to be back.'

Then Bedyr was there beside her, settling his arm about her as Kedryn came to her left and she slid an arm around him, holding husband and son together.

'I have prayed to the Lady for this day. Now let us retire and prepare to celebrate it in suitable fashion.'

'Wynett?' Kedryn extended his free hand and she came towards him, allowing him to hold her as he held his mother, feeling for that instant a part of the group.

'Wynett needs a bath,' Yrla chuckled, 'to warm her. While you two need to scrub the smell of armour and horses away. Come, I have them readied.'

They moved across the yard, slowly to allow for Kedryn's blindness, Tepshen Lahl joining them, one with the family, and Wynett found herself wondering at Yrla's aplomb. Bedyr, she knew, must have sent word ahead so that his wife was not taken by surprise, but even so her control was impressive, for Wynett had sensed the pain she felt at her son's predicament, yet her manner gave no occasion for the anguish of pity; rather, she exuded a real joy that encompassed his blindness, accepting it for the present without allowing it to spoil the warmth of her heartfelt welcome or give Kedryn a chance to feel anything but upraised. The Lady Yrla, Wynett decided, was a most remarkable woman.

That conclusion was reinforced when Yrla joined her after she had bathed. Attendant women had shown her to the chambers prepared for her – warm, cheerful rooms in which she felt immediately at home – and then led her to the bath-house. The steaming water had refreshed her, easing out the aches incurred on the wagon, and she had found Yrla waiting for her with a pewter jug of heated wine and two silver goblets.

'Bedyr wrote that Kedryn has fallen in love with you,' Yrla began, the expression of sympathy on her lovely face leavening the directness of her statement. 'That cannot be easy for you.'

'No.' Wynett sipped the wine, not yet quite sure what tack her hostess took. 'It is not.'

'He also wrote that he sensed reciprocation,' Yrla murmured. 'I do not wish to pry, and I should understand were you to prefer we did not discuss this, but I believe I might aid you in bearing your burden if we can talk openly, without secrets. And I should not carry tales to either my husband or my son.'

Wynett believed her: there was an air to this woman that reminded her of the Sisters. She took another cautious sip of the heated wine and said slowly, 'I chose early to follow the Lady, Yrla. I intend to hold to my vows – that must be understood.'

'It is,' Yrla nodded. 'My dear, I was of Estrevan once, my sole desire to follow the way of the Lady. I had not taken the final vows, of course, but I can understand your dilemma – if dilemma there is.'

She studied Wynett's face with unconcealed concern and Wynett felt a knot tie inside her and then unravel as her words came in a flood that mingled anguish with relief in equal measure.

'There is,' she confirmed. 'I cannot deny the love I feel. But nor can I deny my vows! I would have remained in High Fort had sight not manifested, for I knew that Kedryn would come increasingly to rely on me; to want me with him. And I cannot give him what he wants! I am so afraid of hurting him! And that I would not do. I would not see him hurt further.'

'Poor child.' Yrla set down her goblet and came to where Wynett sat, sliding an arm about the younger woman's shoulders so that Wynett felt the sympathy she radiated and could no longer hold in her emotions. She began to weep, clutching at Yrla as the Lady of Tamur held her and stroked her hair and murmured, 'Poor, poor child. It is so hard for you.'

'What am I to do? What can I do?'

Wynett felt no embarrassment, for there was something about the Lady Yrla that precluded so petty a concern, and she felt that from her she might glean sound advice, perhaps better even than that offered by her fellow Sisters.

'You have explained your position to Kedryn?'

'That I am vowed to the Lady, yes,' Wynett snuffled. 'I have not told him that I love him.'

'That was wise,' Yrla confirmed.

'But what am I to *do*?' asked Wynett.

'What *would* you do?' came the answer, surprising Wynett. 'You need not go on to Estrevan – whatever Bedyr thinks, I believe my son is man enough to make that journey without you – and if you wish, you may remain here a while, then return to High Fort. If that is what you want.'

Wynett stifled her sobs, shock easing the flow of tears. 'I made a promise,' she whispered. 'Kedryn expects me to go with him. Besides, these manifestations of sight come only when he is with me – how could I desert him now?'

'Set that aside for now,' Yrla said gently. 'Kedryn *wants* you to go with him. What do *you* want?'

'I?' Wynett looked up at the older woman, her mind in turmoil from which a single fact emerged, slowly, as though drawn out by the loving sympathy she saw in the calm grey eyes. 'I . . . I want to go with him.'

'Then that is what you should do,' smiled Yrla.

'Can it be that simple?' Wynett wondered; doubtful.

'Sometimes,' Yrla smiled, 'it can. Sometimes the Lady speaks to us through our hearts, rather than in texts or prophecies.'

'It was surely the Text that brought you to Caitin Hold,' Wynett suggested.

'Alaria's Text brought me to Tamur,' Yrla said confidently. 'It was Bedyr brought me to Caitin Hold.'

'But there is nothing in the Text to guide me even so far,' said Wynett.

'Are you sure?' asked Yrla. 'Have you studied the Text?'

'Not at length.' Wynett shook her head.

'Galina gave me a copy before I left the Sacred City,' said Yrla. 'I still have it, and of late I have read and re-read it. There is a part I should like you to consider, but first I wanted you to know your own heart.'

'I think I do,' said Wynett, 'now. I will go with Kedryn.'

'Good,' smiled Yrla. 'Now dry your eyes and ready yourself for the banquet. I will show you the Text on the morrow.'

101

Chapter Five

HATTIM Sethiyan's southward journey was met with more clement weather than greeted the westbound Tamurin. The relentless downpour that marked their departure from High Fort did not catch up with the Galichian's barge save as squalls that his boat captain rode out in safe harbours, anxious to avoid giving his lord cause to vent his increasingly bad temper, and the snow that lay heavy on the uplands remained only a diminishing threat to the north, where the sky was leaden coloured. Along the Idre, wintry sunshine sparkled from a metallic blue sky on the coruscating surface of the river and although the air was chill, and the trees that lined the banks bare of leaves, the harsh reality of winter did not yet strike the southerly reaches.

Nonetheless, Hattim appeared gripped by a spiritual cold that transcended any pleasure he felt at returning home and set him, isolated, apart from those with him.

His barge was larger than the *Vashti* on which King Darr travelled, and considerably slower, a wide-bellied craft of shallow draft that he had had portaged past the cascades dividing Idre from Ust-Idre, more suitable to the gentler waters of Ust-Galich than the swift currents of the upper waterway. Sixty oarsmen manned the scoops thrusting from the sides and ten deckhands serviced the double masts. A cabin rose above the stern thwarts to shelter the boatmaster as he sat at the tiller and amidships there were quarters, small but opulently appointed, for the Lord of Ust-Galich and whatever travelling companions he chose to bring with him. These were more shelter from sun or rain than real sleeping chambers, for the vessel docked at night to afford Hattim the comfort of landbound bed and cuisine, prepared by the cook he included amongst his retainers. There were, also, a handful of courtiers, five in number and the most favoured. Like the captain, they spent a large part of the journey in dread of Hattim's anger.

He had retired to his cabin as soon as the barge, the *Vargalla*, cast off, and had not emerged until they docked that night. The next morning he had loosened three of his barber's teeth for some imagined discomfort and shut himself away again with only wine for company. As he descended the gangplank the following evening, he had pitched a deckhand into the river when the man crossed his path to secure a mooring line and ordered him flogged when he was dragged, near-drowned, from the water. When he boarded again he had instructed the drum-master to beat double time, the *Vargalla* leaving the accompanying retinue of smaller craft behind. Over the nervously-voiced warnings of the boatmaster he had held the pace until the oarsmen flagged, their rhythm growing ragged as fatigue numbed their muscles, and only when exhaustion threatened to make their progress erratic did he permit a return to more normal speed. By then the *Vargalla* rode several leagues ahead of the vessels bearing those officers travelling by water, and the Galichian Sisters, without chance of them catching up.

That night the exhausted crew brought the barge wearily into the harborage of Nyrwan, and Hattim's courtiers hurried ahead to warn the owner of the fishing village's sole tavern that the Lord of Ust-Galich was about to favour his humble inn.

It was a modest hostelry, more suited – and far more accustomed – to the entertainment of fishermen and river traders than the patronage of High Blood, and the tavern keeper grew alarmed at the prospect of quartering, let alone feeding and wining, the Lord Hattim Sethiyan. His wife readily allowed the Galichian cook to take over her kitchen and the innkeeper permitted the courtiers to arrange his best room with stuff brought from the *Vargalla*. Disgruntled fishermen were cast out into the night by the barge's crew as the place became overrun by Galichians, their fear of Hattim's temper outweighing the consideration that they were on Tamurin soil and had no right to usurp the regular clientele.

Hattim entered the low-ceilinged room that occupied most of the ground floor with an expression of disdain on his handsome face, paused, sniffed ostentatiously, and remarked too loudly that the stink of fish pervaded the air. His courtiers laughed dutifully and ushered their lord to a bench by the hearth. Hattim shed his cloak and sprawled in gold-edged tunic and green breeks, his booted feet close to the flames, refusing the plain earthenware mug the innkeeper offered him in favour of his own chased silver goblet.

'You will try my wine, Lord?' the innkeeper asked, thinking that this Galichian fop had no right to scorn honest Tamurin ware, but simultaneously conscious of the gold his visitors might leave in his purse, and of their numbers.

'I will,' Hattim announced, smiling at his fawning courtiers as he added for their benefit. 'We had best conserve our good Galichian vintages for the journey.'

The innkeeper filled the goblet and waited for Hattim's approval.

'It will do,' the Lord of Ust-Galich declared. 'You may leave the jug.'

Maintaining a blandly smiling expression only with difficulty, the innkeeper retired behind his serving counter, happier in the company of the barge's crew than with the nobles. At least the oarsmen and deckhands traded honest coin for the ale and evshan they consumed.

Hattim drank prodigiously, and by the time the meal was ready his face was flushed and his humour morose. His cook produced a vast bowl of river clams, seethed in wine with herbs adding a delicate piquancy. It was met with the same scorn Hattim bestowed on the trout that followed and the cheeses that formed the final course. The cook blamed the paucity of the kitchen, but in private – and with much admonishment to secrecy – he informed the landlord's wife that her ingredients were as fine as any he had used and that if Hattim failed to appreciate them, he had no understanding of the culinary arts.

All about him were glad when the Lord of Ust-Galich rose unsteadily to his feet and announced that he would retire, though had they known what would happen that night their relief would have become terror.

Hattim climbed the narrow stairs to the upper level and paused by the door of his chamber. The incense burned to cleanse the room filled the corridor with aromatic scent and the Galichian nodded in approval, clutching at the jamb to steady himself.

'This Lady-forsaken hovel has doxies?'

His voice was slurred, thick with wine and the fiercer evshan, his eyes as they studied his hangers-on reddened. When the landlord, who stood nervously at the rear of the group nodded, Hattim said, 'Then have one cleaned and bring her to me.'

'My Lord,' murmured Mejas Celeruna, who was a little braver than his fellow sycophants, 'is that wise? There is the danger of disease. And,' he coughed, discreetly lowering his voice, 'you are betokened to the Princess Ashrivelle.'

Hattim's face twisted in a scowl and his eyes seemed to burn a harsher red, as though anger fuelled the glow put there by the alcohol. 'Will any here carry tales?' he demanded ominously. 'Darr is no longer present to cast that disapproving eye, and I have been too long faithful to that icy virgin. Bring me a woman, damn you!'

Celeruna nodded dutifully and turned to the innkeeper. 'Your doxies are clean?'

'Of course.' The landlord was offended. 'Clean as the Idre herself.'

'I will examine them,' announced the courtier.

'Not too closely,' Hattim said, his voice lewd. 'You may take your pick of what's left, but bring me the best.'

'Of course, my Lord.' Celeruna joined the landlord in finding offence in his liege's manner.

Hattim, still sniggering, stumbled into the room and kicked the door closed on the watching faces. He crossed to the bed and threw himself down, groaning as his head spun to transform the beamed ceiling to a whirligig of revolving woodwork and torchlit plaster. He sat up, splashing his face with water from the pitcher set beside the bed, and glanced around. The room was not quite small, the bed, the table beside it, and a cupboard built partly into the wall occupying most of the floor space. There was a window that, when he threw it open and thrust his head out into the chill night air, he saw looked towards the Idre, the masts of the *Vargalla* tossing in the frail light of a new-risen moon. From the streets of the village a cat yowled. Hattim withdrew his head and fastened the shutters. The room was warm, heated by the chimney that ran up from the hall below, and he plucked clumsily at the lacings of his tunic. The jerkin fell to the floor and Hattim began to work at the fastenings of his shirt. He opened that and put a hand to his throat, rubbing. The flea bites had seemed more virulent since his departure from High Fort and when he found a mirror and held it to his neck, he saw a collar of angry flesh. Cursing, he hurled his shirt aside and tugged off his boots. His breeks and underclothing followed, and then, naked, he clambered beneath the sheets, waiting for the doxy.

Ellebriga was nervous. Her usual clientele was comprised of the more successful fishermen of Nyrwan and occasional river captains, and while she prided herself on her nocturnal accomplishments the height of her ambition so far had been to find a captain – or even a mate – willing to carry her to Andurel, where she was sure she could do well in her chosen profession. She had never thought to find herself chosen by a richly-dressed nobleman to service the Lord of Ust-Galich, and the opportunity raised her hopes and her sights.

Surrounded by her giggling sisters-in-trade, she scrubbed herself vigorously in the tub old Emvar provided – together with the admonishment that she perform her best and offer no complaint, whatever the Lord Hattim might require of her – and applied liberal quantities of her most costly perfume. Her favourite robe, a flimsy confection of silk bought with payment in kind from a passing boatmaster, was drawn over her lissome frame and her thick auburn hair dressed by her friends. She took as much time as she dared applying cosmetics to lips and eyes, and set rings on her fingers, a golden necklace about her throat, and the silver chains that denoted her calling about her ankles. Finally she put little slippers of a crimson that matched her robe on her feet and went out to suffer the inspection of the portly courtier.

'You will do,' Mejas Celeruna proclaimed, thinking that with those enormous eyes and lush mouth, she was, indeed, a passable night's entertainment. Youth still bloomed on her skin and her figure, which was largely visible through the fine material of her cheap robe, was engaging, if a fraction underendowed about the bosom. 'Remember to address him as my Lord, unless he instructs you otherwise. And do whatever he asks – you will be well rewarded.'

It was on the tip of Ellebriga's tongue to ask that she be allowed to go with them downriver, but she thought better of it: better to satisfy the Lord Hattim first and ask then, when he would doubtless be so pleased with her that he would instantly grant her wish. Optimism overcame her nervousness and she turned to the stairway, hips swaying as she began to climb.

She paused at the door, smoothing her robe and patting at her hair, then knocked. A hoarse voice called for her to enter and she constructed a seductive smile as she went in.

The man on the bed favoured her with an appraising stare and she did her best to curtsey formally as she, in turn, appraised him. He was younger than she had expected, and pleasing to the eye. His tousled hair was yellow as the gold about her neck and although he clearly suffered the effects of excess wine, he was rather handsome, albeit softer-looking than her usual customers and suffering some unsightly infection that set a ring of ugly marks about his throat. She hoped he had no disease.

'Come here,' he ordered, 'and take off that doxy's gown.'

Ellebriga stilled the pout that threatened to sour her smile at this insult and did as she was bade.

Hattim circled a finger and she turned slowly, raising her arms to unclasp her hair and allow it to tumble loose about her shoulders, pleased by the grunt of approval she heard.

'You will do,' he said, his voice husky now rather than hoarse.

'Thank you, my Lord,' Ellebriga murmured. 'I am glad that I please you.'

'You are honoured,' Hattim corrected, 'and if you please me in other ways I will honour you further.'

'My Lord,' she simpered, and moved with deliberate langour towards the bed.

Hattim threw back the covers and she saw that his body was smooth and white, with the same hint of softness that robbed his features of firm character. No matter, he was the Lord of Ust-Galich and this night would shape her future. She settled herself beside him, reaching for him with expert hands, sighing ardently as she applied her skillful mouth.

Hattim found himself pleased with Celeruna's choice.

So pleased that before long, lulled by her ministrations and the liquor he had consumed, he slept.

Ellebriga lay awake beside him, listening to his snores as she stroked the bruises he left on her and thought of the morrow. He was a vigorous lover, with a taste for pain and, she suspected, a fierce appetite: she did not want him to find her asleep should he awake and require her again. She wanted to please him in every way, that come dawn she might voice her request to sail south, either to Andurel or, if he chose it, on to Ust-Galich. She had heard that his city, Tessoril, was a place of opulence and splendour and she wondered if the lords of the southern kingdom kept seraglios.

She was occupied with these pleasant musings, close to drowsing but sufficiently alert she would respond should Hattim wake, when a movement in the corner of the room caught her eye.

It came from the clothes tossed carelessly against the angle of floor and wall, and when she turned her head she realised that it was less a movement than some strange alteration in the light. A rubescent glow hung about the piled clothing, shimmering as might the flames of a fire, or a fresh-lit torch. The chamber was dark, the lanterns doused, and the shutters denied the wan moonlight entry, yet from the corner came a distinct glow that strengthened even as she watched. Shadows elongated across the floor, creeping to the

107

bed as if possessed of independent life, and Ellebriga turned to see if Hattim sensed them. He remained soundly asleep and she wondered what she should do. Had his clothes taken fire? How could they? Perhaps he had inadvertently tossed them on to a flambeaux that had smouldered through their love-making and now caught flame. She sniffed the air and wrinkled her nostrils as the reek of sulphur pervaded her senses, suddenly sharp and foul as the stench of a midden. Naked save for her jewellery she lifted the covers and set her feet to the floor. Hattim slept on as she moved silently to the weirdly-glowing clothing, the sulphurous stink causing her to gag, her bare skin prickling with apprehension. Tentatively she thrust a hand towards the discarded garments.

Then sprang back, her mouth opening in a scream as fire erupted against the wall, splashing over her so that she felt her eyebrows singe and breathed in malodorous heat that stifled her cry stillborn.

The muscles of her jaw and throat locked; her eyes bulged. Her hands lifted before her face and froze there as, despite the wash of fire, a cold that penetrated to her bones pierced her even as the sweat of pure terror beaded her forehead.

There was no glow now, and the stench was fading, but what she saw was infinitely worse for it had no right to be there. Could not be there. Yet was, emanating an aura of malice that threatened to unlatch her bowels, her reason.

It was a man in delineament only, for the shape was oddly wrong, somehow warped so that the image formed in her dumbstruck brain was that of some gigantic predatory insect. The shoulders humped, thrusting curiously angled arms that ended in taloned hands towards her. The torso descended, a hollowed triangle, to an overly narrow waist, reinforcing the impression of insectility. The skull was maned with hair the colour of snow, or ash, and the features that she saw were less human than those of a mantis, the forehead wide and crenellated above deep-sunk eyes that glowed with hellish fire, as if the sockets opened on to craters of burning coal. The nostrils were slits in a protrusion of bone, and the mouth was a gash that smiled at her with a hideous intent.

Terror paralysed Ellebriga and she stood in trembling silence as elongated legs brought the shape towards her, shifting, changing even as she watched so that she did not know whether she saw a man or an insect or a demon.

That knowledge came as the taloned fingers cupped her chin and tilted her head back so that she looked directly into the pits of the eyes. All will to scream left her then and she could do nothing as the face descended towards her save think that she would never see Andurel now. Do nothing as the mouth came towards hers and the fleshless lips touched her in obscene parody of a kiss. Make no movement or sound as the embrace drained her life, sucked out her very soul, and the creature let her fall, limp, to the floor as it smiled horribly and said in a voice that carried the sussurating malevolence of a serpent's hiss, 'I am Taws.'

The mage stood over the drained body of the luckless doxy, savouring the sweet, strengthening essence he had taken, feeling his power return in full measure. There was no protective magic here, no glamours set to ward against such as he, nor any of the blue-robed women that he could sense in the vicinity. There was only his chosen servant, snoring in drunken sleep on the crumpled bed.

He crossed the chamber in a single stride and hovered above Hattim Scthiyan, peering down at the supine man. It was good to once more possess binocular vision and he stared long at Hattim's slack features, the gash of his mouth twisted in parody of a smile.

Then he bent, knees resting against the bed, and clapped a hand over Hattim's mouth.

The Lord of Ust-Galich grunted and turned on to his back. Against Taws' palm he mumbled, 'Not yet, girl. I will tell you when I am ready again.'

'My Lord,' Taws mocked, his voice soft, colder than the snow to the north, 'I am ready for you now.'

'Damn you,' Hattim grunted, struggling to free his face. 'Leave me be.'

The pressure on his mouth refused to go away and he forced his eyes open. They cleared rapidly of sleep as they focused on the features hanging above him, filling with loathing and a stark terror. He tried to shout, but Taws' grip tightened, stifling breath, and he began to choke, clutching at the wrist of the apparition.

Taws chuckled, a rasping, grating sound more akin to the rattle of dry bones than laughter, and Hattim began to struggle in earnest.

He was a strong man but helpless against the thing that clutched him, the tendons along his forearms bulging as he fought to free the grasp that threatened to suffocate him: uselessly. He tried to kick the monster away, but his legs tangled in the bedding and he succeeded only in arching his back, the blows he directed at the

109

triangular visage deflected casually by a hand that he saw bore only scant resemblance to human digits.

'Be still,' Taws commanded, and Hattim felt his gaze locked by the glowing red orbs, the will to struggle departing, his limbs giving in to a strengthless lassitude.

'What are you?' he gasped when the creature released its grip. 'Do I dream?'

'You are awake,' the mage declared, 'and I am Taws. You know me as the Messenger.'

'May the Lady save me!' Hattim moaned, his features blanched of colour as his teeth rattled between trembling jaws.

'May the Lady roast in Ashar's fires for all eternity,' Taws blasphemed. 'She will not save you. You do not need her.'

Hattim looked to his discarded clothes. His sword was stowed aboard the *Vargalla*, but on his belt there hung a ceremonial dagger, more decoration than real weapon, but long enough of blade, and sharp enough, that it would pierce ribs to find the heart – if this demonic creature was equipped with such an organ.

Taws followed his glance and shook his head. 'It will do you no good. See . : .'

He fastened a hand in Hattim's hair and rose, bringing the Galichian moaning from the bed as he ducked sideways to scoop the blade from its ornate, jewelled sheath. Tears filled Hattim's eyes as his scalp was stretched and he thought he should find the skin torn from his cranium, but Taws tossed him back on the bed as easily as he might have tossed a kitten and sent the blade swirling into the air. As it rose he made a single pass with his right hand and Hattim saw a blue fire dance briefly about the taloned fingers. Then gaped as the dagger spun impossibly long in mid-air, the steel of the blade abruptly red, melting, dripping molten metal that seethed and sputtered on the boards of the floor, the odour of burning wood acrid as the taste of fear in his mouth. The large jewel that decorated the pommel fell loose, shattering into iridescent fragments that were joined by the shards of the smaller stones set into the grip and quillon. Blackened, the hilt thudded to the floor and broke into pieces.

'You can do nothing.' Taws made another pass with his unhuman hand and Hattim felt the cry for help forming in his throat cloy and halt against his chattering teeth. 'Nothing at all save listen to me.'

'Why should I?'

Hattim heard his voice quaver, thin as the mewling of an infant. He could not seem to fill his lungs with sufficient breath to shout, and the numbing lassitude pervaded his limbs so that he found movement impossible; all he could do was lie helpless on the bed as the Messenger studied him, the rubescent eyes hideously fascinating. In that moment, Hattim Sethiyan knew how a rabbit must feel when confronted with the implacable stare of a hunting cat.

'Because I can give you everything you want,' Taws said.

'You are Ashar's Messenger and sworn enemy of the Kingdoms,' Hattim responded, the words thick and slow on his tongue.

'Ashar's Messenger, certainly.' The ashen mane of hair ducked in confirmation. 'But enemy of the Kingdoms? That depends on the definition.'

Hattim stared at the mage, still consumed with sheer terror, but also, now that it seemed his life was not immediately threatened, with a degree of morbid curiosity.

'I am my master's servant,' Taws declared, his voice sonorous, as if he delivered a lesson, 'and consequently the enemy of the Lady and those who serve her. Do you serve her, Hattim Sethiyan?'

'Of course,' Hattim gulped. 'I am Lord of Ust-Galich.'

'But you would be more,' Taws said. 'So much more, would you not? Ambition clogs your pores, Hattim. It oozes from you like the reek of sweat. I can smell it on you, sweet and sickly as the perfume on that doxy.'

'I,' Hattim began, but halted at a gesture from the mage.

'You would take the White Palace,' Taws continued. 'You would claim Darr's throne for your own and take his daughter to your bed. You would extend your rule across Kesh and Tamur until the sun sign rose over all the Kingdoms, from your borders to the Beltrevan, from the Gadrizels to the Tenaj Plains. Did you but think you had the strength of arms, you would take the field against your fellow lords; but you know you cannot, and so you place your hope in marriage to Ashrivelle and the subsequent tenancy of the Andurel throne.'

Hattim dragged a fear-furred tongue slowly across sour lips and knew that those cratered eyes saw into his soul. 'How can you know that?' he muttered.

'Because I am what I am,' answered Taws. 'Do you think the Sisterhood would permit your dream reality?'

'I,' Hattim said slowly, 'I do not know.'

'You do,' Taws informed him. 'You know they would not. They would speak against you. They would side with your enemies. They would lend their influence to Kesh, to the Caitin line.'

An image of Kedryn flashed briefly before Hattim's eyes. He saw the boy as in the duel; saw the kabah swing towards his head; saw Kedryn hailed as victor of the war.

'Oh, yes,' murmured Taws, sibilant, 'you bear no love for Kedryn Caitin, yet the Sisters do. They would see him ascend the throne before you. They are enemy to your dreams, Hattim Sethiyan.'

'You tempt me,' Hattim groaned. 'You put words in my mouth.'

'I take the words I find from your soul,' came the response. 'What I say to you, you have whispered to yourself. Deny them! Tell me you do not want Ashrivelle. Tell me you do not covet the White Palace.'

Hattim gazed with awful rapture into the red-lit pits of the mage's face and felt the answer torn from deep inside him, from the lowermost depths of his being where he hid the truth.

'I cannot,' he admitted.

Taws' laughter seemed to fill the room and Hattim thought that surely his guards must hear it, that courtiers and carls must momentarily burst armed through the door to slay the Messenger. If he could be slain.

But no relief, no escape, came and he could do nothing save face the veracity of the creature's statements. It was indeed as though Taws saw his most hidden, innermost secrets and held them up stark before him.

'Then,' said the mage, 'you cannot deny that the Sisterhood is your enemy. And if those blue-robed whores are your enemy, then so must be the one they follow.'

'No,' Hattim moaned, afraid now for his mortal soul.

'She cannot harm you,' Taws declared negligently. 'Beside my master she is as nothing – a pitiful woman. Would you allow a woman to stand between you and your dream?'

'She is the Lady,' husked Hattim fearfully.

'Ashar is Lord of the Fires,' Taws rasped. 'He is strong. He is power incarnate. He is the granter of dreams.'

'But . . .' Hattim was dreadfully afraid; and horribly fascinated. 'Ashar lent his might to the Horde and the Horde was defeated.'

'By Kedryn Caitin,' the mage snarled, his eyes burning a brighter red as he spoke the name, 'who is your enemy and mine. It will not happen again.'

'They say Kedryn is the Chosen One,' argued Hattim tremulously. 'They say the Lady smiles upon him.'

'He is human – he can die,' Taws responded. 'I will have his soul for my master. Would you not enjoy his death?'

112

Again he struck directly to Hattim's deepest desires and the Galichian nodded: 'I would.'

'Then are we not allies?' Taws asked, his voice calmer, hideously persuasive. 'Do we not seek the same ends?'

'You would see me in the White Palace?' asked Hattim, wonderingly.

'I would put you there and give you dominion over all the Kingdoms,' said Taws. 'I would raise you higher than you dare dream. Come, I will show you.'

He rose to his full height, extending a hand towards the Lord of Ust-Galich, and Hattim felt the torpor leave his body as he stared into the coals of that hellish gaze and reached out to take the offered hand. He felt a shock tingle his arm, and for an instant the hair on his head stood upright, then there was a moment of delirium in which his senses spun and nausea swirled within his belly, only to fade as he felt himself lifted, rising, floating above the floor of the little room, drifting weightlessly, light as a dust mote, filled with a terrifying anticipation.

It was dream-like, yet all too real: he could scarcely dare believe it, even as he knew it happened. He felt himself drawn towards the shuttered window and winced as the hard oak confronted his face. Then he was drifting through the wood, aware of its touch upon his naked body, and out into the night, floating above Nyrwan, rising higher, carried by the mage's power upwards into a sky scattered with stars.

He was vaguely surprised to find that he felt no fear. Instead, confidence filled him, emanating from the spectral figure that flew beside him, and he began to experience an exhilaration as they rose towards the twinkling pinpricks that glittered against the blue velvet panoply of the night. He saw Nyrwan below him, a huddle of buildings no larger now than a child's playthings, receding into darkness as he felt Taws adjust their trajectory and they began to move southwards. He saw that they followed the course of the Idre, the river a moonlit ribbon glistening against the aphotic land. Then, like stooping hawks, they were hurtling downwards and his heart lurched beneath his ribs, his eyes closing as he waited for the impact of hard earth against yielding body.

It did not come and instead he heard Taws command, 'Open your eyes. I would not harm you.'

Obediently he forced his shuttered lids ajar and saw that they hovered now above another riverside settlement, boats rolling on the sway of the river, one of them recognisable as the *Vashti*, the tripartite crown of Andurel on the pennant snapping fitfully at the masthead marking her as Darr's craft.

'The king,' Taws put contempt in the word, 'sleeps yonder. Come.'

And Hattim was drawn forwards, twin of the wraith that led him, over the sleeping settlement to the walls of a tavern hardly different to the one he had so recently left.

He swallowed nervously as they drifted once more through solid wood to stand in a chamber where a man lay asleep beneath rough sheets, the rumpled spillage of his thinning grey hair and his slumber-eased features revealing him to be Darr.

'Do you see him?' Taws said, not really asking a question. 'How easy it would be to kill him now. How easy to snuff out that weak life.'

Hattim stared at the sleeping figure and turned his face slowly towards the mage. A question formed unbidden on his lips, written loud in his eyes, and Taws chuckled, shaking his head.

'You begin to see what I can do for you; but no, not yet. Were he to die now there would be procedures, rituals of appointment that would not favour you. It is not yet time; that will come later, when the moment is more propitious. Come.'

He raised his hand, carrying Hattim with him as they floated back through the window and rose again into the sky, rushing southwards with ever increasing speed, faster and faster until the Idre was a blur below them and it seemed to Hattim they must burn like falling stars. Instead, they slowed after a while and the Galichian saw that the roofs of Andurel spread before them, the walls of the White Palace albescent against the backcloth of night.

Again they descended, invisible to watchmen, traversing walls of stone and doors of wood as spectres unencumbered by corporeal limitation. They entered a chamber Hattim did not recognise until he saw the great bed sheeted with silk and the cascade of wheat-golden hair upon the pillow. Ashrivelle's lips were parted, moist and full; inviting. One slender arm lay atop the covers, pale and smooth. Taws murmured words too indistinct for definition and gestured with his free hand, then released his grip on Hattim and pointed to the sleeping girl.

The exposed arm pushed the covers down and Ashrivelle sat up. Hattim gasped aloud, but his voice appeared as insubstantial as his frame, soundless, for the princess gave no indication that she heard him. Nor did she see him, for her eyes remained tight closed as she slowly swung her legs from the bed to stand upright before the unseen watchers. A gown of smooth, sheer silken material draped her nubile frame, a shining silver-grey in colour, sleek against the contours of her body. Hattim felt excitement rise as her hands reached to the ribbons that fastened the robe about her shoulders and drew the ties loose, the garment slithering to her feet. She stood before him and he drank in the sight, feeling lust stir as his eyes explored the planes of her body.

'I will give her to you when the time is ripe,' Taws promised 'and she will be everything you dream of, and more.'

He shifted his fingers again and Ashrivelle bent to retrieve the discarded gown, veiling herself as Hattim watched, licking his lips, wanting her now. With eyes still closed, she fastened the gown and slid back beneath the covers, drawing them to her chin as the mage took Hattim's hand and they once more drifted away.

'Look,' Taws urged as they hovered over Andurel, 'I show you your future.'

Hattim followed the Messenger's pointing finger and saw the White Palace transformed. The green and gold of Ust-Galich shimmered on the walls and towers, where the sunburst emblem of his kingdom fluttered proudly. On the great gates that faced the avenue leading down into the city he saw the sign, and as he watched, the avenue became lined with warriors dressed in shining golden mail, green surcoats emblazoned with the sunburst. The gates opened and a chariot drawn by two pure white horses came stately through, the charioteer wearing the livery of Ust-Galich. Hattim saw himself standing in the chariot, Ashrivelle beside him, a hand upon his arm and adoration in her eyes. Then his attention was caught by a procession of warriors that came slowly up the avenue, driving a group of men before them with flails. Bedyr Caitin was one, he saw, and Jarl another; Kedryn stumbled between them, and behind him, the heir of Kesh. All were in chains, and bloodied as though taken in recent battle. They came to the chariot and halted, falling to their knees with rank fear in their eyes and manacled hands upraised in plea for mercy. He saw himself spring down, resplendent in regal robe of green and gold, the medallion of the kingdoms upon his breast, and stride towards them. He saw his lips move and Bedyr nod, abasing himself, lips pressed to the boot his conqueror extended. All followed suit and from the watching soldiery and the admiring citizens there rose a great cry. He heard that and recognised his

115

name: 'Hattim Sethiyan! Hattim Sethiyan! Lord of Andurel! Lord of the Kingdoms!'

Then the vision faded and he was again floating in the sky as Taws drew him back to the north over towns where the sunburst of Ust-Galich flew, flickering in and out of his sight, phantasmagoric over Tamur and Kesh, promise of power and prestige beyond his wildest dreams.

Abruptly, the after-image of the chimera still burning in his mind, he was back in the chamber in Nyrwan, sprawled on the bed with Taws standing before him. He shivered, staring at the mage.

'You can give me that?'

Taws nodded without speaking.

'But . . .' Twin doubts clouded Hattim's ambition. 'The Sisterhood? What of them? And Kedryn – if he *is* the Chosen One?'

'Do you doubt me?' snapped the mage, frost in his tone so that Hattim shrank back, shaking his head. 'The Sisterhood is vulnerable – as must be all who adhere to Kyrie – for they place their trust in weakness, in love and brotherhood. How did you vote when Kedryn spoke for peace with the Beltrevan?'

'I spoke for war,' Hattim answered. 'I spoke for a slaughter of the tribes.'

'But Kedryn is governed by the teachings of the Lady,' Taws sneered, 'and he spoke for a sheathing of the swords; for love where blood should have flowed. He is a true follower – and they are all like that. I offer you the Kingdoms, man. Do you want them?'

Hattim licked his lips, his gaze fastened on the mantis-features, no longer held by the hypnotic power of Taws' rubescent stare, but in fascination. He ducked his head.

'Aye, I do.'

'But there is still a doubt,' Taws grated, the words bone on bone. 'You fear the power of Estrevan, but I tell you the Sacred City is far away and I can give you the throne before the blue-robed bitches know it. And when they do, it will be too late. You will sit in the White Palace and you will hold all those in Andurel hostage – Estrevan will not dare move against you.

'Tamur and Kesh will murmur, but neither Bedyr Caitin or Jarl Sestrans will seek civil war. Not while you occupy the city and Ashrivelle sleeps beside you. Not while they know the Sisters of Andurel will die should they move against you.

'And Kedryn Caitin? I have a doom planned for him that will satisfy all your hurt pride. He is blind, is he not? And he travels to

Estrevan in hope of regaining his sight. He will not! Not in Estrevan, nor any place he will think to look. And while he is questing we shall plant the seeds of his downfall. He will come to meet his doom as a lamb to the slaughter!

'You need fear no one whilst I stand beside you, Hattim Sethiyan. You need only do as I bid you and you shall have all that you want.'

The words were seductive and Hattim felt his doubts slip away. Surely not even the Sisterhood could stand against Taws, and was it not the natural way of ambitious men to side with the strongest?

'What must I do?' he asked.

'Obey me,' said the mage. 'No more than that.'

Hattim rose from the bed and stood before the white-maned creature. Then he fell to his knees, lowering his head, ambition slicing a smile across his lips.

'Master, command me.'

Taws looked down on the man, triumph burning in the craters of his face. How easy it was to tempt such as this. How easy it would be to bring the Kingdoms beneath his master's heel.

'Rise,' he ordered, 'What we do requires time. And first I must come on board your vessel, then we must reach Andurel. Once there I will give you Ashrivelle.'

Hattim rose, smiling. 'And Darr?'

'The princess first,' Taws husked. 'Her father after.'

The Lord of Ust-Galich nodded, reminded of practicalities. 'You will require clothing,' he suggested. 'And your presence will be questioned. What shall I tell them? And the doxy . . .' he glanced towards Ellebriga's corpse. 'How shall I explain that?'

'That? It is nothing.'

Taws gestured and Hattim saw the blue fire burn about his fingers again, glowing fiercer this time, and lancing out to encompass the body. For an instant Ellebriga's form was wreathed in dancing light, as though flame consumed her from within. The stench of roasting flesh pervaded the chamber and he pinched his nostrils to shut it out, unwilling to tear his hideously fascinated gaze from the crisping flesh. It blackened as he watched, peeling from bone and bursting organs that burnt and were devoured until only a flaking of ash remained, skirling on the floor as an unholy wind whistled eerily, dispersing them.

There was nothing left. No remnant of the woman or anything she had worn, only the fading odour.

Hattim crossed to the window and threw the shutters open,

breathing in the cold, river-damp air of early dawn. The sky was grey, fetid with rain, and across the Idre faint light pearled the horizon. A cock crowed and a dog barked. Hattim felt sweat chill upon his naked chest and drew the shutters closed again.

'She left you while you slept,' Taws said. 'As for my presence . . . who will question the Lord of Ust-Galich? Once on board, there are glamours I can lay on your party that all will accept me for what I am – you friend and adviser.'

'I will order clothes brought,' Hattim nodded. 'Do you require food?'

Taws studied him somberly, then smiled and shook his head.

'Not such as you offer. In time I will take sustenance.'

The banquet Yrla arranged to welcome home her loved ones was marred only by Kedryn's blindness, for although no reference was made to his disability it remained necessary that his food be carefully prepared that he might eat without the need to employ a knife, and that occasioned some degree of awkwardness. Wynett was seated beside him and helped him as much he would permit whilst all about them jubilantly set to demolishing the delicacies that emerged from the kitchens in a seemingly endless stream.

It seemed to Wynett that the entire population of Caitin Hold and the adjacent town must be present, and that every man and woman there came forward to express their pleasure at having Kedryn safely returned and offer their congratulations on his defeat of Niloc Yarrum. Amongst them were three Sisters, and their interest was directed as much at Wynett as at Kedryn, for Yrla had discussed the letters Bedyr had sent with Darr's mehdri and they were intrigued by her ability to endow sight on the blind hero. One was a Hospitaller, a tall, slender woman in her middle years whose name was Rasha; the second an elderly, dumpy woman who reminded Wynett of Grania, and whose maternal fussing over Kedryn marked her even before she was announced as his tutor, Lyassa. The third was not of Caitin Hold, though only one of the Sorority might have guessed the fact for she appeared much at home and offered no explanation of her presence. She had about her a serenity that Wynett knew came only from long years spent cloistered in the Sacred City, although – despite the grey that streaked her fair hair – she did not seem old; ageless, rather, with a calm beauty that set an aura of stillness about her. Her name was Lavia, and when Wynett essayed a question as to her function she

118

smiled gently and murmured, 'Tomorrow. Let us first celebrate the homecoming.'

Wynett had to be content with that for Lavia refused to be drawn and joined the other Sisters at the end of the high table, too far away for easy conversation. Indeed, any conversation became difficult after a while as the returned warriors expanded loudly on the accounts of the fighting that had already reached the hold and voices became raised in noisy retelling of the battle. Wine flowed freely; jongleurs sang songs newly composed, extolling the heroism of their lord and prince and Tepshen Lahl, whose standing, Wynett saw, was near as great as Bedyr's or Kedryn's. Yrla, who had organised it all, looked on with glowing eyes, reaching often to touch Bedyr's hand or lean past her husband to catch sight of her son. Kedryn, too, appeared lifted by the welcome, smiling and laughing as the minstrels sang his praises and the warriors imposed toasts upon him until he protested that he would sooner fight barbarians than attempt to match his fellow Tamurin in drinking.

It went on long into the night, and Wynett was grateful for the relief of her bed when finally it ended, though not so tired she failed to enquire of Yrla what Lavia's presence meant.

'I trust you will not take it amiss,' Yrla smiled as she stood at Wynett's door, Bedyr's arm about her shoulders, 'but when the mehdri came with word of Kedryn's blindness I felt I understood the meaning of part of the Text. I sent a rider on to Morfah, that the senders there might contact Estrevan. Gerat's response was to send Lavia.'

The explanation confirmed Wynett's suspicion, but failed to enlighten her further. Nor would Yrla, who told her when she asked, 'Lavia imposed a promise on me – that I would not seek answers until she met Kedryn face to face. I believe she will tell us all on the morrow, for she has asked that we attend her. Until then, let us sleep.'

Wynett was pleased enough to accept that, for she was mightily tired, Tamurin hospitality being somewhat more boisterous than that of High Fort, and she had consumed more wine than she was accustomed to. She nodded and went into her room, where within moments despite her curiosity, she was sound asleep.

She woke to birdsong and the brilliance of sunshine on snow, the fire that had warmed her room burned down to embers. The day was well advanced and when she looked from her window on to the courtyard below, she saw the folk of the hold going about their business, clearly more accustomed to carousal than she. Her head throbbed from the liquor she had drunk, and before taking food she had a servant direct her to the bathhouse.

Yrla found her there, bringing a pot of aromatic tisane that joined the steaming waters of the tub in clearing her head. Still replete from the feasting, she ate sparingly in a near-empty dining hall and then went with Yrla to meet Lavia.

The Sister was ensconced in Caitin Hold's library, a pleasingly quiet chamber warmed as much by the rare collection of leather-bound tomes that lined the walls as by the fire that burned cheerfully in the hearth. High windows let in the morning light, shining on polished boards and gaily-coloured carpets, shining on the small book bound in leather dyed the blue of Estrevan that rested on the round table before Lavia. Bedyr sat to her right and Tepshen Lahl to her left. Kedryn faced her and there were two empty chairs on either side. Yrla took the one closest to her husband and Wynett the other.

'Wynett?' Kedryn asked. 'Mother?'

'I am here,' Yrla said, touching his left hand.

He held out his right and Wynett took it, finding pleasure in the touch, and a degree of guilt, for she saw that Lavia's eyes were upon her, studying her as she said, 'And I, Kedryn.'

Lavia smiled then and Wynett felt her guilt dissipate, for there was only approval in the expression. She withdrew her hand gently, murmuring a greeting to Lavia.

'You come on the wings of praise,' said the older woman. 'The reports from High Fort commend you most highly for what you have done, and I bring you greetings from our Sisters in the Sacred City. Most particularly Gerat sends greetings.'

'Thank you.' Wynett bowed her head, flattered and a little embarrassed by such lofty notice. 'I did no more than any Sister.'

'You did your best,' said Lavia, 'and your best appears to be most excellent. In particular, you have proven a boon companion to Kedryn.'

Wynett felt a momentary alarm at this, for she sensed something behind the words and recognised, now that she could see it clearly, that the book before Lavia was a copy of Alaria's Text.

'I will come directly to the point,' Lavia announced, 'for our studies indicate there is little time to be lost.'

'We are to go on to Estrevan?' Excitement rang in Kedryn's voice. 'Or have you found a cure? Is that why you are here?'

Lavia smiled sympathetically and shook her head.

'I must explain, Prince Kedryn. It is difficult to answer you directly without some preamble. Forgive me, but you must understand what lies behind my presence here.'

'I am sorry,' Kedryn bowed his head apologetically. 'I am impatient.'

'Understandably,' Lavia murmured gently, 'for you have suffered a great hurt in service of the Lady and the Kingdoms – one that we of Estrevan hope to remedy.'

Kedryn stirred in his chair, visibly curbing his impatience. Lavia opened the book and glanced at the pages. Anticipation was palpable in the sunny room, Bedyr leaning forward, taking Yrla's hand, she smiling with a mixture of excitement and wariness. Even Tepshen Lahl's impassive features showed interest. Wynett imposed calm upon herself.

'Since first we learnt of Ashar's Messenger the scholars of Estrevan have sought enlightenment in the Text left by Sister Alaria,' Lavia began. 'The writings are enigmatic to say the least, and written in archaic language, for Alaria was a visionary, not a storyteller. What came to her was, we believe, sent by the Lady to warn the Kingdoms of future danger, and because the Lady would not dictate our actions, those warnings were left open to interpretation.

'It was, as you must now know, study of the Text that prompted the Lady Yrla to depart the Sacred City and thus fulfil that part of the prophecy the Paramount Sister Galina had discerned. Thus Kedryn was born and stood ready to defeat the leader of the Horde, ending Ashar's bellicose plan of invasion. However, that does not end the threat: the Messenger still lives and will go about his master's work. In what way, we are not yet sure, but time will doubtless reveal the design.

'We had not, despite all our studies, foreseen Kedryn's blindness, but now that we are confronted with that fact there are parts of the Text that become clearer. Yrla found clues in her studies, and in Estrevan we discovered others. I will not bore you with direct readings of the Text unless you wish a lengthy – and perhaps tedious – lesson in archaism. Will you accept my translation?'

There was murmur of assent and she glanced towards Yrla, who nodded, and then continued, 'It is our belief that Alaria's vision was a prognostication of several possible futures, her Text a maze of words in which paths become clear only as events reveal their course. The only sure facts readily discernable are that Ashar seeks to gain victory over his eternal opponent, the Lady, and to achieve this end he must dominate the Kingdoms – for the Kingdoms represent the benign order of the Lady, and so are hated by the Lord of Chaos. To this end, Ashar raises minions – the Messenger is the one we face now – to work his foulness. He cannot himself enter the Kingdoms, for the Lady set barriers against so direct an intervention, and so he imbues his creatures with ungodly power to do his fell work. The Lady redresses that imbalance by providing situations in which a counter-force comes into being. That force for good is now Kedryn Caitin – the Chosen One of the Text.'

'Blind?' asked Kedryn. 'How may I oppose anyone blind?'

'I come to that,' Lavia said mildly. 'There is a part of the Text your mother brought to our attention. It is the part that concerns our Sister Wynett; and concerned poor Grania, too. Listen . . .'

She turned to the blue-bound book and recited, '*In one shall be three, the pair one, seeing what is and what is not until the one is one.*

'When you joined with Grania on the walls of High Fort a part of her power entered you both. Further reading – I will not try you with the ancient words – indicates that Sister Wynett has become for a while your eyes, and only through her will you regain sight. Further, you will not find it in Estrevan.'

'What?' Kedryn could not hold back the shout, panic ringing in his voice. 'Estrevan cannot help me? Where then? How?'

'*That taken shall be returned,*' Lavia read, '*the thief the giver.* We believe this refers to the one who blinded you. We believe that only he may restore your sight.'

'He is dead.' It was Bedyr who spoke now, his voice hollow. 'He was a baresark. He was slain and his body by now will be in the Beltrevan. Burned by woodlander custom.'

Wynett felt Kedryn's hand close on hers, squeezing. She felt tears fill her eyes as she looked towards him and saw stark anguish on his face.

'I am condemned to blindness,' he groaned.

'No,' said Lavia, her voice firm. 'You may regain your sight – by entering the Beltrevan again to find the one who took it.'

'A corpse?' Kedryn's voice was bitter. 'A body gone to ashes?'

'The sword that robbed you of vision was ensorcelled,' Lavia answered, 'The man who bore it sent by the Messenger, doubtless imbued with some gramarye. Such as he do not find easy peace, and as he failed in his appointed task he is unlikely to have found a welcome in Ashar's domain. We of Estrevan believe his spirit must now wander the netherworld. You must follow him there and seek the restitution of your vision.'

She paused as the five seated around the table stared at her aghast. Kedryn's mouth hung open and Wynett felt the tension in his grip as he demanded huskily, 'How may I do that?'

'You may easily enter the Beltrevan,' Lavia responded, her tone reassuring, 'your status as conqueror of Niloc Yarrum will win you support amongst the tribes. I have brought certain talismans that will grant you a degree of protection from the ... things ... you will face thereafter, and the shamans of the dead man's tribe will know the way you must take. In the netherworld you must seek out the baresark.'

'And then?' asked Kedryn softly.

'Then,' said Lavia, 'you must persuade him to give back that which he took from you – your sight.'

Kedryn laughed, an empty sound. 'You set me no easy task, Sister,' he murmured.

'No,' Lavia agreed, 'I do not. But there is no other way; of this we are confident.'

'Then,' Kedryn announced grimly, 'I depart for the Beltrevan. May the Lady be with me.'

'And I,' Tepshen Lahl declared. 'I ride with you.'

'There is more,' Lavia said. 'Wynett must accompany you. She will be your eyes.'

'No!' Kedryn shook his head, his expression fierce. 'It is too dangerous.'

Lavia looked to Wynett, her eyes unreadable. Beside her, Bedyr drew a hand across his face, hope and horror mingled there. Yrla studied the young Sister as if she already knew what her decision would be. Tepshen Lahl was inscrutable.

Wynett had no decision to make. That fact came to her as she saw Kedryn's eyes lose their blankness, the strength of his emotion bringing another brief return of sight. She smiled at him, then turned to Lavia.

'Of course I will go with him.'

Chapter Six

IT seemed to Kedryn that he was condemned to wander, forever questing, a vagrant in his own land, denied respite in the endless struggle between the opposed forces of Ashar and the Lady, for now he was again preparing to depart his home with scant idea how long this new journey might take, or even whether he would survive it.

Nonetheless, despite all his qualms, he accepted Lavia's word that only in the Beltrevan might he regain his sight, and that thought he kept foremost in his mind, choosing to live by the day rather than contemplate the greater issues raised by the Sister's interpretation of Alaria's Text. That he was the Chosen One foretold by the long-dead sybil he relegated to some hinder compartment of his consciousness, just as he pushed back the thought that at some future date he must fight Ashar's minion. It was enough for now that she gave him hope of sight regained, albeit hope achieved only though arduous travail. The notion was as exciting as his imminent departure from Caitin Hold was depressing, and he knew that he must leave before the wolf-weather closed in to seal the mountain passes so he clove to the promise of Lavia's interpretation, refusing to allow himself the sad luxury of self-pity.

There was a bright side: after explaining Estrevan's estimation of the prophecy and the part he must play, Lavia had suggested that she might increase the bonding through which Wynett was able to restore partial vision. He had instantly agreed, and the Sister had requested a quiet room and sundry items of equipment and herbs that were immediately supplied. She had spent the better part of a day in preparation and then summoned Kedryn and Wynett to join her. He had entered a chamber redolent of materia medica, the air within warm and aromatic, the mingled scents unidentifiable. Lavia had given him something to drink, a bitter brew that left a sour aftertaste, and then dripped some mildly astringent liquid into his eyes. Next she had sat him down and taken his left hand while Wynett took his right, and he had felt the heat of a brazier on his face, its coals giving off a sharp, sweet odour that reminded him of the preparation Grania had burnt on the ramparts of High Fort. He had lost all sense of time, the emanation of the brazier inducing a dreamy, trance-like state through which he heard only faintly the voice of the older Sister as she intoned words that seemed to reverberate with a power of their own in a language he did not comprehend. Then, slowly, as if a mist cleared from before his eyes, burned away by the sun, he had realised that he was looking at a metal pot set on a trivet borrowed from the hold's kitchens; that coals glowed red within; and that the pot was standing on a small, round table of polished oak. He had turned his head to see Wynett smiling at him, her golden hair tinged russet by the brazier's glow, a beading of sweat on her smooth forehead.

'I can see!' he had gasped, tearing his gaze from Wynett to stare at Lavia, seeing for the first time that she was a tall woman with a serene face framed by brown hair streaked with grey, her dark eyes studying him with compassion and anticipation.

'Praise the Lady,' she had murmured, returning his smile as she gently let go his hand. 'If all has gone well, you will now see whenever you touch Wynett. That is why she must go with you – I have strengthened the bonding made by Grania so that it will come into force on a touch, no longer reliant on emotion.'

He had nodded and experimented by releasing Wynett's hand. And, indeed, when he did that his sight instantly faded, returning when the younger Sister reached out to touch him again.

'Praise the Lady,' he had murmured in agreement, though later both he and Wynett found it a mixed blessing. It meant that they were more than ever together, Kedryn's joy at being able again to see his home and show it to Wynett, to look upon the faces of his friends, tempered by his desire to speak his heart to the lovely woman who now accompanied him everywhere, her hand constantly in his. It became increasingly difficult to hold his tongue when he gazed at her beauty, though he did his best, remembering his promise, even as his eyes said the words he would not let past his lips.

Wynett, in equal measure, found it hard, for she saw the love he bore her on his face and felt her own feelings thrown into turmoil by the adoration and the constant proximity. It was not easy to conceal her own affection and she found after a while that the effort drained her, only her resolve to remain true to her vows preventing her from according Kedryn the confession she knew he desired. Despite the dangers, she found herself looking forward to the journey into the Beltrevan: the road would surely provide them with sufficient problems that this emotional impasse might be at least temporarily set aside.

And the preparations proceeded with alacrity. As yet they were touched only by the edge of winter, but soon its full weight would descend upon Tamur and it was, according to Lavia, imperative that they set out as swiftly as possible. In further conclave she expressed Estrevan's fear that the Messenger remained not just alive, but active still and bent on furthering his master's fell design. How, she could not say, for all the efforts of the Sorority had not been able to discover his whereabouts, though the consensus of opinion was that he likely sought to penetrate the security of the Kingdoms to work his glamours from within, having failed to succeed by force of arms. With that in mind, Bedyr reluctantly agreed to her suggestion that he remain in Caitin Hold, entrusting Kedryn to the care of Tepshen Lahl and a select band of ten warriors, two of them familiar with the patois of the woodlanders, and Yrla, bravely concealing her sadness at once more bidding her son farewell, gave them her blessing for a safe journey and a swift return.

'It seems I am to have little part in his life,' she murmured wistfully as she rummaged through closets in search of winter clothing for Wynett. 'He was a boy when he first departed for the Beltrevan, and he has returned a man only to ride out again.'

'He will come back,' Wynett had replied. 'His heart is here.'

'I am selfish.' Yrla had smiled as she said it, laying out a selection of thick, woollen underclothing sweet with the scent of the herbal sachets tucked amongst the garments. 'It is in a mother's nature to forget her children must grow and go their own ways. In Kedryn's case it seems to have happened so quickly.'

'His sight regained, he will come home,' Wynett promised.

'Unless Ashar's accursed creature comes again between us,' Yrla responded, her voice grim. 'It seems we are caught in some cosmic game that takes little account of the desires of mere pawns.'

'If my Sisters' reading of the Text is correct, we all have a duty in that game,' Wynett said slowly. 'We must all play our parts.'

'I know,' Yrla sighed, adding fur-lined leggings to the mounting pile of clothes, 'and my complaints are purely a mother's possessive love. I would not hold him back – and I know he rides in good company.'

She turned to Wynett then, setting her hands to the young

126

woman's face. 'Take care of him, my dear: you hold more than the key to his vision.'

'I know,' Wynett said softly, 'and I shall. Were I not sworn to Estrevan . . .'

'Yes.' Yrla stooped to kiss her brow, then abruptly changed the subject. 'Now, let us see if these things fit.'

Wynett was grateful for the occupation, shedding her blue robe for the winter travel gear Yrla had selected, its warmth and sturdiness attesting to the severity of the season she must soon face on the trail. She giggled as she drew on the stuff, layer upon layer it seemed, until she was sure she must resemble nothing so much as some blonde snow beast. There were the long woollen underbreeches and a vest of similar material, thinner breeks and tunic of soft hide, then the leggings with the fur turned inwards, and fur-lined boots, a thick jerkin, again lined with fur, its collar standing about her face and tickling her, gloves, and finally a furred cloak with holes for her arms and a hood that laced about her face to cover all but her eyes. Yrla added a bonnet and a strange contrivance of carved wood and bone, hinged and thonged, with slits that Wynett did not at first understand.

'It covers your eyes,' Yrla explained, fixing the thing in place. 'You tie the thongs behind your head.'

'I can barely see.' Wynett burst into giggles as she studied herself in the mirror set in a frame beside the wardrobe, seeing the befurred image that confronted her, bulky beneath its coverings, with narrow slit eyes where the mask sat across her nose.

'The snow in the high peaks can blind you,' Yrla warned. 'These protect your sight.'

Wynett remembered the charcoal old Dys had given her and nodded.

'Unguents, too,' advised Yrla, 'lest the wind and frost chafe your skin.'

'I have those,' Wynett said. 'Are winters here so fierce?'

'Worse across the Lozins,' came the answer. 'It will not be so bad crossing the Tamur plateau, but when you climb the foothills to the high peaks you will need all of this.'

'Shall we not pass back through the Lozin Gate?' Wynett enquired, seeing Yrla shake her head.

'No, that would take too long. It seems the woodlander who struck Kedryn was a Drott, and their territory lies north and west of the Gate. Bedyr and Tepshen agreed that the most direct route is to the north, to the Fedyn Pass. It is high and narrow, but it will take you more swiftly than any other trail into the Drott lands. A border fort guards the way and the road there will not be too difficult yet. Though once you enter the pass . . .' She paused, her expression grave. 'Then you will need all this gear. And the Lady's blessing.'

'We have that,' Wynett said stoutly.

'Aye,' Yrla nodded, 'I believe you do.'

Lavia, too, had advice to offer, though it was not to do with the physical journey.

'Take this,' she said as they sat at dinner on the night before their departure, extending a small parcel sealed with the stamp of Estrevan to Wynett. 'It is a talisman that will ward you in the netherworld.'

Wynett broke the seal and took Kedryn's hand as she studied the contents that he might see what safeguard the Sorority offered. There were two small medallions of blue stone, thin and carved with tiny, ancient symbols, suspended from leather thongs, the back of each jagged as if sundered from its obverse side.

'Custom has it these were once one,' Lavia explained, 'and worn by Kyrie herself. When she drove Ashar north and sealed him behind the Lozin Wall the talisman was divided, but the pieces retain power. Keep them safe and wear them when you go beyond – they will guard you and enable you to see the snares that may confront you.'

Dutifully both Kedryn and Wynett hung the stones about their necks.

'You must find the Drott lands,' Lavia continued, 'and claim your right as hef-Alador to their help. Demand of their shamans that they bring you to the burial place and perform the ceremony that will enable you to enter the netherworld. *You must both wear the talismans* – they will bring you to the one you seek.'

'Both?' Kedryn demanded, his grip on Wynett's hand tightening as he stared at Lavia. 'Must Wynett accompany me even there?'

'The bonding applies in both this world and that other,' the older Sister nodded. 'Without Wynett, you will be blind there as you are here. Though without the physical bonds of this world, you will not need to maintain touch – the talismans will establish the linking that grants you sight. And after you confront the one you seek you will require that doubled strength to return. Do not think that Ashar will remain quiescent to this invasion. He will not! Even when you have won back your sight he will doubtless seek to entrap

128

you in the shadows, and for the sake of the Kingdoms you *must* return.'

She faced Wynett then, saying, 'This is a heavy task, Sister.'

'You need not agree,' Kedryn said quickly. 'I would not place you in jeopardy. I will place my trust in the Lady and enter this limbo alone.'

Wynett looked into his eyes and took both his hands in hers as she said, 'I would not allow that, Kedryn. I have begun this journey with you and we shall end it together. You cannot leave me behind.'

'You are brave as you are beautiful,' he murmured, and she blushed, turning her attention to the wine a servant set before her as the others at the table looked discreetly away. All save Lavia, who caught Wynett's eye and smiled enigmatically, her expression one of fond concern and curiosity.

The hall was subdued that night, for there were many present who doubted Kedryn would return, and others who felt it the wiser course to wait out the winter and attempt the crossing of the Lozins in the spring; and all were sorry to bid their prince farewell so soon after his home-coming. Lyassa, in particular, was moved by his going, having believed that he would make the safer journey to Estrevan rather than penetrate the barbarian lands and – worse – the spirit world, and after several cups of wine she found it impossible to hold back her tears.

'I am a disgrace to my calling,' she keened, her plump cheeks glistening. 'The Lady has set you a course to follow and I complain of it, but I cannot help it.'

'I shall return,' Kedryn promised her. 'Do I not ride with true companions? And this,' he touched the blue talisman as his throat, 'will doubtless guard me.'

'But when shall you practise the lessons I taught you?' sniffed the ageing Sister. 'I had thought to see you dance in the White Palace, not ride always into danger.'

'I ride that the danger may be ended,' Kedryn smiled, reaching across the table to take her hand. 'Do not weep, Lyassa; your teachings stand me in good stead and I shall return to show how badly I dance.'

This sally, small though it was, brought a sad smile to the Sister's cheeks and she turned to face Tepshen Lahl.

'Ward him well, kyo,' she admonished. 'He is your charge now.'

'He is his own man,' said the easterner calmly, 'but rest assured my blade will be ever at his back.'

Lyassa shuddered at the war-like promise, but cheered a little and stilled her weeping.

There were other farewells said that night, but they were less emotional for it was not the Tamurin way to make any great thing of danger and the men and women who approached the high table to take Kedryn's hand or kiss his cheek were mostly content to simply express their desire that he come safe home again, his sight fully restored.

They retired early for their intention was to depart soon after first light and the hold was in no mood for prolonged festivity. Wynett went with Kedryn to the door of his chamber, their hands entwined that he might see his way.

'A moment,' Yrla said as Wynett was about to disengage the grip. 'I would have my son see my face.'

Wynett nodded and retained his hand as Yrla hugged Kedryn and then set palms to his cheeks, her head tilted back a little that she might look into his eyes.

'There is nothing I would say to hold you here,' she murmured, 'though my heart aches to see you go. I entrust you to Wynett and Tepshen; and the Lady, who I know will be with you. You have a duty that is hard to bear, but I know you will dispense it as befits a true warrior of Tamur. The heart of Caitin Hold is with you and whatever the outcome, know that I love you.'

'I do,' Kedryn answered, letting go Wynett's hand that he might embrace his mother, setting his arms about her shoulders and holding her close as she rested her face against his chest, 'and I return that love.'

'Aye.' Yrla drew back, quickly brushing a hand across her eyes that he would not see the tears glistening there. 'Go with the Lady, my son.'

Bedyr stepped forward then, his face grave, to place hands upon Kedryn's shoulders.

'I am proud of you,' he said huskily. 'You are a credit to the Caitin blood and I would that I might ride with you.'

Kedryn reached then for Wynett's hand, facing his father, no longer a youth but a man, full grown. 'Your duty lies here,' he said, 'and mine is to ready myself for whatever lies ahead. We shall meet again.'

'I pray so,' nodded Bedyr, and turned to take his wife's arm, steering her towards their own chamber, his back straight and stiff.

'Leavetakings are sad things,' Kedryn murmured.

'You will see them again,' Wynett said. 'And when you do it will be unaided. You will have your own sight.'

'And shall that mean another farewell?' he asked softly, studying her.

Wynett's blue eyes looked into his brown gaze, then she lowered her face to hide the confusion there.

'You look too far ahead,' she whispered.

'Is that an answer?' he chided gently, 'or a promise of hope?'

'I . . .' She shook her head, torchlight glinting golden on the brighter yellow of her hair, 'I cannot say. Please, Kedryn, do not press me. I am a Sister still.'

'Forgive me,' he asked. 'I will not speak of this again until we return.'

That was at least small respite and Wynett essayed a tentative smile. 'Thank you, my Lord. Now – should we not sleep?'

'Aye,' he agreed, and let go her hands, tapping on his chamber door that the servant waiting within might emerge to see him safely to his bed.

It was strange to lie abed in such familiar surroundings yet not see those things he had for so many years taken for granted. He had grown accustomed to his chamber in High Fort, indeed, had set out to learn its configurations with such determination that he needed no help there, but now – in his own home, in his own rooms – he required a housecarl to closet his gear and guide him to the washstand, even to the bed. And when the man was gone he was alone, once more lost in the dark world. He could feel the warmth of the fire banked in the hearth and the stirring of the night wind that came through the shutters, the sheets were pleasantly cool, smooth about his naked body, but he could see neither hearth nor shutters, he did not know if a moon shone outside his window, or even if the carl had left a torch burning. Sightlessness rendered him a stranger to the familiar, and that knowledge pressed upon him thoughts of Wynett. Without her he was lost, doomed to wander blind. Yet his dependence brought her into danger and he loathed that thought. The ride north would be arduous enough, the crossing of the Fedyn pass harder, and after that there was the Beltrevan. The tribes had hailed him as hef-Alador and the chieftains had sworn fealty; Brannoc had seemed confident that their word was good and neither Lavia – who spoke as the voice of Estrevan – nor Bedyr – whom he trusted utterly – seemed to have any doubt but that he would find safe passage through the forests. But would the forest folk extend

131

that hospitality to his companions? Tepshen Lahl and the Tamurin warriors were dangerously able to look after themselves, but Wynett was defenceless. And he knew that if harm came to her, a part of him would die.

He turned in the bed, conjuring a vision of her standing looking into his eyes. She was so beautiful, not merely of visage but of spirit, too. For all that he could not bear the thought of parting from her, he knew what duress he placed her under and he could only admire the way in which she comported herself, with a nobility of spirit that elicited frank admiration of her character.

Were she not a Sister.

Were she but willing to forego her vows.

Had he but met her as his father had met his mother, before those vows were taken.

The thoughts spun headlong about his mind as he drifted into a troubled sleep that was roiled with dreams.

The first was familiar, an echo of that first dream encountered in High Fort, of walking with her in sunlit meadows where birds sang and brooks splashed cheerfully, the sky above blue as her gown, her hair bright as the sun that warmed them. Then it changed with the unnatural normality of such fantasies and the sky became dark with thunder clouds, great storm heads tearing across the azure to obfuscate the purity of the blue behind a pall of livid, lightning-seared darkness as hollow laughter took the place of the thunder and they cowered beneath a tree no longer green with the freshness of spring, but withered and sere, stripped by something more than winter. The birdsong died away and as he gazed about the brooks no longer ran blue-silver, but were sluggish and red, the dark carmine of life's blood. He realised that Wynett no longer stood beside him, but faced him across the meadow, her features riven with grief and terror, though whether for herself or him he could not tell. He moved towards her, but when he stepped from the scant shelter of the tree great bolts of lightning struck down, filling the air with the stink of burning, sickly with the odour of roasting flesh, and the grass was blackened where they hit and fires started up, sparkling small at first, but soon growing to a roaring wall of flame that seemed to reach towards him, driving him back so that he could not go to Wynett and she became lost behind that barrier of incandescence. He heard the laughter louder then and it became a voice that rang from within the flames and said his name, over and over again, a longing in its tone, an awful, hungry anticipation.

He raised his hands to protect his face, but the flames scorched his palms and he cried out, shouting, 'Wynett! Wynett!'

And he felt hands grasp him and struck out as the voice repeated his name and became familiar, recognised as that of the carl set to watch his door.

'Vigrund?' he gasped. 'Is that you, Vigrund?'

'Aye, Prince,' came the answer, 'it is I. You dreamed, I think. I heard you call the Sister's name. Should I fetch her to you?'

'No.' He shook his head, though in that moment he wanted nothing more than to have Wynett by his side, to feel her close, hold her hands, clutch her to him. 'No, do not disturb her.'

'A cup of oenomel, perhaps?' Vigrund suggested, and Kedryn nodded, embarrassed now, for he could feel the aftermath of the tremors that had shaken him and the dampness of sweat-soaked sheets.

He waited, driving his mind to stillness as the carl brought the honeyed wine and set his hands to the cup. The solidity of the plain earthenware beaker reassured him as much as the strong hands that raised him, shaking sweat dampened pillows that he might sit more comfortably.

'Thank you,' he said between sips, relishing the warmth and sweetness of the drink. 'I suffered a disturbing dream.'

'It is not unusual.' He felt the bed shift as Vigrund settled on the edge, informal as any Tamurin. 'I always dreamed before I rode to battle. Terrible dreams, they were, that had me yelling and fighting so that the captain'd often as not set me on night watch just so the rest of them could get some sleep. I remember the night before the Sandurkan put a lance in my leg and made me a housecarl I dreamed I was a boar, but my tusks were broken and I couldn't seem to run when I heard the hunting horns. I tried, but I couldn't, and the dogs sounded me and I was wallowing along when the biggest Sandurkan I'd ever seen came thundering up on one of those hairy ponies they ride and stuck his lance clean through me.

'The captain – Ramur, it was then, though he's long dead now – woke me and told me if I couldn't sleep quiet he'd cut my throat just so the rest of them wouldn't fall asleep in their saddles when they should be fighting Sandurkan. You're finished with that cup? Good, let me have it then. Anyway, that day I got stuck, though I don't suppose it was anything to do with the dream. And after . . .'

He paused as he heard a soft snore from Kedryn and smiled as he rose carefully from the bed, drawing the coverlet up to his prince's chest.

'You sleep sound, Kedryn. For what's ahead of you, you need sleep.'

He stared fondly at the young man, wondering when – or if – he might return again, then shuffled on his twisted leg to the outer chamber where he settled on his own bed and fell swiftly into a dreamless sleep.

Kedryn's rest, too, was unmarred by nightmares for what remained of the dark hours, though when he woke he could still recall with horrid clarity all the details of the dream, and felt the sluggish pull of incomplete sleep. It was early yet and the hold was only just waking as he drew on a robe and shouted for Vigrund to bring him to the bathhouse, trusting in the waters to refresh him. He was not much surprised to find Tepshen Lahl already there, for it was the habit of the easterner to bathe on waking and before retiring.

'What kind of day is it? he asked as he eased himself into the steaming tub. 'Barely light yet,' answered Tepshen, 'but it will be a fine day for a ride.'

Kedryn chuckled: it seemed so typical of the kyo to refer to their journey as nothing more than 'a ride'. 'How long will it take us to reach the Fedyn Pass?' he enquired.

'The Sister will set our pace,' Tepshen said. 'Were we alone, perhaps twenty days, depending on the weather. She may slow us – I do not know how well she sits a horse.'

Kedryn nodded; it had not occurred to him to enquire of Wynett as to her standard of equestrianism. Then a thought struck him and he asked, 'Do you resent her presence?'

'How could I?' the kyo responded. 'You need her.'

'Aye,' he said softly, 'I do.'

Tepshen Lahl heard the double meaning in the statement and squinted through the steam at the young man he looked on as a son. 'What you attempt will not be easy,' he said bluntly, 'and it will be harder if your heart wanders. Regain your sight – then think of other things.'

Kedryn smiled. 'Your advice is sound as ever, Tepshen, and I shall endeavour to take it. But it is not easy.'

'Nothing worth having is won easily,' said the kyo.

'No,' Kedryn agreed, wondering if he heard some hidden meaning behind the words. He was about to ask, but Tepshen climbed to his feet then saying, 'Come, we should not delay,' and he followed his friend from the tub into the cold pool, where the chilling water stung him to full wakefulness.

Tepshen Lahl brought him back to his chambers, where Vigrund had his travelling gear laid ready. He dressed, leaving the carl to see to the packing of his saddlebags, and went cautiously along the corridor, feeling his way, to Wynett's door. He tapped and it opened, and he heard Wynett ask, 'Are you ready for a surprise?'

'Aye,' he said cautiously.

'Then look,' she giggled, and took his hand.

Sight returned with her touch and he smiled as he saw her. Her hair was drawn back from her face, fastened with a twist of blue ribbon so that it hung in a thick tail at the nape of her slender neck. A jerkin of chestnut brown edged with black fur bulked the upper part of her body, drawn in at the waist by a wide leather belt from which a silver-hilted Tamurin dagger hung. Her legs were encased in black hide riding breeches that disappeared into tall boots, heeled for the stirrups, and she seemed more warrior maid than Sister.

'Well?' She raised his hand that she might pirouette. 'Am I suitably accoutred?'

'You are lovely,' he said.

'I am hot,' she grinned.

'It will be cold enough on the road,' he smiled back. 'And Tepshen is anxious to be gone.'

They went down to the dining hall, where the party was already assembling, Wynett's appearance bringing a cheerful barrage of praise from the Tamurin warriors. Bedyr and Yrla joined them and they ate a hearty breakfast before adjourning to the stables where their mounts were waiting, blowing plumes of steam into the chill air.

It was a bright morning, the sky a hard blue-grey with no hint of cloud, the early sun sparkling on the frost that rimed the rooftops and buttresses of the hold. They drew on their cloaks and checked their animals, Kedryn holding Wynett's hand that he might see the lacings of his gear and ensure the security of the various buckles. Yrla hugged him once more, murmuring a blessing, and Bedyr took his hand; Lavia appeared, clad in a long cloak of Estrevan blue, to give formal blessing, and they mounted.

The gates were open and those of Caitin Hold not engaged in pressing duties clustered about the yard and ramparts to shout farewells as they rode beneath the arch on to the hard-packed snow beyond. Kedryn was flanked by Tepshen and Wynett and he took the Sister's hand as they passed out of the citadel, turning in his

135

saddle to wave, seeing his mother and father standing watching, Bedyr's arm about Yrla's shoulders as they saw their son ride away. They returned his wave and he dropped his arm, turning to smile at Wynett and Tepshen.

'May the Lady look with favour on this quest,' he said.

'Amen to that,' Wynett answered fervently, answering his smile.

'Let us ride,' said the kyo.

Kedryn released Wynett's hand and let the Keshi stallion match the easterner's pace, hearing the drumming of Wynett's bay gelding beside him, grinning as he felt the windrush of their passage strike his face, putting thoughts of home behind him as the excitement of what lay ahead drove out regrets, filling him with a fine, wild optimism.

Mejas Celeruna clutched the gold lacquered gunwale of the *Vargalla* and frowned uncomfortably at the seething wake of the barge. Wind tore at his thinning hair, tumbling the artfully teased ringlets in disarray and lashing his plump cheeks with an icy sting that reddened them better that any rouge. Around him the other members of Hattim Sethiyan's retinue clustered in similar discomfort, none daring to voice what lay heavy on their minds.

There was something unnatural about the wind, Celeruna decided, just as there was something unnatural about the latest member of Hattim's court. The two had seemed to arrive together, the breeze freshening soon after the strange newcomer had arrived on board and growing steadily stronger since, dying away only when the vessel put in for the night and then rising again when they cast off in the mornings. The boatmaster had told him it was no seasonal blow, indeed, that he had never experienced such a draught so early in the season, though he had no complaints as it eased the task of his oarsmen, filling the sails and speeding the barge southwards at such a rate they must surely reach Estrevan not long after the king's vessel. Celeruna was less complacent, and more than a little piqued.

They had quit Nyrwan with surprising haste, Hattim appearing uncharacteristically early to summon his courtiers and announce their imminent departure. There had been no sign of the doxy, though Celeruna had left a few silver coins with the landlord, and Hattim had seemed untypically active for one who had spent the night in such company. Then the stranger had appeared on the wharfside, swathed in a voluminous cloak with the hood drawn up so that none had clearly seen his features, and Hattim had greeted

136

him as though he were expected, ushering him to the cabin and shutting out all others. From that day on the retinue was denied access to the lord of Ust-Galich's quarters where Hattim remained alone with the stranger for all the time they were on the water. He would appear at dusk, as they hove to, but always alone, and as best the portly courtier could tell, the mysterious newcomer stayed on board, neither eating nor venturing ashore. He knew better than to press Hattim on the matter, but discreetly casual enquiries had brought no further enlightenment and the courtiers were cast out on to the decks of the barge to suffer the temper of the climate as best they might.

They did not enjoy their reduced status, muttering irritably amongst themselves, but never daring to broach the subject with their lord since Celeruna had requested shelter from a squall and suffered a flung goblet for his effrontery, together with the threat that any who complained of their condition might find their way to shore and travel south as best they could.

It was the wiser course to find what cover they might in the boatmaster's small cabin, or even below decks amongst the rowers, and bear the elements until they halted for the night, when fires and warm food became available in the riverside taverns.

Celeruna did not enjoy it. He was no riverman and had not anticipated spending the entire journey down the Idre on deck, but more than that he was disturbed by Hattim's behaviour. The lord Ust-Galich was customarily of variable humour, and his mood ever since the young prince of Tamur had gained such prominence had been black, but now Celeruna sensed there was more to it. It was as though the ever present wind put a chill in his well-covered bones that winter alone could not account for, a feeling of unease that went deeper than mere physical discomfort, and thwarted curiosity did nothing to lessen his dissatisfaction. He longed to know who the mysterious stranger was, and why Hattim kept him ensconced in the cabin.

He shook his head in weary irritation and made his way clumsily across the deck to snatch a flagon from Bajin Darlath, drinking deep as he stared moodily at the swirling grey water and listened to the others keep up their endless musings.

'Who is he?'

'Where did he come from?'

'Why does he never come on deck?'

'Why are we shut out?'

'What power does he hold over Hattim?'

'Why should he be so favoured?'

'Who is he?'

'Mayhap he is some river demon who has entranced Hattim,' snapped Celeruna, 'and he is leading us all to our doom.'

'Do you think so?'

Bajin's question was serious Celeruna realised as he passed back the flagon and looked into the troubled eyes of the younger man. Lady help us, he thought, the fool's wits are addled. He shook his head.

'No, Bajin, I do not. I do not know who he is, but I do not believe in river demons. Or sprites, or fetches, or goblins.'

'The wind came with him,' said Bajin obstinately, clutching at the idea put in his otherwise empty head.

'Then thank him, because it speeds us homewards,' grunted Celeruna, wondering why Hattim surrounded himself with such nincompoops and unwilling to admit his own unease. 'And the swifter we run, the sooner we shall be off this accursed river and comfortable in our own homes again.'

'Unless he really is leading us to doom,' muttered Bajin.

Celeruna stared at his fellow courtier and considered a reply, then thought better of it and turned his back with a most uncourtly display of rudeness, pacing over to the shelter of the steering cabin, where at least he was out of the wind and the boatmaster went about his duties in silence.

Within the cabin Hattim Sethiyan sprawled on cushions, wiping at the sweat that beaded his chest in the stifling atmosphere. The brazier that Taws insisted be kept lit filled the small chamber with a heat too great even for the chill of winter on the Idre, and the tight-latched shutters allowed no breath of air to disturb the dense miasma. The mage seemed at ease, luxuriating in the turgid thickness, the cloak Hattim had provided wrapped tight about him as he stared into the coals that twinned his eyes.

'We must surely reach Andurel ere long,' the Galichian ventured.

'In time,' the sorcerer agreed, his voice a whisper that still raised a shudder of trepidation in the lord Ust-Galich. 'Your haste is no greater than mine.'

'They will likely spread tales.' Hattim's hand gestured beyond the walls, indicating the courtiers on deck.

'They will say nothing,' Taws promised.

'How can you be sure?' Hattim reached for the decanter set on the

138

low table at his side, the motion a device to avoid the mage's glance. 'Once ashore they will find it hard to hold their tongues.'

'They will find it harder still to loose them,' Taws answered. 'I will see to that.'

Hattim filled his goblet and swallowed a measure of wine warmed by the heat of the cabin, not daring to enquire – not really wanting an answer – how the mage proposed to ensure silence. There were ways, of that he had no doubt, but what they might be he preferred not to know. He had doubts about the bargain he had struck now that he had had time to consider its implications, but the thought of Taws' wrath should he endeavour to renege terrified him. And his ambition remained a spur. Taws was – of this there could be no doubt whatsoever – a formidable ally, but his methods put a chill in Hattim's soul. By night, he knew, the mage stalked the streets of the riverside settlements whilst humankind slept, and in each one he left a carcase drained of more than life. What other practices he might indulge Hattim chose not to think about, knowing that he was now bound to Taws' purpose.

'Do not doubt.' Hattim started, spilling wine, at the words. Did the thaumaturgist read his mind? 'I will give you everything I promised, and it will not be long in the gaining. This waiting is irksome, but we cannot risk swifter passage lest we arouse suspicions.'

'Will your presence not be suspicious?' asked the Galichian. 'There will be Sisters present in Andurel.'

Taws seemed to shrug beneath the enveloping cloak, but it was hard to discern for his body seemed to articulate in ways not quite human. 'They will not see me. Nor sense my presence. I shall enter the White Palace changed, as I came to you.'

Hattim rubbed at his neck in reflex action: Taws had explained how he had penetrated High Fort and although the flea bites had almost faded, the memory still left Hattim a trifle queasy. He had thought to further his ambition through cunning, not sorcery, and whilst he realised that opposition to his claims might well have been such as to deny them, he still adjusted to the notion of committing his fate to Ashar's minion.

'Think of the White Palace,' Taws suggested, the expression Hattim had come to recognise as a smile angling his lipless mouth. 'Think of power. Think of Tamur and Kesh bowed beneath your heel. Remember that I can give you all that.'

Hattim nodded and swallowed more wine, hearing the threat implicit in the statement. He was committed now and there was no turning back. He had given himself into Taws' hands, and by extension to Ashar: the Lady might forgive him, but the Lord of the Fires would not if he attempted to turn his coat.

'I will work a glamour before we dock at Andurel,' Taws said as though to reassure his puppet, 'and your retinue will remember nothing of my presence. You need only proceed as custom dictates – find quarters in the White Palace while you ply your suit with Ashrivelle and I will do the rest. Before you know it you will sit in Darr's place.'

He turned his ashen-maned head to Hattim and the lord of Ust-Galich found his gaze caught by the rubescent glow of the deep-sunk eyes, held. They seemed to burn fiercer, as if some hellish breath fanned magma to a fresh intensity, and Hattim felt his doubts ooze from him as the sweat oozed from his pores. Confidence filled him and he raised his goblet in a toast saying, 'As you will it, Taws.'

'Aye,' the mage replied. 'As I will it.'

The road to the Fedyn Pass was marked with waystops, villages and crossroads inns that were able to accommodate the travellers as those along the road from High Fort had not been large enough to do for the more sizeable party. There were no more nights spent under canvas, the weather holding good and Wynett's equestrian ability proving equal to the swift pace Tepshen Lahl set. They reached Amshold on the first night, riding in as the sun settled behind the western horizon to find warm baths and hot food, comfortable beds and a genial welcome from the villagers who were delighted to host their prince and his party. They left at sunrise and came to a hostelry on the Morfah road before dusk, proceeding to Nigrand and Barshom, Forshold, Wyrath and on to Quellorn at the same swift pace. Between Quellorn and Ramshold, the last settlement before the Lozin foothills, snow began to fall, slowing them, and they found shelter in a lonely farm, throwing the holder's wife into a fine tizzy at the prospect of entertaining the Prince of Tamur. Fourteen days out from Caitin Hold they arrived at Loswyth, with the high peaks of the Lozins towering above them.

This close the mountains were daunting, taller it seemed than at High Fort, great jagged buttresses of stone that swooped upwards as if they supported the sky. Above the winter-clad meadows that surrounded the town the lower slopes were thick with snow-decked timber that thrust from the sweeping whiteness, giving gradual way to bare rock, too steep for snow to grip, like scars on the albescent

140

vastness of the mountain wall. Higher still the Lozins became lost in white mist, cloud and stone merging so that it was impossible to discern where mountains ended and sky began. It seemed equally impossible that they might be crossed, for no pass was visible from Loswyth and it seemed the Lozins stood impenetrable, an unbroachable barrier between Tamur and the Beltrevan.

Wynett and Kedryn walked hand in hand through the streets of the town, snow crunching beneath their boots and the air stinging their cheeks with its chill. The winter gear Yrla had provided came into full use here and Wynett was grateful for its warmth, the very magnitude of her surroundings chilling her with their awesome grandeur. Kedryn seemed at ease, but he had been here before, and was Tamur-bred, accustomed to the majesty of his kingdom and excited at the nearing of his quest's conclusion. He bowed, however, to Tepshen Lahl's suggestion that they rest their mounts before attempting the climb to the border fort and took the opportunity to show Wynett the sights of Loswyth.

It was a spread of wooden buildings flanking the forest that had provided the timber for the low, slope-roofed houses, all overhung balconies painted in bright colours and narrow streets that wound amongst cowsheds and storage barns. In summer, Kedryn explained, the upper meadows were clear of snow and the cattle grazed there, fattening through the warm months before coming down to the shelter of the lower slopes when winter covered their forage. There was a pond, frozen over, with children sliding and screaming on the ice, and as they promenaded they heard the tinkling of the bells that hung from the horse-drawn sleds that were the chief means of winter transport. It was a pretty town, picturesque and welcoming, and after the days on the trail – and the rigours ahead – their brief sojourn assumed the mood of a holiday.

The inn in which they found quarters was homely and cheerful, a fire roaring at all hours in the hearth of the common room, cunningly arranged chimneys spreading the warmth to the sleeping chambers so that even as snow drifted down outside, their rooms were snug. The snowfalls came by night and each dawn the slopes above the village were painted pink by the rising sun, a rosy red at sunset. Wynett thought that Loswyth must be a pleasant place to live, brighter and less damp than the canyon of the Idre containing High Fort. There were two Sisters resident in the settlement, one a healer, the other a teacher, and they welcomed Wynett as both friend and colleague. She was almost sorry when Tepshen Lahl announced that they had

141

rested long enough and should proceed before further snow blocked the pass.

'The going will be harder,' the kyo warned, 'the trail steeper and likely drifted. The Fedyn Fort stands at the entrance, and past it we shall have the full weight of winter against us.'

'How long shall we be in the mountains?' Wynett wondered.

'If we are not delayed, perhaps eight or nine days', Tepshen replied.

Wynett turned then to peer through the window of the common room, looking to where a quarter moon shone on the peaks. They seemed ominous in that light and she shivered at the thought of traversing that vastness of snow and stone.

Kedryn squeezed her hand. 'It will be easier once we enter the Beltrevan,' he promised.

Wynett smiled, dismissing the premonition of danger that seemed to emanate from the great white wall as though she sensed the presence of Ashar beyond, pent behind the barrier the Lady had created.

'Sleep,' Tepshen advised. 'We depart at sunrise.'

His suggestion was accepted and soon after dawn the next day the travellers grouped in the courtyard of the inn. It was another fine day, though the nightly snowfall seemed thicker, reminding them that winter progressed apace, threatening to bar their passage so that they mounted swiftly and rode out to a chorus of good wishes from the landlord and his folk, the two sturdy pack ponies Tepshen had purchased trailing behind on lead reins.

Kedryn's blindness became more of an encumbrance as they began the climb, for once past the easy going of the meadows the trail wound through the timber, rising steadily steeper. It was thick with snow, great drifts built up between the trees so that the horses plunged through, raising great clouds of sunlit powder, the warriors taking it in turns to break trail. Kedryn and Wynett stayed to the rear, the Keshi stallion following the path made by the forerunners and the Sister calling advice when hazards such as low branches or drops presented themselves. By mid-morning she saw how deceptive the view from Loswyth had been, for what had appeared a smooth slope was, in fact, a perilously steep ascent, their path often running alongside near-vertical gradients, or angling up ridges that promised an ugly fall for the unwary. Several times Tepshen Lahl put a rope on the stallion, ignoring the animal's protests as he guided it upwards, and by dusk they seemed to have made little progress.

'We shall reach the fort on the morrow,' Tepshen assured his charge when Kedryn grumbled at their lack of speed, blaming himself. 'We make good enough time. See?'

He pointed back the way they had come and Wynett took Kedryn's hand that he might follow the kyo's direction.

They were halted on a shelf of the mountains, protected on two sides by flanks of naked stone. The tents were up and the animals tethered, munching the oats carried by the pack ponies. A fire had been lit and the air was sweet with the savoury odour of a cooking stew. Far away to the west the sky was crimson flecked with gold, and the peaks above them were brilliant in the dying rays, silver and blue and gilt, iridescent colours glittering and sparkling in a rainbow farewell to the day. Below, the timber lay dark and silent, stark black and white, and beyond full night already filled the land like a brimming midnight lake in which the tiny pinpricks of light that showed where Loswyth lay marked the distance they had come.

'It is lovely,' Wynett murmured, moved by the vastness and tranquillity of the panoply spread out below her.

'It is Tamur,' Kedryn replied simply.

'As an eagle might see it,' she said.

'I wish I were an eagle.' He grinned, turning to face her, thinking that even swathed in furs, hidden beneath her bonnet, she was lovely. 'Then I should fly into the Beltrevan and not subject you to these rigours.'

'I chose to accompany you,' she answered, 'and I have not yet proven too great a burden, have I?'

'No.' He shook his head. 'You could never be a burden to me.'

'You have done well.' Tepshen joined them, presenting bowls of stew.

Kedryn laughed, even though he needed loose her hand to eat. 'Did you but know Tepshen as well as I,' he chuckled, 'you would realise that is high praise indeed.'

'It is merited,' said the kyo solemnly. 'The Sister rides like a Tamurin.'

'Thank you,' Wynett said, studying the impassive features.

'*Gahn-vey.*' Tepshen bowed from the waist. 'In the tongue of my birthland that means deserved praise requires no thanks.'

Wynett smiled at him, surprised that she found such pleasure in his approval. It felt, she realised as he turned and walked to the fire, as though she belonged here, were genuinely an accepted member of the Tamurin rather than a mere necessity, brought along for Kedryn's sake. The feeling warmed her as much as the stew.

143

Next morning the shelf was blanketed with fresh snow and the sky did not brighten. A sullen sun glistened listlessly from behind grey cloudbanks and the air smelled moister than before. An air of expectancy rendered their departure urgent, the warriors saddling their animals hurriedly, looking to the sky as if they expected it to tumble on to them. It did not, but whilst they negotiated the steep rise behind the shelf snow began to fall steadily and soon they rode through a curtain of white, the lead riders hidden from those at the rear. Tepshen called a halt and passed a rope to Kedryn, insisting that he permit himself led.

Their going was much slower through the snowstorm and Wynett began to think they would not reach the Fedyn Fort by nightfall. The terrain grew increasingly precipitous, the mountain flank no longer a steady rise but a jumble of ravines and gulleys that sometimes forced them to dismount and lead the horses. She saw the way the peaks turned and twisted on themselves, less a single line of hills than a great spreading cluster of joined mountains filled with high valleys and dead ends, promising a lonely fate to anyone not familiar with the trail to the pass. Rivers ran up here, appearing in great tumbling falls from lips of water-washed stone all slick with fantastic ice shapes, to disappear in the tortuous undulations of the land. Bare rock like dragons' teeth jutted from the snow, and as the fall continued the animals plunged chest-deep through the drifts that built between. Three times warriors needed to scramble up vertiginous gradients to throw ropes down and manhandle the beasts to the crests, and Kedryn cursed his blindness afresh as he, too, was forced to grasp the cords and allow himself to be drawn up like baggage.

Then, around mid-afternoon, the snow eased off and the cloud above began to break apart, permitting a watery sun to filter through. It was fading as they came in sight of the Fedyn Pass and saw the fort.

They had climbed out of a shallow valley and were standing on a ridge that ran at a slight angle to the mouth of the pass. The downslope facing them curved to form a bowl, too steep save for the spot where they stood to climb, the mouth of the pass directly across from their position. It was a cleft in the rocky wall, the sides vertical and bare of snow, the dark stone forbidding, reaching up until it became lost against the rapidly darkening sky, the interior already shadowed. The fort stood on a promontory jutting from the west side, squat and square, built out to the edges of its vantage point so that it commanded both the pass and the bowl beyond. No trees grew here and even to Wynett's unmilitaristic eye it was obvious that no force could cross the Lozins without first overwhelming the fort, and that that would be a task so costly as to render the attempt worthless. Bonfires burned along the ramparts and the embrasures glowed with light, casting a welcoming radiance against the gloomy rock.

'It is a lonely place,' Wynett murmured.

'It is necessary,' Kedryn replied. 'Or was, so long as the tribes threatened war.'

'Come.' Tepshen was already urging his mount down the slope. 'While some little light remains.'

They followed the kyo down, the horses slithering on the treacherous surface, Tamurin moving in close to flank Kedryn protectively, and began to cross the bottom land.

An angled glacis ran up to the gates, turning back on itself so that any approaching force would be slowed, and when they crested the ascent they were faced with a drawbridge. It was down, but archers manned the walls above, their bowstrings part drawn, and soldiers in heavy fur cloaks faced them across the planking.

'I bid you open the gates for Kedryn Caitin, Prince of Tamur,' shouted Tepshen, and Kedryn threw back the hood of his cloak that the watchers might see his face.

'I bid the Prince and his party welcome,' came the answer, given by a burly figure, bearded and mailed. 'Gann Resyth of the Fedyn Fort is at your service.'

They moved forwards then, clattering over the drawbridge and on to the dressed stone before the gates. The guards formed a gauntlet that closed behind them as they passed through the portals, the thick timbers creaking shut as they came into the yard.

'Prince Kedryn.' Gann Resyth came respectfully to Kedryn's stirrup, white teeth flashing through the dense russet of his beard. 'I am honoured to offer you the hospitality of my command.'

'I thank you, Lord Resyth.' Kedryn dismounted and Wynett saw the commander stare at his eyes, unsure as he bowed and took the hand his prince offered. 'May I introduce my companions? The Sister Wynett and Tepshen Lahl.'

Resyth bowed again, clearly confused by the presence of a Sister amongst the retinue. 'Please,' he said, 'let us make formal introductions in my quarters. Your men will find food and hot baths waiting, and your horses will be stabled.'

Kedryn ducked his head and fumbled for Wynett's hand, further confusing the commander, who led the way across the yard to a door that seemed part of the mountain wall.

They found themselves in a low-roofed chamber that appeared both guard room and vestibule, for they doffed their cloaks there and proceeded through torchlit corridors to more airy rooms, with windows looking across the pass, albeit windows that were cut deep to provide firing points for bowmen. Tapestries coloured the walls and rugs the floor, a cheerful fire burned in a hearth, and as they entered three massive dogs stirred, raising alert heads until Resyth murmured a reassurance and they settled back to their dozing.

'You must forgive me, you were not expected.' Resyth gestured to the chairs set about a table of polished oak and shouted over his shoulder for wine to be mulled. 'Is there trouble? I thought the war ended.'

'It is,' Kedryn assured him as he unlaced his jerkin and shucked out of the fur-lined garment, 'peace has been made with the tribes.'

'The mehdri brought word,' Resyth nodded, 'but I thought you travelled to Estrevan.'

'No.' Kedryn took Wynett's hand that he might see Resyth's face as he explained, outlining Lavia's instructions and Wynett's part in his quest, the commander's ruddy features frowning as he listened.

When Kedryn was done he said, 'I cannot advise you to attempt the pass, Prince. Snow has been falling up here for weeks now and the way is treacherous. There is a danger of avalanches. I urge you to wait until the upper slopes are settled.'

'How long?' Kedryn demanded.

'I cannot say for sure,' Resyth shrugged. 'A few weeks, mayhap longer.'

'If Lavia's interpretation is correct, we cannot afford that long a delay.' Kedryn looked to Tepshen Lahl, who nodded. 'If the Messenger does indeed go abroad to work his magicks I must find the burial place without further pause.'

'But the pass is not safe,' Resyth protested.

'Have there been avalanches?' Kedryn asked.

'Not yet,' said Resyth, 'but even so . . .'

'Then we shall attempt it,' Kedryn declared, 'and trust in the Lady to see us through safely.'

The commander frowned afresh at this and stroked his beard worriedly, as though seeking the words that would convince them of his doubts. Finally he said, glancing apologetically at Wynett, 'It is not wise to place all your trust in the Lady where the Fedyn Pass is concerned. I mean no blasphemy, but you stand on the northern boundary of Tamur and beyond these walls lies Ashar's domain. Strange things happen in the Fedyn Pass – the forest folk may be sworn to peace, but the Lord of the Fires is not.'

Kedryn looked to Wynett, who asked, 'Does a Sister reside here, Lord Resyth?'

'Aye,' the commander confirmed, 'Sister Hospitaller Gwenyl. She will tell you the same.'

'I should like to speak with her,' Wynett said.

Resyth nodded and rose, crossing to the door to bellow into the corridor for Sister Gwenyl.

The resident Hospitaller proved to be a woman of Wynett's age, though the effects of sun and snow and wind made her seem older, her homely face textured like leather, her hair bleached almost white. She greeted them excitedly, listening to Kedryn's explanation of their quest with narrowed eyes and a doubtfully pursed mouth.

'What Lord Resyth has told you is true,' she said. 'This fresh snow is dangerous until it has firmed down, but worse than that is Ashar's presence. I feel it sometimes, like a wolf prowling the night. The Lady erected this barrier to keep him from the Kingdoms but even her power does not extend into the Beltrevan.'

'We are warded by her power,' Wynett countered, fingering the talisman hung about her throat, 'and Kedryn is the Chosen One.'

'All the more reason for Ashar's wrath,' said Gwenyl.

'Is his power not drained by the Horde's defeat?' asked Kedryn.

'Surely,' Gwenyl agreed, 'but it is not ended. You may well be safe from barbarian attack, but Ashar may still bring elemental magic against you.'

'I do not believe I have any other choice but to attempt the passage,' Kedryn announced.

'We entered the Beltrevan when Ashar's power was strong,' said Tepshen Lahl, 'and he could not prevent us. I say we go on.'

'Wynett?' asked Kedryn.

'We must,' she said. 'We must restore your sight and return to face the Messenger. It is likely the fate of the Kingdoms depends on this and I do not believe we have any choice now that we have begun. And I go with you.'

'I will put it to the others,' Kedryn decided, admiration for her fortitude in his gaze.

'They will not turn back,' said Tepshen.

They did not. When Kedryn spoke to them in the dining hall that

147

night they rose as one to declare their loyalty and determination and none of Gann Resyth's or Sister Gwenyl's misgivings could dissuade them.

They rested for a day and a second night in the comfort of the Fedyn Fort and then started into the pass. It was a snowless day, the sky that showed above the narrow walls bright as polished steel, with no hint of wind. Gann Resyth bade them a reluctant farewell and Sister Gwenyl announced her intention of praying for their safe passage. The men of the fort waved from the ramparts as they descended the glacis and wound about the foot of the promontory, the snow underfoot packed hard enough they rode easily into the looming gap.

It was shadowy there, even with the sun over their heads, and soon the pass curved, hiding the fort from sight. The walls seemed to press in above them, the stone rimed with ice, gleaming silver and blue, the way bare of snow so that the horses' hoofs clattered on rock, the sound echoing melancholy from the vertical flanks. There was a foreboding atmosphere, as if the Lozins themselves watched their going with bated breath, or some immeasurable presence lurked, waiting. At sunset they were still within the confines of the ravine and made a cold camp, for no trees grew, nor any undergrowth that might provide fuel. Their talk was muted and they went early to the comfort of their furs, unwilling to admit even to themselves the eerie feeling of being observed.

Dawn came late in that lonely place and they started off again in semi-darkness, anxious to find the egress and ride beneath open sky once more.

At noon the avalanche thundered down upon them.

Chapter Seven

THE wind that had propelled the *Vargalla* so swiftly down the Idre faltered and died before the barge hove in sight of Andurel, prompting the boatmaster to reef his sheets and shout for his oarsmen to man their stations. Before the great sweeps were unshipped, however, Hattim Sethiyan came out on deck accompanied by his mysterious cabinmate to countermand the order. Startled, the boatmaster halted his crew and dropped a drift anchor to hold the vessel on course in midstream. Sunset approached and he had counted on docking by midnight, but if the Lord of Ust-Galich delayed them for any length of time he knew they would face either a night passage or an overnight anchorage at the closest riverside settlement. Both alternatives irked him, for he had a woman in the city and had built up a thirst for good Andurel ale which was shared, he knew, by his crew. Consequently his face, as Hattim came towards him along the swaying deck, was empty of its customary obsequiousness, bland obedience replaced by a frown of irritation. The frown faded as Hattim's companion drew closer and the riverman found himself transfixed by twin points of strangely glowing red light. He opened his mouth to protest the delay, but the words clogged on his tongue and he lowered his gaze, eyes fixing on his boots.

Hattim and Taws climbed the steps to the raised poop, ignoring the curious stares of courtiers and crew alike and took up position beside the captain.

'Listen to me!' Hattim's voice rang over the deck, commanding attention, drawing all eyes to where he stood.

At his side Taws threw back the hood of his enveloping cloak and silent curiosity was replaced with a concerted gasp of horrified revulsion, for every man there had listened to stories of the Messenger and recognised the mage for what he was. Several made warding gestures, but even as their fingers shaped the sign so did Taws' work patterns in the reddening light of the lowering sun, those patterns creating a flickering blue radiance that grew, becoming a

149

steadily enlarging corona of incandescence that crackled and spat like witchfire. Eyes wide with horror locked on that fire, caught by it as the eyes of a rabbit are caught by the hypnotic gaze of a weasel. Not a man moved, either to protest or flee, and the mage shaped his magic like an infernal potter building some blasphemous creation on a hellish wheel. His voice was a sibilation dry as grave dust, the sussuration of bleached bone on bone until the final syllable. That he shouted in a timbre that seemed to rock the *Vargalla* as would a thunderclap bursting low overhead, and as he said it he spread his arms wide, unleashing the blue fire he had built.

It flashed from his splayed fingers in a myriad darting lances of brilliance, illuminating the barge, licking over the horrorstruck features of the courtiers and the crew, filling their eyes with its unholy radiance, leeching them of all expression. Then it was gone and Taws turned to Hattim, the angulation of his mouth approximating a smile.

'They will remember nothing,' he said, 'just as I told you. They will know only that a favourable wind sped them downriver, and that a malaise confined you to your cabin.'

'And you?' Hattim asked softly, the question whispering over dry lips.

'I shall join you in Andurel,' the mage intoned. 'And give you what I promised. Avoid the Sisters when you land – use your malaise as an excuse to find your quarters quickly and await my coming.'

Hattim nodded, then started back as the thaumaturgist began to murmur again in that unfathomable tongue. This time there was no blue fire, only a shimmering of the air, a rubescence more akin to flame than sunset, and a sulphurous reek that grew with the glow surrounding the gaunt figure. Then Taws was gone and Hattim gasped as he saw a black-winged bird standing where the mage had stood, the head turning back and forth to fix him with a beady, crimsoned stare. It hopped on predatory talons to the rudder, stretched its wings wide, and beat upwards, spiralling above the barge before straightening its course and winging southwards towards Andurel.

Hattim shivered, aware that the hair on the nape of his neck stood upright, coldly prickling. He shook himself, tearing his gaze from the dwindling black speck in the sky to the silent deck of the barge.

'Lady curse it, the damned anchor's slipped! Bring it aboard and dip those sweeps. Put your backs into it and we'll make wharfside ere midnight. Jump to it!'

The boatmaster's bellow instilled fresh life in the crew and sent

Hattim starting backwards. He collected himself, seeing his courtiers stir from their rigid stance and move towards him, concern on their faces.

'You are recovered, my Lord?'

He stared at Mejas Celeruna, trying to find in the plump man's solicitous features some memory of Taws, some recollection of the glamour. There was none and he marvelled at the mage's power, saying, 'I am, my friend, and I thank you for your concern.'

'We were all concerned,' Tarkas Verra said quickly. 'Mayhap it was the wind.'

'Mayhap,' Hattim agreed, essaying a wan smile. 'Though that appears to have deserted us.'

'Better a delayed arrival than you suffer river sickness,' beamed Celeruna unctuously, the sentiment echoed by the others.

'We should dock by midnight,' announced the boatmaster. 'If that be your wish, Lord Hattim.'

'Aye,' Hattim nodded, 'it is my wish. Let us make all haste – and if we dock by midnight there's a barrel of ale to be quaffed.'

'Thank you, Lord,' beamed the riverman. Then louder, 'You hear that, lads? Lord Hattim pledges a barrel if you stroke fast enough to dock by midnight.'

A cheer greeted the announcement and the oars went down, carving white water from the sun-crimsoned surface of the Idre as the *Vargalla* leapt forwards and Hattim gathered his courtiers about him, leading the way back to his cabin, where he plied them with his finest wines, accepting their congratulations on his recovery even as he marvelled at the efficacy of the cantrip that had robbed them so effectively of troublesome memories.

How well, he thought, Taws had planned it all, even to their late arrival. At such an hour he would easily avoid the prying Sisters, who might just sense some change in him and alert Darr. At midnight he would easily find privacy and a speedy entry to his quarters; and Taws would meet him there, ready to set in motion the next step. His smile became genuine as he contemplated his ascension: the question of its price did not enter his mind.

His retinue was grateful for the brief comfort of those luxurious quarters after the disagreeable days spent on deck and happy to quaff liberally of the wines there. He ordered the brazier damped now that Taws was gone, explaining the excessive heat as a palliative to his malaise, though he resisted the temptation of drunkenness himself for he wanted his wits about him when they arrived in

151

Andurel. Pleased to find their lord once more restored to good spirits, and fuddled by the glamour set upon them, the courtiers posed no awkward questions, content to lounge on the cushions scattered about the cabin as they listened to the rhythmic splashing of the oars driving them steadily southwards.

Whether by Taws' design or some natural coincidence there was no moon that night, the Idre a nigrescent ribbon on which were reflected the barge's running lights and the myriad stars that shone from the cloudless sky. The oars spilled phosphorescent waves upon the water as the *Vargalla* sped towards the city, the horn mounted on the prow belling a warning even though the river was empty of traffic.

Then the boatmaster's shout brought them to the deck as Andurel hove in sight. At this hour, and at that distance, the great city appeared as a band of canescence across the river, stretching into the darkness on either side as if it floated above the water, a raft. As they drew closer lights became visible along the waterfront, where taverns plied their trade, and farther back, rising to the heights of the White Palace, in houses and salons catering for a trade more salubrious than the sailors and wharfrats frequenting the lower establishments. Hattim found a place at the prow, clutching for a handhold as the boatmaster bellowed, 'Reverse oars! Ship oars!' and put his rudder over to bring the barge gliding smoothly in to the quay. Crewmen sprang across the gap to secure the mooring lines and the gangplank was running out before the curious gathered to see who plied the Idre so late.

Hattim was gratified to see that his unexpected arrival had forestalled any formal welcome, the only officials a trio of harbour bureaucrats who mumbled embarrassed greetings when they recognised the sunburst of Ust-Galich at the masthead and saw that the Lord Hattim stood before them. Hattim dismissed them, calling for Mejas Celeruna to organise litters to bring his party to the palace, and tossed a purse to his boatmaster, who caught it and weighed its value in one expert motion, bowing low in thanks.

'I desire no formalities,' he informed Celeruna. 'I am tired now and would find my bed immediately. See to it.'

'A Sister Hospitaller, my Lord?' Celeruna asked solicitously. 'A palliative for your malaise?'

'No!' Hattim snapped, experiencing a flush of unease. 'A sound night's sleep will doubtless restore me. And as the hour is late, I would not disturb the king. I shall pay my respects on the morrow.'

'As you wish, my Lord.' The portly sycophant bowed elaborately and set to locating palanquins.

Drowsy porters were found and Hattim climbed into a sedan, drawing the curtains as the bearers lifted the poles and began the ascent of the wide avenue leading from the dockside to the palace. As they progressed up the slope he grew wary, nervous of entry into Darr's domain, thinking that if some Sister were abroad she might sense the glamour set upon his retinue or the taint he felt sure his agreement with Ashar's minion must leave on him. He had come too far, he told himself, to turn back now, knowing, too, that he must face Taws' wrath should he renege, and experienced a greater fear of that anger than thought of discovery could arouse. He steeled himself as the outer walls grew visible through the small porthole in the litter's forward wall and he saw torchlight burnish the breastplates of the guards there, lending a roseate coloration to the halberds that lowered in formal denial of entrance.

Then Mejas Celeruna was bustling forwards to announce the arrival of Hattim Sethiyan, Lord of Ust-Galich, and the halberds lifted in salute. Hattim sighed, slumping on the cushions as Celeruna continued on to smooth the way past further watchmen into the central court of the White Palace.

A captain of the royal guard appeared there, armoured and – to Hattim's eyes – menacing, leading a hand of stone-faced soldiers who watched impassively as the Galichian party climbed from the palanquins.

'My Lord Hattim,' the captain bowed briefly, 'you were not expected. The King has found his bed, else he would doubtless have arranged more suitable a welcome.'

'A favourable wind,' Hattim explained vaguely. 'Though one that brought a touch of river sickness. I would not have the King disturbed, but would go immediately to my chambers.'

'As you wish, my Lord,' the captain agreed, and turned to send a man hastening in search of a steward.

Hattim glanced round, pleased that no Sisters were present, and waited for the steward to appear.

He came running, slowing to a more dignified pace as he approached the Galichians, expressing profuse apologies for the absence of suitable formalities, which Hattim waved away, repeating his explanation.

'My Lord is tired,' Celeruna declared pompously. 'His chambers are ready? See that a fire is lit and food and wine set out. He would not be disturbed.'

The functionary favoured the courtier with a murderous glance and bowed in Hattim's direction.

'Your chambers are – as ever – ready, my Lord. It will take but moments to kindle a fire, and I shall have victuals brought. If you will follow me?'

Hattim followed him to the familiar quarters, rousing a bustling horde of servants along the way, and soon found himself alone, a fire blazing in the hearth, wines set to hand, and food laid out on a table in the ante-chamber. He looked around. The rooms were decorated and furnished in the manner of Ust-Galich, just as others were prepared in the styles of Kesh and Tamur for the use of the lords when in Andurel. Ornate tapestries hid the stone of the walls and luxurious carpets covered the floors, the sunburst emblem was carved in the stone above the hearth and the wardrobes contained his own clothing. Ere long, he thought, all of the White Palace would be ornamented in similar style and he would occupy the chambers on the level above, where Darr now doubtless lay in unsuspecting slumber. He chuckled, filling a goblet with sweet Galichian wine, and raised the cup in toast to himself. In the window that looked on to one of the palace gardens he caught his reflection and set an imaginary crown upon his golden hair. It would sit well, he decided.

Then he cursed as the doors to the balcony flung open, causing him to spill wine down the front of his green and gold tunic.

'I startled you?'

There was mockery in Taws' voice, but Hattim ignored that as he stared at the mage. He was growing familiar with the thaumaturgist's powers, but still this shape-shifting unnerved him, and it seemd that Taws was even now in the process of change. Chill night air carried a waft of malodour into the room and Taws' form seemed to flicker, the shoulders hunched like wings beneath the sable cloak, his neck arched, bird-like, emphasising the cadaverous gauntness of his triangulate features. Fire glow set a ruddiness on his ashen skin, but the mane of albescent hair that draped his shoulders was still snow-pale, while his eyes glowed red as furnace pits. He shuddered and crossed to the fire, thrusting out hands too long, too taloned, for any man, peering into the flames as though he sought sustenance there.

'You were not seen?' Hattim refilled his glass, composing himself as he watched Taws' form solidify.

154

The mage turned to fix him with a contemptuous stare and shook his head.

'You encountered no Sisters?'

'None,' Hattim assured. 'But . . .'

'What?' Taws moved a step closer to the fire, surely closer than mortal man would find comfortable.

'I cannot avoid them indefinitely,' Hattim continued. 'And will they not sense the glamour you set on my retinue?'

Taws chuckled, the sound soft and dry as the scuttling of a spider's legs through dust. 'Magic goes often unnoticed where it is not expected. And the cantrip I wrought is minor enough to escape detection. You did as I bade you?'

'Aye.' Hattim nodded, confused, 'I claimed sufferance of a malaise to find these chambers. I have spoken to no one save the watch captain and a steward.'

'And Darr?'

'No doubt sleeps,' Hattim said, glancing automatically at the ceiling. 'I came directly here – just as you bade me.'

'Good.' Taws' fleshless lips angled in horrid approximation of a smile. 'On the morrow you will again claim a malaise, but this time you will ask that a Sister attend you.'

Hattim's confusion grew, his handsome face creasing in a frown.

'I need one,' Taws informed him. 'I can draw much strength from one of the Lady's bitches, and it amuses me to use her power against her.'

'Here?' Hattim gasped, horrified, recalling Ellebriga's fate.

'Do not doubt me!' Taws moved a single step from the fireside. It was sufficient to send Hattim starting back, more wine spilling from his goblet. 'You are committed now, Sethiyan. Do not think to question me – merely obey. When your courtiers come in the morning you will ask for a Sister Hospitaller. Do you understand?'

Hattim nodded, 'Aye.'

'There will be little danger,' Taws declared in a milder tone. 'You will request solitude, and when I am done I shall dispose of the remains in such a manner that none will suspect.'

Hattim nodded again and topped his cup, though this time he ignored the Galichian wine in favour of evshan.

'Do not imbibe too much,' warned the mage. 'I need your wits about you. And your prospective bride will not welcome a drunkard.'

He smiled again as he said it and Hattim found his mind filled

155

with an image of Ashrivelle as Taws had revealed her that night in Nyrwan, lush and suppliant. The promise of that vision – and the promised aftermath – was heady as the liquor and Hattim set down the cup half-drunk.

'Sleep,' ordered the mage. 'I would have you look your best when you meet the princess.'

It occurred to Hattim that Taws spoke as if he were no more than a puppet to be dressed and manipulated at the mage's will, and he felt resentment stir. Stronger, though, than hurt pride was the desire for the reward pledged him, and stronger still his fear of Taws: he ducked his head and turned towards the bedroom.

He doubted that he would sleep, and for a while he lay restlessly, images of Ashrivelle and flames filling his mind, but then a langour possessed him and even as he wondered idly if Taws sent it, he drifted into a dreamless slumber.

He woke to find winter sunlight streaming through the casement of his chamber and the room heady with the warmth of the banked fire. He rose, drawing on a robe of embroidered silk and found the ewer of cool water close by the bed. He laved his face and went into the ante-room, where Taws stood beside the hearth. The mage seemed not to have moved during the night, for his stance was exactly as Hattim remembered, so near the flames that human skin must surely have scorched.

'It is time,' he declared, and Hattim forgot the hunger that cramped his belly. 'Inform your minions that you require a Sister.'

'Will they not see you? Surely she must,' Hattim protested.

'No,' Taws said. 'Now delay no longer. Obey me!'

His tone was such that Hattim sprang instantly to the door, his abrupt appearance startling the servant waiting there.

'Fetch Count Celeruna,' he barked as the man essayed a sleepy-eyed bow.

Celeruna came hurriedly, clearly brought from his bed, for his hastily-donned robe revealed an artfully-embroidered nightshirt and his hair was disarrayed, the usually-coiffed ringlets dangling like rats' tails about a face puffy with sleep and devoid of its customary cosmetics. Tasselled slippers rendered his feet clumsy as he entered Hattim's chamber, even his bow less decorous than was his wont.

'My Lord?' he panted.

Hattim motioned for him to close the door, realising that Taws was nowhere in sight.

'I find myself unwell. Have a Sister attend me.'

156

'Instantly,' Celeruna promised. 'And breakfast, my Lord? What of the King?'

'A Sister,' Hattim repeated. 'No one else. You will inform Darr of my indisposition and present my apologies. I require solitude.'

'Very well, my Lord Hattim.' Celeruna appeared confused, but nonetheless hastened to obey, bustling from the chamber with a flushed face and noisy slippers.

Hattim turned about the instant the door closed, but still there was no sign of Taws, neither in the ante-chamber or the bedroom, nor on the balcony, and the lord of Ust-Galich felt his confidence return, though not so much as to preclude his draining of the glass of evshan remaining from the previous night.

He felt the fire of the alcohol seep into his belly and wondered if he should return to his bed. Somehow he felt unwillingly to lie between the sheets while Taws wrought his will on the Sister and so he dressed hurriedly, foresaking his customary toilette with a grimace of distaste. He combed his long hair and adjusted the earring dangling from his left lobe. Habit set bracelets on his wrists and a modest selection of rings upon his fingers. He had time to fill a fresh cup with evshan and drain it before the Sister Hospitaller arrived.

Sister Thera was surprised by the appearance of the Lord Hattim. The pumpkin-faced courtier who had summoned her had led her to believe his master was close to death, and while she bore no affection for Hattim, considering him an upstart popinjay, she had responded swiftly in accordance with her calling. She had doubted the malaise was quite so dramatic as Celeruna suggested, thinking that – from her knowledge of the Galichian lord – he was most probably suffering the after effects of river sickness exacerbated by excessive consumption of wine, but still she had anticipated a sick man. Instead she found him dressed, albeit in more dishevelled state than was his fastidious custom, and drinking evshan. She studied his face, thinking that he did, indeed, look feverish, his eyes burning bright, and that his manner was extremely nervous.

She dropped an almost indiscernable curtsey as she enquired, 'You are unwell, my Lord Hattim?'

'I . . .' Hattim glanced around the room, 'I . . . Yes! I am . . . unwell.'

Sister Thera wondered why he appeared so nervous. Why his eyes moved everywhere save to her face, almost as though he was afraid to meet her gaze; as if he expected some third party to be present even though his sycophant had made clear his wish to be alone.

'The symptoms?' She set down her satchel as she spoke, unclasping the bag with an eye to some simple nostrum, suspecting that he wasted her time.

Hattim stared at her, turning his head before she could meet his eyes. He did not recognise her, seeing only a young woman in the blue robe of the Sorority, her hair a pale brown, plaited about a vaguely pretty face that now exhibited signs of impatience.

'My symptoms?'

'Aye, my Lord, your symptoms. I cannot prescribe a cure until I know the symptoms.'

'The symptoms,' Hattim muttered, anxiety flushing his features.

'My Lord Hattim, I was summoned from my prayers to tend a man described as sick by that . . .' Sister Thera bit back the insulting description she was about to voice. 'By Count Celeruna. I have ample tasks awaiting my attention and the sooner I am able to prescribe for you, the sooner I may attend them. What exactly do you feel? Nausea? Does your head ache? Do you sweat?'

Hattim heard the impatience in her voice and licked his lips nervously, wondering where Taws was; wondering if he should allow the Sister to examine him, or fake symptoms. Surely either course must lead to discovery of his blasphemous alliance. This woman was a Hospitaller, and so versed in the healing arts rather than the metaphysical, but even so she would, he felt certain, sense some aura about him, know that he lied.

Indeed, Sister Thera was beginning to doubt the truth of Celeruna's description and the nature of Hattim's discomfort. Her talent, as Hattim surmised, was for healing and she had little experience of the magical arts, but Estrevan had trained her to read the signs implicit in a man's body, in the way he moved, in his voice, in his mannerisms. Hattim Sethiyan, she thought, might well be feverish; sweat beaded his upper lip and forehead, and his skin – pale in the fashion of the Galichian nobility – was flushed, but it appeared to her from nerves, rather than river sickness or alcohol. He seemed afraid to meet her eyes. In fact, it seemed he was loath to look at her at all, his gaze roaming the chamber as though he anticipated the momentary arrival of another. She turned from her satchel and took a step towards him. Hattim took a step back, but not before the Sister felt a presence that she could not understand.

She halted, confused. What she sensed came not from Hattim, though she felt he was . . . involved . . . in it, but from somewhere – some *thing* – in the room. She had not sailed with the king's party

158

to the Lozin Gate but Sisters who had had described to her the sense of palpable evil that clouded beyond the walls and she felt intuitively that she experienced that same oppression here. She frowned, telling herself it was ridiculous to even consider that Ashar's malignancy might fester in Andurel, in the chambers of the Lord of Ust-Galich moreover. Yet it *was* there. She felt it in the chilling of her bones; the tingling at the nape of her neck, where hair stood rigid as in a lightning storm.

She said, 'My Lord Hattim', in a faltering tone and then felt her eyes drawn upwards as if by some incontrovertible power.

What she saw there transformed her eyes to wide staring globes of stark horror, springing her mouth open in formation of a scream.

No sound escaped her yawning jaws, however. There was no time, for the great red spider descended a silken line with dreadful rapidity, falling on to her upturned face to clamp its legs about her cheeks and jam her mouth with the obscene bulb of its abdomen.

Hattim leapt backwards, his own eyes wild with revulsion, his own mouth gaping as genuine nausea roiled his belly. He stared, fascinated despite himself, as the spider fastened itself to the Sister's features, seeing every detail of the swollen body, the hairs that bristled rusty as dried blood, the multiple eyes that gleamed a hellish red above the clicking mandibles, the swollen sac that thrust obscenely between her lips. Cold sweat chilled his back as he watched, unable to prevent himself, as the spider turned full circle and lowered itself into Sister Thera's mouth. The head disappeared, propelled by the eight jointed legs, and he saw the Sister's throat bulge, a madness born of stark terror shining in her tear-filled eyes, as the sac dragged over her lips and forced her jaws wide apart. He heard a choking sound and it was too much: he spun about, clutching at his stomach as he stumbled towards the balcony.

He tore the doors open and doubled over, his belly heaving as yellow bile gushed from his mouth. Pain clamped fiercely on his intestines and he clutched at the carved stone of the balustrade to prevent himself pitching into the pool of vomit.

His hands were trembling as he forced himself upright and he heard his own teeth chattering in jaws he could no longer control. For a wild instant he contemplated shouting for guards, for Sisters versed in thaumatology; thought of screaming a warning that the Messenger was come to Andurel, that Ashar's minion stood in the White Palace.

Then Taws' voice jerked his eyes back to the chamber and he

159

knew it was too late. Had been too late from the moment in Nyrwan when he bent his knee to the mage and accepted the compact offered. Slowly, his feet leaden, he entered the chamber.

'They cannot find me now.'

The words came from Sister Thera, sibilant with triumph.

'Taws?' Hattim mumbled, his tongue sour with bile.

'I possess her now.' The voice changed as the Sister – no! Hattim reminded himself, Taws – spoke, losing the sussurant intonation, becoming that of Thera. 'She lives, and that life protects me from discovery. They will not see past her to me, so we are safe.'

Hattim walked falteringly to the ewer and swilled water around his mouth. He stooped, splashing his face, then crossed quickly to the flask of evshan and filled a goblet.

'You find my magic distasteful?' It was fully the Sister's voice now and somehow that was worse: Hattim drained the evshan in a single swallow, gasping as it lit fire in his emptied belly. 'How could I give you what you want if I must hide in these chambers? Now I can go freely about the palace; unsuspected. Now I can fulfil all your dreams.'

Hattim stared, seeking some change in the woman, seeking some sign of Taws, but there was none. The voice was that of the Sister, the movements hers; there was nothing to indicate the body was possessed.

'You will announce yourself recovered,' she – Taws! – said, the voice calm, 'and praise the excellent Sister Thera. You will request King Darr release her from palace service to tend you as part of your retinue. Do you understand?'

'Aye,' Hattim answered hoarsely.

'In all other respects you will behave in your customary fashion,' Taws ordered, 'and proceed with your courtship of Ashrivelle. In a little while you will introduce the princess to your new-found Hospitaller, and then I will make her yours. I will give her to you so that you may possess her as surely as I possess this bitch's carcase, and you may do whatever you wish with her.'

'And Darr?' Hattim asked slowly. 'What of the throne?'

'That, too, will be yours in time,' Taws promised. 'But first, the princess.'

He stepped close to Hattim then and the Lord of Ust-Galich found himself looking into green eyes that dissolved abruptly into red, fiery pits that burned with an awful intensity, driving out doubt with their menace.

160

'As you order it,' said Hattim.

'Aye,' said Taws, and the fires died, the eyes becoming green again, 'as I and Ashar order it.'

The Fedyn Pass remained gloomy late into the morning and even when the sun was risen high enough that it breasted the confining crags the light was poor. It was as though the canyon resented the intrusion of day, preferring sullen shadows, a place of darkness and night. The sky above was dull, metallic with the threat of snow, the sun – when it at last became visible – a faint memory of the brilliant orb that had greeted their entry. They rode in silence, as if the great stone walls denied them the right of speech, and after observing the trail, Kedryn let go his hold of Wynett's hand, content to ride in darkness, letting the Keshi stallion pick a way behind Tepshen Lahl's mount.

He heard the kyo call a halt and reined in as Wynett heeled her bay in close, taking his hand that he might see their stopping place.

It was miserable enough, long sweeps of ice-crusted snow layered over dark rock, the walls rising to meet the heavens, black and grey save for where ice glistened. Breath steamed in the chill air, and Kedryn's cheeks stung with cold. He looked at Wynett and saw her face flushed by the brumal wind that sighed and sang a mournful dirge over the implacable surfaces of the forbidding granite, drawing unbidden tears that trickled over the black smudges beneath her eyes.

'This is a sad place,' he remarked, smiling despite it.

Wynett nodded, drawing the hood of her cloak tighter about her face.

'Grain for the animals and cold food for us,' announced Tepshen. 'We'll find timber once we clear this place and eat hot food again.'

The Tamurin grunted agreement and set to opening the provisions Gann Resyth had provided, spreading blankets over their mounts against the danger of chills. Kedryn allowed a man to take his horse, settling in a crouch beside Wynett, where she huddled in the lee of a boulder. Tepshen joined them there, passing Kedryn a slab of near-frozen meat and a chunk of bread.

'The horses are fretful,' he murmured.

'They like this place no better than us,' said Kedryn.

'It is more than that, I think,' Wynett said softly. 'They sense something. I feel it too.'

'What?' Tepshen Lahl's voice was urgent, his jet eyes flickering over the restive animals, back to the Sister's face.

161

'I am not sure.' Wynett shrugged, the movement almost hidden beneath the bulk of her cloak and fur-lined jerkin. 'Gwenyl said this was Ashar's domain and what I feel here I remember from High Fort, when the Horde drew close.'

'Best we pass through swiftly then,' said the kyo, rising to his feet to shout, 'We move as soon as the horses are fed!'

There was no disagreement and the Tamurin remounted with hunks of bread and pieces of meat still clutched in their gloved hands, their animals no less willing to be on the move again.

'Stay close,' Tepshen advised bringing his grey up alongside Kedryn and the Sister, turning in his saddle to study the men behind.

Wynett nodded, her own mount close enough to Kedryn's that their legs touched as the horses picked up the pace, shod hooves clattering loud in the cathedral silence.

Then she gasped and reached for his hand, not for sake of granting him sight but from innate need of her own. Kedryn took it, looking about him as he sensed her anxiety.

'What is it?'

The sharpness of his question prompted Tepshen Lahl to turn again.

'Do you not hear it?' she asked softly, fearfully, her gaze roving over the surrounding rockfaces.

'Hear what?' the kyo demanded, a hand falling instinctively to his sword hilt as he followed her eyes.

'Aye!' Kedryn's voice was hushed, a question incipient in his tone. 'Laughter.'

'Mad laughter!' gasped Wynett. 'Tepshen! We must ride from here as swiftly as possible.'

The easterner gave no argument, nor sought any further amplification. He rose in his stirrups to shout a single word: 'Ride!'

As one, the Tamurin drove heels to flanks and brought their animals to a gallop, the steady clattering of the hooves becoming a thunder that rang from the stone, echoing down the pass even as the laughter grew louder, rising above the din of their passage so that every man there heard it and felt the chill of its malignancy.

It was as though some insane giant tittered, chuckling and snorting with malicious glee, the sound rising to a weird cackling, then a storm-bellow of wild laughter that rang in winter-numbed ears, filling the Fedyn Pass with its lunacy and its awful threat. It became a pealing of thunder and Kedryn let go Wynett's hand as their

162

horses surged onwards, anxious as their riders to escape the ghastly sound.

It dinned louder and louder, filling their minds until it seemed the madness in it must affect them, terrifying the animals, who galloped with ears laid flat back and eyes rolling, saliva lathering their necks and chests. It grew louder than sound, becoming a vibration of the very air that shimmered about them, the walls of rock seeming to bulge inwards, pulsing with the awful resonance. A man screamed a warning from the rear and Wynett turned, looking back to see the bulging of the rock become a reality, great shards of stone pitching loose from the walls, great slabs of frozen snow hurtling downwards.

'What is it?' Kedryn bellowed.

'Ride for your life!' she shouted in answer.

He heard the urgency in her tone rather than the form of the words, for the thunder that filled the pass drowned understanding, and slammed his heels against the stallion's ribs even though the black horse needed no further urging to speed. Wynett flanked him, Tepshen Lahl slightly ahead, queue flying in the wind of his passage, lashing his face as he craned round to stare aghast at the devastation behind.

It seemed the whole of the Fedyn Pass crumbled beneath the onslaught of that wild laughter, the rimrock sharding as massive blocks broke loose from the walls, crashing down in a tumult of white, the darkness of the granite lost as an unimaginable weight of snow fell, erupting a billowing, storm-driven curtain that gusted with hurricane force along the length of the narrow way. Only the foremost of the Tamurin riders were visible, those behind lost in that wild, swirling mist, and even as the kyo stared, horrified, a monumental slab crashed upon them and they were gone in the coruscating blizzard that accompanied its downfall. Two men emerged, white-shrouded, then disappeared as more snow fell, an avalanche that drowned warriors and horses alike in its irrepressible fury. Snow filled the easterner's eyes and he blinked furiously, trusting in his mount to find its own path, trusting the Lady to protect Kedryn and her acolyte, for he knew there was nothing he could do save ride for his own life, seeking desperately to outrun the tidal wave of snow and stone that roared behind them.

It seemed they rode in the heart of the blizzard, barely visible to one another even though they were so close their animals jostled as they thundered down the pass. Their ears were deaf with the raging of the avalanche, their mouths speechless, their hearts filled with dread, for it seemed their quest was doomed to end here, almost before it had begun. Snow filled their world and the ground beneath their horses' hooves trembled with the destruction that threatened to engulf them.

Then sound returned, the crashing of rock and the sullen roaring of snow fading. The blizzard faltered, the wind dying so that crystals of glittering light filled the pass. There was a final moaning sigh, a frustrated sound, and then only the pounding of hooves.

Tepshen slowed his panic-stricken animal, seeing Wynett and Kedryn clearly again, and shouted, 'It is over. Are we safe?'

This last was directed at the Sister, who raised frightened eyes to look around, her head cocked as though she listened for a recurrence of the laughter before she said cautiously, 'I think so.'

The kyo brought his mount to a halt, rubbing at the trembling neck, soothing the beast. Wynett and Kedryn followed suit, and Kedryn took her hand, seeing for the first time what lay behind them.

He gasped when he saw it, for where the Fedyn Pass had been there was no longer any way through the mountains. Snow-covered stone filled the gap, black slabs of jagged granite thrusting from the enveloping white, great drifts spilling out and down, impassable. He shuddered, his grip tightening on Wynett's hand so that she winced with the pressure, seeing awe and anger mingled in his gaze.

'The others?' he asked.

'There,' said Tepshen Lahl sombrely, pointing towards the barrier that blocked the way to Tamur. 'Entombed.'

'Ashar's work,' murmured Wynett. 'He seeks to halt us. He seeks to destroy us.'

'He will not!' Determination rang in Kedryn's voice. 'By the Lady, I swear he will not!'

'We have more than Ashar to contend with now,' Tepshen said softly. 'Our supplies lie there. We have only what we carry with us. And all the Beltrevan to cross.'

Kedryn turned to face the kyo, his features pale with drifted snow and a heartfelt fury. 'We shall cross it, Tepshen! We shall find the Drott and seek the shade of the warrior who took my sight. And when I have that back we shall return to destroy the Messenger. I swear it in the name of the Lady!'

'We shall try,' agreed the kyo, the grief he felt at the loss of so many true friends not showing on his impassive face. 'For the sake of Tamur and the dead.'

'What chance do we have?' asked Wynett, staring at the Tamurin warriors' rocky tomb.

'We have our horses still,' said Kedryn, fiercely, 'and our lives. The tribes can live through the winter – so can we.'

'Aye,' she responded, drawing courage from his determination. 'And surely the Lady must protect us, else we should have fallen.'

Tepshen Lahl was less sanguine, but nonetheless practical. 'We had best find the egress of this cursed place,' he announced. 'And build a fire – night will be on us soon and we'll likely freeze without timber to burn.'

Kedryn nodded, still staring at the rubble that filled the pass. 'You shall not have died in vain,' he promised. Then turned his mount to follow Tepshen Lahl.

They rode as swiftly as they dared, fearful that the clatter of hoofbeats might dislodge further falls of snow rendered unstable by the disruption, and their mounts winded by the headlong charge. Despite their resolve their spirits were downcast and what remained of the Fedyn Pass grew dark with natural shadow as the day waned. Soon they rode in semi-darkness, hunched beneath their furs, anxious to find the ending of that gloomy place and kindle the optimism of a fire. It seemed to Kedryn that he still heard a faint echo of that insane laughter, as though Ashar mocked him, sneering at his determination, and he ground his teeth in rage at the god's wanton destruction. The cold grew as the light faded and he clung to the candle of his hope in the midst of his darkness, not allowing himself to contemplate failure. So many had died to further Ashar's purpose, not only here, but also in the battle of the Lozin Gate, and now only Wynett and Tepshen Lahl rode with him, his sole companions on the quest that might now end in the frozen wastes of the mountains. Yet they *had* escaped the avalanche, and surely that was the Lady's doing; and with the Lady's aid he *could* succeed. Would! he told himself, just as he had told Wynett and Tepshen. *Would*, no matter what obstacles Ashar might set to block him.

'I will defeat you,' he told the echo. 'Do you hear me, you bloody, hate-filled god? I will bring down your Messenger and thwart your plans. And if the Lady grant it, I shall destroy you!'

He heard a faint whisper of laughter that might have been no more than the first stirring of a nightwind and reached beneath his furs to clutch the talisman that hung about hi: neck. It was warm to the touch and he found reassurance in its feel, a sense of calm pervading him so that he closed the anger from his mind and concentrated on the immediate business of survival.

'Look!' he heard Wynett cry, as if the Lady granted him a sign. 'Is that not light ahead?'

'Aye,' said Tepshen as Kedryn took the hand Wynett offered him.

Sight came with the contact and he saw the trail dip before him, descending towards a cut that showed pale between the darkness of the stone walls.

It grew brighter, more distinct, as they approached, and he saw that it was the egress of the pass outlined by the radiance of a rising moon. The orb was full, hanging low in a clear, cold sky all filled with twinkling stars, its light reflected off snowfields, spilling the long shadows of trees over the moon-sparkled whiteness.

'Timber,' grunted Tepshen. 'Fire.'

'Praise the Lady,' murmured Wynett.

'Aye,' Kedryn agreed heartily, 'praise the Lady.'

They came out of the pass on to a wide slope dotted with wind-stripped pines. The night was even colder beyond the sheltering walls, and snow was drifted in deep banks, treacherous on the gradient that stretched down to the vast, dark sea of timber that was the heart of the Beltrevan. Tepshen Lahl called a halt, surveying the way ahead before he announced that they had best remain close to the mountainside until the sun rose to light their way. He turned his mount along the flank of the crags, studying the moon-washed rock for some sheltered spot. It was hard going, for snow was piled steeply against the hills and the horses plunged awkwardly through the drifts, but in time they found a place where a solitary spur thrust out, the bare rock at its base offering some small measure of shelter.

They dismounted in the lee of the stone and rubbed down the animals, anxious to avoid the danger of chills that might leave them afoot in the wilderness. Then, leaving the three horses draped with saddle blankets, Tepshen set out to gather wood. Kedryn found fresh reason to curse his blindness then, for he was unable to help and could only wait with Wynett as the kyo waded through the snow. He took the Sister's hand, thinking that at least he could assess the contents of their saddlebags and have what food they possessed waiting for the easterner's return. It was little enough: cured meat and journey bread apiece sufficient for one day's travel, a little fruit, but nothing for the animals. Their only blankets were needed more by the horses than their riders and Kedryn huddled close to Wynett as they listened to the thudding of blade against wood.

'It will be easier when we reach the forest,' he promised. 'There will be better shelter there, and game to hunt; forage for the animals.'

Wynett shifted closer, seeking to augment the warmth of their furs with that of their bodies, and Kedryn put an arm about her shoulders, thinking that this was their closest contact since they departed High Fort.

'How long will it take?' she asked, her breath a cloud before her face.

Kedryn took her hand and stared into the night. The moon shone bright on the hoary slopes but it was difficult to judge the distance, snow and darkness robbing the landscape of perspective. No trail was visible and he guessed the descending foothills must conceal ravines and drifts that would inevitably slow them.

'I am not sure,' he told her honestly. 'It will not be easy.'

Wynett made a sound like laughter, or a sigh, and said, 'I did not think it would be. I have cordials that will warm us – give us strength – but nothing for the horses, and we are lost without them.'

'Aye,' he acknowledged, 'we are.'

'But we still have hope,' she murmured, and he turned to study her face, seeing faith there, and trust, and nodded, hugging her closer to him.

'Aye! We are not defeated yet.'

He came close to adding, Not while I have you, but remembered his promise and bit back the words, content to hold her, relishing that contact.

They were huddled like that when Tepshen returned, staggering beneath a weight of timber that he flung down close against the rockface.

'Start a fire,' he advised. 'I will fetch more wood.'

Kedryn nodded amd Wynett fetched a tinderbox from her saddlebag, passing him branches that he broke blind, following her instructions until a cone of smaller limbs was raised over a patch of the dried moss each carried. By the time Tepshen returned with a second load the fire was started, and after three more expeditions the kyo announced a sufficiency of fuel, adding larger branches until a fierce blaze glowed against the rock, the stone reflecting the heat so that the leeside of the spur was almost cosy. Tepshen produced a kettle and set snow to melting, adding meat to make a watery stew that Wynett enhanced with restorative herbs. They ate hungrily, replenishing the energy drained by shock and fear as much as by the cold.

'The horses must keep the blankets,' the kyo decided when they had finished, turning an almost diffident face to Wynett, 'and our tents are lost.'

'So we had best sleep close,' the Sister finished, 'and share our warmth.'

Tepshen nodded, 'If we are to live.'

Despite the gravity of their situation Wynett could not resist giggling at the serious expression on the easterner's face, certain that it stemmed more from a sense of decorum than concern with their predicament. It seemed incongruous that he should consider such matters in the aftermath of disaster and the face of what lay ahead, but she sensed that both he and Kedryn had set the loss of friends behind them with Tamurin stoicism, leaving their mourning for some more appropriate timed as they concentrated on the immediate problems of survival.

'I am sure my honour is safe,' she said solemnly, 'and I have no doubt the Paramount Sister would approve in such circumstances.'

Kedryn chuckled and Tepshen smiled briefly, then settled himself close to the fire. Wynett took Kedryn's hand, guiding him, and stretched between the two men. Their bulky furs negated any real sense of physical contact, though she could feel Kedryn's breath on her face and could not help wondering, in the short time before she slept, what it would be like to wake next to him in a bed.

In that place it was uncomfortable: she woke cramped, jammed tight between them, a rock gouging her back, what little flesh her furs left exposed stinging with the cold. She opened her eyes and gasped as brilliant sunshine lanced her vision. Tepshen Lahl was already awake and rose as she sat up, brushing snow from his furs as he moved to the horses, who snickered in anticipation of food and whinnied plaintively when none was forthcoming. She nudged Kedryn awake and took his hand that he might see the brightness of the day. Where moonlight had glistened, the sun burned, transforming the snowfields to a sparkling effulgence that dazzled sight, watering their eyes. She remembered the masks Yrla had provided as a safeguard against snowblindness and fastened the devices over both their eyes as Tepshen stoked the fire to fresh life and set the kettle to boiling.

They ate breakfast as the sun rose higher, painting the slopes of the Lozins in rainbow hues, black birds wheeling high above them against a sky of startling blue. It was clear that on this side of the mountains full winter held sway. The air was icy, but devoid of threat of snow, and when they started out they found the snowcrust afforded reassuringly firm footing. Even so they were no more than halfway to the timberline when dusk fell and there was no handy spur of stone to shelter them. Their camp was miserable, the trunk of a fallen pine the only refuge from the wind and their fire scantier than before. They devoured what remained of the meat and fed the journey bread to the horses, who snickered protestingly at such meagre fare. They huddled together to sleep, disturbed by the cold and the eerie whistle of the wind, and rose chilled and stiff, weary as they remounted and continued down towards the forest.

They did not reach the trees that day for the lower slopes grew more treacherous, snowbanks forcing them to detour and gulleys causing them to retrace their path. Wynett drew upon her stocks of herbs to brew a cordial that was their only sustenance when they halted and their fire was a poor memory of the blaze that had raised their hopes on the first night. They slept even more fitfully, and when they started again the horses were irritable for want of food. Wynett produced leaves that would usually be applied to wounds, to numb pain, and they chewed them as they rode, the anaesthetic effect going some little way to counteracting the debilitation of hunger and cold.

Then, some time after noon, they saw the slope drop steeply away and end against a great wall of timber that ran in sombre magnificence to the horizon, vast and dark and brooding.

'The Beltrevan,' Tepshen announced through chattering teeth.

'Thank the Lady,' Kedryn shivered, surprised that he found the previously hostile forest so welcome a sight.

They floundered down the slope, the horses skidding on their haunches, and crossed the final drifts into the trees.

There the snow was less, held off by the canopy of branches, and they were able to make better time, driving deeper into the forest, aware that the air grew fractionally warmer, more aware that they could again light a decent fire – and hopefully find food.

The fire came first, a great celebratory blaze that lit the surrounding timber and eased the chill from limbs so numbed the return of sensation was at first painful. Then the horses were hobbled and set to foraging while Tepshen Lahl disappeared into the trees to return with two hares startled from their winter hiding places and a partridge brought down with a lucky throw. It was a feast, and that night they slept contented, though Kedryn missed the feel of Wynett's body close against him.

Chapter Eight

REVIVIFYING though the meal was, it was little enough in that winter-bound wilderness and they awoke to protestations from their stomachs, which craved further sustenance to fuel bodies depleted by cold and hunger. With the sun up and filtering through the canopy of snow-clad branches there was little chance of finding fresh meat and so they made do with a tisane brewed from Wynett's herbs, rebuilding the fire so that at least they had the comfort of warmth as they assessed their situation.

The horses were in slightly better shape, having found some measure of forage amongst the trees, but the overall prospect remained bleak. The euphoria that had followed their narrow escape from the avalanche, and the determination to survive the uplands, had faded, replaced by the stark reality of the fact that they were, effectively, stranded in the Beltrevan with only Tepshen Lahl in good enough condition to hunt or fight. He carried his long eastern sword and Tamurin dirk, and in addition still had a bow and quiver of arrows on his saddle. Kedryn bore a sword and dirk but could hardly use them blind. Wynett wore a small knife on her belt, but that was more for cutting plants that any other purpose. They had the clothes on their backs and the saddle blankets that protected the animals; nothing more.

'We make a sorry party to approach the Ulan of the Drott,' Kedryn remarked.

'If we get that far,' Tepshen grunted in reply.

'Why should we not?' Wynett wondered. 'You can hunt, surely? So we need only press on until we encounter the woodsfolk.'

'The woodlanders are not known for their hospitality towards we of the Kingdoms,' Kedryn told her mildly.

Ever blunt, Tepshen said, 'The tribesmen might well seek to kill us for our horses.'

'But Kedryn is the hef-Alador,' the Sister protested. 'And treaties have been signed. Surely they will acknowledge that?'

The kyo's jet eyes fastened on her face, a small smile that was empty of humour playing upon his narrow lips. 'Does he look like the hef-Alador?' he demanded. 'We look more like some trio of wanderers – and wanderers are fair game in the Beltrevan, treaties or no.'

He turned his gaze to Kedryn, and the young man saw a warning in the look: a woman as fair as Wynett would command a high price as a slave; after her takers had had their way with her. He nodded briefly and asked, 'Do we have the white and red?'

Tepshen nodded in reply. 'For what difference the peace signs will make.'

'We can announce ourselves,' Wynett said, a trifle nervous now, for she sensed the apprehension in the two men.

'We have no Brannoc to translate,' the kyo answered. 'Lethyn and Durn were to be our spokesmen, and they are buried in the Fedyn Pass.'

'And we speak no Drott,' Kedryn amplified. 'I have a few words of the forest argot, but scarce enough to explain our presence or our purpose.'

'I speak the *byavan*,' the Sister declared.

Tepshen Lahl grunted approvingly. The byavan was the *lingua franca* of the Beltrevan, the common tongue that made communication between the tribes and traders possible; that Wynett might thus speak for them was a considerable advantage.

'So,' he exclaimed, 'we have a spokeswoman, a bow, and our animals. We need only continue northwards until we encounter the tribes.'

His face was impassive, expressionless as he spoke, and it was impossible to tell whether he voiced cynicism or determination. Kedryn grinned, squeezing Wynett's hand encouragingly. 'So we have little to worry about.'

'Save living,' replied the kyo. But this time he smiled as he said it.

'Then we should delay no longer,' Kedryn said firmly. 'Let us find whoever rules the Drott now and state our business.'

'In the byavan,' Tepshen nodded, bowing formally to Wynett.

They saddled their horses, fastening ribbons of white and red to the bridles, and ploughed snow over the fire, mounting the still-hungry animals and moving out in a northerly direction. There were no maps of the Beltrevan, for it was the domain of the woods folk and Kingdomers had never penetrated deep enough to chart the forest ways. They knew they were already in the territory of the Drott, and that the approaching equinox would find the clans joined for the winter Gathering around the mound that marked the burial place of the first great overlord, Drul. That, they knew from Brannoc, lay to the northwest, deep within the forest's confines. To find it, they must rely on luck.

It was a dismal journeying for Kedryn because the trail they followed was narrow, forcing them to ride in single file and thus denying him the contact with Wynett that granted him sight of their surroundings. As it was, he allowed the Keshi stallion to plod after Tepshen Lahl's grey whilst the Sister called warning of low branches and commented on the landscape from behind. Mostly she spoke of trees, for they move through an arboreal world, mostly pines here, where the slopes of the Lozins still ran down to the heartland of the woods, and what little animal life existed amongst the looming conifers fled from their approach. He heard occasional snatches of birdsong and once, far off, the howl of a wolf. Deeper into the wood lands he knew they might well encounter the great forest cats, or the fierce bulls with their harems of cows, and the contemplation of such meetings rendered him nervous in his darkness, for he knew he would be helpless to defend his love or himself.

That glum thought transformed to fresh determination as the day wore on, and he resolved anew that he *would* penetrate the forest kingdom to Drul's Mound and call upon the sworn allegiance of the Drott chieftains to enter the netherworld and regain his sight.

Then determination became fresh hope as Tepshen called a soft warning and the horses halted.

'Deer tracks,' the kyo announced. 'Wait here.'

Kedryn heard the rustle of furs as the easterner dismounted, then the faint twang of waxed cord as a bow was strung. He swung down, accepting blind the reins Tepshen thrust into his hand and reaching for Wynett as he heard her step close behind him. Before her touch restored his sight Tepshen was gone, and all Kedryn saw was the channel of trampled snow that marked the game trail disappearing between thick stands of pine like pallisades all around. He looked to the sky, finding a watery sun to his left, its light sparking off the snow that bent the limbs of the lofty trees, glistening faintly through the near-impenetrable wall of perpendicular trunks. The air was still and silent, sepulchral, and he turned to smile at Wynett, finding joy in the sight of her cold-rosed cheeks and calm, blue eyes, the strands of wheat-fair hair that escaped the confines of her hood. She smiled

172

back, close to him as she cupped his hands, and he fought the urge to bend and kiss her.

'Fresh venison would be good,' she murmured, deliberately turning her face from the adoration she saw in his gaze to study the trail.

'Aye,' he responded, staring openly at her profile, thinking that she was surely the loveliest woman he had ever known, or would ever know.

'And a fire,' she added, stamping her feet as the cold began to bite through the fur-lined soles of her boots.

'Let us prepare one,' he suggested. 'If Tepshen succeeds we'll travel no further today, and gathering wood will keep us warm.'

'Will that not frighten the deer?' she asked, and he shook his head.

'No more than our presence.'

'Very well.' Wynett's smile was brighter than the sun and he wound the reins of their horses about a low-hanging branch, retaining her hand as they waded through the snow in search of windfelled limbs.

It was a pleasant diversion and it did, indeed, keep them warm as, hand-in-hand, for all the world like two lovers, they gathered branches and dragged them to the trail.

Dusk was settling and they had a sizeable pile built ready for kindling when Tepshen returned, dragging a yearling buck, his customarily emotionless features beaming at the prospect of such an abundance of fresh meat.

'You show great confidence in my hunting,' he remarked, glancing at the readied fire.

'We never doubted,' Kedryn grinned.

'Then use your tinder,' suggested the kyo, 'while I butcher this stag.'

No further bidding was needed and soon a blaze was melting sufficient snow; the horses found winter grass as the deer was quartered. The hide and entrails were buried under snow some distance away and the choicest cuts set to roasting, the remainder – sufficient to last them several days – stowed in their saddlebags.

The meat was excellent, restoring their spirits as much as their strength, and the prospect of traversing the Beltrevan seemed less daunting as their bellies filled and they began to experience the soporific comfort of satisfied appetites.

'We had best mount a watch,' Tepshen declared, wiping grease from his lips. 'Such a feast may attract wolves, or worse.'

Kedryn's cheerfulness dimmed slightly at this, for he knew he would be useless, but Wynett cheered him by saying, 'You had best share mine – to keep me awake after this kingly repast.'

He nodded, smiling at her, even though he recognised it was merely a gesture to keep up his spirits. Wynett, after all, was accustomed to the long watches over hurt men in the wards of High Fort. Nonetheless, he sat with her, happily silent as they watched the moon flirt cold brilliance through the lattice of branches and Tepshen slept beside the fire. They heard mournful wolfsong as the silver orb crept higher, and towards the end of their watch a scuffling from the direction of the buried entrails, followed by a noisy gulping that was counterpointed with low, chesty growls.

'What is it?' Wynett whispered, her hand tightening on Kedryn's.

'A forest cat, I think,' he told her, tossing fresh branches on the fire so that the flames rose, hurling stark shadows over the surrounding snow, 'It will likely come no closer, but if it does, wake Tepshen.'

A horse snickered nervously and was joined by its companions, then the Keshi stallion screamed a challenge, rearing on its tether line with hooves pawing the chill air. Its scream was answered by a coughing roar from the timber, the sound rebounding off the trees to fill the night with savage feline menace.

There was no need to wake Tepshen Lahl for he was roused by the sound, rolling from the comfort of his furs to stand with naked blade, staring into the darkness.

'It was at the offal,' Kedryn called.

The kyo nodded, replacing his sword with the bow, and moved to the edge of the firelight, arrow nocked ready to fly.

'Quiet that warhorse,' he commanded, and Kedryn went with Wynett to the tether line, soothing the frightened, stamping beasts.

The bay and the grey gentled readily enough, reassured by the familiar presence of humans, but the black stallion was angered by the implicit threat of the cat, its ears flattened back and its eyes rolling as it sought an outlet for its fury. Kedryn seized an ear, releasing Wynett's hand as he dragged the plunging head down and murmured softly to the belligerent animal.

'Kedryn, stay with the horses,' Tepshen called. 'Wynett, bring a brand to me.'

The Sister was loath to leave Kedryn, but the kyo's tone brooked no argument and she hurried to the fire, snatching a blazing branch.

'Throw it,' Tepshen ordered, indicating the direction with a thrust of his chin.

Wynett flung the brand into the trees, sparks trailing and

sputtering as they hit the snow. The burning wood cast random shadows and before it died she saw a tawny shape slink back from the flame, the impression brief but frightening, for it was one of glaring yellow eyes and gnashing fangs, of raw power and ferocity.

'Another,' Tepshen said and she obeyed instantly.

The second brand burned longer, but showed no sign of the cat save a shadow that seemed to move, shifting back into the timber, leaving behind a rasping growl.

'It is gone,' Tepshen announced after a while, and Wynett sighed, suddenly aware that she had been very frightened.

She returned to Kedryn, taking his hand to lead him back to the fire. Tepshen Lahl eased his bowstring down and replaced the arrow in the quiver, announcing that he would take sentry duty for the remainder of the night. Kedryn nodded without speaking and Wynett sensed a tension in him as they huddled in their furs and reached to take his hand again.

'What is it?' she asked. 'The cat is gone.'

'Were it here I should be of no use,' he answered, the bitterness she remembered from High Fort in his voice. 'Save, perhaps, as bait.'

'You are of great use,' she responded gently.

'Blind?' he rasped.

'Remember Lavia's words,' she urged, reaching across the gap between them to touch his cheek. 'You are the Chosen One – the only one able to defeat the Messenger. Were it not for you, we should not be able to approach the Drott – you were the one forged that peace, so already you have proven your worth.'

'And brought you into danger,' he replied.

She smoothed his tousled hair and smiled. 'I came of my own free will, Kedryn. There was no coercion.'

'Save this accursed blindness.' He turned his face so that his lips brushed her palm. 'I would see you safe, Wynett. I would *see* you! I would defend the woman I . . .'

He bit off the word, but she knew what it would have been and felt a sudden, heady flood of emotion that, unbidden, before she even knew what she did, had placed her arms about his shoulders, drawing him to her so that she felt his cold cheek against hers, his mouth against her skin.

'I know,' she whispered into his hair, and almost said, *And I love you*, but caught herself in time, the vows she had made again interposing between them, 'but we have a duty to the Kingdoms. We must remember that.'

'My feelings will not change,' he said, though more calmly now.

'Regain your sight,' Wynett murmured, knowing she should draw back, but unwilling to end the closeness, feeling guilty that she could not, 'and then let us talk of feelings.'

It was Kedryn who drew back then, lifting his head that he might look into her eyes, the beginnings of a smile stretching his mouth.

'You promise?' he asked, excitement in his voice, making it husky.

Wynett gazed back, resisting the impulse to draw his head down that she might feel his kiss, remembering the intoxication, the confusion, she had experienced before, wanting it again, and frightened by the wanting.

'Aye,' she agreed, and placed a gentle finger on his lips before he could speak again, 'I promise.'

Kedryn's smile spread, his even white teeth glinting in the fireglow, his handsome features leached of bitterness as he nodded and settled contentedly into his furs.

Dawn found them sleeping hand-in-hand, the sight eliciting a wry smile from Tepshen Lahl as he tossed branches on to the fire and began to carve meat from the haunch roasted the night before. Shared hardship, shared danger, he thought, forged bonds far stronger than those formed in easier times, and when this quest was ended the Sister Wynett would likely find it difficult to remember her vows. He climbed to his feet and went to examine the tracks left by the forest cat, leaving the star-crossed lovers to wake of their own accord.

He found them risen on his return and wondered what that whispered conversation had been to make Kedryn so happy. He posed no questions, however, nor offered any comment, content to see the young man he regarded as a son in such good spirits.

That mood continued as they progressed steadily deeper into the Beltrevan, though it was marred the next night by the return of the forest cat.

'The creature paces us,' he decided as the great coughing roar echoed through the trees again. 'Mayhap it is maimed and seeks easy prey.'

'Will the fire not keep it off?' asked Wynett.

'Hopefully,' the kyo told her.

'Should we – you,' Kedryn corrected himself, 'kill it?'

'They are not easy creatures to kill,' Tepshen shrugged, 'and that would take time we can ill afford. Perhaps we may placate its hunger.'

Without further ado he took a cut of venison from his saddlebags and a brand from the fire and strode into the trees. He tossed the meat far into the shadows and returned to the camp, listening to the growling of the cat as it consumed the offering.

The following day he surprised a deer floundering through drifted snow and brought it down with a single well-placed arrow, leaving the carcase for the prowling cat. That night they were not troubled, nor was there any sign of the predator for several nights after, though they continued to maintain a watch and rode always with ears straining for sound of the hunter.

The days grew steadily shorter as they moved into the heartland of the woods, the pines giving way to more varied timber, massive beeches spreading cathedral branches above them, gnarled oaks standing like wise old men, birches silvery slender. Animal life became more abundant and their diet of venison was enhanced with hares and wild birds, the roots and winter berries Wynett found. There was increasing forage for the horses and their speed picked up. It seemed they had left the cat behind, though Tepshen still left a haunch to placate the beast whenever he brought down a deer, and they relaxed a trifle as their strength and confidence grew.

They were some weeks into the forest before they sighted the first Drott.

They had forded a river and decided to make camp on the far bank, building a fire to dry their boots and furs as the kyo strung a line in the water, hoping to add fish to their diet. The sun was poised above the trees with a little daylight still in hand, and the blaze crackled merrily as the companions shivered, clustering close to the flames. Their furs were hung on frame works of branches and they had changed their undergarments, modesty dictating that Wynett use the draped furs as a makeshift screen, all three wrapped in the saddle blankets as they waited for the fire to work its heat into their outer garb. Kedryn wiped carefully at his blades as Tepshen Lahl checked his bowstrings and Wynett examined the contents of her satchel, but despite the discomfort there was a festive mood to the halt and they called promises to one another that in future they would find shallower crossing places.

Then their badinage was interrupted by a harsh shout and four men emerged from the surrounding trees with nocked bows and hostile expressions.

They were short, burly men, their stocky frames rendered bulkier by the furs they wore, jerkins of wolf and otter drawn tight by swordbelts, their lower limbs encased in leather-bound leggings.

Two bore shields strung on their backs and all were heavily bearded, bare-headed, with dark skin and narrow, darker eyes.

Tepshen Lahl set a hand to his sword's hilt, then halted the movement as two arrowheads levelled on his chest. Kedryn was already holding Wynett's hand and his grip tightened as he saw the surly eyes appraise her blondeness. '*Ka emblan pasa,*' he called, dragging the phrase from his memory, 'We come in peace.'

'*Ka emblan pasa,*' echoed the foremost warrior, his gutteral tone mocking. '*Ku emblan estro, chaddah. Emblan dyla vistro serra wird.*'

The others guffawed, moving closer.

'He says we have come to die,' Wynett said quickly, her voice low. 'Because we are strangers with no right to be here.'

Kedryn stepped back from the fire, seeing from the corner of his eye that Tepshen was ready to attack should the chance present itself; doubting that even the kyo, for all his lethal speed, could move faster than four arrows.

'Tell them who we are,' he urged.

Wynett spoke rapidly in the byavan and her words halted the barbarians for a moment. Then the spokesman frowned and stepped closer, still holding his bow nocked and ready to fire, more of the harsh speech bursting from his lips as he studied Kedryn's face.

'He says the hef-Alador is blind,' Wynett translated, 'and as you are not, you cannot be the hef-Alador.'

Kedryn let go her hand, bringing down his personal darkness, and pointed to his eyes. '*Yi hef-Alador,*' he cried, then could summon no more of the forest argot.

'He *is* the hef-Alador,' Wynett declared, drawing the saddle blanket closer, conscious of the lustful glint in the warriors' gaze. 'He is come to the Beltrevan to regain his sight, and I am come with him because my touch allows him to see.'

'I should welcome your touch,' leered the barbarian.

'I am a Sister of Kyrie,' she responded, struggling to hold her voice firm, 'and sworn to celibacy. It will go ill with you if you harm any of us.'

'We will not harm you, little one,' the man promised ominously. 'You are worth too much as a slave. But these . . .' He gestured carelessly at Kedryn and Tepshen Lahl, 'they are worth nothing so I think we shall kill them.'

'The Ulan of the Drott will carve the blood eagle on you for such a crime,' Wynett warned him, calling on all the training of Estrevan

178

to put iron in her tone. 'And your souls will wander for all eternity in limbo.'

'For killing strangers who trespass?' sneered the warrior, though an element of doubt had entered his voice and his bowstring eased a little.

'For killing the hef-Alador and his chosen companions,' Wynett snapped. 'For preventing the hef-Alador from presenting himself to your Ulan.'

'I see only a blind man,' came the answer, 'and there are many blind, but only one is the hef-Alador.'

'This one!' Wynett cried. 'Harm him and your soul is in peril!'

The barbarian glared at her, chewing on his moustache, then stepped close, raising his bow until the arrow was aimed directly at Kedryn's face. The tip of the arrowhead almost touched the sightless orb of Kedryn's right eye. Kedryn sensed the presence of the man, caught the sour odour of ancient sweat, and held his ground, wondering what it was Wynett had said.

'Mayhap he is,' the barbarian allowed at last, 'though he does not look like the slayer of Niloc Yarrum to me.'

'Did you see him defeat the hef-Ulan?' Wynett demanded. 'Were you there when he faced your chieftain?'

The tribesman glanced at her and grimaced, lowering the bow. 'No,' he allowed, 'I was not, but . . .'

'You had best tread carefully,' Wynett interrupted, seizing the advantage she saw in his doubt. 'Unless you are anxious to embrace the eagle. You slay the hef-Alador at your peril.'

The man licked his lips and turned his head towards his fellows, barking a question.

One shrugged and said, 'Kill them anyway. Who will know?'

The others appeared less sanguine, though one shrugged and said, 'It would be easier than guarding them. And we should still have the horses.'

The last frowned and said, 'Mayhap we should take them all prisoner. If he is the hef-Alador it will be as she says.'

The first spat and said, 'They ride fine horses. We could sell them, and none the wiser.'

'You would kill the woman?' asked the shortest of the four. 'What if she is a holy woman?'

'If she is, then she is a holy woman of the Kingdoms, not the Beltrevan,' was the answer, 'and she is still formed like a woman. I have never had a holy woman. We could kill her afterwards.'

179

His eyes appraised Wynett with a horrible frankness and she shivered, fighting to keep fear from her voice.

'Take us to your Ulan,' she suggested, 'and let him decide. If he decides against us – which he will not! – then you still have slaves, but when he sees the truth you may well find yourselves rewarded.'

'Cord will have those horses for himself if we go to the Gathering,' said the barbarian in favour of rape.

'And give us to the eagle if she tells the truth,' argued the doubter.

'We could trade with the Caroc,' opined the third man.

'Do you trust the Caroc?' said the leader.

The warrior frowned and shook his head.

'I must think about this,' the leader decided. 'Bind them.'

'Do you dare lay hands on the hef-Alador?' Wynett cried.

'Until he proves himself, aye,' grunted the barbarian.

'Then at least allow us to dress,' she asked. 'We shall freeze else, and there will be no profit.'

The man thought for a moment, then nodded. 'Very well. But tread carefully, strangers!'

The four woodsmen moved back, ringing them with arrows as they climbed into their furs and pulled on their boots, then one bound their wrists behind their backs as the others levelled shafts at their chests. After they were secured they were pushed roughly to the ground, their weapons tossed aside as the barbarians set to debating their fate.

Kedryn was doubly frustrated, for he could neither study the faces of their captors nor understand what they said. Wynett outlined the argument she had put up and the responses it had brought, and – as best she could – translated what she could hear of the conversation.

'One argues for killing us,' she murmured, 'another for bringing us to the Ulan – Cord, he is called – whilst the third is unsure. Their leader is eager for profit, but afraid that you might be the hef-Alador.'

'If only he could be convinced,' Kedryn muttered.

'Perhaps he can,' Tepshen Lahl whispered.

'How?' Kedryn was dubious.

'By swordright,' answered the kyo.

'Swordright?' Kedryn shook his head, his voice bitter. 'I am blind, Tepshen – I cannot fight.'

'The hef-Alador would not fight a common warrior,' said the easterner, 'but a member of his Gehrim might.'

Hope sparked in Kedryn's darkness and he said, 'It might work.'

'How goes the argument?' asked the kyo.

'I am not sure,' Wynett answered, 'but I suspect that greed wins. They fear that Cord will take their profits if they bring us to him, and that if we prove to be only wanderers they will have wasted time. One still fears the eagle, but the rest seem careless of the danger.'

'Then speak before they reach a decision,' urged the kyo.

'What shall I tell them?' she wondered.

'That the hef-Alador forswears to soil his blade on a commoner,' said Tepshen, 'but presents the leader of his Gehrim in his place.'

'You might well face three blades,' warned the Sister.

Tepshen Lahl snorted dismissively.

'Tell them.'

Wynett paused, marshalling her thoughts, then called out, startling the barbarians who turned towards her, clearly irritated by the interruption.

'The hef-Alador challenges you,' she cried. 'He will prove himself by swordright.'

'A blindman?' chortled the would-be rapist.

'The hef-Alador would not soil his blade on such as you,' she retorted, praying she did not overdo the insult, 'but the leader of his Gehrim will stand in his place.'

'The yellow-face?' demanded their leader.

'The kyo, Tepshen Lahl,' Wynett confirmed. 'The hef-Alador grows angry at his confinement and if you will not bring us to your Ulan, then you must face the wrath of his champion.'

'Kill them now!' urged the sanguine one.

'Would you doubly despoil the honour of the Drott?' Wynett said, putting contempt in her tone. 'To kill bound men is the work of cowards, not warriors. To kill the hef-Alador bound must surely condemn you to limbo. After you have known the embrace of the eagle!'

'There is truth in that,' said the short warrior.

'Aye,' grunted the spokesman. 'Let us vote on it. Who favours killing them now?'

Two hands pawed the air.

'Ragnal and Narr vote for death. You, Wyll?'

'I say we bring them to Cord,' said Wyll. 'I think the woman speaks the truth.'

'It depends on you, Kalar,' Ragnal said. 'How do you cast it?'

Kalar combed dirty fingers through his beard, dislodging little pieces of food as a slow, ugly smile spread across his face. 'There are four of us and only three horses,' he murmured. 'Three slaves if she lies. And what reward they will bring if she speaks the truth will go farther should two of us die.'

'You think that slant-eyed creature can kill me?' Ragnal sneered.

'I do not know,' answered Kalar, 'but if he does I shall claim your woman.'

'If he does, you can have her,' said Ragnal, 'and welcome.'

'And mine,' added Narr.

'Very well,' Kalar decided, 'I have seen no honest combat since Cord took the torque.'

Ragnal and Narr were on their feet in the instant, shields slipping from their backs to be secured about their forearms, wide-bladed swords sliding from their sheaths. Kalar rose, producing a knife, and cut Tepshen's bonds. The kyo rose fluidly, massaging his wrists.

'This pretty thing is yours?' Kalar hefted the long eastern blade in its ornate scabbard and tossed it to the kyo.

Tepshen caught the sheath, nodding.

'I would see this,' Kedryn said, and Wynett translated.

Kalar ducked his head in agreement and said, 'Hold your shaft on them, Wyll,' slicing the ropes as the other warrior nocked a fresh arrow.

Kedryn and Wynett rose, standing hand-in-hand as Tepshen paced gracefully towards the waiting barbarians.

'Can he win?' asked the Sister.

'Aye,' said Kedryn, confident in his friend's ability.

The sun was closing on the tree-tops, elongating the shadows, the fire brightening as the light grew dusky. Rangal and Narr moved away from one another, crouching behind the cover of their bucklers, shifting to come at Tepshen from either side. Ragnal brought his blade up, ready to strike on the downswing, whilst Narr held his close against the circle of cured bullhide, preparatory for a stabbing thrust.

Tepshen slid the longsword clear of the scabbard and let the container fall to the snow. He gripped the eastern blade two handed, extended before him at waist height, slanting upwards, his stance deceptively casual.

'You are dead,' Ragnal bellowed, the words falling uncomprehended on the kyo's ears.

Kedryn watched, guessing the content of the challenge and doubting its veracity, his gaze fixed on the trio as the barbarians began a circling movement, seeing the stance Tepshen assumed and knowing how the easterner would respond to the double attack.

Then Narr shouted and both men rushed in, intent on bearing the kyo down before their shields.

Tepshen Lahl remained still for what, to anyone unfamiliar with his deadly style, would appear too long. Kedryn felt Wynett stiffen; heard her sudden intake of breath. Then the kyo shifted, fluid as a cat, darting forwards the three paces needed to take him between the shields, spinning as he passed with the long-bladed sword swinging in a double-handed cut at Ragnal's spine. A tail of wolfskin hung abruptly down the barbarian's legs, bloody where the sword had slashed to the bone. He jerked, his descending blade hacking empty air, and screamed in pain and rage. Only the thickness of his furs had saved him from mortal injury and as it was, he was slowed, gore pulsing from his wounded back.

Narr was less fortunate – or more, for his death was swift. He stabbed at Tepshen's side and found no target, the kyo continuing his turn so that he pirouetted, the long blade rising above his head, falling as he faced the second warrior. Narr was unbalanced by his clumsy charge and struggled to bring his shield up, foregoing swordwork as he saw that defence was his only hope. It was a forlorn optimism, for Tepshen's edge came down to strike his shoulder, hacking with terrible force at the joint of neck and collar bone. Narr's sword arm dropped as a gout of crimson drenched his face and torso. His eyes opened wide, the scream that would have erupted from his mouth only a liquid gargling as he fell to his knees, then pitched face-down on the snow, his draining life spreading an ugly darkness over the white.

Tepshen wrenched his blade loose and paced back as Ragnal came forwards, limping, his bearded features contorted. He held his buckler high, his heavy sword out to the side, its weight straining the weakened muscles of his back. Kedryn saw that the lower part of his jerkin and the backs of his fur breeks were stained with blood. Tepshen Lahl's face was calm, indifferent to the carnage he had wrought, and that seemed to infuriate the barbarian. He bellowed a war-cry and charged a second time as the kyo faced him with upraised sword.

Tepshen's timing was exquisitely precise, even more delicate than that first lethal manoeuvre. He let Ragnal's swing begin, then sidestepped, his own blade descending and turning to cut beneath the defensive buckler, a single step taking him clear of the warrior's sword as his own carved across the man's belly. Ragnal gasped, doubling and scything wildly with his blade as the kyo turned again and almost casually reversed his stroke to bring the edge down against the man's exposed neck. Ragnal's head fell forwards, the whole of his jerkin drenched now, his neck stretching to expose bone through the red lips of the wound. He went on to his knees, weight resting on his out-thrust hands, his long hair touching the snow. He seemed to stare at the crimson that pooled beneath his face, steaming in the cold air, then slumped full length, his feet kicking for a while before the stillness of death overtook his body.

Tepshen Lahl spun to face Kalar, menace in his obsidian gaze.

For an instant it seemed he might charge the two remaining woodlanders and Kalar took a step backwards, hand fastening on his own sword hilt.

Kedryn saw Wyll shift his aim to cover the kyo and tensed to spring forwards, thinking that he could at least prevent the tribesman from putting a shaft into Tepshen. Then a coughing, angry roar filled the ominous silence and Kalar's swarthy face paled under its coating of grime. Wyll's hands trembled on his bow, his eyes rounding in amazement, and he shouted something to his fellow. Kalar replied in a tone that Kedryn recognised as awe and dropped to one knee, his hands extended towards Tepshen. Wyll eased his bowstring down and followed suit as a second roar bellowed from the darkening trees.

Both woodlanders babbled, turning from Tepshen to Kedryn, then to Wynett as she translated.

'They say you are truly the hef-Alador, and Tepshen your champion. They say the forest cat tells them this – he proclaims your right to ride the Beltrevan. He threatens to take their souls in the night if they do not bring you to Cord. They offer you their allegiance. They believe that only with you will they be safe.'

Kedryn came close to smiling then as he watched the barbarians unsheath their swords and hold them towards him, hands on hilts and blades in token of obeisance.

'Tell them I accept their fealty,' he responded. 'But not that the cat expects us to feed him.'

'He will have meat aplenty,' murmured Tepshen, glancing at the bodies.

'And we have guides to Drul's Mound,' Kedryn added.

'You are certain of this?' King Darr asked his daughter, displeased by her request but unable to conceive any valid objection beyond the personal antipathy he felt for Hattim Sethiyan.

'Aye, I am.' Ashrivelle ducked her blonde head, so much like

Wynett's, Darr thought, yet lacking that soundness of judgement, that strength of character, that marked his elder child.

'I had thought you viewed the young Prince of Tamur with favour,' Darr said, seeking to purchase a little time in which to marshal his thoughts. There seemed such an escalation of events he felt himself caught up in a flood he appeared incapable of slowing. The Lord of Ust-Galich had appeared in Andurel far earlier than the king had anticipated – almost as though propelled by magic, yet he had no Sisters in his retinue to work the weather spells that might have summoned a wind – and the malaise that had brought a guilty flush of pleasure to Darr had abated under the ministrations of Sister Thera, who now occupied an honoured place amongst Sethiyan's followers, leaving the Galichian clearly able to press his suit of the princess with such force as to persuade her.

If only, Darr cogitated, Kedryn had come south, rather than seeking the cures of Estrevan, then perhaps Ashrivelle would have found her interest rekindled, and Hattim's ardour held at bay. Kedryn would, without doubt, make a finer husband, for no matter how he viewed the matter, the king could find little to please him in the Galichian's character. The man was handsome enough, and that counted for much in Ashrivelle's eyes; and he was wealthy, fashionable, the king supposed, and certainly eligible. But there was that overweaning ambition in the man and Darr doubted that Hattim's motivation was purely that of a lover: doubted that Ashrivelle, for all her beauty, would be so pleasing to him were she not of the highest blood, a potential stepping stone to the throne.

'Kedryn Caitin is pleasing enough,' Ashrivelle agreed with irritating candour, 'and when he fought the trajea I did, indeed, feel a stirring of interest; but Hattim is a man and I love him.'

'He is somewhat older than you.' Darr fingered the medallion of his office hung about his neck, the tripartite crown raised in silver from the golden disc, but it gave him no inspiration.

'Father,' Ashrivelle responded with fond scorn, 'what matter? A few years makes no difference to us.'

'He is the Lord of Ust-Galich,' Darr said, stroking a beard gone fully grey these past months, 'and it is more usual for a princess of Andurel to wed a son of the Kingdoms. Wed to Hattim you bind Andurel and Ust-Galich; you create an imbalance. Our custom has always been to marry sons to daughters, the partner not of Andurel renouncing inheritance that no Kingdom might rise above its fellows.'

'Father!' Ashrivelle struck a pose, pouting dramatically. 'I know all this. It is common knowledge. But I love Hattim and there is no one else.'

'There is still Kedryn Caitin,' Darr said hopefully.

'He is blind,' answered Ashrivelle, undeterred, 'and gone to Estrevan. He may never return. And Prince Kemm is bandy and smells of horses, which I believe he loves far more than women.'

Darr could not help smiling, for there was some measure of truth in what she said and he doubted that Kemm would agree to forsake his beloved herds even for a woman as lovely as his daughter. Besides, Kemm was no statesman, and the throne required a diplomat – such as Kedryn had proven himself to be.

'I doubt Kedryn will remain in Estrevan for ever,' he tried.

Ashrivelle wound a ringlet of honey-coloured hair about a finger and smoothed an invisible fold in her pink gown. 'He is blind,' she argued, 'and so *young*.'

'He is a hero,' her father countered, 'He slew the leader of the Horde and saved the Kingdoms, and he is of marriageable age.'

'He is not Hattim,' answered Ashrivelle, her voice sulky.

'Would you not consider him?' Darr saw that he fought a losing battle: in some ways Ashrivelle was as firmly purposed as her sister. 'Could you not wait a little?'

'For what?' Ashrivelle let go the ringlet and took her father's hand. 'I love Hattim and that will not change no matter how long I wait.'

Darr stroked her palm thoughtfully, marvelling at the smoothness of her pale skin. He had voiced objections when Wynett announced her intention of remaining in Estrevan to become a full-fledged Sister and lost then; now it seemed he had another daughter – albeit less sensible, in his eyes, than her sibling, but nonetheless determined – who would go her own way no matter what objections he raised.

'There is still the problem of power,' he murmured. 'Andurel and Ust-Galich bound by marriage? Would Hattim renounce his Kingdom?'

Ashrivelle's blue eyes opened wide, her generous mouth forming a moue of surprise. 'We have not discussed it,' she said. 'Why should he? Do you not think it possible he can rule both?'

'Tamur and Kesh might object,' her father opined mildly.

'We could . . .' Ashrivelle thought for a moment, then smiled as if she stumbled on a perfect solution, 'establish a regent.'

'Who would doubtless be Hattim's man,' Darr pointed out.

His daughter pouted again, snorting dismissively. 'I think you harbour some secret dislike, some animosity towards Hattim.'

She removed her hand from his grasp, turning an amethyst ring in a gesture Darr recognised as irritated. 'I have no animosity towards Hattim Sethiyan,' he said slowly, mildly ashamed that he lied, 'but I do dislike the notion of vesting such a weight of power in a single lord.'

Ashrivelle stamped a silver slipper. 'You deny me my love!' she cried melodramatically. 'Perhaps we should elope!'

'I doubt Hattim would agree to that,' Darr retorted, then added tactfully, 'He would not shame either of your lines with such an action.'

Ashrivelle allowed herself to be mollified, turning an appealing face to the king. 'Surely there must be some way to overcome this tiresome objection? Surely I may marry the man I love?'

'I expect there is,' Darr agreed. 'But I must think on it.'

'Then you are not – in principle – against our wedding?'

The king looked at the princess and shook his head, seeing no alternative that would not be an insult to Ust-Galich. Outright refusal could make an outright enemy of the ambitious Sethiyan, and Darr had no wish to foment civil war; especially not with the Galichian forces marching south while the armies of Tamur and Kesh disbanded.

'Then I may tell Hattim he is free to approach you,' pressed Ashrivelle, 'formally?'

'You may,' Darr nodded.

'Thank you!' The princess rose to kiss her father on the cheek, hugging him briefly before running in a most unregal way to the door, blonde locks streaming behind her.

Darr watched the door thud closed and sighed. If only Grania lived, he thought, she could prognosticate the outcome, perhaps even suggest a solution. But Grania was dead and Bethany the Paramount Sister of Andurel, and Bethany, for all her undoubted virtues, was not a whit the politician Grania had been.

He rose from the plain carved chair and paced to the window, his simple grey robe rustling as he crossed the flags. Cold winter sunlight sparkled on the white of the palace walls, stark shadows hiding in the angles and corners of the yards below. Frost shone on the gardens, silver against the white canopy of snow, the shrubbery dark, seeming to crouch against the frozen earth. A squad of pikemen marched orderly to their watch station, sunlight glinting bright on their cuirasses, on the polished heads of their bills, the steady pounding of their boots a metronome cadence that echoed against the windows of the chamber. They might hold the palace, Darr thought, but the city would fall should Hattim employ his southwards-marching army, then shook off the thought as unworthy. Surely not even Hattim Sethiyan would risk civil war.

He wondered if he should have spoken more honestly with Ashrivelle – told her that her lover was overweaningly ambitious and lusted for the throne as much as for her – but doubted she would have listened, let alone agreed. She appeared enamoured of the Galichian; entranced, as though bound by some love potion, and his doubts would, doubtless, have been reported, resulting in . . . He was not sure, but there was something about the whole affair that left him uncomfortable.

He was caught in a dilemma. Ashrivelle was bent on marriage to the Lord of Ust-Galich and Hattim had done nothing so overt as to provide reasonable cause for refusal. The traditional balance of power was a possible obstacle – neither Tamur nor Kesh would take kindly to such an aggrandisement of Galichian influence, but if Hattim did agree to renounce his kingdom that objection could be overcome, at least at face value. Hattim might declare a regency, but it would be a puppet show, whoever assumed the title a Sethiyan adherent. Yet who could object without chancing internecine strife? Should either Tamur or Kesh voice disagreement, Ust-Galich would have justifiable cause to complain and the hard-won unity of the Three Kingdoms be shattered. Corwyn might have found an answer in armed might, aligning Tamur and Kesh against the southerners, but their armies were scattered, homeward-bound, and the Galichians moved, albeit peaceably so far, towards Andurel. And Darr was no Corwyn, nor had any wish to be. Corwyn had welded unity from chaos and to take his path now was to risk plunging the Kingdoms back into those dark ages.

There was, of course, the possibility of agreeing to the marriage but not to a Sethiyan succession. To permit Hattim Ashrivelle's hand, but refuse him the right of lineage that would lead to the throne. Let him take Ashrivelle back to Tessoril, where they could rule Ust-Galich together. But what of Andurel then? The succession passed down through the blood, the sons and daughters of the White Palace wedding the scions of the Kingdoms, those thus bound to the throne renouncing their inheritance for the greater duty of that heavy crown. And with Ashrivelle wed to Hattim, Wynett sworn to the Sisterhood, there was no other heir. Thus the throne would stand empty on his death – and that way, too, chaos threatened.

Darr moved from the window, crossing the chamber to the table of Tamurin oak on which rested decanters and goblets. He poured a measure of rich Keshi wine, carmine as spilled blood, and drank it down, his high brow creased in a care-worn frown.

No such expression decorated Hattim Sethiyan's brow, though his agile mind foresaw many of the problems that dogged the king. His was smooth, his smile carefree, exultant as he embraced Ashrivelle and whirled her about, listening to her laughter as she showered kisses on his face and told him her father had agreed to formal presentation of his suit.

Taws' – or Thera's – potions had worked their physical magic on a willing subject, drawing, as the transformed mage had promised, on the attraction already present to consume the princess with love. She adored Hattim, could find no fault in him, thought him the most handsome man she had ever known. She was virtually his slave, already – discreetly, lest discovery offend her father and dash their hopes – his lover. There remained only the formality of the wedding, after that the fulfilment of Taws' promise: the throne.

He set her down and kissed her, feeling himself stir as she pressed against him, reminding himself that he must still exercise caution, appear an honest suitor, a suitable husband. Taws had explained that to him as the love potion was readied: it was not a glamour, for such would be too easily detected by the Sisters present in the city, but a nostrum that by its natural, physical nature might go unnoticed, enhancing, magnifying an attraction already present.

He drew back, holding her in his arms, smiling.

'He did not object?'

'Oh, he spoke of power, of imbalance.' Ashrivelle nestled tighter into his embrace. 'That Kesh and Tamur might dispute the union.'

'They might,' said Hattim. 'They might envy my fortune.'

Ashrivelle laughed. 'I told him you would doubtless appoint a regent should there be such opposition.'

Hattim held the smile on his face, brushing her hair with his lips that she should not see the cold light in his eyes, 'Aye, I could do that. But why trouble ourselves with such petty considerations? The marriage is the important thing. Jarl and Bedyr will doubtless attend and we can settle such matters then. We shall find a solution, my love – nothing shall stand in our way.'

Or my way to the throne, he thought, as she lifted her face, presenting her lips to his kiss again. Your father will no doubt seek to put obstacles in my path, but I shall overcome them. Taws and I will overcome them! And with Taws, I am invincible. Tamur and Kesh shall not prevent me, nor that decrepit fool, Darr.

He disengaged his mouth and took her hands, kissing them, murmuring, 'Perhaps you should go now, lest my passion overwhelm me and we create a scandal.'

Ashrivelle's smile became mischievous. 'I care not,' she declared. 'Let all Andurel – all the Kingdoms! – know that I am yours.'

'I know that,' he told her smoothly, 'and whilst I long to proclaim it openly I do not think we should so disturb your father.'

'Oh, my dearest,' she sighed, 'how thoughtful you are.'

Hattim beamed, steering her gently towards the door.

'I shall see you again when we eat, my love.'

'I cannot wait,' said Ashrivelle, but she allowed him to direct her through the door, where her attendant women waited, eager to hear her news. They saw her flushed, excited features and began to press her with questions as they escorted her down the wide, flagstoned corridor.

Hattim closed the door on the babble of their voices and turned to face the entrance of the sleeping chamber. The figure of Sister Thera emerged, the pretty features smiling in a way that Thera never had.

'You heard?' asked Hattim.

'I did,' said Taws. 'It goes well.'

'Darr will seek some way to deny me the succession.' Hattim said.

'That does not matter,' Taws responded. 'We need only firm a time for your marriage and ensure the lords of Tamur and Kesh attend. Before they arrive Darr will be dead and you will have the throne.'

'And you your vengeance,' smiled the Lord of Ust-Galich.

'Aye,' said the mage. 'In full measure.'

190

Chapter Nine

THE snow that had fallen with increasing regularity over Andurel since the arrival of Hattim Sethiyan layered the city with an achromatic blanket that matched the canescent purity of the White Palace. The avenues and alleyways were cleared, but the parks and gardens and roofs lay unsullied, save for the tracks of laughing children – and not a few adults – who gloried in the opportunities for play afforded by the wintry conditions. Such deep and early snowfall was unusual in the island city and it seemed to Darr, as he proceeded through the frosted avenues, that this uncustomary turn of weather matched the political shifting he sensed in process. He allowed his eyes to wander as he rode, letting his charger, a stallion with coat as pale as snow, pick its own way, following the mounts of the Palace Guard ahead, studying the shouting children with a fond smile as they sent toboggans hurtling down the slopes, or hurled snowballs at one another. The air was chill and clean in his nostrils, the north wind blowing off the Idre bleached of the wharfside odours that frequently assailed the senses, the sky a steel-hard blue, silvered by the sun that reflected in dazzling rainbow hues from the whiteness. There was an air of excitement, of joy in this unexpected diversion, and it contrasted with the sombre mood of the king so that the smile he assumed as he raised a hand in greeting to those who cheered him as he passed was a façade hiding his real discomfort.

Whether the Sisters could help him or not, he was not sure; any more than he was sure of the course he should take, but they were his only hope at present. He had thought of despatching mehdri to bring word to Caitin Hold and Keshaven but held back: once the wedding plans were set afoot the lords of Tamur and Kesh would, by custom, be summoned to give their blessings to the union, and to send riders out into the winter now would merely impose a double burden on the royal messengers – and possibly provide Hattim with grounds for assuming insult. Darr did not want that – not yet – and

191

so had decided to seek the counsel of the Sorority College, to which he now went.

His musings dimmed his vision and it was with a start of mild surprise that he realised the white stallion had halted, taking its cue from the horses ahead as if, accustomed to ceremonial procedures and an absent-minded master, it acted of its own accord. He snorted brief laughter at himself and climbed from the saddle, passing the reins to a waiting guard as he walked across the swept dark blue flags of the square that surrounded the college building. It was a structure imposing in its stark simplicity, a cube of pale blue stone only two storeys high beneath a gradually angled roof that was now the purest white, patches of darker tiling showing about the squat chimneys that wafted pale smoke into the winter air. Balconies ran evenly around the walls, the wood painted the blue of Estrevan, as was the ever-open door that gave entrance to the interior.

Darr halted there, wrapping his fur-lined cloak closer about him as the captain of the guard pounded three times on the woodwork and cried in ringing tones, 'The king asks entrance.'

The answer was prompt and amused, as if the youthful Sister who gave it considered such protocol to be exactly what it was – mere formality.

'The king is welcome, as are all who come in peace.'

'Thank you,' Darr smiled, and turned to the captain. 'I am not sure how long this will take, Corradon, but doubtless the Sisters will find you and your men some warm place to wait.'

'Majesty,' Corradon responded, bowing.

Darr nodded vaguely and said to the Sister, 'Bethany received my request?'

'She awaits you, King Darr,' the Sister said. 'If you will follow me?'

She clapped her hands and another blue-robed acolyte appeared to lead the escort away as Darr followed the young woman down the low-roofed passage that gave egress to the inner courts. There were gardens here, given mostly to the production of the herbs that provided the Sisterhood with its remedies, but also to shrubbery and trees that in warmer times would blaze with colour, lending the college the air of cheerful serenity Darr enjoyed so much. He glanced about as the Sister led him briskly along a cleared path towards the far end of the yard, feeling, despite his foreboding the calm that seemed to emanate from the very stones of the place.

Beyond the gardens they entered the building again and the

192

Sister brought him up a wide, stone stairway to an interior balcony overlooking a well in which a fountain played, the steady trickling of its water musical, tinkling softly from the smooth stone walls. They halted at a plain wood door and the Sister tapped twice, opening the door with a smile as a voice bade them enter.

Darr went in and ducked his head as the door closed behind him.

'Sister Bethany, I trust you are well?'

The woman who faced him was outlined against the window at her back, the light giving the prematurely-whitened hair that curled about her head the appearance of a halo. She was tall and thin, rather than slender, the eyes on a level with Darr's, studying him with a hazel intensity that, had he not known her, might have made him feel uncomfortable. There was an air of austerity about her, emphasised by the hollow planes of her cheeks and the straight, thin line of her mouth. Those who did not know her frequently did feel uncomfortable in her presence, for until she smiled she appeared severe, almost disapproving.

She smiled as she answered, and the expression seemed to shine brighter than the illumination from the window.

'I am well, King Darr. But I sense . . . discomfort? in you.'

Darr answered her smile and nodded, shrugging clear of his cloak to toss it carelessly over a high-backed chair. Bethany, Paramount Sister of the college, gestured at the table set close to the fire blazing in the hearth and the king took one of the unadorned seats surrounding the smooth-polished wood. A carafe and several earthenware mugs sat on the table and Bethany poured wine already heated and spiced with herbs, its taste simultaneously sweet and savoury, warming as the king swallowed.

'You see through me,' he murmured.

'I see the set of your shoulders, the lines on your face,' Bethany replied. 'We of Estrevan are taught to read such things. It is no great feat.'

'Would that I had such skills,' Darr sighed.

'Tell me,' the Sister urged, coming with typical bluntness to the point.

'Ashrivelle has come asking permission for Hattim Sethiyan to present formal court,' Darr told her. 'I could see no course but to agree.'

'You had rather refused?' Bethany asked.

Darr sipped wine and shrugged, the corners of his mouth turning

193

down beneath his grey moustache. 'The Lord of Ust-Galich would not be my first choice.'

'Kedryn Caitin? Jarl's Kemm?' Bethany queried.

'Kedryn, not Kemm,' Darr nodded.

'Who goes to Estrevan in search of sight,' nodded the Sister, 'and the princess will not wait.'

'She is in love,' Darr spoke the word as though it left an unsavoury taste. 'Hattim Sethiyan is the only man for her! It is as if she were bewitched.'

'I doubt that,' smiled Bethany. 'Were there magicks afoot we should have sensed them. Sister Thera is close to the Lord of Ust-Galich and would doubtless have sent me word.'

'Sister Thera appears to have become the confidante of our Galichian cousin,' grumbled Darr. 'As you know, he marks her amongst his retinue.'

'Which is no bad thing,' Bethany commented mildly. 'Hattim Sethiyan had little to do with the Sorority ere now, and to have a Sister so close can only provide a benign influence. That is why I agreed to her secondment.'

'I do not dispute that,' Darr agreed, 'but I doubt the wisdom of the union.'

'He is eligible.' Bethany sipped delicately at her wine, adding, 'You cannot dispute that.'

'His eligibility, no,' Darr said. 'But the wisdom? Ust-Galich bound to Andurel?'

'Darr must renounce one throne,' came the even answer. 'Either he forfeits liegedom of the southern kingdom, or the High Seat.'

'It is not so simple,' Darr murmured, thinking that Grania would have seen it in the instant. 'Should Hattim relinquish Ust-Galich to some fresh bloodline it will inevitably be to some loyal follower. A Sethiyan puppet! I do not believe he would agree to forego the White Palace.'

'Tamur and Kesh have a say in this,' Bethany interrupted. 'Will they accept Hattim Sethiyan as ruler of Andurel?'

'Were he wed to Ashrivelle, they might have no choice,' Darr answered. 'The line continues through marriage.'

'And is Kedryn Caitin so much better an heir?' The Sister demanded. 'He is the hero of the Lozin Gate and commands the loyalty of Tamur. That kingdom wed to Andurel might pose a union threatening to Kesh and Ust-Galich.'

'Kedryn would renounce Tamur and I should trust his word,'

Darr said, shaking his head. 'Bedyr Caitin still lives and might well father another child, even late in life. Jarl of Kesh trusts both father and son.'

'But Hattim Sethiyan is not to be trusted?' Darr stared at the Sister, unsure whether she spoke ingenuously. She smiled, setting down her mug, and continued, 'I say what others might ask, Darr. I am no Grania, to foresee the future, but I know the Galichian army marches south and must even now close on the city, and that Hattim Sethiyan is quick to find offence. Is this not what troubles you?'

'Aye,' the king sighed. 'Should I refuse this union, Hattim might well find reason to secede – or promote his case by force of arms – and thus foment civil war. Should I agree, then Tamur and Kesh might stand in opposition and Ust-Galich take arms in defence of Sethiyan honour. I seem caught betwixt high water and quicksand whichever way I step.'

'It is no easy decision,' Bethany agreed.

'It is a quandary,' Darr said mournfully.

The Sister nodded, her hazel gaze becoming distant. She stared at the king without seeing him and he waited, knowing that she considered the options, hoping she might arrive at some answer that would provide a solution to his problem. In this, at least, she was Grania's equal, for where the dead Sister had been able to prognosticate, weaving each thread of a situation to its logical outcome in such a way that she seemed capable of reading the future, Bethany had a talent for finding compromise. And kingship, Darr reminded himself, was so much to do with compromise.

'Ashrivelle is set on this union?' she asked at last, her eyes focusing again.

'She will consider no other,' nodded the king.

'And you can scarce refuse. Yet neither you – nor I! – trust Hattim Sethiyan to renounce Ust-Galich.'

Darr nodded again.

'So you are trapped in this dilemma. But not Tamur or Kesh! And both Bedyr and Jarl have the right to a say in this.'

'Opposition will likely foment war,' Darr said, prompting a cursory wave of the Sister's hand.

'*Say*, not opposition. Bedyr Caitin will bend rather than see the Kingdoms consume one another; and his counsel – as yours – stands high with Jarl. Therefore put these arguments to Hattim. As yet he offers no open dispute, and as a loyal lord he must, on the face of it at least, set premium on the unity of the Kingdoms. Express your doubts tactfully – the weight of leadership rests on your shoulders and Hattim must accept that – so that you do not object, but fear for Hattim's smooth succession. Consequently you act in Hattim's own best interests, and those of your beloved daughter, when you suggest the lordship of Ust-Galich be decided by yourself, Tamur, and Kesh.'

'Aye,' Darr said softly, digesting her suggestion, 'that might work.'

'Further,' Bethany went on, 'the marriage cannot take place until the lords of Tamur and Kesh attend Andurel. All precedent demands they be here – and in this winter that will take time.' A certain wickedness entered her smile, 'Your messengers might even suggest they make no great hurry. By then, perhaps, Kedryn will have regained his sight and accompany his parents.'

'To change Ashrivelle's mind?' wondered the king.

'Mayhap,' shrugged the Sister. 'He is a handsome young man, is he not? And women's minds do change.'

Darr almost said, But he loves Wynett, but did not, assuming that to be a hopeless cause and anxious to seize whatever straw of optimism he could find. Perhaps – if Kedryn did attend – he might be swayed by Ashrivelle's beauty. And she by him.

'That is not any great hope,' Bethany added, promptly dashing the king's, 'we must chiefly rely on delay. Hold off the wedding until the lords may attend; and then delay further whilst the succession is decided. For the sake of unity! I do not believe Hattim can argue that.'

'He is ambitious,' Darr said. 'He will not like it.'

'But he can scarcely argue it,' said Bethany.

'No,' Darr allowed, 'I do not suppose he can.'

'I will ponder this further,' Bethany promised, 'but for now that seems your safest course.'

'It seems my only one,' Darr said, 'if I am to avoid civil war.'

'Aye.' Bethany's face was grave as she studied the king. 'Unless Ashrivelle should change her mind.'

'I do not think she will,' sighed Darr. 'She appears enamoured of the man.'

'Then let it be as we have said,' the Sister urged. 'And pray we do aright.'

'Amen,' said Darr, solemnly.

He took his leave then, refusing the Sister's invitation to eat in the college, thinking that the sooner he broached these matters with Hattim the better, and certain the Galichian would be anxious to approach him. Some inner voice suggested that it were best Hattim had no inkling he had sought the advice of the Sorority, and certainly none that he sought to delay, and that he should, therefore, return to the White Palace without prevarication.

He found Corradon and the squad of guardsmen supping mulled wine in one of the spacious receiving rooms, feeling almost sorry to drag them from the hearth-warmed comfort of the chamber to the chill outside.

Dusk was falling as they returned to the palace, the metallic brightness of the sky fading to a dull grey that shrouded the distant waterfront behind a veil of mist, and large flakes of snow began to descend, skirling leisurely from the lustreless heavens. The children he had seen earlier were gone, summoned to firesides and food, and as he rode the broad avenue that climbed to the palace the grey grew steadily darker, shadows lengthening over the gardens, lamps glowing like faraway promises behind windows and tight-closed shutters. The king felt melancholy.

'Your business went well, Majesty?' Corradon enquired, the question unusual enough that Darr realised his mood expressed itself physically.

'Well enough, thank you, my friend,' he murmured, bracing his shoulders and drawing himself more erect in the saddle.

'I am pleased,' said the captain, his kindly eyes on his master's face, the doubt behind them masked.

'Well enough,' Darr repeated to himself, composing his features into what he hoped was an expression of calm confidence, regal self-assurance. Knowing as he did so that a world of difference lay between outward appearance and inner reality. 'But there is something I would have you do, Corradon.'

'Majesty?' asked the captain. 'You have only to command.'

'This requires discretion,' Darr murmured, his voice low enough that only the officer might hear him. 'I would have scouts sent out to advise me of the position of Galichian forces. How far are they from the city? When might they arrive?'

Corradon's eyes grew troubled beneath the beak of his helm and Darr added quickly, 'I would have this done secretly, my friend. Use only your most trusted men, and tell no one of their mission.'

Corradon was far too disciplined to question his king, so he merely nodded once and said, 'It is done, Majesty.'

'Thank you,' said Darr.

He essayed the same composure as he prepared himself for the dinner at which, he was sure, Hattim would make formal presentation. It was the obvious time, when the nobles of Andurel and the Galichian's own retinue would be present to hear the announcement, such public declaration forcing the king to an equally public response. Consequently he forewent his customarily simple garb in favour of more regal vestments, donning a tunic of scarlet silk and breeks of black picked with silver thread, draping a belted overrobe of blue with the tripartite crown sewn in gold and silver on chest and back about his shoulders. He took particular care combing his thinning hair and groomed his beard to an unusual perfection, hanging the pendant of his office about his neck as he surveyed himself in the mirror and smiled wryly at the effect. He had never considered himself very regal, but he hoped that he might, when required, rise to the occasion.

Ashrivelle, certainly, felt that he had. She clapped her hands and smiled with delight when she saw him, crying, 'Father! You look splendid.'

'Thank you,' he murmured, offering her his arm.

'You have done this for me,' she whispered. 'You know that Hattim will speak with you tonight, and I thank you for it.'

'I thought he might,' Darr agreed, patting her hand. 'The Lord of Ust-Galich is not one for wasting time.'

'He *is* decisive,' the princess nodded, mistaking the tone of the comment. 'It is one of the things I admire about him.'

'Indeed,' said Darr, proceeding at a stately pace towards the stairwell that descended to the ante-chamber of the banqueting hall.

The court, as was customary, waited there, swelled by the ranks of Galichians, their embroidered finery contrasting with the simpler styles of the White Palace, Hattim standing out amongst them.

He was dressed in gold, tunic and breeks and the short cape that was the latest fashion, all glittering in the light of the flambeaux set about the walls. His hair was oiled and coiffed, bound back by a circlet of matching metal, even the hilt of the ceremonial dagger and the belt that sheathed it picked with gold.

'Is he not magnificent?' Ashrivelle whispered as they approached.

'He is very . . .' Darr paused, 'pretty.'

His daughter glanced at him, then love swayed her judgement again and she chuckled. 'Pretty is not the word I would have chosen, but yes, he is.'

Darr assumed a friendly smile as the Lord of Ust-Galich bowed low before him and said, 'King Darr, greetings.'

'And to you, my Lord,' the king responded, meeting Hattim's green-eyed gaze with an even stare.

'Princess.' Hattim bowed afresh to Ashrivelle, his earring dangling as he stooped over her hand. 'You are breath taking.'

Ashrivelle was radiant as she studied him. 'As are you, my Lord.'

'I am shadowed by your beauty,' Hattim declared. 'I am dazzled.'

'Let us eat,' Darr suggested abruptly, feeling mildly sickened by these excessive compliments.

Dutifully, the Galichian fell into step behind the royal couple as they led the way into the hall and assumed their places at the High Table.

By custom, Ashrivelle sat to the king's right and Hattim to his left. The Galichian nobles were seated along the table to either side, whilst those of Andurel occupied the lower places in deference to their guests. Musicians plucked the strings of balurs and theorbos, accompanied by the soft drumming of a tabor and the higher-pitched notes of rebecks, and Darr noticed that Ashrivelle, whose duty it was to select the tunes, had chosen melodies of Galichian origin. Servants poured wine into goblets of crystal, a red southern vintage to accompany the gamey soup that was the first course. Through that Darr felt as might a wall interposed between lovers, Ashrivelle and Hattim exchanging compliments and conversation across him. A richer vintage was served with the hare that followed, the meat marinaded and spicey, and Darr wondered if Hattim hoped the wines would ease the way into his presentation as he waited for the man to speak.

It came as the king chewed on the boar meat that was the main course, silk-smooth and confident as steel.

'I can contain myself no longer,' Hattim declared. 'May I ask your permission to speak frankly, Darr?'

The king swallowed and nodded, aware of the gradual stilling of conversation around him.

'My Lord King,' Hattim said, raising his voice a fraction, projecting it sufficiently that it was heard by all the nobles, 'I would ask your permission to present my suit to your daughter, the Princess Ashrivelle.'

Darr washed down the boar meat with a goblet of dark red wine, surprised that it was a Keshi vintage, and turned to face Hattim. He wanted to say, No, you may not, but knew that chaos lay in that direction and instead answered solemnly, 'You have my permission, Lord Hattim.'

The silence that had fallen was broken by a sudden rush of conversation and that by a cheer from down the table, where Mejas Celeruna raised a brimming cup in toast, eagerly followed by the other Galichians.

Hattim motioned them to silence and said, 'Thank you, Darr.'

Ashrivelle clapped hands to her mouth, her eyes ablaze as she looked past her father to her would-be husband.

'My feelings for the princess are, I believe, known,' Hattim continued, 'and I venture to hope that I find favour in her eyes. Should she accept me, I swear to you now, in the presence of all here, that I shall endeavour to my utmost to make her happy, to prove myself worthy of her.'

'You are,' Darr heard Ashrivelle whisper. He said, 'I would not stand in the way of my daughter's happiness, my Lord.'

'Then, if you will forgive my impatience . . .' Hattim rose dramatically to his feet, pushing back his chair that he might turn and look across the king to the princess. 'My Lady, I ask you now to be my wife. I pledge you my love and my life. I ask your hand in marriage.'

The strumming of the balurs faded; a dying note from the rebeck hung briefly on the air. Ashrivelle rose, blonde and beautiful in gown of aquamarine, a golden coronet in her hair. 'My Lord,' she said, her smile incandescent, 'I accept your pledge, and thank you for it. And should my father agree, I do most happily accept your suit.'

Both turned then to face Darr, and the king knew that every eye in the hall was on him. I should feel happy, he thought. My daughter loves the man: she radiates happiness and I should find pleasure in that. But I do not, and if I could, I would halt this here. But I cannot: I must take the path I feel safest for the future of these fragile kingdoms.

He rose in turn, looking first to Ashrivelle, then to Hattim, then out over the watching, waiting faces.

'I do agree,' he announced. 'Let it be known that my daughter, the Princess Ashrivelle, is now betrothed to the Lord Hattim of Ust-Galich. And may the Lady bless their union.'

He took Ashrivelle's hand and Hattim's, bringing them together across his chest, placing his own upon them as they joined, oddly aware that the Galichian wore as many rings as his bride-to-be.

'Thank you,' murmured Hattim.

'Father,' Ashrivelle beamed, 'I am so happy.'

Mejas Celeruna was the first to cheer, but only by an instant, his shout drowned by the uproar from the Galichian retinue, that by the hubbub that rattled throughout the hall. Goblets were raised in toasts; dagger hilts thudded on tabletops; servants beat platters; and the musicians promptly struck a lively tune.

'There are things we must discuss,' Darr murmured through the shouting.

'A dowry is of no importance,' Hattim smiled.

'Not that,' the king replied. 'There are certain . . . problems that we must resolve.'

'The succession?' Hattim's smile was guileless, so innocent that Darr knew instantly he had pondered this and found his own solutions. 'I shall be guided entirely by you, Darr.'

'Later,' said the king. 'We shall talk later.'

'As you wish,' Hattim agreed easily.

'A kiss!' Celeruna bellowed, face flushed by wine and excitement. 'A kiss to seal this joyous compact!'

Darr held his smile with an effort as he motioned for a servant to draw back his chair and watched as Hattim Sethiyan took Ashrivelle in his arms and kissed her soundly. He maintained the expression throughout the remainder of the meal, accepting the congratulations of all who presented themselves, seeing in many eyes the same doubts he held, knowing that he would shortly be bombarded with objections. And knowing that he must still them as he stilled his own: for the sake of the Three Kingdoms.

He endured the spontaneous celebration until the night grew old and it seemed politically acceptable he suggest they retire. Ashrivelle argued, but allowed herself to be persuaded by Hattim, who took her arm to escort her to her chambers. After she was gone in he turned to Darr.

'When would you discuss these matters?' he asked, still polite.

'On the morrow, I think,' the king responded.

'As you command,' Hattim nodded. 'At what hour?'

'I shall send word when I am ready.' Darr could not resist that small reminder of authority, but it went uncontested, running smooth as oil over Hattim's satisfaction.

'Of course,' agreed the Galichian. 'I shall await your summons.'

Darr nodded and bade the man good night.

'Sleep well,' beamed Hattim.

Darr doubted that he would.

Hattim had no such doubts, nor cared if he did not. It had gone far smoother than he had hoped, for he had been unable to prevent himself wondering if the king might not trump up some argument

201

despite all Taws' reassurances, knowing Darr to be a wily man and well-versed in the art of diplomacy. But it had gone exactly as the mage had prophesied, and Hattim's spirits swelled to elation as he dismissed his retinue and the servants with the final request that Sister Thera be sent for, explaining that he was so excited he would require a sleeping draft were he to sleep well enough to be ready for the royal summons.

Inside his quarters he filled a goblet with wine and presented the draugh to his reflection, admiring himself as he imagined the tripartite crown upon his brow, the medallion about his neck.

He turned as the door hissed open and the woman Taws had become appeared. She – or he, Hattim could not make up his mind how he thought of the sorcerer – set down the satchel of unneeded curatives and studied the Lord of Ust-Galich.

'I assume it went well?'

'As you told me it would.' Hattim turned from the mirror, finding it far easier to face the mage in this form. 'Just as you told me it would.'

'Did you doubt?' Taws asked. 'What choice was there for Darr? He cannot risk offending you.'

'He spoke of problems,' Hattim remarked. 'That he will discuss on the morrow.'

'He will seek to deny you the succession,' said Taws. 'Or ask that you relinquish Ust-Galich. If the latter, he will seek to subvert your choice of regent in favour of his own.'

'And how should I respond?' Hattim wondered.

'Agree,' said Taws. 'No matter what conditions he may set, you will agree. Let him stipulate all the clauses he wishes – they will make no difference.'

He paused, and Hattim saw the face of Sister Thera contort, the muscles of the neck stiffening, the eyes widening and rolling until white showed, the female form shuddering beneath its blue robe. Then a strangled sigh escaped the wide-stretched lips and they smiled again, the voice that came from them husky, as if possessor and natural owner fought for control.

'I have it,' Taws declared. 'She fought me then, for she sees the way of it, but her knowledge is mine now. What protocols appertain?'

'Those we have discussed,' Hattim said, 'though I have dispensed with a lengthy courtship – thanks to you.'

The figure of the Sister shook its head impatiently. 'No! How may Darr prevaricate?' Taws asked.

Hattim shrugged. 'It is customary for the liege lords of Tamur and

202

Kesh to attend, and that may take time.' He gasped, nodding. 'And Darr may seek their advice in the matter of the succession. Yes! Of course.'

'Of course,' said Taws. 'And custom dictates you may not wed Ashrivelle until they attend.'

'Aye,' said Hattim, an expression of lupine triumph creasing his lips. 'But what matter? Kill Darr before they arrive and I'll greet them from the High Throne.'

'No,' said the mage, freezing the triumphant smile on the Galichian's face, 'you will await their arrival. As I have told you, you will agree to all Darr's terms.'

'And have them gainsay me?'

The mage laughed at the chagrin on the man's face. Could he see no further than that? Were all these creatures so short-sighted?

'They will find a man humble beyond their belief,' he said. 'A man willing to relinquish his kingdom or the High Throne for love of the princess. That he is also a man with an army camped at the gates of the city is by the way – it can scarcely be considered your fault that the forces of Ust-Galich, marching south from their loyal duty, wish to see their lord celebrate his wedding. They will witness the wedding, and after that Darr will die. Then you will become king! And the lords of Kesh and Tamur will find themselves prisoners.'

Hattim paled somewhat: 'And *their* armies? Do you believe they will stand idly by whilst their lords are imprisoned?'

'Given choice between that and the death of their lords, aye,' said Taws. 'Do you not see it? We bait a double trap – first your wedding for those most able to oppose you, and then their imprisonment for Kedryn Caitin.'

Hattim's colour returned and he began to smile again. 'I see it,' he murmured. 'With his parents' lives at stake, Kedryn will doubtless come seeking to free them.'

'Indeed,' said Taws, 'and when he does, we have him.'

Hattim began to laugh then, the sound triumphant.

When Darr sent for him late in the morning of the following day he appeared, as Taws had ordered, suitably humble. He sat quietly as the king outlined the potential problems of an extant ruler marrying his daughter, nodding his agreement as the grey-haired man suggested the possible objections of Tamur and Kesh, indicating modestly that he would accept the king's decision in the matter.

'Were you a son of Ust-Galich there would be no problem,' said Darr, surprised – and suspicious – at Hattim's untypical acquiescence. 'Had I another son or daughter of marriageable age there would be no problem.'

'Indeed,' murmured the Galichian, laughing inwardly at the older man's discomfort, 'and how may we resolve this dilemma?'

'I would suggest,' Darr said, toying a trifle nervously with the medallion about his neck, 'that you should relinquish Ust-Galich. Should Ashrivelle forsake the White Palace, the throne must stand empty on my death. That cannot be, so it must fall to you to assume that seat by her side. Tamur and Kesh must, of course, agree to this, but with the royal line ended at Ashrivelle, I cannot foresee their refusal.'

'And to rule both Andurel and Ust-Galich would be unthinkable,' said Hattim, unctuously.

'Quite,' Darr agreed, his agitation growing at Hattim's continued assent.

'So I must renounce all claim,' Hattim smiled.

'But there can be no suggestion of patronage,' said the king. 'I intend no slur, but the man who succeeds you must not be one of your choice, lest folk speak of puppets. Therefore, I would ask that you abide by the decision of the lords in council – let Tamur and Kesh, and I, choose the one who shall rule Ust-Galich in your stead.'

'As you will it,' nodded Hattim, further surprising Darr. 'The suggestion is eminently sensible.'

'You have no objection?' Darr asked, finding it difficult to keep the disbelief he felt out of his voice.

'None,' Hattim confirmed equably. 'I shall willingly abide by whatever ruling my fellow lords may reach.'

'Then,' said Darr, wondering why he felt no relief at this seemingly amicable compact, 'we have little else to discuss, save the details of the wedding itself.'

Hattim smiled and nodded, stroking idly at his earring as if he had not a care in the world.

When he was gone Darr sent for Corradon and learnt that the scouts had been despatched, ordered to observe the Galichian army and return without making contact. The king then composed messages for Bedyr Caitin and Jarl of Kesh, advising them of Ashrivelle's betrothal and requesting their presence in Andurel with retinues suitable to a wedding celebration. He added the suggestion that neither lord make undue haste, and of Bedyr enquired as to Kedryn's whereabouts. There seemed little more he could do, save wait.

*

Tepshen Lahl shared neither the trust Kedryn and Wynett showed in the barbarians' word nor their faith in the Lady. He knew the forest folk as savage enemies and the Lady as a vague concept too much given to forgiveness and good will. Consequently he rode with hand on sword hilt as the two woodsfolk trotted before him, his cold, dark eyes never leaving their backs lest they turn to reveal their true natures. At night he slept with the blade cradled in his arms, lightly as a cat, his ears attuned to sound of movement for fear the warriors should seek to flee or slit sleeping throats.

Kedryn and the Sister were far less concerned with betrayal, for they pinned their hopes on Kalar and Wyll, trusting in the men to bring them to the Gathering far more swiftly than they might have managed unguided. And it seemed they were the wiser in this, for neither man sought to flee and offered only respect to their charges as they progressed through the winter-decked timber of the Beltrevan along paths the questers might never have discovered unguided.

Even so, it took long days before they approached the great clearing that surrounded Drul's Mound and their guides halted.

'We had best tread carefully now,' Kalar told Wynett, waiting as she translated his words, 'for your presence will be unexpected. I had best go before, announcing the coming of the hef-Alador.'

Wyll cut poles as he spoke, lashing bunches of the red and white peace feathers to the ends, fixing more to the bridles. Tepshen Lahl fastened ribbons of the same colours to his sword hilt and Kedryn's.

'There will be dogs,' Kalar warned, reminding Kedryn of the vicious hounds that had flooded into High Fort, 'and folk wary of your presence. Offer them no offence, but follow us to Cord's lodge.'

Wynett translated this and Kedryn nodded, clasping her hand as he glanced to Tepshen. The kyo grunted his assent and they mounted, Kalar taking Kedryn's bridle, Wyll marching beside him, each holding aloft the feather-hung poles.

They smelled the Gathering before they saw it, the sweet odour of burning wood mingling with the less pleasant stench of discarded bones and rotting meat, the palpable odour of a myriad unwashed bodies, of curing hides, of dogs and horses, the skin lodges. The air darkened with the smoke drifting from the hogans, transforming the sky to a yellowish hue as they crested the rise and paused above the encampment.

Kedryn remembered the vast camp he had seen spreading down the valley as he spied on the Horde and knew that what he saw now was smaller, but somehow even more impressive, for that other grouping had been viewed by night and this he studied in day's light, able to see its details.

It seemed the great hollow about that central mound sprouted a thousand mushrooms of giant size, a vast spread of mottled hides, barbarically splendid, for they hung with skulls and shields and bright pennants. They radiated from the mound that stood higher than the tallest shebang, a massive fire blazing at its apex, spreading back in ranks that suggested some kind of chaotic hierarchy, those closest to the mound more grandiose than their fellows, the structures declining in size and magnificence the farther from the centre they were. Narrow lanes ran between them, like the spokes of some enormous wheel, and they were filled with people, men and women and children jostling one another as they moved, kicking dogs from their path, the air loud with their chatter.

'The Ulan's lodge is there,' said Kalar, pointing, 'about it, those of the ala-Ulans. Beyond lie the shamans' and the bar-Offas'. Mine is there.'

Wynett relayed his words and Kedryn followed his finger to a hogan of medium size as Wyll tugged on a stirrup and said, 'And mine stands there.'

Kedryn was more interested in the lodge of Cord, the Ulan, which stood closest to the mound and consequently farthest from him. To reach it they would need to traverse the entire section of the Gathering on this side, and the lanes were too narrow to allow the horses passage together: to reach the Ulan he must relinquish Wynett's hand and ride blind through the massed ranks of the Drott.

He took a breath and said, 'Let us proceed.'

Wynett, equally impressed, said, 'May the Lady stand with us.'

Tepshen Lahl said, 'If they offer treachery, ride. I shall cover your back.'

'Come,' said Kalar, and began to descend the slope.

Dogs came running as they caught the scent of strangers and the two woodsmen began to curse and kick, using their poles to drive the animals away. The horses grew skittish, and Kedryn found himself struggling to hold the Keshi war-horse from striking out at the troublesome hounds. The two barbarians shouted what he took to be an announcement of his presence, for he caught the word hef-Alador as though in answer to the cries that rebounded from all sides and heard it repeated, echoing about him as they rode deeper into the spread of hogans. His nostrils clogged on the stench as they moved amongst the lodges and his ears strained for sound of blade sliding from scabbard, or axe rasping on shield. But Kalar kept a firm grip on his bridle, grunting as the stallion snickered and sought to bite at the dogs – or folk, for all Kedryn knew – as he led the way towards the centre of the encampment.

There was a great babble of noise then, and Kedryn felt the horse halt and Wynett's hand fumble into his, bringing back sight.

He saw the mound before him, and to his side a lodge even grander than it had appeared from the rim of the bowl. It was avenued with tall poles on which skulls stood, some still with tatters of hair and flesh adhering, leading to an awning beneath which grim-faced men with shaven heads and mail shirts stood clutching swords. They parted as a warrior he recognised from the peace talks strode between them, a squat man, his shoulders brawny beneath a cape of otter skin, his black hair bound in a long tail that swung with the rolling motion of his walk. His chest was bare beneath the cape, as if he scorned the cold, and marked with a lattice work of scars. About his neck circled a torque of interwoven gold and silver, its brightness contrasting with his dark skin. His face was flat, the nose broken, and a scar newer than the others ran from the point of his high cheekbone into the unruly mass of his raven beard. He wore breeks dyed a garish red, ending in hairy boots, and about his waist there was a wide leather belt from which hung a sheathed longsword. He stared at Kedryn and said in gutteral, hideously accented Tamurin, 'I am Cord, Ulan of the Drott. I bid you welcome, hef-Alador.'

'I thank the Ulan,' Kedryn responded. 'And offer him my congratulations on his elevation.'

Cord laughed then, a deep, rasping sound, and said, 'There were those who denied it. Now their skulls decorate my trophy poles.'

He pointed to the staff farthest from the entrance, where two globes of bone, fresher looking than the rest, hung.

'Threnol and Farlan. Now I own all the horses you gave us.'

'I wish you well of them,' Kedryn said.

Cord grunted, beckoning, 'Climb down and enter.'

He shouted something in the language of the Drott as they dismounted, and when Kedryn took Wynett's hand again he saw the shaven-headed Gehrim had sheathed their blades and stood in formal ranks, something close to respect in their fierce eyes as they studied the new comers. Kalar and Wyll stood close by, basking in the attention of the on-lookers who crowded round, whispering and pointing.

'These men brought us to you, Ulan,' Kedryn said. 'Should you find it acceptable to reward them for that service, I would see you compensated.'

Cord glanced carelessly at the two warriors and barked a question that was answered with a flurry of explanation. When they had finished he looked to Tepshen Lahl and nodded speculatively, then said, 'It shall be done as the hef-Alador wishes. For recompense . . . an ungelded stallion, perhaps?'

Kedryn's jaw tightened a fraction: although he did not share Tepshen's near-total distrust of the forest folk he had no wish to see them mounted on thoroughbred horses, for so equipped they would make formidable enemies. Nonetheless, he could see no way to avoid the gift without offending the chieftain and thus endangering his mission and all their lives. He nodded.

'It shall be so. I shall give word to the Warden of the Forests.'

'To Brannoc?' Cord chuckled. 'Make it clear word, then, lest that halfbreed wolfshead try to cheat me.'

'The bargain will be honoured,' Kedryn assured him, and Cord ducked his head.

'So be it, now enter.'

He led the way into the lodge, two of the Gehrim holding back the hide flaps that covered the entrance, letting them fall closed behind the quartet, shutting out sight and much of the sound of the Gathering. Cord took them through what appeared to be a kind of vestibule, or guard room, to the interior of the place and Kedryn found himself surprised at its barbaric opulence.

Thick wooden columns wound with multi-coloured ribbons supported the roof, leaving ample room for even one so tall as Kedryn to stand comfortably. The floor was scattered with rugs of cloth and animal skin, concealing the packed dirt beneath, and braziers gave both warmth and light, the charcoal that burned in their containers sprinkled with herbs that lent an aromatic scent to the air, masking the underlying odour of leather and sweat. Colourfully woven tapestries hung from the walls, and on a frame to one side stood a superb shield and scabbarded sword, a helmet chased with silver and gold, and a breastplate on which the design of a bull's head was worked in bas-relief. A table and chairs of ingenious design stood at the centre, their frames constructed in a manner that allowed them to be folded for travelling, on the table a silver jug and several cups of bone.

'Sit,' Cord said bluntly and clapped his hands.

A red-haired woman appeared from behind a curtain, her eyes curious as she glanced at the visitors, down-cast as she turned to the

Ulan. Cord said something to her and she disappeared, returning moments later accompanied by two other females carrying food.

The repast was set on the table and the women vanished again. The three Kingdomers shed their heavy furs and followed the Ulan's suggestion that they eat.

'Kalar says that the cat hailed you.' The Drott addressed himself to Tepshen Lahl, who merely nodded, grunting an affirmative.

'I might have killed you else,' the Ulan remarked negligently.

'You might have tried,' returned the kyo, eliciting an appreciative snort of laughter from the barbarian.

'He is your champion?' This to Kedryn, who nodded in turn and said, 'And my friend.'

'And she,' Cord looked appreciatively at Wynett, 'is your woman.'

'My eyes,' Kedryn said, feeling Wynett's grip on his hand tighten. 'She is a holy woman of the kingdoms, devoted to the Lady.'

'This is Ashar's domain,' Cord grunted. 'Though I respect the blue-robed ones. How came you here, and why?'

His eyes were set deep beneath craggy brows and as they fixed on Kedryn's face they sparked with a curious light.

Kedryn licked his fingers clean and said, 'We came through the Fedyn Pass, which closed upon us killing many of our companions. We come to regain my sight, which was taken by the ensorcelled blade of the warrior sent against me by the Messenger.'

Cord's right hand shaped the three-fingered gesture of warding; his left scratched in his beard. He said, 'The dead are sacrifice to Ashar, I think – a toll on your passing. The Messenger deserted us at the Lozin Gate and would not aid you were he here.'

'I seek the shade of his man,' Kedryn replied. 'I would enter the spirit world to ask his quadi to return that which he took.'

Cord's eyes grew wider and his hand ceased its burrowing. For long moments he stared at Kedryn as he might stare at one gone mad. Then he said slowly, 'That is a most perilous venture.'

'Nonetheless I would chance it,' Kedryn said, more calmly than he felt now that the reality approached so much closer. 'I have spoken with a most holy woman of our land and she has told me I must do this, accompanied by the Sister Wynett.'

Cord's dark gaze turned to Wynett. 'Ashar is mighty in the nether world, and Ashar has little love for your kind. Would you risk this?'

'I would,' she said simply, her calm impressive.

'I salute you!' Cord raised a bone mug in toast, the beer leaving

209

a frothy whiteness on his beard that he wiped away with the back of one huge hand. 'But to do this you must know the name of the one you seek. Do you?'

Kedryn shook his head.

'He was Borsus,' said Cord. 'He brought the Messenger to us as Kalar and Wyll brought you. But there was something else – wait.'

He rose, quitting the inner sanctum of the lodge and the waiting trio heard a muttered conversation before he returned, a frown on his broad features.

'He had a woman.' The Ulan's voice was low and troubled, as though he doubted the wisdom of imparting this information. 'Her name was Sulya. She wore another's torque and it is said the Messenger gave her to Borsus. Then took her life to put the glamour in Borsus' blade. I do not know what weight this knowledge may carry, but it is something.'

'Then you will aid us?' Kedryn asked.

Cord nodded ponderously. 'Because you are the hef-Alador,' he said slowly, 'and because of that I am Ulan of the Drott. And because I hope – if you survive – that you will give me a mare to match my stallion.'

'Done!' said Kedryn, without hesitation.

'That is not the whole of it.' Cord raised a hand. 'I want your word, spoken before your champion that he may carry it back, that if you die here your promises to me will be honoured. That the terms we agreed in your fort will remain. And that the Kingdoms will seek no revenge.'

Kedryn placed a hand over his heart, staring at the Drott. 'As hef-Alador and as Prince of Tamur, I give you my word, Cord. Whatever may transpire here you shall have your horses, and there will be no gainsaying the accords we made at High Fort.'

'And you?' the dark face turned to Tepshen Lahl. 'You will carry this word if need be?'

'I will,' the kyo promised.

'Then I will do what I can to aid you,' the Ulan said. 'It is a thing for the shamans, but I will tell them to prepare you and to open the way.'

Kedryn looked to Wynett. 'You are sure of this?' I should not blame you were you to dissent.'

She answered his gaze with firm, fond eyes and said, 'I am sure.'

Kedryn squeezed her hand, the love he felt tingeing his decision with fear. 'So be it,' he announced. 'When may it be done?'

'I will summon the shamans now,' Cord promised.

Chapter Ten

THE walls of Caitin Hold were built to withstand more than siege and even in the depths of such a wolfish winter as now gripped Tamur they held out the worst of the cold. Fires blazed in hearths and braziers stood strategically, giving the halls and chambers and corridors of the keep an air of cheerful comfort.

It was not a feeling shared by Bedyr Caitin as he lounged on the cushion-strewn bay of an embrasured window, idly watching the activity in the courtyard below. Grooms exercised that spring's foals there, turning the eager young horses from the comfort of the stables, watched by the mares, to gambol on the hard-packed snow. They were sturdy youngsters for all their gangling legs, the hardiness of the indigenous Tamurin stock mingled with Keshi bloodlines to combine endurance and speed, and they frisked and raced with the carefree joy of all young things. They reminded Bedyr of his son.

He turned to look towards his wife, feeling as he always did that surge of pleasure as he studied her profile, bent over a sampler. Yrla's raven hair was unbound, falling smoothly over the shoulders of her russett gown, gleaming in the light of the sun that shone through the frost-rimed glass and the glow of the fire that heated the chamber. Her hands were deft on the needlework, a tiny frown of concentration creasing her unblemished brow. It was odd to think that she approached her middle years, for time had marked her little, and while he knew that grey showed more prominently in his own thick, brown hair, hers remained as he remembered it from the first time he had seen her, stepping from the wagon in the Morfah Pass, come from Estrevan to meet her destiny. He had loved her on the instant, scarcely daring to hope she might return that love; overjoyed when the attraction proved mutual. He had thought his life must approach its peak when she agreed to marry him, and known it did when she presented him with a son. That there had been no more children had mattered little to either of them, for their delight in Kedryn was unalloyed, their pleasure in one another a source of constant delight.

He felt a need to touch her, to reassure himself with physical contact, and slid from the embrasure to cross to where she sat, setting a gentle hand on her shoulder.

Yrla smiled at the contact, turning her head to press a smooth cheek against his hand.

'You are worried.'

She set the frame of her needlework aside, shifting in the high-backed chair to look up at her husband. He was so handsome, this man she had chosen, tall and straight, the grey strands that showed in his dark hair serving only to lend him an air of dignity that was reinforced by the hawkish set of his features, the lines marking his tanned skin those of character rather than advancing years. She took his hands so that he stood before her, clad in simple shirt of thick linen, creamy, and plain brown breeks, the dirk that was the emblem of all Tamurin warriors sheathed on his belt. She looked into his eyes, seeing the hazel clouded as he smiled wryly and nodded.

'It has not been that long. And Tepshen rides with him. And the squadron.'

'I know.' Bedyr hooked a seat close and settled himself in it, still holding her hands, his thumbs moving absently to stroke the smooth flesh. 'But I still fret.'

'Inaction was never your strongest suit,' she murmured, 'but there is nothing we can do save wait.'

'Would I had been able to ride with them,' he frowned.

'Leaving me alone again?' Yrla's coquettish smile stole years, making her girlish. 'Do you tire of me so swiftly?'

Bedyr laughed, shaking his head. 'I shall never tire of you, my love. But . . .'

'But you had no other choice,' she interposed. 'You have a Kingdom to govern and Kedryn is a man now.'

'A blind man,' he sighed.

'Aye, but not for long if Lavia spoke aright.'

'Even so, he must enter the Beltrevan.' Bedyr stretched back in his chair, craning his neck to study the vaulting of the ceiling, 'And for all the promises of peace made at High Fort I cannot entirely trust the forest folk.'

'He is the hef-Alador,' she murmured, 'and they will respect that. Besides, do you think Tepshen would allow harm to come to him?'

212

'Not whilst he lives,' Bedyr answered, 'but Tepshen cannot go with him into the netherworld.'

'Nor could you,' she said. 'Only Wynett may accompany him there, and then they will be protected by the talismans.'

Bedyr nodded, smiling fondly. 'Would that I had your calm; your trust.'

'I was Estrevan trained,' Yrla reminded him, 'and I believe the Lady watches over him. She must if he is the Chosen One.'

'Aye,' Bedyr allowed, 'but does the Lady's strength extend into the forests? The Beltrevan was ever the domain of Ashar.'

'I think that power was weakened by the Horde's defeat,' she said thoughtfully. 'The strength of gods depends to large extent on the belief of men, and Kedryn slew Ashar's chosen champion. No sign was found of the Messenger, and the woodsfolk accepted peace. That, I am confident, must sap the potency of their god.'

'But Lavia – Estrevan – is confident the Messenger lives, still a threat,' Bedyr argued.

'And that is another reason Kedryn had to go,' Yrla countered. 'There was no other way, and so it is fruitless to fret over that which is inevitable.'

Bedyr ducked his head in agreement, loosing her hands that he might rise and go to the hearth, where a copper jug seethed gently, the wine it held giving off an aromatic steam, redolent of lush grapes, cinnamon and spices. He took the dipper and filled two plain clay mugs, passing one to his wife, raising the other to his lips.

'Where is the Messenger?' he queried rhetorically.

'I do not know.' Yrla sipped and shrugged. 'Lavia offers no insight, and there is no word from Estrevan.'

'Nor will be,' Bedyr grunted, looking to the window. 'This winter has closed the Morfah Pass, and the plains beyond must be icebound. I wonder sometimes if it had not been wiser of Kyrie to site her city in some more accessible location.'

'Too easy,' Yrla said. 'Too easy to reach, too easy to influence. Those who would study the way of the Lady must make an effort to reach the city, and those who would suborn Estrevan's influence must find it hard.'

'I know,' Bedyr grinned ruefully. 'I fret, and I cannot help it.'

'What news of Hattim's army?' she asked, seeking to divert his troubled mind.

'At last report it marched south,' he replied. 'Hattim, as you know, went ahead down the Idre. He is likely at Andurel now, and plying his suit. The army had reached Arvenna when last I heard, but reports are slow in this wolf-winter.'

'Will Darr agree – should Ashrivelle accept?' Yrla wondered.

'Darr spoke of Kedryn as a prospective bridegroom,' said Bedyr, 'but Hattim had already found favour in Ashrivelle's eyes; and he is there. As to Darr's agreeing – he will have little choice, I think, though adjustment will be required.'

'Hattim must relinquish one throne,' Yrla nodded. 'But which?'

'He wants the High Throne.' The frown returned to Bedyr's brow and the corners of his mouth descended in a disapproving curve. 'A council will be needed to decide the matter.'

'Would Hattim make so bad a king?' asked Yrla.

'He is vain and ambitious,' Bedyr shrugged, pouring more wine. 'Were he to renounce the marriage-right it would be no great problem, but the High Throne cannot stand empty and Darr has no other heir, save Wynett.'

'And Wynett is of Estrevan,' said Yrla, softly, wonderingly. 'Unless . . .'

'You think she may renounce her vows?' Bedyr shook his head, his voice dubious. 'She knows of Kedryn's love – and I know she reciprocates in some measure, at least – but she is a woman of great will and her dream was always to serve the Lady.'

'Even so, they share so much,' said Yrla, unconsciously echoing the thought that had passed through the mind of Tepshen Lahl. 'Hardship, danger – these things might well fan the flames of that attraction. And it is not unknown for one dedicated to Estrevan to change her mind.'

'Thank the Lady,' smiled Bedyr, touching her cheek. 'But you had not taken your final vows.'

'Even had I, you would have changed my mind,' Yrla responded, turning her face into his hand that she might brush his palm with her lips. 'And for all the emphasis Estrevan places on free will, there is a pattern to these things.'

'Do you say that Kedryn and Wynett are brought together by some design of the Lady's?' Bedyr asked, his voice thoughtful now.

'Mayhap,' said Yrla, slowly, as if she voiced thoughts gradually shaped and not yet defined clearly, 'I do not know. I do not believe Lavia knows, or Estrevan. But think on it – we are agreed that Kedryn *is* the Chosen One, the only one able to defeat the Messenger – wherever he may be now – and Wynett is the only one able to grant him sight, albeit temporary. Had they travelled to Estrevan

I think Wynett's determination to serve the Lady as a Hospitaller would have been reinforced, but events guided her away. Was it not thus with me? I intended to remain in the city until Galina showed me the Text, and then – of my own free will – I chose to travel east. And met you. And wed you. And gave birth to Kedryn. Now Wynett goes not to Estrevan, but with Kedryn – of her own choice, mark you – and perhaps out of that comes a resolution.'

'Lavia intimated that Wynett was necessary to Kedryn's regaining sight,' Bedyr said, slowly as his wife, 'but I had assumed once that was achieved she would return to her analeptic duties.'

'Maybe she will,' nodded Yrla, 'but do you not see the possible shape of a pattern? Should Wynett find her love for Kedryn – and I assure you it is there – stronger than her devotion to Estrevan, the Sisterhood would not object and she would be free to marry him. Thus presenting Darr with an alternative heir to the High Throne. Then Hattim could carry Ashrivelle off to Ust-Galich whilst Kedryn and Wynett stood ready to occupy the White Palace on Darr's death.'

'Do you think the Lady plans it this way?' Bedyr asked wonderingly.

'I do not know,' Yrla told him, 'but remember my own talent was similar to poor Grania's: that of foretelling. And the Lady guards these Kingdoms, and her vision was and is far deeper than ours.'

'My own Lady,' Bedyr raised his mug to his wife, marvelling at her ability to still surprise him, 'I toast you.'

Yrla smiled serenely, setting down her mug to resume her embroidery. 'I may well be wrong,' she murmured, 'but there are possibilities.'

'Hattim would take it ill,' Bedyr said quietly, enjoying the thought, 'but it would resolve the problem of the succession.'

'Indeed,' said Yrla. 'Now will you cease your fretting?'

Bedyr nodded, smiling, and settled again in the chair, stretching his long legs towards the fire, content to watch his wife as he contemplated the potential of her suggestion.

They sat like that as the afternoon extended towards evening, conversing idly, happy in one another's company, Bedyr's doubts stilled, at least for a while.

As the sun touched the western ramparts of the hold, painting the cold, grey stone with fire, that calm ended.

A knocking rang loud on the chamber's door, something in its clamour starting Bedyr from his tranquillity so that he was on his feet, left hand clamping instinctively on the sheath of his dirk even

215

as he called permission to enter. Yrla, too, felt it, setting down her sampler as she turned towards the door.

It flung open, a wide-eyed servant flattened against the wood as a burly man, his russet beard unkempt, strode past. He was bare-headed, sweat plastering his hair to his broad forehead, his cloak and boots attesting to long hours in the saddle, his grey eyes troubled as he gave brief salute, something close to fear in them.

'Gann Resyth?' Alarm edged Bedyr's voice as he recognised the chatelain of the Fedyn Fort. 'You have word of Kedryn?'

'Lord Bedyr,' Resyth ducked his head, the motion curt as his salute, 'Lady Yrla. I bring sad news.'

'Kedryn!' Yrla fought to maintain some semblance of calm as she studied the distraught face. 'What news, Gann Resyth?'

The stocky commander spread his hands wide, looking from man to woman, his lips pursing beneath the concealing bush of his beard.

'An avalanche,' he said helplessly, anguish hoarsening his voice. 'There was an avalanche.'

'Come, sit.' Bedyr fought his own trepidation, gesturing at his recently vacated chair. 'Drink, man, and compose yourself.'

He filled a mug with the mulled wine and handed the beaker to Gann Resyth, who gulped it down and wiped his beard, sighing gustily.

'Now,' Bedyr stood behind his wife, setting a firm hand on her shoulder, 'what has happened?'

Yrla took the hand, seeking comfort in the touch as she studied the chatelain's troubled features and prepared herself for the worst.

'They reached the fort,' Resyth began, 'some moons ago. Your son, the Sister, Tepshen Lahl and the escorting squadron. They announced their intention of entering the Beltrevan and even though Sister Gwenyl warned them of the danger, they proceeded into the Fedyn Pass.'

'What danger?' Bedyr asked curtly. 'Have the forest folk reneged on their promises?'

'Not the tribes,' said Resyth. 'Ashar! Sister Gwenyl warned them of his fell power; that it was strong in the pass.'

Bedyr felt Yrla's hand tighten its grip, unaware that his own clamped harder upon her. He said, 'Continue.'

Resyth nodded, took a deep breath, and said, 'They were two days out from the fort when we heard ... Lady preserve me, I am not sure what was heard! ... It was like laughter. Awful laughter. The tittering of a mad god! Sister Gwenyl declared she felt an evil presence and I led a troop into that dark place. I felt fear then, for I, too, felt . . . something.'

He shuddered, his hands clamped on the beaker he held as though he would crush the clay. Then he shook himself and straightened his back, stilling the tremor in his voice with visible effort.

'There was a storm of snow. A blizzard that howled between the walls, driven from ahead, not falling. For the better part of a day we rode blind, then the snow cleared and we saw a single horse. There was no rider; only the one horse, and that so panicked it took three men to hold it. We pressed on. And then we saw it: a wall of snow and stone that filled the pass. It was as though the Lozins had fallen! We could not climb it and nothing could have survived its tumbling. Kedryn – all of them! – must lie beneath that cairn.

'May the Lady forgive me that I should be the one to bring you this news, but your son must be dead.' His voice faltered, tailing off, and he shook his head, his eyes moist.

'I could come because the fort is no longer needed. The Fedyn Pass no longer exists.'

'No,' Yrla said softly. 'It cannot be. I cannot believe it.'

'My Lady,' Gann Resyth said mournfully, 'it is. It must be: nothing could have survived that downfall.'

'You saw no sign?' asked Bedyr, his voice slow with anguish. 'No smoke of camp fire? No sound?'

'Bedyr,' said the chatelain, 'there was no pass! The mountains fell down upon it, pushed by Ashar's hand. There was nothing to see because nothing *could* have survived. Kedryn is dead.'

'I will not believe it,' Yrla said.

Bedyr put both his hands upon her shoulders, seeking both to give and find strength. 'I will send word to Brannoc to search the forests,' he promised, 'but . . .' His voice broke, husky with held-back tears, 'I fear Gann Resyth is right.'

'No!' Yrla shook her head. 'The Lady would not permit it.'

'The Fedyn Pass is Ashar's domain,' said Resyth quietly.

'No!' Yrla repeated as tears coursed down her trembling cheeks.

There were five shamans, one for each clan of the Drott, and their presence filled Cord's lodge with a sour odour of unwashed flesh and rancid hides. Each one, the Ulan explained, represented a forest beast, taking that creature's strength and cunning for his own that he might employ it for the good of his clan. Bear, bull, cat, wolf and boar were represented, the hides of that animal that was the clan totem decorating the shamans' bodies, cut bloody from the sacrificed beast and adding greatly to the stink that radiated from the men. Two were venerable, the others younger, and all suspicious of the trio of Kingdom folk.

Cord spoke with them at length, and from their responses Kedryn surmised that they were dubious of his venture. Equally, he guessed that the defeat of the Horde and the subsequent disappearance of the Messenger had weakened the power of the medicine-men, for Cord became voluble as he spoke, several times drawing his dagger part way from its sheath. Finally, he shouted down the objections and summoned members of his Gehrim, who heard him out and then hurried from the lodge, returning with the ala-Ulans, their presence filling the hogan to bursting point.

More argument ensued, the gutteral language of the Drott echoing within the confines of the hide walls as horns of beer were passed about and Cord clearly found himself engaged in a struggle for supremacy. It seemed to Kedryn – as best he could tell from the tone of the dialogue and the way the men looked at one another – that the ala-Ulans sided with Cord, likely not from any great desire to aid him but in order to aggrandise their own secular power, whilst the shamans appeared to consider the request blasphemous. He clutched Wynett's hand, Tepshen Lahl to his right, thinking that had he the opportunity he would learn the byavan, or the language of the Drott itself, that in future dealings he might take vocal part, for it was frustrating in the extreme to know that his fate was debated whilst he could do nothing save wait, wondering at the outcome.

He studied the current speaker, an old man clad in the skin of a boar, the skull fashioned into a helmet, the lower jaw fastened below the wearer's own so that as he spoke the great curving tusks shifted before his seamed face, the eyes shadowed by the overlapping carapace. He saw those eyes turn towards him, taking in Wynett, and endeavoured to understand the expression there, but too soon they swung back to Cord and the argument was taken up by a younger man, muscled near as large as the bear whose skin he wore. An ala-Ulan spoke, his voice low, seeming pitched between deference and defiance, then Cord, then a shaman whose head was engulfed by the horned skull of a forest bull, another chieftain, then the Ulan again.

Round and round it went, the words seeming to fill the lodge with a palpable sensation that combined with the heat and the miasma of hides and bodies to produce an almost hypnotic air. Kedryn's head began to ache and he longed to stand, thrust aside the entrance flap and walk out into what he guessed must by now be the night. Instead, he willed himself to patience, gently easing out legs that threatened to go numb with too much sitting. He caught Wynett's eye and she smiled slightly, her face serene, her composure communicating to him so that his impatience eased, stilling into a determination to wait calmly. To his right Tepshen sat cross-legged, his face blank, still as an icon, appearing unmoved by the debate.

Then, abruptly, there was silence, falling so suddenly that Kedryn started, staring as Cord turned and said, 'They agree.'

'When?' he asked.

The Ulan scratched in his beard and said, 'Two nights from now they say the signs are most propitious.'

Kedryn ducked his head and said, 'I thank you, Ulan. And them.'

Cord apparently relayed this to the shamans, for they stared at the trio from beneath the frameworks of their masks and the bull-head nodded as though in acknowledgement, then the medicine-men rose and filed from the lodge, followed by the ala-Ulans.

Cord snorted when they were gone and tossed back a horn of ale.

'They were loath to aid you,' he remarked conversationally, 'and I needed to remind them you are the hef-Alador, and that I am their Ulan. I think the promise of the eagle persuaded them.'

He laughed at this, pounding a meaty fist on the table until it seemed the portable frame must shatter under his blows. Kedryn felt nervous that such threat had been needed and asked, 'They will do it? There will be no dissent?'

'When you go beyond?' Cord shook his head, recognising Kedryn's concern. 'No – I explained to them that should any ill befall you through their offices, I shall offer them as sacrifice.'

This amused him further, and he chuckled. 'There will be no treachery, my friend. You will be safe as their gramaryes can make you.'

'Thank you,' Kedryn murmured, not entirely reassured.

'It is nothing.' Cord waved a dismissive hand, his words confirming Kedryn's earlier suspicions, 'The shamans grow too proud and I welcomed the opportunity to remind them of my own power. The ala-Ulans, too, were with me – too many died storming your fortress on the word of a messiah who deserted us.'

Kedryn nodded, stretching stiffened legs, and Cord rose to his feet, beckoning them. 'Come, let my people see the hef-Alador; then we shall eat.'

They followed him from the lodge and the Gehrim fell into step around them as they were promenaded about the Gathering, warriors staring with open-eyed curiosity, women holding children aloft that they might see the slayer of Niloc Yarrum. It was dark and fires burned before the lodges, their glow overwhelmed by the blaze of the great pyre topping Drul's Mound. The light washed against the sky, driving back the night, though Kedryn saw that the moon approached its full corpus.

'When Mother Moon is bellied,' Cord told him, 'then it will be done.'

Kedryn ducked his head in agreement, his heart beating faster.

For the two days that followed they were the wonder of the camp. As it had been in High Fort, after the battle, Kedryn was required to relive his fight with Niloc Yarrum; women brought babies that he might touch them; Kalar and Wyll, basking in the glory of their finding, invited him into their lodges, showing him the possessions they had gained from Ragnal and Narr; Tepshen Lahl warily showed his sword; and Wynett replenished her stock of herbs; they ate heartily, and at night slept in Cord's lodge, Wynett modestly separated from the two men by a curtain.

And then came the night of the full moon.

During the day a lodge was erected between Cord's hogan and the mound. It was small and contained only one chamber, the hides that formed its roof and walls laced tight to the uprights, the floor the hard dirt of the clearing. The shamans appeared one by one to daub the outer walls with runes and symbols and the Gehrim set a circle of torches on ribboned poles about the structure. There was no evening meal offered Wynett or Kedryn, nor any beer, and as dusk fell the medicine-men presented themselves before the Ulan's shebang.

'It is time,' Cord said as rattles dinned outside, counterpointed by a thin wailing. He gestured at Tepshen Lahl and said, 'They go alone. No other may be present.'

Kedryn rose, clutching Wynett's hand, smiling at Tepshen.

'May your Lady be with you,' said the kyo gravely, his face unmoving.

'Aye,' Kedryn answered. 'And should we not return, remember my promises to Cord.'

The easterner nodded his agreement and Cord said, 'You have

courage. Both of you. May your gods and mine look on you with favour.'

They went out of the lodge then, to find the Gehrim, full-armoured and clutching spears, lined to form a narrow avenue between the hogan and the smaller structure, beyond them the watching, anticipatory mass of forest folk. The shamans stood at the entrance to the smaller construction and save for the noise of their rattles and the ululation there was no sound, even the roaring of the bonfire atop the mound seeming dimmed. Kedryn felt Wynett's hand tighten and he smiled at her.

'Lady bless us,' she whispered as they walked between the Gehrim towards the waiting medicine-men.

The shamans were painted now, their faces decorated in sem-blance of the beasts they took as spirit kin, their torsos bare and striped with bars of yellow, green, red, white and black. They ceased their wailing as the two drew close, then moved with shuffling, terpsichorean steps to surround them, shaking the rattles close to their faces, then down, and up again, in a movement akin to sweep-ing. Kedryn and Wynett stood silent, awaiting instruction, and the man wearing the guise of the bull beckoned them forwards as the wolf-skinned man held back the entrance flap.

Inside the lodge a fire burned in a low metal brazier, giving off a heat fiercer than was natural for the amount of coals therein, the flames granting the pictograms on the inner walls a life of their own, so that the cat and the bear, the bull, the wolf and the boar painted there seemed to move, prowling restlessly. The shamans entered behind them, the last drawing the flap tight, and each one delved. in his belt pouch to produce a handful of powdery leaves that they scattered into the brazier.

The fire flared then, long tongues of incandescent red and yellow lapping towards the roof, and a sickly-sweet odour filled the con-fined space. Kedryn and Wynett were motioned to the far side of the lodge, facing the entrance, and ordered by gestures to sit. Sweat began to course down Kedryn's cheeks, his eyes stinging as aromatic smoke coiled about his head. He felt Wynett's palm grow slick, and from the corner of his eye saw her brush strands of darkened blonde hair from her face.

The five shamans settled cross-legged around the brazier, the cat-man to Kedryn's right, the bull to Wynett's left. Again they fumbled in their pouches, this time producing sticks of dyed wood that they used to mark the cheeks and foreheads of the nervous pair. Then each in turn chanted in high-pitched syllables, dropping the sticks into the fire, the chant taken up by the next man until they sang in unison.

The strange singing ceased as though cut off in mid-sentence and five fists thrust towards the initiates, the fingers opening slowly, like the petals of a flower at dawn, to reveal tiny mushrooms, the pale flesh blotched with red. The bull-man nudged Wynett, touching his lips, and she took the mushroom he offered, swallowing the fungus with an expression of distaste. Kedryn followed suit, seeing that the bear-shaman facing him across the fire held two of the growths. He took one, Wynett the other. The mushrooms were slimy on the tongue, faintly bitter, but there was no immediately noticeable effect. He waited, aware of the painted faces watching him, wondering what would happen, how they would pass from this corporeal world into the insubstantiality of the netherworld.

The shamans began to sing again, but now it was a low, crooning sound, dirge-like and soporific. The heat seemed to grow, and the cloying odour filled his nostrils, extending tendrils of scent that became colours that danced before his eyes. He felt Wynett slump against him but could not turn his head because his gaze was fastened on the boar painted on the flap of the lodge, fascinated by its movements, by the way it raised its head and flung up its tusks. He turned his head slowly, the effort tremendous, but before Wynett came within his line of vision he became caught by the sporting of the painted wolf and heard it howl as it threw back its head, the jaws opening wide. Dimly, feeling that he should be surprised but not, he realised that he could no longer see the fire; it was a faint glow at the lower periphery of his vision, a dull redness that barely marked the shadowy darkness that now appeared to roil and shift of its own accord within the tent. He blinked but it did nothing to clear his sight, though, as if dreaming, he grew aware that he no longer held Wynett's hand, feeling her slump lower against him, her head a faraway pressure on his thighs.

He tried to shake his head, but his neck seemed held, too solid to move and all his attention was caught by the shifting of the shadows, the weird dance that slowly resolved into shapes he recognised, yet could not define.

Across the fire sat a bear. Not a man dressed in the creature's hide, but a massive, ivory-fanged bear, thick brown hair flowing over huge shoulders that extended into short arms ending in taloned paws. Next to it a wolf crouched on its hindquarters, studying him through cold, yellow eyes, a pink tongue lolling from jaws lined with wicked fangs. On the bear's other side sat a forest cat, all reddish yellow fur and slitted eyes, the blunt muzzle whiskered and toothed, the canines curving over black lips, a paw reaching as though in salute, claws extended towards him. His eyes flickered sideways and saw a grizzled, grey boar, tiny red orbs implacable as death behind the upthrust tusks, the flattened snout pulsing pinkly, one blunt-toed hoof pawing at the ground. Beside that was a bull, seated but still massive, all glistening black hide and swooping horns, its bovine gaze fixed solemnly on his face.

It said, 'Come,' and the sound was thunder that dinned against his ears, ringing in his head, allowing no refusal.

He rose and felt Wynett take his hand, knowing that it was for comfort rather than the granting of sight, for he was aware that they both realised he could see, or had no need of eyes in this place, or that to which the beasts took them.

The bull lurched to its feet and he saw that it stood on its hindlegs, a minotaur, a human hand gesturing that they follow. He obeyed, Wynett moving beside him, the animals that were also men forming about them as though a guard of honour, or protective, for he sensed awe in them, and fear.

'Come,' said the bull again, and they began to walk through the darkness, through the shadows, to where a light burned very bright, so radiant it seemed they approached the sun itself, though it gave no heat.

As they drew close the brilliance diffused, spreading and softening like the sun at dawn, driving back the shadows so that when the bull creature halted they stood in a penumbra, the half-light hinting at the contours of a cavern, or a tomb, the outlines not quite clear, lost in the mists that swirled restlessly at the edges of their sight. Before them was a dais of stone, on it a sarcophagus, ancient runes marking the sides. The light was brighter there and the were-creatures stood before it, respectfully.

'We ask entry to the portal.'

Again it was the bull that spoke, though now the booming voice was echoed by the others, each in turn, their request ringing from whatever walls confined the place, echoing into dying whispers that hissed away into silence.

From the sarcophagus there came a creaking as of ancient armour stirring, of unoiled leather stretched close to breaking point, and something rose, slowly at first, as if brought from a long sleep, but then swifter as it flung a hand to the stone and hauled itself clear of the kist. It stepped to the ground, if ground it was on which they stood, and faced them. Kedryn stared at it, seeing a harness of a style unknown in long ages. The helm descended in sweeping wings to the metalled shoulders of a brigandine, curving forwards to encompass the face, leaving only a lightless gap where nose and eyes and mouth should have shown. Vambraces moulded with indiscernible, eroded figures were belted to the arms, extending into gauntlets that hid most of the hands, save that no hands were visible, only a darkness that gripped a massive, wide-bladed glaive. Beneath the brigandine the legs were warded by grieves latched over boots to which plates of rusted metal were sewn. Of physical feature there was no sign: it was as though the creature consisted of shadow, blackness where flesh should be.

It spoke, and its voice was rusted as its armour, sending a waft of putrescence billowing noisome across the strange chamber.

'Who would enter that is not dead?'

'These two,' the bull-man answered, gesturing briefly at Kedryn and Wynett.

'Living flesh.' It seemed a condemnation. 'What business has living flesh here in the realm of the dead?'

The great sword rose as the thing spoke, swinging ponderously to its shoulder, poising there as the empty helm turned eyeless gaze on the intruders.

'He is the hef-Alador,' the bull-man said, his voice nervous, his own eyes flickering towards the upraised blade. 'He lost his sight to one dead, and would ask its return. She is his boon companion, and needful to his quest.'

'You have no need of eyes in this place. Stay and help me guard the gate.'

Kedryn felt the power of the creature as the blank casque faced him. He felt fear, and Wynett's hand tight in his. He said, 'I have a duty to those still living, and my time is not yet done. I was blinded by one now dead and would ask him for my eyes that I might dispense that duty. Wynett stands with me because I need her. Let us go by. I ask as hef-Alador.'

Noxious laughter rang through the chamber and the thing said, 'The one you slew is here. And many others. Perhaps some you would rather not face. I know you, hef-Alador, and I tell you – go back!'

'I cannot,' Kedryn answered, not sure where the words came

from, knowing only that they were right and that he must say them. 'I have travelled far to come to this place, and lost good friends in the coming. Did I go back now it would betray their trust, and that I will not do.'

'Said well,' declared the shadow creature, 'but know that if I grant you passage, you may not return. He who rules here is not a friendly master. A price may be demanded. Will you pay it?'

'I do not know what that price may be,' Kedryn replied, 'so I cannot say that I will pay it.'

'You tread dangerous ground,' the thing warned.

'All ground is dangerous to the blind,' said Kedryn. 'I would have back my sight – and I will risk much for that.'

Again the laughter echoed, foul stench reeking, the corruption of flesh, the words coming thick through it.

'You are brave, and you are the hef-Alador. For those things I will let you by. Though you may regret the passing. And you may not return.'

'I will chance that,' Kedryn said.

'Then go.' The thing nodded its ornate helm, the great blade lowering, the shadow-filled armour turning back to the sarcophagus, clambering heavily into the stone coffin.

'You have passed the first test,' said the bull-shaman. 'It is not the hardest, and we can go no farther. We return now to await you; you go there.'

Kedryn followed the direction of the pointing arm and saw beyond the kist an opening. 'My thanks for what you have done,' he said and moved with Wynett towards the orifice.

It seemed no more than a gap in the rock of the funerary chamber and he halted before it, looking back. The shamans were gone and the light began to fade, darkness creeping oily about the dais, no exit visible. He experienced a flood of panic, hope evaporating. From the opening before him came the nauseating stink of corruption, of decayed flesh and ordure, a growing, sussurating sound as if a myriad blowflies feasted on corpses. It rang in his ears, filling his head as the charnel reek filled his nostrils, and he felt his legs weaken beneath him.

'The talisman!' Wynett said, her voice thick as she gagged on the stink. 'Trust in the talisman and the Lady!'

He saw that she had drawn her own from the neck of her tunic and held it clasped firm in her left hand. He fetched his out and held it in his right, taking Wynett's free hand in a firm grasp. Instantly he felt a return of confidence, optimism surging, and, his eyes watering with the horrible odour, he stepped into the opening.

It was dark there, black as his blindness, but filled with shifting, writhing things that pulped beneath his feet and brushed against his face so that he held his mouth tight closed for fear they might enter and contaminate him with their corruption. Wynett pressed hard against him and he let go her hand to curve an arm about her shoulder, feeling her reach across her breast to link their fingers again. The smooth surface of the talisman was warm to his touch and as they proceeded into the occultation it began to glow, gradually lighting their way with a soft blue radiance that in itself was comforting.

He saw that they passed along a tunnel, the roof curving low above them, the walls slimy with moisture and reeking as if the midden of the Gathering drained there. The things that had touched them went with the light, as if creatures of the blackness and unable to bear the effulgence of the talismans. Before them, and behind, on the edges of the soft-hued illumination he caught glimpses of them, white wormy undulations like the maggots that cluster in untreated wounds, in the eye sockets of dead things, loathsome to observe and emanating a sightless malevolence. They slithered from the glow and Kedryn, still clutching Wynett hard against his side, trod more swiftly down the ominous passage.

It ended abruptly in a vast, grey-lit cavern, the way ahead sloping down, the walls sweeping up to immeasurable heights, the roof lost in opalescent mist that seemed to rise like fetid steam from the lake that filled the entire centre of the vault. All was grey and gloomy, walls and floor and water mingling in viscid union so that perspective was impossible to judge, the descent before them seeming simultaneously gradual and horrendously steep. Grey things with wings like tattered cloth flapped painfully in the heated air, emitting shrieking cries that stabbed at ear-drums, whilst from the lake came a steady moaning as though a thousand thousand souls wailed in hopeless remorse. Confronted with some degree of light, the talismans lost part of their radiance, and as Kedryn began the descent he let go the stone, needing his arm free for balance as he felt the surface beneath his feet slick and treacherous. He brought his arm from Wynett's shoulder, taking her hand again that they might support one another on the gradient.

The bat-like flying things fluttered close as they descended, the proximity revealing human faces set between the ragged wings, tiny eyes filled with tears, little hands extending from the grey membranes. 'Go back,' their shrill voices called, 'go back before you are lost.'

It was hard to ignore them, for there was an imperative in their warnings that struck deep into the soul, but as the slope flattened, the two intruders in this land of the dead touched the talismans again and found fresh strength, blocking their ears to the shrieking cries and ignoring, as best they could, the unpleasant closeness of the winged beings.

They reached the shore of the lake and saw wavelets lap turgidly against the limitless extent of that doleful strand, each one leaving a foul grey froth on the dripping stone. Things moved beneath the surface, glutinous bubbles rising and bursting to release sharp gasses that stung their nostrils, threatening to cramp their bellies with nausea. There appeared no way across and Kedryn was loath to enter the colloidal liquid so he began to walk along the shore, still plagued by the bats that fluttered about their heads, maintaining their fluting warnings like some horrible air-borne chorus. How long they walked he did not know, for time had no meaning here and there was no way in that depressing uniformity to estimate distance or duration, but finally they saw a difference in the shore and the surface of the mucous lake. A slab of stone intruded on the mere, and beyond it others, extending out into the mist-shrouded distance, precarious stepping stones. They were rugged and uneven, like ill-formed teeth, offering at best a dangerous footing, and lapped by the viscous, bubbling stuff. Kedryn studied them dubiously, unsure whether to risk a crossing or continue along the doleful strand.

'We might march forever,' Wynett suggested, 'and these at least offer a way forwards. I think we must cross.'

'Or try,' he nodded, remembering the warning of the guardian.

She smiled encouragingly and he touched her cheek, wondering if he could have found the courage to attempt this awful quest without her.

'Go on,' she urged, and he stepped up on to the first extrusion of stone, taking a deep breath as he trod across to the next, his arms thrust out to the sides, the blocks beneath his feet uneven, threatening to spill him into the menacing fluid.

Wynett followed close behind and they moved warily out over the lake. The spacing of the stones was irregular as their surfaces and they proceeded in steps and hops and jumps, often teetering on the verge of falling, aware that whenever they seemed poised to plunge into the reeking brew the moaning grew louder, anticipatory, the bubbles rising faster, as if creatures breathed below, eager to drag them down. The shoreline was lost to sight when something huge rose to the right. A massive, crenellated back humped from the surface, then a triangular head that dripped tentacular whiskers that waved, questing of their own accord, about a wide lipless mouth in which rows of saw-edged teeth glinted. Eyes the colour of smouldering coals turned towards the travellers and a sigh, more awful for its longing its loudness hissed from the gaping maw. The monster's neck undulated as it dived, and wide-spreading ripples marked its passage towards the stepping stones.

'Quickly!' Wynett called. 'Mayhap we can escape it.'

'No!' Kedryn's answer was firm. 'It will reach us ere we reach the far shore. We must face it.'

He smiled at her, more confidently than he felt, bracing his legs on the bumpy surface, studying the advancing crest of ripples.

This time the head appeared first, the long neck serpentine, writhing up until the jaws hung above him, the red eyes glaring down, liquid cascading from between the ghastly teeth as the feelers fluttered towards him. Kedryn clutched the talisman in his left hand, raising the right as though to command the leviathan.

'You defy me?'

It was not possible for jaws so shaped to speak, but words came out, sibilant, menacing.

'We seek to cross,' Kedryn answered, not knowing what else to say. 'We offer you no harm.'

'Nothing can offer me harm,' the creature boasted, breath redolent of rotted fish gusting about Kedryn's face. 'I destroy all.'

'We are not of your realm,' Kedryn shouted into the piscine stink. 'You have no right to take us. The guardian at the gate gave us entry.'

'That suit of stinking armour?' Fishy contempt sprayed Kedryn. 'That is nothing! I am everything.'

The neck thrust higher, the jaws opening, poised to descend, wide enough to swallow Kedryn whole. He opened his left hand, extending the talisman to the length of its retaining cord.

'Can you swallow this?'

The great head snatched back, turning from side to side that each eye in turn might study the faintly pulsating jewel, and angry breath hissed from the craggy nostrils.

'What are you?' it demanded.

'I am a man,' Kedryn said. 'I am Kedryn Caitin. I am the hef-Alador. And I would pass with my companion.'

'So,' the thing hissed slowly, 'you are the one. I know of you, and I know that you are awaited. There is one has greater claim on you than I – so I shall let you pass. You and yours. But I hunger, so you had best go swiftly.'

Kedryn nodded, unsure of the creature's meaning, but unwilling to risk questions or delay longer. If something waited for him, it would appear in time, and for now the imperative was to cross the lake and leave this thing behind. He turned to Wynett, seeing that she, too, held her talisman out towards the monster.

'Come,' he called. 'Come quickly.'

Wynett needed no further bidding and followed him as he leapt from stone to stone across the mere, not turning to see the leviathan sink slowly back beneath the surface, not seeing the smile that decorated its impossible mouth.

Their legs ached from the jumping before they saw the farther shore and sprang gratefully to drier ground, hard, grey gravel that was hot to the touch beneath them. They halted, throwing themselves panting down, at last daring to look back over the sullen grey lake. It still bubbled, but now there was no sign of the monster, and they felt almost relieved, happy to have escaped its threat.

'I have awaited your coming,' said a husky voice behind them. 'It will be good to have companions in this place.'

Their breath caught then and they drew back from what stood before them, for it was recognisably human and that rendered it, somehow, more awful than the nightmare creations they had so far encountered. It stood on two blood-streaked legs, its loins wrapped in gore-soaked furs, bones visible through the wounds that gashed its sides and chest, its arms lacerated, tendons showing. Maggots crawled in the wounds, blind and white and fat. Around the neck was a gash lipped with old, still-oozing blood, the head set at a curious angle, as though barely connected. The lips were dried and curled back from yellowing teeth, the nostrils gone to ugly holes either side of a rotted jut of bone, the cheeks hollow, stretched like ancient leather between the thrust of the jaws, from which hung the mangy remnants of a beard. Worst of all were the eyes, for they were no longer there, only sockets in which worms crawled, and more maggots, falling loose as the apparition spoke. It plucked one absently from its ravaged chest and popped the wriggling obscenity between its fleshless lips, gulping it down casually as if it were a sweetmeat.

'Do you find me so distasteful?' The carrion creature laughed, spewing maggots. 'There are worse than I here. And it was your father did this to me. Your father and the one called Brannoc.'

It touched its neck, fingering the wound there, and its head tilted, more crawling things dropping from the opened wound.

'You are Borsus,' Kedryn said softly, his gaze transfixed in horrible fascination on the vermiculate face.

'I am,' the creature nodded, the movement threatening to topple the skull from its fragile connection, 'and you are Kedryn Caitin.'

Kedryn saw then that the shade of Borsus was not alone, for across the gravelled shore, where the stones seemed hotter, steam rising to form a reddish mist, shapes moved, shuffling within the fog. They were unclear, and he was thankful for that mercy, for they had the delineaments of madness and they emanated a terrible lust, as if they waited for some sign, the giving of which would propel them forwards to slake the ghastly hunger he felt in them.

'You took my sight,' he said.

'The sword that Taws gave me took your sight,' Borsus responded, and there was an echo of grief in his voice. 'It took the life of the woman I loved – as you love her.'

A hand rose to point at Wynett, standing slightly behind Kedryn, to his right.

'That was how Taws put the glamour in it,' the worm-eaten cadaver continued. 'He took the blade and drove it through her heart; through mine in the doing. I was his man, yet he condemned me to this.'

His gesture encompassed the seething mere and the steaming beach, grubs falling like tears from the sockets of his skull.

'I would end such things,' Kedryn said. 'Give me back my sight and I shall give you a revenge.'

'Revenge?' Borsus shook his head. 'How can you revenge me? Taws is the Messenger; Ashar's creature.'

'He deserted the Horde,' Kedryn said urgently, seeing the things that skirted the edges of the mist creep closer, sensing that all depended on this argument. 'I slew Niloc Yarrum and Taws' magicks failed against me. You took my sight, but not my life, and the Horde was defeated. The Messenger fled and has not been seen again. Your people hail me as the hef-Alador. I have the support of Cord, Ulan of the Drott. The shamans of your people brought me to this place, that I might find you and gain back my sight.'

'Such doings,' husked Borsus, 'belong to the world of men. The world of the living. We are the dead here.'

'You do not find peace here,' Kedryn said, 'and in the world of men the power of Ashar is weakened. There is peace between the forest folk and the Kingdoms. Give me back my sight and I shall seek out Taws and slay him, and you will be revenged.'

'You promise much,' the cadaver murmured drily, 'and I lost much. Perhaps I will make a bargain with you.'

'What?' asked Kedryn.

Beyond the ghastly mummy the advancing figures halted, closer now, but momentarily unmoving.

'I lost my woman,' Borsus said. 'Give me yours and I will give you back your sight.'

'No,' Kedryn replied without hesitation.

'Then you shall remain here,' said Borsus. 'Give her to me and you shall return, sighted again.'

'I will not,' Kedryn said.

Wynett stepped past him then, her face pale in the opalescent light of the cavern, set in grave lines, a hand clasped firmly about her talisman.

'If I remain, you will return his sight?' she demanded. 'And send him safely back to the world of the living?'

'I will,' Borsus promised.

'No!' Kedryn shouted.

Woman and corpse ignored him. Borsus said, 'If you will stay and be my woman, I will do this.'

Kedryn reached out, fastening firm hands on Wynett's shoulders, thrusting her back. 'This cannot be!' he yelled. '*I* will not agree to this! I had rather remain blind than condemn you to this place.'

Wynett struggled in his grip, tears in her eyes, though her jaw was set firm and fierce determination blazed in her blue eyes, hot as the light that pulsed, unnoticed, from the two talismans.

'You are the Chosen One,' she said, fighting to break loose, 'and you have a duty, a destiny that you must fulfil. You *must* regain your sight.'

'It is too great a price,' he gasped, fighting a fear greater than any he had known. 'Your life for my sight? No! If my destiny demands that, I spurn it. I will not bargain you away. I love you!'

'And I love you,' she said, the tears welling now, spilling over her cheeks, though her voice remained firm. 'I love you with all my heart, and if I must, I will sacrifice myself. I am not important – you are.'

'I am nothing without you,' he groaned. 'Without you there is

231

nothing for me. I had sooner remain here with you than live without you.'

He clutched her to him, pressing her to his chest, his arms protective about her, his face haggard as he saw the unacceptable enormity of the bargain offered. She clung to him, weeping and shaking her head as he pressed his lips to her hair, her cheeks, her mouth, turning so that he faced the wormy figure of Borsus again.

'I will not accept this bargain,' he said. 'Return Wynett to the living and keep me here.'

'No!' Wynett fought free of his encircling arms, turning herself that she, too, might appeal to the shade of the warrior. 'Do not listen to him! I *will* remain if you will send him back.'

'Do you love him so much?' Borsus asked, wonder in his grating tone.

'I do,' she said.

'And you,' the cadaver asked of Kedryn, 'would you truly condemn yourself to this netherworld for her sake?'

'Aye,' Kedryn answered, unhesitating, 'I would.'

'Such love,' Borsus murmured. 'Taws gave Sulya to me with a glamour, but I loved her for all of that. Would that I had her now; whole. Would that we could love as do you.'

He paused, head lowered, so that the rear of his neck split open, tumbling writhing grubs to the gravel at his feet. Then, slowly, he raised his awful visage to fasten the wormy sockets on the two before him.

'Go back,' he said hoarsely. 'Such a love deserves to live. Go back sighted, Kedryn Caitin, and take this woman to you.'

He reached out then, savaged arm extended towards Kedryn's face, something that might have been a smile stretching his withered lips as he touched fingers to Kedryn's eyes.

As he did so the light of the talismans pulsed fiercer, the blue radiance growing until it encompassed the three figures standing on that bleak shore, surrounding them with its effulgence. Kedryn held Wynett close, feeling something change within him, conscious of the watching shades retreating into the fog even as a sense of well-being filled him. The light grew brighter, driving back the grey shadows until the three of them stood alone in an enclave of peace. Borsus lowered his hand, a rasping sigh escaping his cankered mouth, and for an instant Kedryn saw him whole, full-fleshed and smiling through a thicket of beard. Then he was gone and there was only the light, blue-bright as a summer sky, glad as Wynett's eyes.

232

It pulsed faster, filling his vision until he was blind again and he blinked, aware of tears on his cheeks, aware of a dully-glowing brazier that was red, and of five masked figures hunched within the confines of a smelly lodge. Aware of Wynett stirring beside him, lifting her head from where it had fallen against his thigh, raising her face towards him. Aware that he held her about the shoulders, their hands not touching. And that he saw her.

'Kedryn?' she asked wonderingly.

He raised his hands, deliberately breaking the contact between them. And still he saw her.

'I see you,' he said. 'I see you and I love you.'

'And I,' she answered, almost fearfully. 'I love you. I cannot gainsay it – I love you, Kedryn.'

He took her face between his hands then, staring into eyes blue as the radiance that still burned in his memory, but lovelier, for in them he saw the confirmation of her words, the undeniable promise, and that filled him with a soaring joy greater even than the regaining of his vision.

He bent his head towards her and she put her hands about his neck, drawing him closer, her lips parting as he kissed her, the response of her mouth the final testament, and a promise of the future.

233

Chapter Eleven

THE mehdri despatched to bring word to Caitin Hold was not privy to King Darr's wish for procrastination and so pressed on, as was the custom of his guild, with all speed. Nonetheless, he found his going slowed by the rigours of winter, the more so the farther he travelled from Andurel. He proceeded, at first, by river craft, embarking from the city on a sleek brigantine christened the *Vallanna*. She tacked into a howling north wind that by the time they reached Rostyth, a mere five days from Andurel, was threatening to shred the brigantine's sails. The mehdri stayed on the Idre another three days and then opted to take his chances travelling overland, disembarking at Larns, where he collected a horse from the guild stables and struck out for Amtyl. There he exchanged his near-exhausted animal for a fresh mount and continued on in stages to Kryst, Borwyth, Cadula and Norren. In the latter town he waited out a blizzard that gusted down from the Geffyn, closing the roads for five days. Then, fresh-mounted and equipped with a pack animal, he began the journey to the foot of the plateau. He was almost frozen by the time he reached Ganthyl, and spent two days easing the black threat of frostbite from his fingers and toes before attempting the ascent of the Geffyn. He was gratified to find sunlight awaiting him when he crested the massif and changed his mount and packhorse in Wyrren. Four days later he reached Caitin Hold.

The Lord Bedyr and the Lady Yrla were not there. They had received word, the mehdri learnt, that their son, Kedryn, had likely fallen victim to an avalanche whilst attempting entry into the Beltrevan through the Fedyn Pass, and had gone to High Fort to seek information, and the help of the Forest Warden. The mehdri changed animals once more and started east to High Fort. At least, he thought, as he crossed the snow-shrouded plain, he would be able to take ship from the fort.

As he rode, Bedyr and Yrla were ensconced with Rycol, chatelain of High Fort, and his wife, the Lady Marga Cador na Rycol, in a chamber high above the great canyon of the Idre. It was dark and the shutters were closed over the windows, rattling as the wind blowing out of the Beltrevan gusted eerily about the tower. A fire blazed in the hearth, lending the wood-panelled room a cosy air that was not reflected in the faces of the occupants. Two rangey hunting dogs dozed restlessly by the flames, the mood of the humans communicating so that the heavy-jawed heads rose periodically to study them, the thick tails flicking. They were ignored, as was the wine and sweetmeats the Lady Marga had brought in.

She, Yrla and Rycol sat in cushioned chairs about a carved-legged table. Bedyr could not, and paced the room restlessly, thumbs hooked in the dagger belt encircling his black leather tunic. Crescents of shadow hung beneath his eyes and there was a gauntness to his handsome features that was magnified by the careless combing of his long brown hair. His wife appeared better composed, though visible to any who knew her well was the fear that lurked in her seemingly calm grey gaze. She sat with hands folded in her lap, still against the dark blue of her gown.

'He will arrive soon,' Rycol promised, watching Bedyr turn before the door and retrace his steps. 'Word is out.'

'I know.' Bedyr smiled a wan apology, his tension unrelieved. 'You have done all you can, old friend, but – Lady help me! – I cannot bear this waiting.'

'Sit down,' Yrla advised, her voice weary, 'your pacing serves only to disturb us all.'

Bedyr sighed and nodded, dropping heavily into a chair. 'Where might he be?' he asked.

'Brannoc comes and goes,' answered Rycol, 'and few know exactly where he might be at any given moment. But I have despatched riders to every known haunt, and they will have sent word on into the forests. He will be here ere long.'

Bedyr grunted and reached for the silvered jug of wine, raising it questioningly towards his wife, who shook her head, before pouring himself a glass. He sipped and set the glass down, staring moodily into the rich, red liquid.

'It has been six days.'

'And may be six more,' Yrla said quietly. 'We can do nothing but wait.'

'I should have gone with him,' Bedyr muttered.

'And left me to wonder about you both?' Yrla shook her head, reaching across the table to take his hand. 'Gann Resyth said an avalanche blocked the Fedyn Pass. He had no proof Kedryn fell beneath it.'

'But we do not *know*,' Bedyr retorted miserably. 'That is the rub of it.'

'Is that worse than confirmation?' she enquired mildly, hiding her own fears. 'Would you rather Gann Resyth had brought us back a body?'

'No!' Bedyr's answer was fierce, startling the dogs into nervous watchfulness.

'Then we still have hope,' Yrla said. 'Hold on to that. Trust in the Lady, for she was surely with them.'

'In Ashar's domain,' Bedyr grunted, then shook his head, enfolding his wife's hand between both of his. 'Forgive me, but I am more accustomed to action than this damnable waiting.'

'You waited well enough when we sat in darkness, besieged,' the lady Marga said mildly.

'I had my son with me then, and an enemy I could face,' retorted Bedyr, sharper than he had intended, paling the rosy cheeks of the plump little woman. He saw her smooth her greyed hair nervously and smiled placatingly. 'My apologies, Marga. It seems I can do nothing but offer apologies for my fretting.'

Marga smiled, regaining her composure. 'There are none needed, Bedyr. I share your concern – we all do.'

'I know,' he said, and climbed to his feet again, walking to the hearth, where he stroked absently at the two brindle heads that rose enquiringly at his approach. 'Would, though, that I had word. Of whatever has transpired.'

Rycol rose, lean and hawkish, his stern features set in carefully measured lines, and went to join Bedyr, setting a hand to his friend's shoulder.

'Is it not as it was then?' he asked. 'We could not see our enemy then, or know what he planned, but we rode it out.'

'Aye, with Kedryn,' came the answer, Bedyr's gaze fixed on the flames that danced and fluttered within the confines of the stone. 'And for all the gramaryes of the Messenger we knew our enemy was physical. We knew we should face warriors in the end. This is different.'

'It is another kind of waiting,' Yrla said. 'A kind you men know little of, and we women much. You ride off to war whilst we wait behind, not knowing if you will return. Or if you will come back maimed. When you rode into the Beltrevan with Kedryn, did you think of me then? Did you think how I worried whilst you were gone? Not knowing if I should see my husband and my son again? Now you share that unknowing, that woman's fear.'

Bedyr's head rose slowly from his contemplation of the flames. Yrla's voice had been mild, and he knew her well enough to know there was no condemnation in her words, only truth, but that verity cut deep. He turned towards her, his eyes moist, and when he spoke, his voice was grave and full of love.

'You are right, my Lady, and I stand guilty of selfishness. You and our son are the two most treasured things I have, and I had not seen these matters from your side. I ask again that you forgive me.'

Yrla made a dismissive gesture. 'We need not speak of forgiveness for there is no accusation or guilt. We deal with gods and their ways are unguessable, implacable. We are caught in a web of too complicated a pattern for our mortal eyes to discern, and we can do nothing but hold to our faith and maintain our hope. Until such time as we know beyond doubt that Kedryn is dead, we must believe he lives.' She smiled at her husband and then said in a brisker tone, 'Now, I shall go to the chapel to pray.'

'I will accompany you,' said Marga.

Bedyr crossed the room to hold Yrla's chair, and when she rose he took her hands, kissing her cheek. 'Thank you, my love,' he murmured. 'You give me strength.'

Yrla reached to smooth his unkempt hair. 'He cannot be dead,' she said softly. 'I do not believe the Lady would allow that.'

Bedyr nodded and watched her go from the chamber, the shorter Marga bustling beside her. When the door was closed he turned to Rycol.

'No word from Fengrif?'

'The signal towers report nothing,' answered the chatelain. 'Fengrif has sent out riders from Low Fort, but . . .'

He spread his hands helplessly and Bedyr nodded, turning his back as he went to a window and threw open the shutters. A blast of winter-chilled air rustled his hair as he leant against the embrasure, staring into the darkness. Behind him the dogs growled softly at the intrusion of cold and Rycol murmured them to silence, pouring himself a measure of wine that he sipped as he studied Bedyr's back, seeing the tense set of the broad shoulders, wishing there was more he could do than advise patience; knowing there was nothing else, and that patience was the hardest thing.

Bedyr found no answers in the night, only the mockery of

the wind. The sky was clear, the orb of a full moon pooling a tracery of pale light over the canyon walls, silvering the restless surface of the river below, its lapping a counterpoint to the melancholy draught. Watchfires sparkled crimson on the ramparts and occasionally through the gusting he heard the chink of mail and the sound of voices, too wind-blown, too far away, to be discernible. He envied Yrla the faith that gave her calm, his own in more material things: the edge of a cared-for blade, the buckling of sound armour, the strength of a good horse. Lady, he thought as the night air chilled the tears that pressed from his eyes, forgive my lack of piety and hold it not against my son. Let him live, I beg you.

As if in answer to the silent prayer he heard a knocking at the door and spun about as the portal opened to reveal a soldier swathed in heavy winter cloak, his hair windswept.

'My Lord Rycol, my Lord Bedyr,' the man announced, 'the Warden of the Forests requests an audience.'

'Brannoc? Send him in, man. Quickly!' Rycol barked, startling the warrior so that he jumped back to reveal the figure waiting behind him.

'Brannoc!' Bedyr echoed. 'Where have you been?'

'My Lords?' The Warden of the Forests stilled the elaborate salute he had been about to execute, the smile on his tanned features dying still-born. 'What is wrong?'

He entered the room and shucked off his wolfskin cloak, tossing it carelessly to a chair as his midnight eyes studied their faces, the long lashes rising in surprise. He ran a careless hand through his braided hair, setting the feathers and shells that decorated the raven locks to fluttering. As was his custom, he wore motley leather, a Keshi sabre hung across his back, a throwing knife at his hip, another revealed strapped to his left forearm. Rings of Keshi origin shone on his left thumb and the third finger of his right hand, and a hoop of silver hung from his left ear, a necklace of leather and beads about his throat. He wore no badge of office, and to those who did not know him he would have appeared what he was, and had been: a halfbreed wolfshead, part Keshi, part Tamurin, part barbarian.

'Kedryn,' Bedyr said.

'Kedryn?' Brannoc crossed to the fire, absently dislodging the hounds that he might present himself closer to the warmth. 'Surely Kedryn travels to Estrevan with the lovely Sister?'

'They are in the Beltrevan.' Bedyr faced the former outlaw across the table, pausing as he marshalled his thoughts, reminding himself that he was, in addition to a distraught father, the Lord of Tamur. 'Estrevan deemed it wiser he travel to the Drott in search of his eyes. It seems only the shade of the warrior who took his sight may restore it, so he went to the Drott. Wynett, Tepshen Lahl – a squadron – accompanied him. Then Gann Resyth brought word from the Fedyn Pass that an avalanche had buried them. The Lady Yrla and I came here, to seek you out.'

'Gann Resyth brought no bodies?' Brannoc's voice was flat, slightly accented.

'No.' Bedyr shook his head. 'He saw only a single horse. The fort's Sister sensed evil – Resyth presumed Ashar's work.'

'The fire god has power there,' Brannoc nodded. 'It had been better they came here, that I might have escorted them.'

'Estrevan deemed there was little time to waste.' Bedyr clasped a chairback, frustrated by the need to explain. 'The Sacred City believes the Messenger is abroad; that he works Ashar's design. And Kedryn is the only one able to defeat him.'

'Where?' asked Brannoc, instinctively shaping the warding gesture of the tribes.

'That they could not surmise,' said Bedyr, impatient. 'They know only that he lives. For that reason it was paramount Kedryn regain his sight.'

'And he went into the Fedyn Pass,' said Brannoc as though digesting the news, 'and there was an avalanche that was likely Ashar's doing, and you wish me to enquire of the Drott whether he lives.'

He omitted, Or not, and Bedyr nodded. 'I would not chance the upset of our peace treaty by entering the forest with the men we should need to find them.' Like Brannoc he did not speak the alternative. 'And you are likely to get word faster. Hence, Rycol's summons.'

Brannoc ducked his head, tugging thoughtfully on a braid. 'The Drott territories are a long ride west and north,' he murmured. 'And it is the time of the Gatherings – there will be little intercourse between the tribes, so little hope of word filtering down. I had best leave at dawn, alone. I shall travel faster without the encumbrance of an escort, but even so it will take a while to reach the Drott. And return with word.'

'At dawn?' Bedyr asked.

'I need a sound night's sleep,' said Brannoc. 'I have some hard riding ahead of me.'

'Thank you,' Bedyr said.

'Your son is my friend,' answered the halfbreed. 'Now, I need a bed, and before that food and drink.'

Without further ado he settled himself at the table and downed a glass of wine, rapidly followed by a second as Rycol shouted for servants to bring victuals and prepare a bed.

Yrla and Marga returned while he was eating, and he rose, bowing courteously.

'My wife, the Lady Yrla Belvanne na Caitin. Yrla, this is Brannoc, Warden of the Forests. The Lady Marga you already know.'

Bedyr effected brief introduction and Brannoc nodded, smiling at the two women. 'Lady Marga, you are well, I trust. And Lady Yrla – I regret the circumstances of our meeting, but assure you I shall do all in my power to bring Kedryn safely to you.'

Yrla paused, somewhat taken aback by so courtly a greeting from a man she had heard described as wolfshead, who wore the appearance of some mixed-blood forester. Then she smiled and said, 'Good Warden, I thank you. My husband has spoken of you, as did my son, and both in glowing terms.'

'I am flattered.' For all the gravity of the situation Brannoc could not keep the bantering tone from his voice for long. 'But that weighty title sits a trifle heavily on my shoulders and I would ask you to call me Brannoc, as do all my friends.'

Yrla nodded gravely and said, 'Then Brannoc it shall be, for I am glad to count you friend.'

'He leaves at dawn,' said Bedyr, adding, as he saw the question in his wife's eyes, 'Alone.'

'I shall travel faster that way,' Brannoc explained, resuming his seat and continuing to eat with a gusto the others could not muster. 'The forest folk trust me and it is early yet to send armed Tamurin into the Beltrevan.'

Yrla nodded, taking a chair across from the Warden. 'You have heard nothing from the woodsfolk?'

Brannoc shook his head. 'It is the time of Gatherings, Yrla. The clans of each tribe come together and there is little intercourse between them until First Day, when they return to their hunting grounds.'

'How will you go?' Rycol demanded.

'Through the pass and then due west,' said Brannoc. 'Along the

Lozin wall until I reach the Saran, then north and west along the line of the river to Drul's Mound. That is where the Drott gather, and where Kedryn must go to find the quadi.'

'Do you think the shamans will agree to help him?' asked Yrla.

Brannoc shrugged. 'It is hard to predict what a Drott shaman will do, but – yes. The defeat of the Horde weakened their hold, and now Cord is Ulan, and he was never fond of the medicine-men. Kedryn is the hef-Alador and I think that Cord will respect that.'

'Is Ashar's power weakened?' she demanded.

Again Brannoc shrugged. 'If his power depends on worship, then it might well be. When the Horde broke and the Messenger disappeared, there were many who felt they were betrayed by their god.'

'Do you hear?' Yrla turned towards Bedyr, fresh hope in her eyes.

'I hear,' Bedyr nodded. 'But we should not underestimate his strength.'

'No,' Brannoc agreed. 'Ashar is a vengeful god and he will fight for what he considers his.'

A silence fell then and Brannoc finished his meal, taking a last cup of wine before rising and asking that Rycol indicate where he might sleep. 'I shall do my best,' he promised.

'My thanks,' Yrla said.

Bedyr smiled grimly and nodded.

The next morning dawned grey, the sky leaden with threat of snow, the sun a faint promise behind the low cloud. Wrapped in cloaks, Bedyr, Yrla and Rycol gathered to bid the Warden farewell. Brannoc was mounted on a sturdy dun horse, built more for endurance than speed, a piebald animal of similar physique laden with his supplies. Both animals wore the red and white peace feathers woven into their bridles, and Brannoc had fastened more into his braids, a cluster lashed to the hilt of the sabre that thrust up behind his shoulder. He was clad in his wolfskin cloak and heavy boots covered his feet. A bow and quiver of arrows were sheathed on his saddle. He smiled, white teeth flashing against the nutbrown of his skin.

'If they are with the Drott, I shall find them and bring them back,' he said.

'May the Lady go with you,' said Yrla.

'Be careful,' admonished Rycol, his concern eliciting a grin from the halfbreed.

'Find him,' said Bedyr. 'Find them for the sake of friendship.'

'I will,' Brannoc said, and without further ado heeled the dun out through the postern, hooves clattering as he cantered down the frosted surface of the Beltrevan road.

They watched until he was gone from sight, and then there was nothing they could do save wait. Bedyr found employment about the fort and Yrla spent much time in the company of Marga, or in the chapel, praying. Time passed slowly, the days merging into one another. Urstide came and went, its celebration dulled by the absence of knowledge, and then, out of a flurry of windblown snow, confusion arrived.

It came in the form of a weary mehdri on a tired horse.

He approached the gates of High Fort with shoulders slumped, his stance indicative of too many days in the saddle, riding through one of the worst winters Tamur had known. He straightened as he crested the glacis, lifting his head with visible effort to call the traditional demand of his guild.

'A mehdri asks entrance. I bear a message.'

The gates were open but he halted nonetheless, for so custom dictated, waiting until the captain of the watch gave formal response.

'Enter and be welcome, mehdri.'

Soldiers came out to greet the rider as he came through the gates, reaching to help him from the saddle. He shook his head, waving them back as he kicked clear of the stirrups and swung to the ground. His legs trembled then and he clutched at his saddlehorn for support, pushing himself upright as the captain enquired for whom the message was intended.

'The Lord Bedyr Caitin of Tamur,' the mehdri answered, 'and the Lady Yrla Belvanne na Caitin.'

'I will bring you to them,' the captain offered.

The mehdri stroked the bowed head of his mount and asked, 'You will see my animal stabled? Rubbed down and fed?'

'Of course,' the captain promised, turning to bark orders at his sergeant.

'Tend him well,' the mehdri added, 'he deserves care.'

'He shall have it,' the sergeant said, taking the bridle.

The mehdri straightened his soiled blue cloak, adjusting the hang so that the tripartite crown emblazoned on the thick material was spread for all to see and set a hand to the pouch secured to his belt. 'Lead on,' he nodded.

The captain set off across the courtyard, studying the man as he led the way through a door and up a winding stairwell that brought them to the labyrinthine interior of High Fort.

242

'You have travelled far?'

'Andurel to Caitin Hold,' the mehdri grunted. 'Then on across the Geffyn to here.'

'A hard road in this winter,' the captain murmured sympathetically.

The mehdri merely nodded: it was his experience that few roads were easy when travelled on the king's business.

The captain halted outside a carven door and tapped three times. A voice granted entry and he thrust the door open, seeing Bedyr and Yrla seated either side of a cheerful fire, leather-bound books in both their hands. It crossed his mind, briefly, to wonder what it would be like to have such learning that time might be passed reading and, although he was far too well disciplined to express the thought, what message the rider had for them.

He said, 'A mehdri has arrived with a message, Lord Bedyr,' and ushered the weary man inside, closing the door as Bedyr rose.

'My Lord Bedyr, Lady Yrla,' the mehdri said formally, 'I bring word from King Darr in Andurel.'

Bedyr took in the man's exhaustion at a glance, gesturing at his vacated chair: 'Sit down.'

Yrla reached to the dipper of the jug set beside the hearth, filling a mug with the mulled wine.

'You have come far. Please, seat yourself and take wine with us.'

The mehdri nodded gratefully and eased himself stiffly into the chair. He took the cup that Yrla offered, smiling his thanks, but set it down, reaching instead for his pouch.

He brought out a folded parchment, sealed in three places with yellow wax in which the royal signet was imprinted. Bedyr took the sheet from him, and only then did the mehdri lift the mug and sip the spicy brew, his duty done.

Bedyr broke the seals and studied the message, a frown forming. He passed it to Yrla. Her own features grew disturbed as she read the words set there in Darr's familiar hand and the mehdri recognised concern, or fear in her look. He pushed upright, wincing as he straightened, and said carefully, 'My Lord, my Lady, you will excuse me?'

Bedyr recognised his tact and smiled thanks, nodding. 'Of course. You have come far, and must be weary. A bath? or a bed? Food first?'

'A bath, I think, my Lord,' the mehdri smiled ruefully. 'Then food. A bed last.'

Bedyr nodded again and flung the door open to shout for a servant

243

who escorted the rider away down the corridor. Bedyr closed the door and turned to Yrla.

'We cannot go,' she said, still clutching Darr's message. 'I *will* not go!'

Bedyr's expression grew tortured and he crossed to stand before her, his back to the fire. 'I think we have little choice.'

'Darr does not know we await word of our son,' she answered. 'He cannot know that, or he would not impose this on us.'

'An imposition lies on him,' Bedyr said slowly. 'He has not sought this – he has no choice in the matter.'

'He suggests delay.' Yrla tapped the parchment.

'He has delay,' Bedyr said, regret in his tone. 'Had that man found us in Caitin Hold we should have been en route ere Urstide. We should be closing on Andurel now.'

'E'en so,' Yrla shook her head. 'We can send word back down the river – tell Darr what transpires.'

'And would Hattim understand?' asked Bedyr, gently.

'I care not a jot whether the Lord of Ust-Galich understands,' Yrla responded fiercely. 'Or Ashrivelle – who shows little sense in her choice of husband! – or anyone. I have waited too long for word of our son and I would not put more distance between us than this.'

'The Galichian army must close on Andurel by now,' Bedyr said, his voice thoughtful. 'This winter will have slowed the march, but still it must be close. Or there. Camped about the city.'

'What of it?' Yrla demanded.

'Hattim is ambitious,' Bedyr answered. 'He has secured Ashrivelle's hand and now waits only for the formality of marriage. By custom our presence is required at that ceremony – and Darr clearly seeks our help in the deciding of the succession. Should we not attend - for whatever reason! – Hattim may insist the ceremony proceed. And with his army in place, Darr may have no choice but to agree.'

'He would not dare!' Yrla gasped, seeing the direction of her husband's argument.

'I have dealt with Hattim,' Bedyr murmured, 'and I believe he would dare. And should he consequently take the High Throne, it would suit Tamur ill to have such an enemy.'

'You are not afraid of him.'

It was a statement and Bedyr shook his head in agreement. 'No, I do not fear Hattim Sethiyan, but I fear for the Kingdoms should such as he lay claim to the White Palace.'

'You would go?' asked Yrla. 'Without word of Kedryn?'

'Jarl has but one voice,' Bedyr said, 'and Darr's hands are somewhat tied. He needs me there.'

'And Kedryn needs us here,' said Yrla defiantly.

Bedyr sighed, sinking to his knees before the raven-haired woman. He took her hands in his, his eyes troubled as he studied her lovely face.

'If Kedryn is alive, then Brannoc will find him and bring him out of the Beltrevan,' he said. 'He can follow us down the Idre, perhaps even in time to attend this wedding. If not . . .' He paused, not wishing to voice the alternative. 'In either event, there is nothing we can do here save wait. In Andurel we might serve the Kingdoms better. Serve Kedryn better, too.'

'He is our son.' Yrla's tone was dogged.

'Aye,' said Bedyr. 'He is our son and I love him. But he has a destiny to fulfil and so do we. I love these Kingdoms, too, and it is my duty to serve them as best I can. I think that Darr has need of me – of us both – and I think that perhaps that need is greater now than Kedryn's.'

Yrla stifled tears, imposing on her troubled mind the tranquillity instilled by the years of training in Estrevan, seeking to unravel the complex threads of impending fate she felt gathering about her.

'Did you not say there was a pattern we could not read?' asked Bedyr, and she nodded slowly, regretfully.

'Aye, I did. But it had not occurred to me that it would require my desertion of our son.'

'We do not desert him,' Bedyr said urgently. 'We do our duty, and he would understand that.'

'You are decided,' Yrla said softly.

'I believe it is decided for us,' said Bedyr, just as quietly. 'I like it no better than you, but I see no other choice than to answer Darr's summons.'

Yrla studied her husband's face, seeing on it regret but none of the irresolution that had earlier shown there. He was, without doubt, a man of action and while his concern for Kedryn was undoubted, he was able to set aside personal emotions in service of his greater duty. And, she had to admit, his arguments were unpleasantly valid: they could do nothing for Kedryn save sit and wait, whilst in Andurel they might well serve both Kingdoms and son far better. It was a question of priorities that gave rise to dilemma: as a mother, her instinct was to remain in High Fort, to stay as close to her son as possible; as the Lady Yrla Belvanne na Caitin, wife of the Lord of Tamur, her duty was to serve the Kingdoms, to obey the king. She closed her eyes and sighed, then forced a wan smile to her lips as she nodded.

'You are right, and I prevaricate. We must go to Andurel.'

Bedyr rose to his feet, cupping her face between his hands. 'The Lady blessed me when she sent me you,' he murmured. 'I will find Rycol and arrange passage.'

Yrla watched him go from the chamber and turned to face the fire. It blazed merrily but did little to warm the cold that chilled her heart.

Rycol, when Bedyr outlined the gist of Darr's message, saw the danger instantly and sent men to enquire in the town of available boats. As luck would have it a late-season trading barque had recently docked with a cargo of fruits and wine from the south, the master delighted to offer the Lord and Lady of Tamur passage down the Idre. The tiny midships cabin was prepared for them and they embarked a day later. Rycol and the Lady Marga, surrounded by Bedyr's Tamurin escort for which there was not room on the vessel, saw them off, standing huddled in thick cloaks on the wharfside. It was a sullen day, the canescent sky matching the mood of their departure, the wind that screeched from the canyon lashing the undulating surface of the river to a foaming greyish white. Bedyr, trusting in the medicaments provided by Rycol's Sisters to quell his river sickness, stood beside Yrla at the taffrail, watching the massive walls of High Fort fade into obscurity against the greater bulk of the Lozins as the oarsmen dipped their sweeps, bringing the barque rapidly into the current, where the master shouted for them to ship oars as the sails unfurled and the wind took them fast southwards.

The mehdri sent to bring word to Jarl found easier passage than his westbound comrade. A ferry took him across the Vortigen and he rode north and east towards Keshaven across the sweeping plains that were the domain of the horse lords. Kesh was thin on towns, but farms and ranches were plentiful, affording him ample shelter as he crossed the windswept grasslands, using the network of roads and trails that were largely reserved for such as he, and whilst his fellow struggled with the rigours of the Geffyn he came in sight of Keshaven.

The capital of the eastern kingdom was a sprawl of low, stone buildings to the south of one of the few forests in Kesh. A Tamurin would likely – and a barbarian certainly – consider the forest little more than a sizeable wood, but to the inhabitants of Keshaven it was a most welcome defence against the wind that scoured the savannahs, a useful source of fuel, and a diversion from the seemingly endless expanse of grass. It was for those reasons, and the stream that flowed out of the timber, that Yathyn, the first lord of Kesh, had chosen to site his ranch there. That ranch had long since become a palace, and around it had grown a town, though the land beyond remained the personal property of the Keshi lords.

The town was built on both sides of the stream, bridges spanning the water so frequently that large tracts were virtually hidden, the largest leading directly to the palace. The mehdri, his coming observed by black-clad townsfolk, clattered over the wooden bridge and found himself confronted by a wooden gate and guard post. He halted, cupping his hands to send his voice over the wailing of the wind, and shouted, 'A mehdri asks entrance. I bear a message.'

A man who would have been tall had his legs not been so bowed stepped from the shelter of the guard post and replied, 'Enter and welcome, mehdri,' and two men trotted out to swing the gates wide.

The mehdri rode through and halted as the bow-legged man approached him. 'I bear word from the king for the Lord Jarl,' he said.

The officer nodded and called over his shoulder, bringing two men on big Keshi stallions from the stable behind the post building.

He said, 'Take him to Jarl,' and the riders fell in either side of the messenger, their horses lifting to an easy canter with no apparent instruction. They were dark, hook-nosed men, typical of the Keshi, their hair braided, clad in sable breeks and padded tunics, curved sabres slung across their backs. They spoke not at all and the mehdri studied the land about him as they rode towards the palace. A vast meadow separated Jarl's home from the town of Keshaven, the grass sere, but still foraged by herds of the long-legged horses that were the pride of the kingdom, turning curious eyes to the trio of riders, the stallions snickering tentative challenges that went ignored by the disciplined war-horses.

A high palisade, wooden save for the watch towers spaced at intervals along its length, surrounded the palace and the escort slowed to a walk as they approached. A gate swung open and they rode beneath its arch on to a lawn where the mehdri's two companions reined in, giving him into the care of a third man who nodded and mounted a horse to lead the messenger forwards. He wondered if the Keshi ever went afoot.

The palace was a mixture of stone and wood, its central buildings comprised of great blocks, with timber-built substructures extending from the sides. Save for a tall tower nothing was more than a single storey, though the ornate railings that ran the length of the upper levels attested to roof gardens. A verandah shaded the forefront from the mid-afternoon sun that shone fitfully from the cold, steely sky and the mehdri's escort halted there.

'Give me your horse,' he said, 'and I'll see her bedded.'

'My thanks.' The mehdri climbed down, passing his reins to the Keshi, knowing the animal would be well tended.

He stepped on to the verandah and smoothed his cloak as a silver-haired man with skin like aged leather and a dragging foot limped towards him.

'Mehdri, eh?' He spoke before the messenger could give formal greeting. 'You'll be wanting Jarl. Well, come this way.'

He beckoned, leading the mehdri into a spacious, low-ceilinged hall that was a surprising contrast to the austerity of the building's exterior. Gaily-patterned tiles formed the floor, warmed by the pipes of the hypocaust beneath, a marble fountain at their centre splashing a tinkling trickle of water into a series of bowls in which fat red and gold fish swam lazily. Trailing plants hung in baskets from the roof beams, colour on colour against the tiles of the walls. Light fell in filigree patterns from the ironwork of the windows and the beaten copper of the dangling lanterns. The air was warm and spiced with foreign scents.

'Come,' the old man said, too familiar with the hall's exotic charms to share the mehdri's wonder, and stepped through an archway on which designs that should have clashed formed a harmonious pattern.

They went down a narrow corridor lit by slender windows and emerged into a smaller hall, all alcoves and cushioned benches, a great golden cage at the centre containing a profusion of small, brightly-coloured birds that filled the room with their high-pitched song. The old man paused before double doors of polished wood inlaid with chasings of silver and tugged on a tasselled cord of green silk. The mehdri heard a bell chime, and the doors opened.

'A mehdri with a message for Lord Jarl,' the oldster announced, and turned away.

The mehdri found himself facing two burly Keshi in flowing black pallia, the horse head of their kingdom shaped in silver against a green background on the left breasts. Sabres were sheathed at their

248

waists and as they turned to announce him, their voices in perfect unison, he heard the faint chink of mail beneath their robes.

Beyond them he saw a chamber fine as any in the White Palace, grander than many. The floor was of brilliantly-polished wood, its sheen reflecting the glow of the lanterns hung about the walls, rugs scattered casually, and cushions that served as seating. The ceiling was vaulted, intricately carved arches swooping gently to a great disc of coloured glass that pooled a rainbow over and around the three musicians squatted beneath. Two held Keshi flutes, the third a balur, its final note lingering on the expectant air. Past them, sprawled on cushions, the mehdri recognised Jarl of Kesh. He wore a simple robe, black as was the custom of his people, the horse head emblem silver against dark green, his beak-nosed face alert as he swept strands of glossy black hair from his tanned forehead and beckoned the mehdri towards him.

On his left sat a younger version of himself, plumper, but unmistakeably Jarl's progeny, Kemm; on his right, four women of varying ages, dressed in rich gowns, their fingers bright with rings, the gold circles in the left nostrils of three declaring them concubines, the fourth Arlynn, Lady of Kesh. She studied the mehdri and then glanced at her husband, who raised a ringed hand, whereupon she rose in a swirl of coloured skirts and ushered the other women before her from the chamber, the musicians following on their heels.

'Sit,' Jarl said. 'Take wine with us.'

The mehdri smiled his thanks but made no move to accept the invitation, reaching instead to his pouch, from which he took Darr's message, handing it to Jarl. Only then did he settle on the cushions and accept the jewelled goblet Kemm passed him.

Jarl broke the seals and read in silence. Then thrust the parchment at his son.

'There is no other message?' he asked.

'No, my Lord.'

Jarl nodded slowly, as if appraising something in his mind, turning bird-bright eyes of a startling green to the mehdri.

'Lord Hattim prepares for his wedding?'

'He does, my Lord.'

'And his army?'

'Marches south. It had not reached Andurel when I left the city.'

Jarl grunted, then: 'You will wish to bathe, no doubt. And eat.'

Recognising polite dismissal, the mehdri nodded. 'Indeed, my Lord. A bath would be most welcome.'

Jarl motioned at the two doormen. 'Show this weary traveller to our baths and have food prepared for him. Ask my wife to attend me.'

The mehdri rose, bowing his thanks and followed the guards from the chamber. When he was gone Jarl filled a goblet with wine and drank deep. 'Well?' he asked his son. 'What do you make of it?'

'Hattim's desire to wed Ashrivelle is well known,' said Kemm.

Jarl sighed, staring at his son with fond exasperation. 'As is his ambition.'

'He cannot be Lord of Ust-Galich and take the High Throne, both,' Kemm said.

'No.'

Jarl paused as the door opened and the Lady Arlynn came in. She was a woman in her middle years, still handsome, but tending to plumpness. The grey that streaked her black hair was hidden by dyes, and cosmetics concealed the lines on her face; the intelligence that shone in her eyes could not be hidden. Jarl took the parchment from Kemm's hand and gave it to her.

'What do you think of this news?' he demanded.

Arlynn studied the message and clicked her tongue against her teeth.

'Hattim looks to the White Palace. He will offer some protege as Lord of Ust-Galich.'

'Is that so bad?' asked Kemm.

Jarl sighed, addressing himself to Arlynn rather than his son: 'He is so good with horses. Would that he understood men as well.'

Arlynn smiled and patted Kemm's knee. 'If Hattim Sethiyan is able to take the High Throne whilst some puppet occupies Ust-Galich he will, for all effect, rule both Andurel and the southern kingdom. He will control the heart of the Three Kingdoms, with greater power than either your father or Bedyr Caitin. He will control the centre of trade and command both the Ust-Idre and the Vortigen – he will have a stranglehold on the Kingdoms.'

'But he cannot lay claim to the High Throne without the blessing of Kesh and Tamur,' Kemm said, frowning.

'Darr has no other child, save Wynett,' Arlynn explained, 'and she is sworn to service of the Lady. If Ashrivelle chooses Hattim, Darr can neither refuse nor prevent Hattim's claim to right by marriage.' She turned to her husband. 'You cannot prevent the wedding.'

'No,' Jarl agreed, 'that would be tantamount to declaring war.'

'Nor – by custom – with only Ashrivelle in rightful line, can you prevent her husband from assuming the High Throne at her side.'

'No,' Jarl said again.

'But mayhap you and Bedyr can find some appointee to Hattim's kingdom sympathetic to your wishes.'

'That is doubtless what Darr seeks,' Jarl agreed.

'Surely Ust-Gallich could not stand against the union of Kesh and Tamur,' Kemm offered.

'Neither Bedyr nor I wish to see the Kingdoms descend to civil war,' Jarl said wearily, wishing that his son might have inherited less of his skill with horses and more of his mother's acumen. 'We, and our fathers before us – theirs before them – have worked too hard to bring unity. Our armies are scattered and we stand in the grip of winter. Should we give Hattim reason to find offence – to take up arms – his forces could seize Andurel before we have hope of rallying our own warriors. And with Andurel in his grip, and Ashrivelle at his side, Hattim would occupy a vastly strengthened position.

'Such a war might last for years. And while we fought, the forest folk might forget their vows of peace and come down through the Lozin Gate; the Sandurkan move from the west. No, we cannot risk war. We must do as your wise mother suggests and seek to find some claimant to the Galichian throne of less ambitious a bent than Hattim. Or circumvent his ascension by some means I cannot now foresee.'

'Towards which end we must journey to Andurel,' said Arlynn. 'And the sooner the better.'

'Aye,' said Jarl grumpily. 'Though I had looked to spend a quiet winter here.'

'It will be exciting,' said Kemm, 'to visit Andurel.'

Jarl glanced at him, then looked to Arlynn, who nodded slightly, recognising the question in his eyes.

'You will not accompany us,' he said, stilling the smile on his son's face. 'You will remain here to tend the affairs of Kesh.'

'Father!' Kemm protested.

'Kesh needs a lord,' said Jarl, modulating his tone that Kemm might see the sense in his words, 'and I may have need of you. Should this affair . . . let us say, go less smoothly than I hope, then Kesh may have need of a rallying point.'

'You believe Hattim would attempt such treachery?' Arlynn demanded, her voice suddenly sharp.

'I do not know,' said Jarl, 'but I had rather know my back protected and my kingdom secure.'

'Should he harm you I will bring all Kesh against him!' Kemm vowed loyally. 'I shall bring down a storm about his ears.'

Jarl smiled, nodding. 'I do not doubt it, my son. But avoid precipitate action. For now I had rather keep my eggs in several baskets than bring them all to Andurel. Should aught befall us, seek counsel with Tamur before you sound the war drums. I am, mayhap, overly suspicious.'

'But none too cautious,' murmured Arlynn.

Jarl took her hand, toying with the rings that covered most of her fingers. 'Darr has not pressed urgency upon us, so shall we dally a while? Set out in a few days time? It will doubtless take Bedyr longer to come south.'

Arlynn smiled her agreement. 'And meanwhile perhaps it would be as well to send scouts west, to see where the Galichian army stands.'

'Do you hear your mother?' Jarl laughed, turning to Kemm. 'Is she not a wonder amongst women?'

The barque carrying Bedyr and Yrla southwards ran for three days before a storm that precluded docking. Then they put in and spent a day repairing damage. Their passage was smoother after that, though little to Bedyr's liking, the Idre restless, her banks white with fallen snow and her waters a forbidding grey. As they approached Andurel they saw the tents of the Galichian army massed along the western shoreline and Bedyr experienced both apprehension and a flush of anger.

'They occupy Tamurin land,' he complained as he stood beside Yrla at the rail, 'and doubtless consume Tamurin food. Word should have been sent; permission asked.'

'Doubtless Hattim will claim winter as an excuse,' Yrla suggested, holding her wind-streamered hair from her face. 'And say his men wait merely to celebrate his wedding.'

'Doubtless,' Bedyr agreed irritably, 'But still they could have gone over the Ust-Idre into his own kingdom. I do not like it – from that position Hattim might take Andurel. His army commands the western approaches, and if they seize the bridges the city is his.'

'He cannot have warriors in Kesh,' Yrla said, 'so surely Jarl's men would oppose such a venture – should it come to that.'

Bedyr shrugged, hugging his cloak tighter about him. 'Mayhap I see the worst,' he allowed, 'but remember that Jarl's army, like ours, is disbanded. At this moment only Hattim has full strength in the field.'

'And Darr's forces?' she asked.

'Are not enough,' said Bedyr. 'Little more than a bodyguard. They might hold the White Palace, but not the city.'

'Could it really come to that?' Yrla shivered, prompting Bedyr to drape his cloak about her, an arm spanning her shoulders.

'Likely not,' he sighed. 'Likely I fret too much. But I like none of this.'

'Nor I,' said Yrla, leaning against him.

They turned then from their observation of the Galichian encampment to study the island city swelling before them. As ever, it impressed with its size and its beauty, sparkling snow-decked in the afternoon sunlight, the bridges that connected the cantons and the banks seeming, at this distance, miraculous webworks suspended above the waters that swirled on the west side into the Idre cascades, and on the east to the wider sweep of the Vortigen. The roads and avenues were dark traceries against the whiteness, the parks and gardens lost, so that all appeared some fairy tale construction, rising in sweeps and undulations to the simple grandeur of the White Palace set atop the apex of the highest islet. The horn mounted on the barque's prow belled a warning and the river master shouted for the sails to be furled, the oars brought out. The sweeps slowed their approach and they came into the harbour area gentle as a falling snowflake, the barque turning to come up against a mole, where longshoremen waited to take the mooring lines.

The gangplank was run out and their baggage transferred to the shore. There was little enough of it and within moments Bedyr was thanking the master for their passage. Harbour officials came from their offices to check the inbound vessel and one enquired of Bedyr what business he and his lady had in Andurel.

'Lord Caitin,' he gasped when he was apprised of their identities, 'Lady Yrla, forgive me. You are expected. Please, follow me.'

Bedyr was surprised, for their arrival could not have been timed, and he had anticipated no formal welcome until they reached the palace. Yet in the warmth of the harbour office they found a captain of the Royal Guard waiting.

He was a young man, burly beneath his silver armour and purple cloak, a helm under his arm as he saluted. His hair was short-cropped on a square skull, his nose broken. Bedyr recognised him vaguely from the battle of the Lozin Gate but could not put a name to the homely face.

'My Lord Bedyr, Lady Yrla,' the captain said, 'I am Corradon. King Darr sent me to greet you.'

'How could you know when we might arrive?' Bedyr asked.

'I have been waiting some time,' said Corradon. 'The king is most anxious to speak with you. He bade me wait until such time as you did arrive, then bring you instantly to the White Palace.'

Bedyr nodded, his sense of unease growing. 'Then let us not keep the king waiting longer,' he said.

Chapter Twelve

HORSES were brought from the shelter of the harbour offices, a hand of the Royal Guard rather than the customary *venta* forming about Bedyr and Yrla as they rode through the bustle of the dock area to the quieter streets beyond. Corradon took the lead, guiding them not to the avenue that led directly to the palace, but through the maze of thoroughfares surrounding that broad roadway. Cloaked against the cold they went largely unnoticed, arriving at one of the lesser gates, where more silver-armoured guardsmen waited to take their animals whilst Corradon murmured an apology for the informality of their entrance and hurried them to a small door that Bedyr recognized as leading to Darr's chambers by a circuitous route that avoided the more public areas of the White Palace.

It seemed they came in the manner of conspirators rather than honoured guests and Bedyr found himself loosening his sword in its scabbard, his ears attuned for sound of attack, his eyes scanning the narrow corridors as if in anticipation of ambush. Yrla kept close to his side, her eyes wide, a small frown wrinkling her brow, not speaking as they traversed the ill-lit, empty passage.

No ambush came and Corradon halted before a plain oak door, producing a key that he turned in the lock, offering further apologies that served to heighten their sense of unease. He thrust the door open and bowed them inside, a somewhat embarrassed smile on his lips as he said, 'King Darr will be with you shortly. Please wait for him here.'

They entered and the door closed behind them, cutting off the sound of Corradon's retreating footsteps as they looked curiously around the deserted chamber. It was a place Bedyr had visited seldom and Yrla never, the dust that lay on the ledge of the narrow window and the bare flagstones of the floor attesting to its lack of use. Bedyr removed his cloak and draped it over his left shoulder, his hand still on his sword hilt.

'What intrigues go on?' Yrla murmured, trailing a finger through the grey coating of a small table.

'I know not,' grunted Bedyr, 'but this secrecy troubles me. This chamber connects to Darr's quarters and few know of its existence: it would appear he does not wish Hattim to know of our arrival.'

'Why not?' asked Yrla. 'It must eventually be made public.'

Bedyr shrugged and moved towards a door in the far wall.

It opened before he reached it and his sword was sliding from the scabbard as Darr appeared. The king wore his favoured robe, old and grey, with no sign of his office other than the token about his neck. Yrla saw that his hair was completely grey now, and that his face was deeper etched with lines of worry, though his eyes sparkled with pleasure as he spread his hands and smiled at them.

'My friends,' he said, 'Yrla – you are lovelier than ever – and Bedyr – you will not need that blade – please forgive this secrecy, but I am anxious to speak with you before Hattim Sethiyan presents himself.'

He stood back, beckoning them to the stairway on which he stood and leading the way up to another door that gave access to a more used chamber. He waited until they had entered and then closed the door, its frame blending invisibly with the carved wooden panelling of the walls. This room was banked with west-facing windows through which pale sunlight streamed, rendering the parquet of the floor lustrous, glowing on the spines of the books that filled the shelves lining all four walls. A fire burned in a low-mantelled hearth and six wooden chairs stood around a circular table on which rested several decanters and five crystal goblets. Three were already filled, as were two of the chairs.

Jarl of Kesh said, 'Bedyr, Yrla, welcome to our circle of intrigue,' in a sardonic tone.

Beside him, her gown an explosion of colour against the sombre black of his robe, Arlynn smiled and said, 'Hail, old friends. Have you word of Kedryn?'

The expression on both their faces alerted the others to the disturbance of expectations, Arlynn's smile freezing on her lips, Jarl's eyes narrowing. Darr said, 'What has happened?'

Bedyr took the cloak that Yrla doffed and tossed it with his to the empty chair as she sat down. 'He sought to enter the Beltrevan,' he said hoarsely, 'and Gann Resyth brought word the Fedyn Pass fell about his ears. Brannoc has gone into the forests in search of him.'

'Wynett was with him?' Darr asked, his face abruptly paled.

Bedyr nodded, 'Aye, and Tepshen.'

256

'They are . . .' Jarl hesitated awkwardly, embarrassed for all his bluffness, 'dead?'

'We do not know.' Bedyr dropped into a chair, his features grim. 'We know only that the Fedyn Pass is blocked and the Sister there sensed evil.'

'Ashar's work,' Darr said softly.

Arlynn reached to take Yrla's hand, concern in her eyes. 'You do not know for sure?'

'No,' murmured Yrla, shaking her head, 'Gann Resyth knew only that they entered the pass and that the pass fell. We hope . . .'

Her voice trailed off and Bedyr continued, 'That they live. Somehow. We can only trust in the Lady – and hope that Brannoc finds them.'

Darr poured wine, his hand trembling so that droplets of the ruby liquid splashed on to the table. He passed the goblets to Bedyr and Yrla and said, 'Had I known, I would not have summoned you.'

Bedyr squared his shoulders, smiling sadly.

'Your message suggested some urgency. As does the manner of our arrival.' He glanced at Yrla and said, 'Let us leave Kedryn for the moment. What transpires here that you wish to speak with us so secretly?'

Darr swallowed wine, absorbing the news, and said earnestly, 'I pray that they all live – the Lady knows, Wynett is of my blood, and Kedryn . . . Well, I spoke of my hopes.'

'There is no point to picking at such a scab,' Yrla said, the firmness of her tone concealing the pain she felt. 'We place our faith in the Lady and for now can do no more. Let us, then, apply ourselves to the immediate business.'

'Aye,' Bedyr echoed decisively. 'What of this impending wedding?'

The others looked at them in silence for a moment, sharing their distress as they recognised behind the Tamurin stoicism the grief they felt, respecting the solidarity that had brought them south despite such calamitous news. Darr sighed.

'These are troubled times,' he murmured, 'would that winter did not cut us off from from Estrevan, for the guidance of the Sorority would be most useful now.'

'There is some plot afoot?' Bedyr demanded, grateful that the conversation moved from that painful, personal ground.

Darr shrugged, stroking at his beard. 'I do not know. In all honesty I cannot say there is, but there is something in me that screams it. I have consulted with Bethany, but she offers no great guidance other than the political. She senses no magic abroad, yet I have the feeling I am trapped in a web, with some malign creature drawing in the strands.'

'Hattim Sethiyan is malign enough,' Jarl grunted.

'He employs sorcery?' Bedyr asked in a shocked voice.

'No.' Darr shook his head. 'At least, none that any can define or feel. But . . .'

He paused, refilling his glass, looking from one face to another before he continued.

'Hattim returned from the battle of the Lozin Gate to woo Ashrivelle. She is utterly enamoured. I had no choice but to agree to the marriage – overtly I had no reason to object – and so Hattim stands in line to the throne. Or will, once the ceremony is concluded. I raised the matter of the succession with him and he assured me that he will abide by whatever decision we make. His concern, he tells me, is solely for Ashrivelle and the Kingdoms.'

'That carries the ring of untruth,' said Bedyr.

'Aye,' Darr agreed, 'yet I cannot fault Hattim. His behaviour so far has been impeccable.'

'Which is unlike our Lord of Ust-Galich,' Jarl grunted, tapping his beak-like nose. 'I smell something rotten.'

'But cannot define it,' Darr said. 'Hattim has agreed to allow we three to decide his successor; or to relinquish claim to the High Throne.'

'What?' Stark incredulity rang in Bedyr's voice. 'Did I not hear this from you, I should not credit it.'

'Yet it is what he promises,' said Darr. 'He is the very paradigm of compromise. He will stand by any appointment we make, or any disposition.'

'I believe him confident of the High Throne,' Jarl offered. 'He knows that Ashrivelle is the key – unless we change the customs of our forefathers, Ashrivelle's husband *must* become king.'

'Or Wynett's,' Yrla said quietly, her words drawing all their attention. 'Wynett is the elder daughter.'

'Wynett is . . .' Jarl caught himself in time, amending the sentence: 'lost. And besides, she is sworn to celibacy.'

'Perhaps not,' Yrla said. 'If she lives, then mayhap her mind will change on the matter of her celibacy.'

Darr stared at her, his eyes narrowed. 'I saw them together in

High Fort, but Wynett's devotion remained strong. Have you valid reason to suspect some alteration in that situation?'

'Intuition,' Yrla murmured, her shoulders rising in an almost imperceptible shrug. 'Nothing more.'

'That,' said Darr sadly, 'is not enough. We are forced to deal with the immediate situation, and that is that Hattim will wed Ashrivelle and become the rightful heir to the High Throne. Our purpose – and this is why I sought to speak with you privately, that we might decide and act in conclave – is to determine what safeguards we can place upon that succession.'

'How we can draw Hattim's teeth,' said Jarl, blunt as ever.

'He will accept whomever we suggest?' Bedyr asked.

'So he has said,' Darr confirmed.

'It needs be someone less ambitious than Hattim,' said Bedyr, thoughtfully, 'someone more concerned with the unity of the King-doms than with personal advancement or the aggrandisement of Ust-Galich.'

'Aye,' Darr nodded. 'I had thought of Hattim's cousin, Chadyn Hymet.'

'A possibility,' Bedyr allowed. 'Or perhaps Hyjal Forwyn?'

'Too weak,' said Jarl, 'He borrows too much, and stands in debt to half the merchants of Ust-Galich.'

'I did not know,' Bedyr said.

'Naryl Domme might be a likely candidate,' Jarl suggested.

Arlynn laughed. 'You might as well appoint that wife of his, for she controls him as if he were stringed. And she is – or was – Hattim's mistress. One of them, at least.'

Her husband's bushy brows lifted at this tidbit of gossip. 'You had not told me that,' he complained.

'I do not tell you everything,' Arlynn replied, archly innocent.

'Then neither Domme nor Forwyn are acceptable,' said Darr. 'Are there other candidates?

'Lerwyn Chanyth is a sound man,' Bedyr said, 'and he commands the respect of the army.'

'But is childless,' countered Darr, 'and if he were to become lord, would have no heirs. That would open the way to Hattim's appointee after his death.'

Bedyr and Jarl nodded their agreement. Darr said, 'What we need do here is establish a dynasty that may not be challenged later by Sethiyan claimants. We need a man we can trust. One whose posi-tion is unassailable.'

'So far as any Galichian may be trusted,' Jarl sniffed.

'I offer Chadyn Hymet again,' Darr said. 'Hattim's cousin he may be, but that relationship is by marriage rather than blood, and he is young yet, and already the father of three.'

'I could accept Chadyn,' Jarl nodded. 'Unless my wife has some further information from the bedrooms of Tessoril.'

'Chadyn is a model of probity,' said Arlynn. 'In fact, he is rather boring.'

'He grows more acceptable,' smiled Jarl. 'How say you, Bedyr?'

'He fought well at the Lozin Gate,' Bedyr responded, 'and I have heard no ill of him. He is wealthy enough to withstand the temptation of bribery and the succession of his children should secure his resistance to any pressure of Hattim's.'

'Are we then agreed?' asked Darr. 'Yrla, you have not spoken.'

Yrla smiled absently, as if her thoughts were far away. 'Let it be Chadyn,' she nodded. 'On those occasions I have met him he has struck me as a sensible young man.'

'Then Chadyn it shall be,' Darr said. 'We shall put his name to Hattim with a concerted front.'

'There remains the question of his army,' Bedyr said, remembering the cantonment spread along the west bank of the Idre.

'He has spoken of that. He came to me with apologies and the offer of levies.' Darr's words surprised Bedyr, for he had not anticipated such civility from the Lord of Ust-Galich. 'What his men eat, they pay for; and they pay a tithe on the land they occupy. The location is justified by the cascades – Hattim would have his forces accessible for his proposed triumphal journey after the wedding. He said that he wished to provide Ashrivelle with a fitting escort when he proceeds into Ust-Galich. I could not fault him.'

'He has become a diplomat,' Bedyr said, his tone dubious.

'And you like it no more than I,' Jarl remarked. 'It is too great a change in the man.'

'Mayhap Ashrivelle has changed him,' suggested Arlynn.

'I doubt that,' her husband said, returning his keen gaze to Bedyr. 'And to that end I left Kemm in Keshaven with instructions to raise a modest force – just sufficient to oppose the Galichians should such measures become needful.'

'My Tamurin are disbanded,' Bedyr said.

'I do not believe it will come to that.' Darr spoke optimistically. 'If Hattim plays some underhand game, I do not think it includes civil war.'

260

'He would be foolish to attempt that ploy,' Jarl agreed. 'Your palace guard could defend this place long enough for Kemm to bring our cavalry south, and we have access to the city from the Vortigen side. Thus reinforced, we could hold Andurel until Bedyr's Tamurin were raised.'

'It is some other game,' murmured Darr. 'Though what, I cannot surmise.'

'Then we can do no more,' said Bedyr. 'We are agreed on Chadyn Hymet as our candidate, and Jarl's foresight offsets the Galichian army. If Hattim pays for what his men eat, I have no valid quarrel.'

'But still you like it no more than I,' Jarl rasped.

'No,' agreed Bedyr, 'but it seems Hattim has manoeuvred us into a corner.'

'We cannot oppose him, not without the risk of such insult as might bring down civil war,' Darr nodded. 'We can only seek to bind him.'

'Mayhap the High Throne is all he seeks,' Arlynn suggested, 'and he will be content with that. Once on it, he is constrained by those same rules as appertain to all our kings.'

'Mayhap,' said the incumbent, doubtfully.

'We might do more,' suggested Bedyr slowly, continuing as all turned towards him, waiting. 'were we to establish a fixed council, precipitate decisions might be circumvented.'

'How so?' asked Darr.

Bedyr thought for a moment, then: 'This winter – indeed, our tardy arrival for so propitious a ceremony as our cousin's wedding – emphasises the difficulty of travel. Were there representatives of our kingdoms, and of Ust-Galich, resident in the palace then regal business might be decided in concert, and more swiftly.'

'A council!' Darr nodded approvingly.

'One that would serve to bind Hattim,' Jarl grinned.

'Purely in the interests of unity,' smiled Bedyr.

'An excellent suggestion,' said Darr.

They fell to discussing the nature of the council and its composition, selecting candidates of character stern enough to resist pressure, devising a format that would bind all future rulers that no one man might impose his will upon the Kingdoms.

Finally they were done and Bedyr said, 'Our business is finished, I think. We can do no more for now'.

'Aye,' Darr agreed, 'I shall inform Hattim in due course, but now you doubtless wish to bathe and rest. You will meet Hattim at dinner,

261

and perhaps then you will see changes in the man. Or see what I have missed.'

Bedyr nodded, rising. 'Until dinner, then, my friends.'

Yrla rose, too, and Darr called for servants to escort them to their quarters, where baths were already drawn and clothes suitable for the palace laid out.

As were the chambers occupied by Hattim, and by the Lord and Lady of Kesh, so were these designed in the style of the occupants' homeland, and the familiarity of the fitments brought a pang of homesickness to them both. They bathed separately and met again in the dressing room, their surroundings reminding them painfully of Caitin Hold and High Fort, and consequently of their missing son.

'You were withdrawn,' Bedyr remarked as Yrla brushed her long black hair before the fire. 'Do you think of Kedryn?'

'Aye,' Yrla replied, 'but not as you suspect. I am convinced he lives, and Wynett, too. I cannot explain it, but that conviction has grown since we arrived in Andurel.'

'Intuition?' queried Bedyr.

'I am not sure.' Yrla paused in her brushing, sweeping raven strands from her face that she might see her husband clearly. 'I cannot put a name to it, but the feeling is more than that, I think. I should like to speak with Bethany.'

'That should be easy enough.' Bedyr slid a shirt of cream silk over his head, the material muffling his words.

Yrla resumed her toilette. 'Darr spoke of sensing a web about him. And I thought – do you remember? – that perhaps some pattern exists.'

'Concerning Kedryn and Wynett?' Bedyr drew on dark grey breeks of supple leather.

'Aye,' Yrla confirmed.

Bedyr grunted, seating himself on the bed to pull boots of black hide up his legs. 'Kedryn is not here,' he said. 'And as best we can know, Wynett remains true to her vows. And that supposes they live.'

Yrla tugged her lower lip between her teeth, knowing he intended no infliction of pain with his bluntness, and said, 'I know that. But still I feel . . .'

'Something,' Bedyr concluded as her voice tailed away into a pensive silence, 'and I respect that. But as Darr pointed out we are faced with immediate problems that we must resolve here and now.'

'I shall discuss it with Bethany,' Yrla declared.

'Mayhap she can clarify your feelings,' Bedyr smiled, rising to cross the room and run his fingers through her hair. 'Certainly clarification would be welcome, for Hattim Sethiyan appears to act in most uncharacteristic a manner.'

'Indeed,' murmured Yrla, 'he has done nothing to give offence. It seems he acts with the utmost correctitude, and that is unlike our Lord of Ust-Galich.'

'Most unlike,' agreed Bedyr, selecting a dark blue overrobe, the clenched fist of Tamur embroidered in silver on back and chest. 'It is all so . . . *neat*. There is no evidence of Hattim's usual high-handed behaviour.'

'Mayhap he has matured.' Yrla set down the brush and began to select clothing, Bedyr watching, enjoying as he always did the supple movements of her body. 'Mayhap Arlynn was right.'

'Arlynn did not believe her own words.' Bedyr watched as she slipped off the silken dressing robe and lifted a chemise to the light. 'Do you?'

Yrla was silent for a moment as she slid the chemise over her head, smoothing the soft material over her body, then: 'No, I do not.'

'Do you suspect some plot?' he asked.

Yrla cast a critical eye over several gowns, finally choosing a bod-iced dress of pale blue stitched with heavy silver threads. 'I do not see what plot he might hatch,' she said. 'If he *is* prepared to accept your nomination of successor, then what can he do? He cannot share the throne until Darr is dead and Ashrivelle announced Queen. Long before then his army will disband. Would he now employ force of arms? He must know that Jarl guards his back, and that all Tamur would rise against him should he venture down such a path.'

'Exactly,' Bedyr grunted, frowning. 'It is too neat.'

Yrla fixed a circlet of silver in her hair and a chain of matching design about her slender neck.

'Perhaps Bethany will shed some light.'

Bedyr nodded somewhat doubtfully and belted the waist of his overrobe, settling the Tamurin dirk on his left hip. 'Perhaps,' he said. 'And perhaps we shall learn more when we speak with Hattim.'

Speaking with Hattim, however, served only to confuse him further. They found the Lord of Ust-Galich in the great salon leading to the dining hall. He was resplendent in pale green robe edged with gold, his shirt of matching silk and his breeks silver, the boots, too, gold. He glowed, basking in the unalloyed adoration of Ashrivelle, whose gown resembled his attire as though she

263

sought to identify with him totally, the two of them the focus of an admiring throng of nobles, most of them Galichians, Hattim's original retinue now swelled by those come south with the army. He greeted Bedyr and Yrla as if they were old friends, enquiring solicitously after Kedryn and expressing dramatic concern when he heard of Gann Resyth's news from the Fedyn Pass. Bedyr could not fault him, though it seemed to the Lord of Tamur that some emotion less than friendly lurked behind the Galichian's eyes, and he wondered if it was not satisfaction at Kedryn's apparent fate. Of Chadyn Hymet there was no sign, and when Bedyr enquired as to his whereabouts, he was told the young noble remained with the army.

'He seems polite enough,' Yrla whispered as they followed Darr into the banqueting chamber.

'Aye,' answered Bedyr, 'yet he bears no love for Kedryn.'

'Mayhap he is merely glad our son is not present,' she responded.

'Mayhap,' Bedyr nodded.

They took their seats at the high table, occupied now solely by the lords of the Kingdoms. Darr was at the centre, Ashrivelle to his right and Hattim to his left. Bedyr and Yrla sat beyond the princess, whilst Jarl and Arlynn, her gown now a veritable rainbow, were to Hattim's left. Ashrivelle spoke only of the impending wedding, voluble in her delight that now all those required by custom were present it might proceed. Bedyr was forced to endure her paen of praise to Hattim, smiling politely as she regaled them with the details of the celebration she planned. She was, as Darr had suggested, utterly besotted. Toasts were drunk to the betrothed couple, to Darr, to the victory at the Lozin Gate, and it was Hattim who rose with filled goblet to shout for silence, saying,

'My friends, you drink to my future, and I thank you for that, for with the Princess Ashrivelle at my side it can only be joyous. I ask you now to raise your goblets in toast to the Lord and Lady of Kesh, and to Lord Bedyr Caitin of Tamur and his Lady Yrla. Yet while you do, let us not forget their son, Kedryn, whose sad plight denies us his welcome presence.'

He turned, his goblet lifted first to Jarl and Arlynn, then towards Bedyr and Yrla.

'Let us drink in hope that Kedryn shall return.'

A great shout of approval met this announcement and after he had drunk, Hattim turned to speak across Darr.

'We have had our . . . disagreements . . . in the past, Bedyr, but now I hope we may be friends. My wish that Kedryn may return is sincere.'

Bedyr nodded, a rigid smile on his lips. 'My thanks, Hattim,' he answered.

'Is he not the most wonderful man?' Ashrivelle asked Yrla.

The answering smile was noncommittal, for like her husband, Yrla felt she detected the ring of falsehood in the Gallichian's unctuous manner.

The toasting went on, great roasts of venison and boar carved below the high table, fishes from the Idre and delicate vegetables from the gardens of Ust-Galich and Andurel offered to the feasters. The musicians worked busily, their tunes a selection from the three Kingdoms. Dancing followed the feasting and it was late before Darr suggested an end to the festivities. Ashrivelle protested, declaring her wish that so congenial a gathering continue until at least dawn, but Hattim took her hand, murmuring softly in her ear so that she affected a pout before kissing his cheek and agreeing to find her bed.

.'I would speak with you,' Darr murmured, a hand restraining Hattim from following his betrothed. 'There is business we must discuss and it is best settled as soon as possible.'

'I am at your command,' Hattim smiled.

'I will see you in my chambers,' nodded the king. 'With Bedyr and Jarl.'

Hattim's smile remained firmly in place; it was still there when he entered Darr's rooms, offering formal salute as the king motioned him to a chair. Lanterns cast warm yellow light over the polished chairbacks set about the hearth, sparkling from the facets of the crystal decanters resting on the low table. Jarl lounged with slippered feet close to the fire, a goblet of Keshi *lyr* in his right hand, the left toying with the ornate hilt of the curve-bladed dagger sheathed on his belt. Bedyr sat beside him, sipping evshan, his features stern in the fireglow. Darr sighed and arranged his purple robe as he sat down, selecting a pale wine of Andurel vintage. Hattim took evshan, looking from one man to another with an open, facile smile.

'The wedding may now proceed,' Darr began, 'and if Ashrivelle has her way it will be within days.'

Hattim nodded without speaking, attentive for all the wine he had consumed, seeming unaffected by the fierce liquor he was now drinking.

Darr was somewhat nonplussed by his calm, and did his best to

265

hide it. 'We must, therefore, agree the matter of your succession. That announcement needs be made before the wedding.'

'May I first speak on another matter?' Hattim enquired.

Darr nodded his assent and the Lord of Ust-Galich turned towards Bedyr.

'I ask your forgiveness for my presumption in leaving my forces on Tamurin land. Our king has, perhaps, explained it to you, but I would have you hear it from my own mouth – I offer no threat, nor intend insult. The portage down the cascades is arduous and my people expressed a desire to remain close by, wishing to celebrate my marriage. Once that is done, they will escort my wife and I south to Tessoril and disband. Meanwhile, we have accepted those terms good Darr suggested for our tenure. Do you agree this?'

Bedyr found himself taken aback by such reasonableness from a man he knew as arrogant, overbearing. What Hattim said was logical, and to respond in the negative would be to proffer insult. He ducked his head.

'The cantonment will depart after the wedding?'

'Of course,' said Hattim.

'Then I have no objection,' Bedyr agreed.

'My thanks.' Hattim smiled afresh, turning politely to Darr. 'My apologies for interrupting you, my Lord King. You spoke of the succession?'

'Aye.' Darr was as confused as Bedyr. 'I have spoken with our Lords Bedyr and Jarl and we are agreed on Chadyn Hymet. I would suggest he be summoned here and informed of our decision. If he is agreeable, then we may announce him as Lord of Ust-Galich, his assumption of that post becoming effective in the moment you take Ashrivelle as your wife. Do you agree?'

'Chadyn Hymet is a most excellent choice,' said Hattim. 'No one can dispute his loyalty to the Kingdoms; or claim he is my man. I am in full agreement.'

So smooth was his acceptance that Jarl could not stifle a gasp of surprise. Indeed, Bedyr found himself staring at the Galichian with wonder in his eyes.

'Shall I send for him on the morrow?' Hattim asked innocently. 'Or shall the summons come from the White Palace?'

'From,' Darr said slowly, 'you, I think.'

'So be it,' Hattim beamed.

They spoke then of ceremonies and residencies, Hattim agreeing easily to all suggestions, offering no resistance when asked that he voluntarily strip himself of all holdings in Ust-Galich, disassociate himself from all political ties there, and make his home from henceforth in Andurel. He agreed to the council, and that representatives of all three Kingdoms be domiciled in the White Palace to ensure fair and concerted government. He was a very paragon of moderation, giving none cause to object or find fault. It was so unlike him that when they were finally done he was the only man present at ease. He was magnanimous in his promises and effusive in his assurances, wishing them each a courtly goodnight that sent them troubled to their beds.

That politic demeanour continued as he at last made his way to his own chambers, where Mejas Celeruna and the other courtiers waited eagerly to hear what had been agreed. Hattim told them of the conversation and smoothly dismissed their sycophantic complaints that he should remain Lord of Ust-Galich and king, both. He assured them of his continued affection and sang Chadyn Hymet's praises, knowing that reports of his words would rapidly circulate throughout the White Palace.

Only when they were gone did he allow his delight to show.

He threw off his overrobe and filled a cup with wine, standing before the balcony windows as his eyes roved over the rooftops of Andurel, the smile already on his fleshy lips growing ever wider, until it occupied the larger part of his face. He raised the cup high, his arm flung out as though he would embrace all he saw, then drained it in a single gulp and threw back his head, howling laughter. Tears ran down his cheeks and the muscles of his jaws ached. Still laughing, a hand pressed to his belly, he recrossed the room to tilt the decanter over his cup. It filled with wine, and he was so consumed with self-satisfaction that the yellow liquid spilled over, pooling on the table. Uncaring, he raised the cup again and drank deep, wine trickling down his chin as he chuckled.

'It went well?'

Hattim turned, beaming at the Sister who entered silently from the adjoining chamber, feeling no unease now at sight of the possessed body.

'It went as you promised,' he chortled, and raised his glass in toast. 'I drink to you, Taws. I did all you said and they were exactly as you told me they would be. Oh, it was delightful to watch their unhappiness! They had their candidate ready to present and I accepted him without demur. I apologised to Bedyr Caitin! I asked his permission to leave my army on Tamurin soil and he could do naught but agree.

I thought Jarl might draw his dagger and seek to slay me, so amenable was I. He hated it! And Bedyr could do nothing save squirm and seek to conceal his displeasure. It was just as you promised.'

'And Kedryn?' asked the transformed mage. 'What of Tamur's prince?'

Hattim spun in a circle, his feet moving in parody of a victory dance, wine slopping from the outthrust cup, the alcohol he had drunk beginning to affect him now, combining with his joy to slur his words.

'Prince Kedryn is lost, it seems. He entered the Fedyn Pass and was, so far as Bedyr knows, buried beneath an avalanche. Was that your master's work, Taws? Was that Ashar's doing?'

The physiognomy of the woman Taws had possessed was not disposed to expression of anger, so the set of the features became disapproving rather than vexed, but the eyes grew brighter, firey, flashing an ominous red as they studied Hattim, the intensity of their gaze stilling his drunken swirling.

'What?'

The voice was now entirely that of the mage, icy as the north wind, sibilant as the threat of a serpent. Hattim froze abruptly, wine dripping unnoticed to the carpet.

'He is lost in the Fedyn Pass, Taws. Buried! Is that not what you want?'

'The Fedyn Pass?' The words seemed as hoar frost in the air, chilling Hattim. 'Why did he seek to enter the Beltrevan?'

'To regain his sight.' The Galichian's voice was no longer slurred: the mage's rubescent stare impressed sobriety on him. 'It seems a Sister awaited him in Caitin Hold with word he must seek his sight in the Beltrevan. Some necromancy was involved.'

'Borsus,' husked the mage, his tone unreal from female lips. 'He seeks the shade of Borsus.'

'But the pass fell down upon him,' Hattim said, cautious now, choosing his words more carefully. 'He must be dead.'

'*Must?*' snarled the blue-robed figure. 'Do you know that? Was his body found?'

'He frightens you!' Hattim gasped it, afraid of his own insight. 'You fear Kedryn Caitin!'

The mage moved a step towards the man and Hattim started back, rank fear in his eyes, his hands lifted as though to ward off whatever spell Taws might cast. His shoulders struck the mantel of the hearth and he shifted to remove his body from the heat, the cup dropping unnoticed to shatter on the flags. Taws' movement was swift as a striking snake, his strength not that of the woman's frame he occupied but far greater, supernatural. A hand fastened on the frontage of Hattim's silken shirt and the Galichian felt his feet leave the floor. He opened his mouth to scream for help, but Taws' gaze aborted the cry, drying it stillborn in his throat. Crimson fire burned in that stare and then the thaumaturgist lowered his arm, Hattim sighing with relief as he felt solid floor beneath him again. The sigh became a cry of alarm as he was bent backwards, his knees buckling as he struggled to remain upright, his hands fastened on the slender wrist that extended from the blue robe. He was no weakling, but against that force he was powerless, helpless as a babe, Taws driving him down and backwards until his spine arched and he felt the heat of the flame lap at his head and shoulders, his golden hair scorching, crackling and spitting, the stink of it in his nostrils.

'Was his body found?' rasped the unhuman voice.

'No!' Hattim wailed. 'For the Lady's sake, Taws, let me up!'

'For the Lady's sake?' the mage snarled. 'Do you not yet understand? You no longer serve that mistress, fool. You have a new master now.'

'For Ashar's sake, then!' moaned the Galichian. 'For our master's sake, Taws.'

The pressure eased a fraction and Hattim felt the heat lessen. He tried to draw himself up, but still he was held, poised before the flames, aware that if Taws let loose his grip he would plunge backwards into the fire.

'Do you feel the heat?' the mage demanded, an awful satisfaction in his voice. 'It is as nothing to what you can suffer should you fail our master; should you fail me.'

'I have not failed you!' Hattim moaned. 'In Ashar's name, I did everything you told me.'

'And brought me unwelcome news of Kedryn Caitin,' Taws husked. 'You say he sought to enter the Beltrevan?'

'Aye,' Hattim whimpered, incomprehension adding to his terror. 'To regain his sight, they said.'

Abruptly he was snatched forwards, lifted and flung across the room. He crashed against a chair, overturning it, unaware of the pain that burst in his shoulder at the impact, huddling close to tears, frightened eyes turned towards the mage. Taws stepped towards him again and he scrabbled away, crab-like, over the carpet. Taws halted and gestured for him to rise. Hattim climbed awkwardly to his feet, rubbing at his neck, his aching shoulder. He did not dare to speak for there burned in the ensanguined orbs so terrible a rage he was afraid any words of his might bring down that threatened fate.

'So, we know not whether Kedryn lives, or is dead.' The voice was softer now, a little less sibilant, musing almost. 'But if dead, surely I would have known. Even here I should have known. Or not? Had he slain him, could even his power reach so far?'

He paused and Hattim took a tentative step back, seeking to put distance between himself and the woman who was now Taws. A knocking sounded at the chamber's door and he gasped, awareness of the outside world intruding on his private terror. Taws turned at the sound, the red glow fading from his eyes, their colour returning to Sister Thera's natural green. He motioned at Hattim and the Lord of Ust-Galich swallowed, fighting to make his voice normal as he went to the door and called, 'What is it?'

'My Lord?' He recognised the lisping tone of Mejas Celeruna. 'Are you well? A servant reported a noise.'

Hattim looked to the door, thinking that perhaps palace guardsmen were also present, that if he cried for help they might enter before Taws had a chance to slay him, that in the ensuing confusion he might escape the mage's presence. And even as the thought flitted across his panic-struck mind he knew it was useless: he was bound to Taws now, to Ashar, and he could not escape the fate he had chosen.

'I stumbled,' he answered. 'No harm is done. A little too much wine. Leave me.'

'As you wish, Lord Hattim,' Celeruna called. 'Sleep well.'

'Aye,' Hattim responded.

When he faced Taws again the mage had calmed, become once more the Sister, blue-robed and seemingly harmless. Had I summoned guards, Hattim thought, what would they have seen? Sister Thera, no more. And if I denounced Sister Thera, if I told them she is possessed by the Messenger, what fate for me then? Condemnation as an apostate? Vilification? The loss of all my dreams? Execution, even?

'You see it,' Taws said, menacingly soft. 'You are in my web and you cannot wriggle loose.'

Hattim licked his lips, smoothing his rumpled shirt, seeking to regain some measure of dignity. 'I chose it,' he said hoarsely. 'I chose to serve Ashar.'

'Indeed,' the mage agreed with a horrid equanimity, 'and so you

270

are committed to a path from which there is no turning back. Remember that always.'

Hattim nodded.

'The matter of Kedryn remains,' Taws continued. 'If our master has slain him, then so be it. If not . . . Well, mayhap the tribes will kill him.'

'They proclaimed him hef-Alador,' Hattim ventured, 'and swore peace.'

Taws grunted. 'Then mayhap he will succeed in regaining his sight. If so, he is a greater threat.'

He paused and Hattim found the courage to ask, 'Is he truly the . . .' He broke off, afraid to complete the sentence.

'The Chosen One?' Taws spat the words as if they pained his borrowed lips. 'These blue-gowned bitches believe him so, and mayhap he is, but that matters little. He has been out of this game too long and our hand is too strong. We proceed as I have planned.'

'What if he does live?' Hattim asked nervously.

'Then he will come south into the trap we set,' Taws promised. 'He will find you in control of Andurel; his parents bait in our snare. Chosen One or not, he will be but one man against my power and the might of your army. This candidate the lordlings presented, he will obey you?'

'Chadyn Hymet?' Hattim felt a return of fear, his eyes flickering nervously. 'He bears no great love for me.'

'I did not ask that,' Taws snapped. 'Will he obey you?'

'In the matter of Kedryn?' Hattim hesitated. 'I am not sure. He is loyal to the Kingdoms.'

'Then he must not have command,' Taws declared. 'He must die.'

'You will kill him?' asked Hattim.

'When will they announce his ascendancy?' Taws countered.

'At the moment of my wedding to Ashrivelle,' Hattim answered. 'The proclamation that declares me rightful heir will also declare Chadyn Hymet Lord of Ust-Galich in my place. I agreed to that as you told me to agree to all their suggestions. I am to inform him on the morrow.'

Taws nodded. 'Then it must be before your wedding.'

'How?' Hattim wondered.

'No magic can be used,' said Taws, 'lest Kyrie's bitches sense it. You are to summon him here? Then when he comes, you will toast his good fortune with cups I shall prepare for you. He will not survive that.'

'Poison?' Hattim frowned. 'What if the Sisters provide a remedy? Or detect it?'

An obscene chuckle tittered from Sister Thera's lips as Taws shook his head. 'They will not. There is no remedy, and the potion I shall prepare will leave no trace. All who drink will suffer – and the vintner will be blamed for his tainted wine.'

'All?' Hattim asked warily.

'Aye.' Taws laughed again, the sound ugly. '*Suffer*, not die. That fate I shall reserve for Chadyn Hymet alone – the others shall have a remedy.'

'If Hymet dies,' Hattim said, confident that Taws would have the answer ready, 'then some other of Darr's choosing will be selected.'

'What you will drink will not act immediately.' Taws confirmed the Galichian's certainty. 'It will curdle slowly and he will die scant hours before the ceremony. There will be no time to select another. The rest will suffer a little, but survive – after all, am I not a Sister Hospitaller?'

Hattim nodded, wondering if there was any eventuality for which the mage was not prepared. Had he truly thought Taws afraid of Kedryn? How could he be when he was so powerful? Chosen One or not, Kedryn must surely fall before such might.

'Sleep now,' Taws suggested. 'There is business to be done ere long, and you must ready yourself for your wedding.'

'Aye.' Hattim smiled as his confidence returned, watching the blue-robed figure turn and walk to the door that connected their chambers. 'Our master's business.'

The door closed behind Taws and Hattim Sethiyan filled a last cup with wine, drinking deep before he went into his bedroom, the ache in his shoulder forgotten as he thought of his ascendancy and the power it would bring him.

He slept well and long, waking to winter sunlight and the announcement that the Princess Ashrivelle waited in the antechamber, eager to decide the day of their marriage now that all was settled favourably. He rose, bidding the servant comb his hair as he set rings on his fingers and fastened a pendant in his pierced ear. He dressed modestly in a shirt of plain gold and dark green breeks, boots of pale green and a tunic of white, admiring his reflection before he went out to greet his betrothed.

Ashrivelle ignored the servants setting breakfast for Hattim as she flung her arms about his neck and pressed her lips to his mouth.

272

'I have seen my father and he has told me all is agreed,' she declared gaily, 'so we may set the time.'

'As soon as possible,' Hattim said, smiling. 'I would make you my wife today if I were able.'

Ashrivelle affected a pretty frown. 'It cannot be so soon,' she giggled, 'for there is much to prepare. But in five days' time?'

'So be it,' Hattim agreed. 'In five days' time.'

From the corner of his eye he saw the face of Sister Thera move from the slightly opened door between their chambers and knew that Taws was gone to prepare his poison.

'I cannot believe him dead.'

Yrla turned from the window of Sister Bethany's chamber, the sun striking blue light from her raven hair. Her face was concerned, yet determined, her voice fierce.

'Did winter not cut us off from Estrevan I might be in better position to answer you,' Bethany said, 'but all our communications are limited by this weather, so I can do little save join you in prayer.'

'He is the Chosen One, is he not?' Yrla spread the wide skirt of her russet gown as she sat, smoothing the folds across her legs her grey eyes intent on the face of the Paramount Sister. 'Do you believe the Lady would let him die?'

'It may not be a question of *let*,' Bethany answered. 'I intend no hurt – and I share your fervent hope – but the Beltrevan *is* Ashar's domain and it may be that the mad god succeeded.'

'No!' Yrla said. 'I will not believe that.'

'Because he is your son?' Bethany asked gently, 'or because of something else?'

'I feel . . .' Yrla paused, marshalling her thoughts, seeking to impose logic on feelings she knew she must admit might be no more than maternal optimism, a natural reluctance to admit Kedryn's death. 'I feel that some pattern unfolds.'

'Kedryn and Wynett?' Bethany nodded. 'It is possible. I had thought of that myself – even hoped it, though it would lose the Sisterhood a devotee likely to become Paramount Sister of Estrevan itself. But then you brought this news from the Fedyn Pass.'

'They found no bodies,' Yrla said doggedly.

'But Gann Resyth saw a rocky tomb.' Bethany sighed, smoothing strands of white hair from her stern brow. 'And no word has come down the Idre.'

'It is too soon,' Yrla said, continuing when Bethany frowned a

273

question, 'If they survived the avalanche they had still to find the Drott Gathering, and then to seek the aid of the shamans. To enter the underworld and find the shade of the warrior. To return – to High Fort, now that the Fedyn Pass is sealed. To come down the Idre. It is too soon to know.'

'And too soon to hope he might appear before the wedding,' Bethany murmured, her tone provoking a sharp glance from Yrla.

'You do not approve?'

The white-haired woman played for a moment with the blue gem on her third finger. 'I do not believe Hattim Sethiyan to be the stuff of which kings are made. I had hoped Kedryn might find favour in Ashrivelle's eyes.'

Yrla smiled tautly and shook her head. 'Kedryn loves Wynett; he would not, I think, consider Ashrivelle.'

'Who appears besotted with the Lord of Ust-Galich,' Bethany nodded. 'Swiftly and totally.'

Yrla heard the doubt in her voice and asked, 'You suspect some deviousness?'

Bethany shrugged. 'There is nothing I can detect. No taint of magic, and I can hardly ask to examine the princess for evidence of love potions.'

'What of this Sister Hattim favours so?' asked Yrla.

'Thera?' Bethany shrugged again. 'I have had little contact with Sister Thera of late so close does Hattim keep her. She is a Hospitaller who attended him on his arrival – so well, it seems, that he requested her permanent presence in his retinue. She was agreeable and I felt her proximity would be a beneficial influence on the man.'

'Certainly he appears changed,' Yrla murmured.

'Does he not?' said Bethany. 'Do you not approve of the change?'

'If it is genuine,' Yrla said carefully, 'then yes. But I find it hard to credit so drastic a shift in behaviour.'

Bethany nodded. 'As do I. It is too unlike Hattim.'

'Think you that he plays some secret game?' Yrla wondered.

'If so, it is well hidden,' answered Bethany. 'He appears the very ideal of reasonableness. He has given offence to no one and agreed to every measure suggested by Darr.'

'And in so doing given no one opportunity to question him,' Yrla said. 'My husband feels it is all, his word for it was, too neat.'

'Indeed,' Bethany agreed. 'Do you think that part of this pattern you sense?'

'I do not know.' It was Yrla's turn to shrug. 'What I feel is so vague, so open to question.'

'Explain it to me,' Bethany asked, 'as best you can.'

Yrla was silent for a moment, then: 'Estrevan believes the Messenger alive still, working Ashar's design in some way we do not yet comprehend. If Alaria's Text is correct, then only Kedryn – as the Lady's Chosen One – may defeat him. The battle of the Lozin Gate left Kedryn blind, yet that very blindness drew Wynett closer to him – she loves him, whether she admits that to herself or not – and Wynett is Darr's elder daughter and thus a candidate for the High Throne. Did she renounce her vows in acceptance of her love, then wed to Kedryn she would make him candidate for the White Palace, rather than Hattim Sethiyan; and my son would make a better king.

'Yet now it seems that Hattim will take that prize with such alacrity that nothing can stand in his way, prevent what many consider a succession detrimental to the Kingdoms.'

'Do you say that Hattim works Ashar's design?' Bethany demanded, her voice sharp with disbelief. 'Surely not. Surely it cannot be. Whatever his faults, Hattim Sethiyan is no acolyte of that evil god.'

'I do not know,' Yrla admitted. 'I do not see how it could be, and yet . . .'

She broke off, helplessly, her lovely face creased by a troubled frown. Bethany stared at her, her own stern features worried. For long moments they sat with only the crackling of the fire burning in the hearth to disturb the silence.

Then the Paramount Sister said, 'You were amongst the most promising of the acolytes, and you have studied the Text: mayhap there is something in what you say. Certainly there seems, as you have put it, some kind of pattern, though still I cannot credit this notion that Hattim Sethiyan has sold his soul to Ashar.'

Yrla shrugged again, shaking her head. 'Mayhap not. Mayhap the possible loss of my son confuses me. But I had felt that so long a time together would surely clarify Wynett's feelings, and that such clarification would lead to marriage. And did that but happen, we should not sit here speaking as we do.'

'No,' said Bethany, cautiously, 'for we should celebrate the ascendance of a most welcome heir. But Kedryn is not here, nor can we surmise Wynett's intentions.'

'And so we must accept Hattim Sethiyan?' Yrla said softly. 'Even though we doubt him? Even though he might – knowingly or not – work Ashar's design?'

'What other choice have we?' Bethany asked.

'To trust in the Lady,' said Yrla. 'And in Kedryn as the Chosen One, for if this pattern I sense is real, then only Kedryn may break the web, and if Alaria's prophecy is true, then Kedryn *cannot* be dead.'

'But we cannot know that,' said Bethany sadly.

'But if we do not believe it, then we do not credit the Text,' Yrla said.

Bethany sighed, toying again with her ring, her expression one of grief and confusion. 'The Lady leaves us the gift of choice,' she said, very slowly, 'and so no prophecy is binding. Alaria had a greater gift than any other Sister, but even the Text is not a guarantee, it is not a thing of certainty. It is possible that Ashar can circumvent its guidance.'

Yrla stared at her then, finally, said, 'No, I must believe that Kedryn lives to save the Kingdoms.'

'I pray that you are right,' came the quiet answer, 'but I cannot share your confidence.'

When Ashrivelle at last quit his chambers, eager to set in motion the preparations for their wedding, Hattim despatched a messenger to fetch Chadyn Hymet from the cantonment. Once that was done and his rooms emptied, Sister Thera came in with two flasks of wine. One, Taws explained, was envenomed, the other the antidote. The Lord of Ust-Galich should toast his cousin's appointment and after he was gone, administer the remedy to those who remained. Hattim stared at the flasks, for all the world no more than a particularly ancient Galichian vintage, suitable for so momentous an occasion. He set the poisoned brew at the centre of the table and awaited Hymet's arrival, somewhat surprised to find himself so calm as the closest of his court gathered about him, anxious to curry favour with the Lord-to-be and the future King.

Hymet arrived a little after noon, wrapped in a heavy winter cloak. He was a tall, homely man, his clothes drab in comparison with the finery sported by Hattim and his sycophants, his brown hair severely cut, his jewellery limited to a simple earring and a mere two finger rings. He saluted Hattim courteously enough, though his expression suggested he had rather remained with his men. It changed to one of surprise when Hattim told him that he was to become Lord of Ust-Galich.

'Lord Hattim,' he gulped, 'I had not expected this. I do not deserve such favour.'

'He is modest,' lisped Mejas Celeruna.

'Modesty becomes a Lord,' beamed Hattim, 'and you will, I know, rule our Kingdom wisely, dear Chadyn.'

Hymet bowed, confused by his sudden acceleration to so lofty a position.

'A toast!' Hattim cried. 'I have found a suitable vintage in which to drink your health.'

Smiling hugely he broke the seal of the poisoned flask and began to fill goblets.

'To Chadyn Hymet, Lord of Ust-Galich!'

He raised his cup, watching as the others followed suit, echoing his toast. The wine sat smooth upon his tongue, subtle as the vintage promised, with no hint of poison.

'To the Lord Hattim,' cried Mejas Celeruna unctuously. 'To our future king.'

Each cup was drained to the full.

Chapter Thirteen

TEPSHEN Lahl squatted beneath the awning of Cord's lodge throwing knuckle bones with the Ulan's Gehrim, his fulvous features impassive as he raked in his winnings. He had waited there for three days, refusing invitations to hunt or engage in the combats that occupied much of the Drott's time, calmly declaring his intention of remaining until his charges should emerge from the medicine tent, or be declared lost, and the barbarians had given up their efforts to divert the solemn easterner, choosing finally – to their occasional regret – to gamble with him. He had amassed a selection of excellent furs and a handful of gold coins and held the bones ready to throw when a movement from the small structure at the foot of Drul's Mound caught his eye and he sprang to his feet, the dice falling unnoticed, though had anyone looked they would have seen he had won again.

The entrance flap was thrown back and the shamans came out, the paint decorating their bodies and faces streaked with sweat, their eyes wide with wonder. They formed a semi-circle about the entrance, their rattles chattering triumphantly. Then Kedryn and Wynett emerged and the kyo saw that they were changed in ways both obvious and subtle. They were smiling, joy shining radiant in their eyes, and their hands were entwined, that physical proximity seeming to Tepshen symptomatic of a deeper closeness. They lifted their faces to the afternoon sky, drinking in the Gathering's odoriferous air as if it were fine wine, and he knew as he studied them that Kedryn could see again unaided, and that the linking of their hands, the glances – almost secrective – that they gave one another, spoke of union, a joining at last admitted openly. He walked down between the skull-hung poles to greet them, his own lips curving in an expression of unalloyed pleasure.

'You can see,' he said, simply.

'Aye,' Kedryn let go Wynett's hand, beaming at the kyo, studying him from head to toe as if for the first time. 'We found Borsus and he gave me back my sight. Gave me more than sight.'

He reached out taking the Sister's hand again and Tepshen Lahl bowed in elaborate eastern fashion, knowing what else it was the quadi had given them as Wynett, shyly, pressed close to Kedryn's side, her smile bright as the rising sun.

'You must be hungry,' Tepshen remarked practically. 'You have been gone four nights and three days.'

'So long?' Kedryn was surprised. 'It seems . . . I do not know – it was hard to estimate time there.'

Cord emerged from his lodge then, drawn by the rattles and the growing hubbub as news of the return spread through the camp and the forest folk began to gather, gazing in awe at the pair.

'You are truly the hef-Alador,' he declared, his voice husky with respect. 'Come, rest – you must be tired after so long and I would hear what went on in the shadow land.'

Kedryn nodded and allowed the Ulan to escort them, proprietorial, into his lodge as the shamans struck the medicine tent and consigned its hides and poles to the flames of the great fire that burned on the tumulus, the Gehrim forming a deferential honour guard about them.

Inside Cord's hogan wine was brought, and beer, both in great quantities as the ala-Ulans crowded in, eager as their chieftain to hear an account of the descent into the underworld. Food appeared, and Kedryn and Wynett both realised, as their stomachs announced vocal anticipation, that whilst their spirits seemed to possess no sense of time, or require sustenance, their bodies did, indeed, crave food and drink. They ate well, recounting between mouthfuls what had transpired, aware of the growing reverence with which the barbarians regarded them, seeing in the dark eyes the same awe that had possessed the common folk outside. It became a feast, Cord's thralls delivering an increasing variety of dishes, lingering themselves to hear the story, the ala-Ulans shouting questions, demanding the re-telling, until at last the Ulan, himself more than a little the worse for his celebrating, declared a triumphal progress in order. Kedryn protested, but was shouted down, and found himself, an arm protective about Wynett's shoulders, hustled out of the lodge, where the Gehrim, as though they had been awaiting just this event, raised their shields to form a platform on to which Kedryn and Wynett were hoisted by the eager chieftains.

They crouched upon the overlapping bucklers as Cord, his own arm companionably flung around Tepshen Lahl, strode out in front, bellowing in the language of the Drott. The procession circled Drul's Mound three times, then wove amongst the massed ranks of lodges, the dense throng of forest folk parting to give it way, the dark faces turned to observe the wondrous couple, their voices rising in a tumult of congratulation, the excitement communicating to the great hounds that freely roamed the Gathering so that they, too, added their belling to the din. It seemed to Kedryn that all the Beltrevan must ring with the clamour, the shouting carrying to the Kingdoms themselves, and he smiled, delight filling him as his eyes roved, sighted, over the beaming faces and the mushroom-like growths of the hogans. Up and down the avenues they went, circling the outer perimeter of the camp, then down again amongst the tents, at last returning to the tumulus and the entrance to Cord's lodge.

Afternoon had become dusk and that turned into night before the procession ended and the Gehrim lowered their shields, allowing the two to step down on to firm ground again. The fire on the mound burned bright against the star-pricked sky, the great orb of the moon that had heralded their entry into the nether world flattening as time carved slices from its girth. The crowd eased, shifting and departing, and Kedryn experienced an unfamiliar nervousness as he took Wynett's hand, leading her back into the hogan.

The remnants of the feast were cleared away and the hide curtains that gave access to the sleeping quarters lifted. Cord was swaying on his feet, and when he downed a horn of beer in toast, his eyes glazed and he shook his head like some troubled bear, grunting an apology as he stumbled towards his furs and crashed face-down, snoring instantly, oblivious of the slaves who came to undress him. Kedryn found himself alone with Wynett and Tepshen Lahl, and felt the nervousness grow.

'Would that there were baths here,' Wynett murmured.

'Wait.'

Tepshen was gone on the word. Kedryn drew Wynett close, holding her, and whispered, 'I am ... I feel as I did before my first battle. Afraid? I am not sure ... but ...'

'I know,' she replied, her face against his chest. 'I, too. Let us bathe as best we can, and then ...'

Her voice tailed off into silence and Kedryn held her, content to feel her in his arms, not speaking, still filled with that sense of triumph mingled with almost frightened anticipation.

Tepshen returned then with thralls in tow, dragging in a construction of hides and circular wands that rapidly became a small tub. With equal rapidity it was filled with hot water and the kyo, a slight smile on his face, suggested that Wynett be allowed to lave herself, discreetly removing Kedryn to the outer chambers of the tent.

They sat at the table that had held the feast and Tepshen filled two mugs with wine.

'You are changed,' he said. 'As is Wynett.'

Kedryn nodded: 'She loves me. She has said it.'

'At last,' murmured Tepshen. 'It has taken long enough.'

'Was it so obvious, then?' asked Kedryn, frowning.

'To all who saw you,' smiled the kyo, raising his mug in a toast. 'I drink to your future.'

'She has not yet said she will forego her vows,' Kedryn said thoughtfully.

'She does not need to,' replied Tepshen. 'Do you not see it in her eyes?'

For a moment Kedryn looked mournful, then he smiled wryly.

'I do not have much experience of love. What should I do?'

'Do?' Tepshen chuckled. 'You are a man and she is a woman – you will know what to do.'

'She is still a Sister,' argued Kedryn. 'And we are not yet wed.'

'You do not need to be wed,' Tepshen responded, still chuckling. 'And I do not think Wynett will remain a Sister for long.'

'You think we should ... ?' Kedryn stared at his friend, who nodded.

'I do.'

'Before ... ?'

Tepshen nodded again.

'I am not sure,' said Kedryn.

'Then let Wynett decide,' suggested the kyo. 'She is the one who must agree to loss; you, only to gain. Let her decide.'

Kedryn nodded, then: 'I am nervous.'

'That is understandable,' said Tepshen, his voice serious now, although the smile remained. 'You will overcome that.'

'If Wynett decides ...'

'Aye, if Wynett decides.'

Wynett called then that she had vacated the tub and Kedryn rose.

'I will find quarters with the Gehrim,' Tepshen said softly, smiling at the young man he loved so well. Kedryn returned the smile and pushed aside the curtain.

He found a steaming tub in an empty chamber and stripped off his clothing, climbing gratefully into the water. No thralls appeared and he scrubbed himself clean, then dried himself and bundled his clothing. The lodge was quiet, save for Cord's soft snoring, and he took a deep breath, aware of his heart pounding drum-like against his ribs.

Let Wynett decide.

He licked his lips, his feet slow on the fur-covered floor as he crossed to the flap concealing the sleeping chamber.

Let Wynett decide.

He pushed the flap aside and stepped into darkness as it fell closed behind him. Sighted now, he was blind again, dropping his gear to the floor as he fumbled his way to the mound of cushions and furs that made his bed.

He slipped beneath the coverings with his new-found vision adjusting to the absence of light. It seemed to him that he held his breath while all his body tingled, each nerve ending alert, anticipatory. He was not sure whether he wanted to find Wynett there, or whether it would be easier were she beyond the dividing curtain. Perhaps it was best they talk. Wait until they were returned to the Kingdoms. Wed formally.

He felt smooth skin, warm, brush his thigh, and gasped, startled despite himself.

'Wynett?' he whispered.

'Kedryn,' she answered, and he felt her hands upon his shoulders, his face, drawing him towards her.

'I love you,' he said.

And she said, 'I love you.'

Then her lips were on his and he held her hard against him, feeling all the length of her body soft and smooth and warm, moulding to him, her arms encircling him, the scent of her hair and skin in his nostrils, the smell and the touch of her driving away the nervousness and replacing it with a soaring sense of joy, of triumph, greater by far than any he had known.

'Your vows?' he husked against the tenderness of her neck, feeling it arch beneath his caress.

'The Lady grants us choice,' she gasped, her hands in his hair, pushing his lips lower until they were moving with gentle excitement over the mounds of her breasts. 'I have chosen.'

She moaned then, as his mouth touched the apex of her bosom, and he said against the hardened nub, 'I am glad.'

They spoke no more after that, save in wordless sounds of love and pleasure. They had no need, for they knew they were joined, not only in physical mingling that lifted them to undreamed of heights, but deeper, in private ways, with welcome bonds that could not be severed.

For that night their world became joyfully limited. The Gathering, the Beltrevan, the Kingdoms, did not exist: there was only the darkened sleeping chamber, no Messenger, no malign god, no danger or threat; only the two who gave themselves freely to one another, wanting nothing save that commingling that was, for them, a truer marriage night than any ceremony could bestow.

It ended all too soon with the ruckus that marked the awakening of the Gathering. Cord's voice, shouting hoarsely for food, brought them from slumber, waking to the unfamiliar sensation of a shared bed, of limbs that twined enticingly, blonde hair spread wide on furry pillows, smiles of shy modesty. Kedryn studied Wynett's drowsy face and kissed her gently, glorying in the cornflower eyes that shone into his.

'You are lovely,' he said.

'As are you,' she answered, her lips inviting further caresses. 'But I knew that.'

Kedryn smiled a question, his eyes drinking in her body.

'Do you not remember?' she giggled. 'When you came wounded to High Fort? When I found you naked in my hospital?'

Kedryn laughed, taking her in his arms again, speaking against her hair.

'I did not think then that we should come to this, but I loved you then. I think I loved you from the first moment I saw you.'

'I think,' she said, her mouth against his, 'that I loved you, but I did not know it. Or how great was my love.'

'You do not regret anything?' he asked, knowing that soon they must rise and enter a more public world.

'Nothing,' she answered, her voice confident. 'Whatever I have lost, I have gained more. I saw that when we faced Borsus.'

'Praise the Lady,' Kedryn said fervently,'

'Aye,' Wynett agreed, 'praise the Lady.'

They dressed then and went out of the sleeping chamber to find Cord and Tepshen Lahl eating breakfast, the smells of fresh-baked bread and roasted meat awakening their appetites. Cord turned a dishevelled head towards them and smiled blearily.

'You . . . slept . . . well?'

Kedryn felt the skin of his face grow warm at the good natured innuendo and realised, uncomfortably, that he was blushing as he nodded and said, 'Aye, thank you.'

He glanced at Wynett as the Ulan began to laugh and saw that she, too, was flushed, though her smile remained radiant as she said solemnly, 'Very well indeed,' thus reducing Cord to table-pounding merriment.

Tepshen Lahl behaved as though nothing had changed, rising to his feet to bow courteously and indicate the empty chairs, asking, 'Are you hungry?'

'Ravenous,' Kedryn said, and began to laugh simply because he felt so happy.

It was a glorious winter day, the sun that shone through the open tent flap seeming to bestow its own blessing on their joining, the sky a blue so pure it dazzled the eye, streaked here and there with streamers of white cloud run out like celebratory pennants on the wind. The air was crisp, stifling the noisome odour of the Gathering, the woodsmoke smell of the fire on the mound lending a homely scent. They sat and ate, no longer embarrassed, for in Cord's laughter and Tepshen's smile there was only approval, expression of pleasure in their happiness.

'What now?' asked the Ulan, reality intruding. 'Do you remain here, or return to the Kingdoms?'

'We return,' Kedryn said, then looked to Wynett for confirmation.

'We must,' she nodded. 'There are tasks yet to accomplish.'

Cord's smile dulled then, for he knew what those tasks were and for all his opposition to the shaman's power he was wary of offending the god who still ruled the Beltrevan.

'You ride against the Messenger,' he murmured in his heavily-accented Tamurin.

'I must,' Kedryn confirmed. 'It is my duty.'

'I cannot help you in that,' Cord said. 'You have strengthened my position — and I thank you for that — but I cannot ask my people to go against the elect of Ashar.'

'I would not ask it of you,' said Kedryn. 'I ask only that you observe the agreements we made and keep the peace.'

'I will,' Cord promised, 'and I will give you an escort to the gates of High Fort. When will you leave?'

Kedryn looked to Wynett and Tepshen and said, 'Today?'

Cord nodded. 'So be it. I will have provisions readied, and my own Gehrim shall furnish your escort.'

284

'Thank you,' Kedryn said, wondering that such bonds of friendship could be formed so easily when men spoke openly together.

They were once again the centre of attention as they prepared to depart the Drott Gathering. It seemed the whole tribe clustered about their path as they rode between the lodges, Cord slightly ahead on one of the geldings donated at the peace talks, and Tepshen Lahl behind, flanked by the escorting Gehrim, now armoured beneath their heavy furs as befitted the convoy of the hef-Alador. The shamans, won over to a new respect, capered before them, shaking their rattles and blowing noisily on bone flutes in what, Cord explained, was a ceremony of prayer for their safe return.

On the rim of the great hollow that held the camp Cord reined in, a hand lifted in salute.

'Go in safety,' he said, 'and may your goddess be with you. Whatever should transpire, know that Cord of the Drott is your friend. And do not forget those stallions you promised.'

'I shall not,' Kedryn averred.

Cord's eyes, still bloodshot from his enthusiastic drinking, twinkled as he added, 'And take care of your woman – she is a prize.'

'I know,' Kedryn said solemnly. 'Farewell, Cord. Farewell, my friend.'

The Ulan nodded and waved them away, the Gehrim rising up to take the lead as they wound their way amongst the trees over snow frozen hard now, the figures on the ridge soon lost as the great woods of the Beltrevan swallowed them.

The horses, rested and well-fed after their sojourn, made a good pace and Kedryn saw how much he had missed in his blindness. For all that Wynett's touch had granted him sight, it had not been possible to maintain that necessary contact throughout their entry into the forests, and now he was able to see with his own eyes the magnificence of winter's mantle. The massive, ancient trees were hung with cloaks of snow that sparkled under the brilliance of the sun, glittering with a myriad frosty colours that danced and swirled, rainbow cascades of shimmering flakes falling as birds started from their path. The undergrowth took on new forms, like crystalline statuary, limbs draped with icicles like pendant jewels, their shadows dramatic on the unsoiled albino ground. Breath steamed in the cold air and from the pounding hooves exploded clouds of drifting white. There was a wild beauty to the place that filled him with awe, a feeling of reverence, and a deep resentment that so wilfully evil a god as Ashar claimed sway over so lovely a domain.

It occurred to him that the god might yet seek to block their way, preventing their return to the Kingdoms, for if he had been able to bring the Fedyn Pass down about their ears, then surely he must be able to conjure some obstacle here, so much deeper into his territory. Yet, even though good companions had been lost to the avalanche, he and Wynett and Tepshen Lahl had survived, and then Tepshen's sword skill had won them a way to the Gathering; and there Cord had overridden the objections of the shamans to open the way into the shadow world; and there the talismans and Wynett's love had seen them safely through. Perhaps then, he thought, Ashar's dominance was indeed weakened, and the god would not be able to prevent their return. And in the Kingdoms, where the Lady ruled, surely Ashar's power must be weaker still, his Messenger an enemy capable of defeat.

The thought, allied with the certain knowledge of Wynett's love and the sheer magnificence of their surroundings, cheered him and he threw back his head, laughing at the sky.

The sound prompted Wynett to turn from her own contemplation of the scenery, her eyes twinkling from the enfolding cowl of her cloak's hood, tendrils of sun-blonde hair curling over the edges of the fur.

'Will you share your happiness?' she asked.

'I feel that we shall win,' he told her. 'I feel that nothing can prevent us now.'

'We have achieved much,' she agreed, though a trifle more soberly, 'but the Messenger remains.'

'Aye,' Kedryn smiled at her, their mounts matching pace, the windrush exhilarating, 'but we have braved the underworld, you and I, and I feel that nothing can defeat us.'

'The Lady grant you truth,' Wynett shouted back, then answered his smile with a radiance that stilled his breath. 'And I believe she will.'

They continued on, halting at noon to eat and rest the horses, then proceeding until dusk, when the Gehrim set up tents in the shelter of enormous oaks. They ate, seated around a blazing fire, and then retired, Kedryn and Wynett delighted at the privacy afforded by the shelter of hide, climbing swiftly beneath the furs to rediscover the intoxicating pleasure acknowledgement of their love had introduced.

The reserve Wynett had affected, the restrictions imposed by her calling, were gone now, as if, having come to that inner resolution of purpose, she gave herself to Kedryn as fervently as she had embraced the duties of a Sister. There were no regrets, no doubts or second thoughts, but rather a whole-hearted acceptance of their new-found relationship that found ardent expression in their shared bed. Her pleasure, as his, was unalloyed, and when finally they slept, it was in one another's arms, innocently, free of any qualms of conscience, justified by the deep inner conviction that what they did was right, approved of by that deity to whom they still gave service. They did not see, though perhaps they sensed, the gentle pulsing of the talismans that shone with a soft blue effulgence as they slept.

They rode on through days of fine weather. Occasional flurries of snow served only to enhance the beauty of the forest, the Gehrim leading them swift and sure over the woodland trails to the river called the Saran, whose course they followed south and east. Five days along that trail they met a solitary rider.

At first they did not see him, for he was hidden behind the dark boles of massive beech trees, dismounted, with a nocked bow in his hands until he recognised them. Then he shouted:

'Hail, friends! You are well-met.'

The Gehrim formed a protective phalanx about their charges, bows with the red and white peace feathers still attached lifting to cover the shadowy figure. Tepshen Lahl eased his shaft down and called, 'Brannoc?'

'None other,' declared the Warden, emerging from the trees with lowered bow and a huge smile.

Wynett called out in the byavan to the Gehrim and they set their weapons at rest, those who recognised the former wolfshead shouting to the others that he was a friend.

Brannoc sheathed his bow and fetched his horses from the trees, coming out of the shadows to study the trio of Kingdomers and their escort.

'I would surmise,' he remarked, casually as if they met on some street corner, 'that your quest was successful.'

'Aye, it was,' Kedryn grinned, dismounting to embrace the furclad man. 'But what brings you here? Do you come as Forest Warden?'

'As a seeker after truth,' beamed Brannoc, affecting an air of mystery and clearly enjoying the surprise he read on their faces. 'Sister Wynett, Tepshen – you are well?'

'Aye,' the kyo replied. Then, bluntly, 'Why are you here?'

'The truth I seek concerns you,' Brannoc said, ignoring Tepshen's gesture of impatience as he studied Kedryn's face. 'You have won back your sight. You found the quadi?'

'Aye,' Kedryn nodded. 'Wynett and I entered the nether world and found him, and he returned my vision.'

'I am glad,' said Brannoc simply.

'Why are you here?' Tepshen repeated.

'You are lovelier than ever, Sister.' Brannoc continued to ignore the kyo, addressing Wynett. 'This quest appears to suit you.'

'It does most excellently,' Wynett replied, 'though I am no longer a Sister.'

'So!' Brannoc's smile grew wider still. 'You saw the light at last. It makes you radiant.'

'Thank you,' Wynett said, smiling in return. 'But why *are* you here?'

'Word came to Caitin Hold that the Fedyn Pass had fallen,' Brannoc announced, ducking his head slightly as Tepshen Lahl grunted approval of his at last coming to the point, 'and Kedryn's parents travelled to High Fort to ask that I find you. More precisely, to discover whether you still lived, or had fallen to Ashar's hand.'

'They must be wretched,' Wynett declared, concern in her voice.

'They are, indeed, mightily worried,' said Brannoc. 'But now we may return together with this happy news.'

'They are at High Fort?' Kedryn asked. 'Is there word of the Messenger?'

'They are,' said Brannoc, 'and no, there is no word. Winter grips the Kingdoms and all is quiet.'

'That, at least, is good news,' Kedryn signed, 'but now we must make haste to set their minds at rest.'

'Then let us ride,' grunted Tepshen, 'and let this babbler prattle from his saddle.'

'You have lost none of your charm,' grinned Brannoc.

Tepshen Lahl smiled back. 'Mount, friend, and let us be gone.'

'Aye, and as we ride you can tell me of your adventures,' Brannoc agreed, swinging astride his dun and casting a mischievious glance at Kedryn and Wynett. 'At least, of those suitable for my ears.'

Under Ashrivelle's eager command preparations for the wedding proceeded apace. The seamstresses of the White Palace were busy with the gown she designed, the musicians occupied with the creation of new melodies, each one requiring her approval, the cooks excelled themselves in the devising of menus. The cellars were checked and re-checked in the search for noble vintages of an excellence and antiquity suitable to so momentous an occasion.

The Galichian contingent occupied the clothiers of the city with their search for garments, and a procession of mehdri rode out with invitations to the nobility of Kesh and Tamur domiciled close enough to attend. Traders in jewels and cloth enjoyed a boom unprecedented since Darr's coronation, whilst those selling foodstuffs found their purses swelling as the servitors of the palace ensured sufficient viands were readied for the celebration. Hattim Sethiyan was liberal in his own preparations, commissioning outfits and jewellery in abundance, and all of Andurel was gripped with excitement.

Those who doubted the wisdom of the impending union felt almost guilty as the princess rushed about the palace, alight with anticipation, and Hattim continued suavely diplomatic, offering no cause for criticism. Yrla reported her conversation with Bethany to Bedyr, who in turn, discussed it with Darr and Jarl, but none could find it in themselves to give credence to her suspicions, and even she began to genuinely wonder if distress at Kedryn's fate clouded her judgement. To make matters worse she found herself, with Arlynn of Kesh, required to share in Ashrivelle's bustle. Her opinion was sought on the wedding gown and the form of the celebrations, on the choice of music and of wines, and all the time she was forced to listen to the princess sing a paen of praise to her husband-to-be, unable to express to the besotted girl her doubts.

For Darr, Bedyr and Jarl it was no easier, Hattim's ready accept-ance of the strictures they set about his assumption drawing the teeth of any objections they might have raised. Whatever their personal opinions of the Lord of Ust-Galich, they could not disagree with his right to marry Ashrivelle, nor fault his behaviour as the day of the wedding drew inexorably closer and they were drawn into the preparations, the ceremony itself requiring their official approval, the billeting of the Galichian officers needing management, a myriad duties calling for their guidance.

No news of Kedryn came as the day approached, though one old friend appeared to brighten Bedyr's and Yrla's carefully concealed apprehension.

They were alone in their chambers, Bedyr studying a list of those Galichian warriors quartered in the palace and about the city, Yrla examining the gown she proposed to wear, when a servant announced the arrival of Galen Sadreth.

The river captain filled the door as he entered, his bulk greater, if anything, than before, his ruddy moon lace beaming. He flung

289

back a fanciful cloak of oiled green cloth trimmed with black fur and doffed his feathered cap, his bald pate gleaming as he bowed.

'My Lord Bedyr, Lady Yrla,' he declared, his booming voice echoing about the room, 'Greetings.'

'And to you, Galen,' Bedyr smiled, beckoning the huge man in. 'You are well?'

'As anyone,' Galen said. 'Though this news – or its absence – of Kedryn troubles me.'

'He will return,' said Yrla firmly, motioning the riverman to a chair that he filled to overflowing. 'Brannoc seeks him e'en now.'

'None better suited to find him,' Galen nodded, easing off his cloak to reveal a tunic of startling crimson, with breeks to match and boots of gleaming black leather that might serve as buckets, 'and I pray that he will be successful.'

'You appear to be.' Bedyr indicated the captain's extravagant outfit.

'I like to dress well whilst ashore,' Galen declared modestly, 'and with so many Galichians thronging Andurel like peacocks I see no reason why they should outshine me.'

Bedyr chuckled, lifting a decanter of evshan in enquiry. Galen nodded, beaming as he watched a goblet filled. He took it and drank deep, sighing as the fiery liquor went down.

'Excellent,' he murmured, 'just the thing to hold out this wolf weather.'

'Does it affect your enterprise?' Yrla asked.

Galen nodded, 'There is little commerce whilst this north wind blows, and ice has been reported on the Idre. Consequently I am without a cargo – which may be fortunate.'

He emptied his goblet, accepting the replenishment Bedyr offered with a grateful smile.

'How so?' asked the Lord of Tamur.

'It occurred to me that you may wish Kedryn to join you here,' said Galen, 'and with the Fedyn Pass blocked he must surely find his way to High Fort. Should the *Vashti* be waiting for him there, I could bring him south far swifter than any horse.'

'Galen!' Yrla clapped her hands delightedly. 'You are sent by the Lady!'

'Mayhap,' said the riverman, scratching his pate, 'the idea did come upon me most suddenly.'

'It is an excellent idea,' Bedyr agreed, 'though I would suggest a slight amendment.'

Galen raised one enquiring eyebrow, the expression lending him the appearance of a massive owl.

'The wedding takes place two days hence,' Bedyr said. 'Delay your departure until the third day and we shall accompany you. Rather than bring Kedryn to us, take us to him.'

'Can we?' asked Yrla, excitement in her voice. 'So soon?'

'Our presence is required for the ceremony and at the banquet after.' Bedyr shrugged, smiling at his wife. 'Whether Hattim remains in Andurel or takes Ashrivelle into Ust-Galich, they will have no need of us. Darr will understand and there is no insult in it.'

'I had thought we should remain to see how Hattim will behave once announced as heir,' murmured Yrla.

'He will be heir, not king,' Bedyr said. 'Darr will still rule and he will welcome news of Wynett no less eagerly than we seek it of Kedryn.'

Yrla nodded, doubt fading from her grey eyes. 'Then let us do it!' she laughed.

Bedyr turned to Galen and said, 'Can you be ready to sail the morning after the wedding?'

'The *Vashti* is ready now,' the riverman confirmed. 'Fresh caulked and refitted for winter. My crew grow idle in the taverns – a brisk trip up river will put an edge to them.'

'Then so be it,' smiled Bedyr. 'Three days from now.'

'I drink to our departure,' beamed Galen, holding up an empty goblet for Bedyr to refill.

That night alarm spread through the White Palace as Hattim Sethiyan and his closest courtiers – all those present to drink a toast to Chadyn Hymet – fell victim to a mysterious illness. It was reported that the Lord of Ust-Galich was afflicted with the most painful of stomach cramps, that he vomited blood, that he was close to death. Those of his retinue who had joined him in the poisoned toast were no better and the palace rang with their moaning.

Ashrivelle was distraught, insisting that she attend her beloved. Darr, Bedyr and Jarl were roused from their beds, the latters' wives asked to attend the panicking princess, whom they had almost to drag from Hattim's bedside.

The Galichian did, indeed, appear sick unto death as he lay tossing on his bed, attended by Sister Thera. His face was ashen, sweat matting his golden hair, his eyes hollowed, his body racked by tremors.

291

'I will send to the College,' Darr announced. 'Bethany will send her most accomplished hospitallers.'

'No,' moaned Hattim, 'let Sister Thera attend me.'

Darr looked to the brown-haired Sister, who administered a draft to Hattim's pallid lips. 'Do you require help?' he asked.

The woman shook her head, setting the cup aside and mopping Hattim's brow.

'No, Majesty,' she said confidently, 'I can cure my Lord. I believe he has drunk tainted wine. He will recover.'

'He appears most ill,' said Darr, worried.

'It seems worse than it is,' replied Thera. 'I assure you, Majesty, that he will be well again ere morning.'

'Should he die,' Jarl murmured, so soft that only Bedyr might hear, 'our doubts would be resolved.'

Bedyr nodded, his conscience torn between the spiteful wish that Jarl be right and genuine sympathy for the pain-racked Galichian.

'See, he sleeps.' Thera lowered Hattim's head to the pillows, his eyes closing as a vomit-tainted sigh escaped his lips. 'I will attend the others.'

She bustled from the chamber, carrying her satchel of medicaments. Darr, Bedyr and Jarl stood staring at the supine lord, each entertaining his private thoughts as servants changed soiled sheets, Hattim still now, his breath coming more evenly. Finally Darr said, 'The Sister's remedies appear to work.'

'More's the pity,' Jarl grunted.

Darr sighed and shook his head. 'I bear no great love for Hattim, but I would not wish such a death on him.'

'You are too kind,' said the Lord of Kesh, his eyes cold as he studied the Galichian.

'He sleeps,' said Bedyr, 'Let us find our own beds.'

The others nodded and they quit the chamber with instructions that servants watch over Hattim and send instantly for Sister Thera should further seizures strike.

'I had best advise my daughter,' Darr said, 'and free your wives.'

They found Yrla and Arlynn comforting Ashrivelle, who would not be mollified until she was allowed to observe her sleeping lover, only then, after she was satisfied he slept and nothing more could be done for him, permitting them to settle her in her own bed, singing the praises of Sister Thera.

Indeed, when dawn broke, it seemed the Sister Hospitaller had performed most excellently. Hattim and his courtiers lived, albeit a trifle uncomfortable of digestion, refusing food but declaring themselves recovered from whatever malady had struck so dramatically. They were somewhat weakened, but when Darr, accompanied by the Lords of Tamur and Kesh, attended him, he expressed his resolve that the wedding should proceed as planned. Ashrivelle was seated by his bedside as he gave this news, and she smiled at his words, turning a grave face to her father as she asked, 'Is he not brave?'

'I would not disappoint you,' said Hattim gallantly, his own smile wan. 'And I am selfish – I would let nothing stand in the way of my own happiness.'

Ashrivelle laughed with delight, smoothing his hair. Darr asked, 'You are sure of this? The ceremony may be easily delayed.'

'No,' Hattim shook his head, taking Ashrivelle's hand, 'let nothing delay our union.'

Darr nodded. 'Then we shall leave you.'

'I am in most excellent hands,' said Hattim, indicating with a gesture the solicitous Ashrivelle and the hovering Sister Thera.

'A pity,' Jarl remarked as they quit the chamber.

'Mayhap the Lady saves him for greater things,' said Bedyr, clapping his disappointed friend on the shoulder.

Jarl's disgruntlement was vastly increased later that day when a servant brought urgent word that King Darr required his presence in the quarters occupied by the Lord of Ust-Galich. At first the Keshi's spirits rose, thinking that Hattim had suffered some relapse and the wedding might, after all, be transformed to a wake. He hurried to answer the summons, allowing himself the luxury of optimism, only to find Bedyr and Darr grave-faced by Hattim's bed.

The Galichian was propped against a mound of pillows, most of his natural colour returned, but his own features set in lines both stern and mournful that, to Jarl's cynical eye, seemed utterly false.

'There is disturbing news,' said Darr, fidgetting with the medallion of his office in a manner that, to Jarl, suggested acute discomfort.

'I have received word from the army,' Hattim said when Darr made no move to continue. 'Chadyn Hymet is dead.'

'What?' Jarl barked, his mind turning instantly to thoughts of poison.

'This malady,' Hattim gestured vaguely in the direction of his stomach, his face solemn, 'appears to stem from the wine we drank in toast to his ascension. Lady forgive me, I chose that vintage myself!'

He broke off, his lips clamped tight together as if in prevention of some wail of grief, shaking his head as though he could not believe what he had done.

'You cannot blame yourself,' Darr murmured. 'You, too, might have suffered that fate.'

'Had Sister Thera not attended me,' Hattim nodded, his voice pitched low. 'If only I had sent her to Chadyn.'

'You could not know,' said Darr, 'not then.'

Jarl frowned, confused by his own suspicions. 'Chadyn is dead? What is this talk of wine?'

'It would appear that Hattim selected a tainted vintage,' Bedyr explained. 'When he sent for Chadyn to apprise him of his appointment they drank a toast. The wine was fouled.'

'Have Sisters examined it?' asked Jarl, making little effort to conceal his suspicion.

'It was all drunk,' said Hattim, his voice pitched low, 'and the bottles destroyed. There were but two. The vintage was ancient – the very reason I chose it.'

Jarl grunted without offering comment.

'I have made enquiries,' said Darr, sensing the drift of the Keshi's thoughts, 'and there can be no question of foul play.'

'Who would wish to poison Chadyn?' asked Hattim sadly. 'Who would wish to poison so many?'

'All who drank fell ill last night,' Bedyr expanded. 'It would seem that only the prompt attendance of Sister Thera saved Hattim's entire court from death. Unfortunately there was no Sister to attend Chadyn.'

'Poor Chadyn,' keened Hattim.

'This leaves us with a problem,' Jarl said bluntly.

Hattim nodded listlessly, for all the world a man stricken with grief. 'You must select another to take my place.'

'The wedding is tomorrow,' Jarl said. 'Shall it be postponed?'

Darr clutched his medallion in a tight-locked fist and shook his head. 'I think not,' he announced. 'All is ready and whilst we mourn the demise of the Lord Hymet I do not think we should delay the ceremony.'

'Would it not be disrespectful to continue?' Hattim asked.

'I think not,' said Darr. 'Things have gone too far to halt them now. What we must do is choose another candidate.'

'Who?' Jarl demanded.

Darr sighed. 'I cannot readily offer another.'

'We must debate the matter,' suggested Bedyr.

'I shall, as before, accept your nomination,' murmured Hattim. 'Though for now I feel too weak to offer suggestions. I leave it to you, my Lords.'

'Very well,' Darr nodded. 'We shall apprise you of our choice once it is made.'

Hattim ducked his head in agreement as they turned from his bed, making their way from the chamber. Once they were gone and he was alone he threw back the covers and rose to his feet, rubbing at a belly still sore from the discomfort of the previous night, smiling as the door opened to admit Sister Thera.

'Taws,' he chuckled, 'your design is masterly! They cannot suspect me – nor will they find a candidate so suitable as Chadyn before the wedding.'

'Ashar's will be done,' said the mage. 'You are fully recovered?'

'A somewhat painful stomach,' shrugged Hattim, dismissing so small a price for so large a gain, 'nothing more.'

'That will remedy itself,' Taws remarked. 'It was needful you showed the signs of illness, lest any suspect.'

'And it worked!' Hattim shrugged into a brocade dressing gown, his eyes alight with triumph. 'They saw me suffering – they heard the others. Jarl doubted – I saw that in his eyes! – but what could he say? What accusation could any of them level against me when I lay so sick? They could only offer me sympathy; and how that hurt them! They had rather I died.'

He chuckled at the thought, shaking his head in amusement.

'And tomorrow,' said Taws softly, 'you will be married.'

'Aye,' smiled Hattim, 'too soon for them to select another to take my place. I shall become heir to the High Throne and remain Lord of Ust-Galich.' His smile faded as a thought intruded on his jubilation: 'When shall Darr die?'

The slight shoulders beneath the blue robe shrugged as Taws said, 'The same night, I think.'

'So soon?' Hattim's eyes expressed doubt. 'Should we not wait a while longer?'

'To what purpose?' asked the mage. 'That they may decide upon another candidate? No, we strike while Ashar's fires burn bright still. You will wed your little princess and all Andurel will celebrate. Your men will throng the city and that night Darr will die. The dawn will see you king, with an army at your back to quell any who oppose you. The High Throne and Ust-Galich both will be yours.'

'And the objections of Bedyr and Jarl will brand them traitors,' Hattim nodded.

'As I have set it out,' agreed the mage, his woman's face smiling exultantly, 'their incarceration will forestall any move of the Keshi's spawn, and if Kedryn Caitin lives still, his parents will be bait in our snare.'

If he does not?' Hattim enquired.

'When we know that, they die,' smiled the mage.

Hattim burst into a fresh gale of laughter. 'Taws,' he declared, 'we have them! We cannot lose now! The Kingdoms are ours!'

'And Ashar's,' said the mage softly. 'The time of the Lady's bitches draws to a close. Soon our master shall rule here.'

Hattim swallowed, his face becoming serious, for still he felt some trepidation at such open acceptance of the god, but he had come too far along this path to turn back now, and he knew with an awful certainty what fate awaited him should he renege on his apostasy, so he nodded, echoing the mage: 'And Ashar's.'

The dawn that broke over Andurel on the day of the wedding was a glory of gold and crimson that crept along the edge of the eastern horizon as if a fire burned there, driving back the night. The curtain of gloom that lingered still was steadily illuminated with a clear blue effulgence that spread across the heavens as the sun rose, a great disc of candescent citrine. There were no clouds and the north wind that had buffeted the city dropped, swinging around to become a milder afflatus that set the pennants and buntings decorating the streets and houses to rustling and fluttering gaily, the boats moored along the wharfsides to bobbing on the gentled sway of the Idre. Those abroad at that hour declared it a blessing of the Lady on the union to be celebrated that day, and many who had doubted the wisdom of the marriage revised their opinions, allowing themselves to be persuaded that Hattim Sethiyan was, indeed, a suitable candidate for Ashrivelle's hand and the tenure of the White Palace.

Neither Bedyr nor Yrla was so easily dissuaded, and there remained in their minds, as in those of Jarl and Arlynne, and King Darr himself, lingering doubt concerning the untimely death of Chadyn Hymet.

They had sat late, discussing the selection of a fresh candidate for Hattim's kingdom and finding themselves unable to agree on a suitable nomination. This man was too old, that too young; the one too loyal to the Sethiyan line, another too weak to oppose it;

blood relationships abrogated many claims, lack of support others. Their suspicions were brought into the open, but none could lay valid accusations at Hattim's door, nor produce real reason for condemnation. Finally, still without a decision, they had agreed to find their beds and continue their debate after the wedding. Consequently they had had little sleep as they prepared for the lengthy festivities for which not one of them could muster much enthusiasm.

As custom dictated, the betrothed couple breakfasted alone before praying in company of a single Sister, Thera in Hattim's case, Bethany in Ashrivelle's. Then they were dressed, the bride-to-be in gown of Estrevan blue, hemmed with gold, her hair bound up in a mesh of silver threads, the groom in tunic and breeks of purest white, an overrobe of silver with matching boots. At noon the Ladies of Tamur and Kesh, in company with those of the High Blood able to attend, joined Ashrivelle, whilst their husbands went to fetch Hattim from his chambers. They escorted the Galichian to the quarters of the princess, where Jarl, as the elder Lord, pounded thrice on the door, demanding entry. Three times Sister Bethany called out, demanding that Hattim be sure in his intent, and three times Jarl was required to answer that he was. Then the door was flung open and Bethany granted them entry.

Hattim, flanked by Bedyr and Jarl, dropped to one knee before the seated princess and said in ringing tones, 'I ask that you come with me now that this night we may be man and wife before the eyes of the Lady and the good folk of the Kingdoms.'

And Ashrivelle replied, 'I will come with you and take you to be my husband.'

She rose then, her attendant women about her as Hattim turned, Jarl and Bedyr beside him, and left the chamber, striding through the corridors of the White Palace to the throne room, where Darr waited, dressed in purple and gold, the tripartite crown upon his greyed head, the Palace Guard resplendent in burnished armour to either side of the High Throne.

The high-vaulted rotunda was packed as the Lords brought Hattim in and left him standing alone before the King as they took their places on the lesser thrones a step below the king's on the marble dais. Yrla and Arlynn came in with Ashrivelle, leaving her beside Hattim as they joined their husbands. The Sisters of Andurel grouped behind the pair as Bethany moved to take her place at the foot of the dais and silence filled the room. She raised her hands, palms towards the two, and invoked the blessing of the Lady, then Darr rose to ask, 'Hattim Sethiyan of Ust-Galich, do you in good faith and loyalty take this woman, Ashrivelle, to be your wife?'

Hattim said, 'I do,' and Bethany demanded, 'in the name of the Lady, do you cherish and respect her?' and again Hattim said, 'I do.'

The questions were repeated to Ashrivelle, who answered firmly, her eyes alight with joy.

Then Bethany announced, 'These two are joined as one before the Lady. Let all here know that and ask her blessing on their union.'

Darr said, 'These two are joined in the eyes of the Kingdoms. Let all here know that.'

Hattim turned then to take Ashrivelle in his arms and kiss her, chastely, his face solemn, as Darr and Bethany in unison pronounced the ancient formula, 'You are wed in the eyes of the Lady and of the Kingdoms. Be you faithful one unto another from this day hence.'

The Sisters invoked a prayer, and when it was done the chamber rang with the shouting of Hattim's Galichians as their lord took his wife on his arm and led the way from the Throne Room to the banquet that waited in the hall beyond. The triumphant smile that curved his lips was, the celebrants assumed, because he had won so lovely a bride and now stood in line to the High Throne when – might the Lady make it a long time hence – King Darr should die.

Chapter Fourteen

CANDLELIGHT darkened the hollows of Darr's cheeks, etching deeper the lines that striated his forehead and pooling shadow beneath his eyes. He caught a glimpse of his reflection as the attendants eased off the heavy ceremonial robe that had seemed to become increasingly burdensome as the wedding celebrations continued, and thought that he looked old. He was long accustomed to the remorseless thinning of his hair, and its greying he accepted, but as he studied his features they seemed for the first time to assume the lineaments of venerability. Was this the price of the tripartite crown that now sat in lonely splendour on its velvet cushion, this acceleration of the ageing process? Or would he have grown old just as quickly had he not wed Morenna and come to the High Throne? Bedyr was his junior by scant years, yet he still seemed young despite the streakings of grey that now winged his brown locks; and Jarl, who was older, seemed ageless. Did the burdens of kingship sit so heavily upon him that the years marked their calendar passage more savagely? Or did more recent matters carve him with their dolours?

He sighed, prompting an enquiring look from the servant now working on the lacings of his stiff shirt that he answered with a dismissive gesture, essaying a slight, wan smile, indicating that the man should continue, shrugging into a sleeping robe as the trappings of his kingship were carefully folded and settled into the wardrobe. If only he could set aside his cares as easily. But he could not, and he carried them with him as he climbed into his bed and dismissed the attendants, who snuffed all but the one candle standing beside his sleeping couch as they retreated from the room.

Sleep, he knew, would come slowly this night, for he had much to ponder, and none of it the happy concerns of a father who had just seen a beloved daughter wed to the man of her choice. There was the matter of the Galichian succession still to be decided; and the dispersal of the Galichian army. Hattim had offered assurances on

299

both items, but no suggestions, and whilst Darr was thankful for the free hand the one allowed him, he was mildly worried that no date was set for the disintegration of the forces camped on Andurel's doorstep. Hattim had proven vague on that count, promising the cantonment would break up without setting an exact time, and Darr was troubled by the thought of so large a body of armed men concentrated so close to the city gates. Kemm, he knew, had obeyed his father's word and brought a striking force of Keshi to the banks of the Vortigen, but their numbers, even allied with the Palace Guard, were less than the muster of Galichians. Yet why should that disturb him? Hattim had offered no threat – presumably had no need, now that he was legally heir to the throne – yet still Darr did not trust the man. There was, making it all the worse, no valid reason for his mistrust. He knew Hattim to be ambitious – it was something the Galichian had never hidden – but surely not even Hattim Sethiyan would chance the wrath of Tamur and Kesh by seeking to forcibly accelerate his ascension. That must come automatically when Darr should die and marriage to Ashrivelle elevate Hattim to the throne.

He sighed noisily, wondering if he should summon a Sister Hospitaller and request a sleeping draught, then dismissed the notion in favour of a small cup of evshan that he sipped as he cogitated, thoughts drifting at random through his troubled mind. Had Chadyn Hymet not fallen victim to that tainted wine matters would be less unsettled. Could that have been planned? No, surely not, for had not Hattim and most of his court fallen victim, saved only by the fortunate presence of Sister Thera? That was an unworthy suspicion! Yet Yrla, in whose judgement and cognitive abilities he had much faith, had spoken disturbingly of a pattern, albeit one she did not clearly perceive. Yet he could not grant credence to her tentative suspicion that Ashar worked somehow through Hattim, for that must surely have required the presence of the Messenger – if, in the first place, one allowed the blasphemous possibility that Hattim had sold his soul – and there was no sign of Ashar's minion. He had discussed the subject at length with Yrla and Bethany, and the Paramount Sister had expressed her own doubts so eloquently that even Yrla had admitted her suspicions might find their source in maternal concern for Kedryn and Wynett.

He drank more evshan as the one thought gave way to another, this of more personal concern. Did Wynett live? Or did she lie with Kedryn beneath the tumbled wreckage of the Fedyn Pass? And if she lived, what was her relationship to the Prince of Tamur? That love burgeoned he had seen, as had all who saw them together. Yet Wynett had always possessed a strength of character greater than her sister's, pursuing her dream of service to the Lady despite all his blandishments, all his reminders of her place and heritage, so perhaps she would – did she live still – refuse the calling of her heart for continuance of the more abstract love. But if not . . .? He raised the cup again, thinking that if not, then likely Wynett and Kedryn would emerge from the Beltrevan lovers, to marry. And as the elder sister, Wynett's claim would supersede Ashrivelle's, rendering Kedryn heir to the White Palace. He sighed afresh, aware that he dallied with *ifs* and *mayhaps* while the real problem lay in the marriage chamber of Hattim Sethiyan on the level below, but nonetheless unable to prevent himself reviewing those tempting alternatives. *If* Wynett and Kedryn lived, and *if* their unspoken love had come to fruition; *if* they emerged safely from the Beltrevan, and *if* they wed; then Hattim, with no slight or insult to claim, must relinquish his ambition and carry Ashrivelle back to Ust-Galich where, Darr hoped, they would live happily, leaving Wynett and Kedryn to possess the White Palace in due course, and doubtless rule more wisely.

There were too many *ifs*, too many *mayhaps*. There was no news and it seemed Hattim must eventually come to the throne. Consequently the more immediate problem was the selection of his successor and Darr's mind turned again to that; with as little success as before. Weary now, his stomach tight with the weight of food eaten at the banquet, he emptied the cup and snuffed the candle, composing himself for sleep.

Outside, the wind had started up again, rustling about the towers of the palace, rattling shutters and sighing in chimneys. Darr listened to it, remembering that once it had seemed a restful sound, a reminder that he slept snug, secure in the heart of the peaceful Kingdoms. Now it seemed an omen, a threat of lurking discontent, as if some gusty beast prowled the land, its very breath sowing the seeds of malcontentment. He shivered despite the warmth still imparted by the glowing hearth and drew the covers higher about his ears.

Then pushed them down as he heard a faint sound from the antechamber. He listened for a moment, then shook his head, telling himself he was childish. Did Palace Guards not stand sentry at his door? And servants sleep beyond? And who would offer him harm, here in the heart of the White Palace? He drew the covers up again, willing himself to sleep.

And heard the door open, the hinges soft on oiled bolts, dim light showing briefly the shape that entered.

'Who is it?' He sat up, the covers falling from his chest. 'Who are you?'

No answer came from the figure that glided across the room, but in the red glow of the hearthfire he saw blue robes, brown hair drawn back from a face not quite pretty.

'Sister Thera? I did not summon you.'

'No,' said a voice that hissed far colder than the north wind, 'but we have business, you and I.'

Darr stared, hair prickling on his neck, cold dread chilling his very soul, for that voice could not have issued from the slight frame of the Sister who now stood beside him, her lips stretched wide in a smile that was a snarl of feral satisfaction. His mouth was suddenly dry, although cold sweat burst upon his brow and chest as he stared aghast into eyes that glowed red as the coals limning the figure, their intensity sapping his strength, his will.

'What are you?' he choked, the words coming slow and thick around a tongue that seemed to fill his mouth as if swollen with the mortal dread he felt.

'Do you not know me?'

The question held a terrible finality, terminal as the bite of gravedigger's spade in earth, and as its sibilance still rang in his ears Darr knew the answer, knew that Yrla had been right, knew that an awful pattern unfolded, too late, before him. He opened his mouth to shout, to summon guards, but that rubescent gaze flowered, burning brighter, stilling the words unspoken in his throat.

'I am Taws,' said the creature. 'You know me as the Messenger. I am come to do my master's work.'

Darr stared, his eyes trapped by that horrendous glare, hearing the triumph in the declaration, the gloating tone in the voice that had no right to issue from the lips of a Sister.

'So weak, so foolish.' A hand stroked the king's face and he groaned at the obscenity of its touch, the hypnotic carmine eyes robbing him of will as the mage savoured the moment. 'There are none can aid you, Darr. No guards will come, nor Kyrie's bitches. We are alone, you and I.'

'How?' Darr managed to gasp.

'How?' Taws chuckled, the sound dry as long dead, grating bones. 'Easily. Into High Fort with those weakling turncoats who gave up

302

my master's work and from them to the one who would accept me. One of your own then, Ashar's now.'

'Hattim!' Darr moaned, cursing himself even in the depths of his terror for failing to recognise the veracity of Yrla's insight.

'Aye, Hattim Sethiyan,' the mage confirmed. 'A useful puppet; a soul ready for the plucking. And now Hattim Sethiyan is your daughter's husband and will soon be king – for you will soon be dead.'

'You,' Darr said slowly, forcing the words out through the numbing lassitude that gripped him, 'shall . . . not . . . win.'

'How can I not?' Taws chuckled exultantly. 'The future king is mine. Mine and through me my master's. He is Ashar's creature now, Darr, and soon all the Kingdoms shall belong to Ashar.'

'No!' Darr husked. 'Kedryn . . .'

A hand clamped about his jaws, covering his mouth, the face that was no longer quite that of Sister Thera but something else, something infinitely older, infinitely evil, leaning closer to gust breath that smelled rank with innate wickedness into his nostrils.

'Can do nothing! Be he the Chosen One or not, he is lost now. Dawn shall see Hattim Sethiyan on the throne and my master's enemies in chains, pawns in my game. If Kedryn lives I shall have him for a plaything, for a little while. And your daughter, Darr! Shall I have her, too? Or shall I give her to Hattim? Shall he enjoy a harem, his claims redoubled by the subservience of both your daughters?'

Darr's eyes started from his head as horror filled him and he struggled uselessly against the supernatural strength of the mage's grip. He could not break it and after a while his writhing subsided.

'There is nothing you can do,' Taws leered. 'You are lost.'

'The Lady,' Darr mumbled against the restraining hand. 'The Lady . . .'

'Can do nothing,' said Taws. 'Her day is over and Ashar's night begins. Such a long night it shall be, Darr, with my master supreme over all the Kingdoms. Such a night as this petty world of yours has never known, with your death to mark its twilight.'

The hand left Darr's mouth then, but all he was able to utter was a single, rasping moan of despair, for Taws gripped his shoulders and forced him back against the pillows as the distorted face of Sister Thera descended, the lips parted, the visage of a succubus filling the king's final moments of life. He felt that ghastly mouth touch his and in the instant of his dying screamed out to the Lady to forgive him,

303

and to save his soul. Then a swirling redness clouded his eyes and there was nothing.

Taws drank deep, luxuriating in the stolen essence that tasted so fine after so long an abstinence, relishing the moment of triumph, feeling Darr's spirit strengthen him. He rose slowly from the bed, leaving behind a husk, drained, more than life taken, and crossed leisurely to the door.

In the antechamber servants slept a deep and dreamless slumber, beyond them, in the corridor outside, the guards, still upright, sightless eyes staring at the shadows that flickered about the candle sconces. Taws passed them unseen, moving silently towards the stairs that descended to the lower level where Hattim Sethiyan consummated his marriage.

The mage went unnoticed down the stairs, the red glow fading from his eyes until they were again the green that belonged to Sister Thera. He entered his own chamber and piled fresh logs on the fire, standing close to the flames as he contemplated the furore that must erupt when servants went to rouse their king and found him dead. Before then – though only the chosen should know it – Hattim would be ready, the most loyal of his officers already in the palace, prepared to support their lord in his immediate assumption of the throne.

Nothing, Taws thought, could now stand in his way. Not the Sisters, or Tamur, or Kesh, not Kedryn Caitin; nothing.

Bedyr and Yrla were roused from slumber by the clamour that seemed to fill the corridors of the White Palace. They heard feet pounding beyond their chamber and the shouting of servants, the answering cries of guardsmen, weeping women and grieving men. They rose swiftly, Bedyr delaying only long enough to don shirt and breeks and boots, buckling his swordbelt about his waist as he hurried to the door, accompanied by Yrla, who had merely thrown a robe over her night attire.

All was confusion and Bedyr caught a sergeant by the arm, forcing the man to halt as he demanded what was amiss.

'The king is dead!' the sergeant gasped. 'May the Lady preserve us, Lord Bedyr – King Darr is dead!'

Without further ado Bedyr took his wife's hand and began to run towards the royal chambers, thrusting servants and soldiery aside, his features grim as they raced up the wide stairway and hurried along the swarming corridor.

A crowd was bunched tight about the doors of the king's quarters, held back by guardsmen, their faces pale with shock beneath the beaks of their helmets. Bedyr shouldered a way through and was granted entry to an antechamber only slightly less populated with nobles and Sisters and soldiers and servants. At the bedroom door two stern-featured officers stood with drawn swords, hesitating before permitting Bedyr and Yrla to enter, closing the door behind them on the babble that filled the outer room.

Inside a grim calm barely contained the grief and anger of the figures grouped about Darr's bed. Sister Bethany was there, leant over the supine form of the monarch, Corradon on the far side, his homely features drawn tense, his left hand clenching rhythmically on the hilt of his sword, Jarl, his chest bare beneath a black robe, his long hair uncombed, at the foot. He turned as they entered, his eyes narrow with suspicion.

'Darr is dead,' he said harshly. 'Murdered in his sleep.'

Bedyr looked past him to the corpse. Darr was stretched back on his pillows, his body possessed of that slackness, that total absence of muscular tension that announces death. His face was grey, his mouth gaping wide, his eyes staring sightlessly, no light in them.

'Murdered?' Visions of chaos, of war, roared in Bedyr's mind. 'How do you know?'

'How else?' Jarl grated. 'He was not sick, he was not old, but he is dead. This is Sethiyan's work.'

'Guard your words.' Bedyr set a hand on the older man's arm, his voice urgent. 'It is early yet to level accusations.'

'Who else?' snapped Jarl. 'Who else benefits from this?'

'What killed him?'

Bedyr addressed the question to Sister Bethany, stepping past Jarl to come close to the bed, gazing down at the face of his friend with anguish filling him, a desire to weep moistening his eyes even as he steeled himself, knowing that the stability of the Kingdoms must rest tremulously on her verdict, on the events of the next few hours.

'I am not sure,' answered the Sister, her voice careful, held in control by the disciplines of her training, 'His heart has burst, but . . .'

She touched the wide-spread lips, indicating their pallor, the blueing of the surrounding flesh. Bedyr clamped his teeth tight on the nausea that welled as he saw the swollen, blackened tongue that protruded there.

'But?'

'I cannot be sure. I think . . .' The Sister turned brown eyes in

305

which tears welled to the Lord of Tamur, confusion and disbelief in her voice. 'I think I sense magic.'

'The pattern!' It was Yrla who spoke, her voice thick with grief and tinged with fear. 'It is as I thought.'

'Yrla!' Bedyr turned to face his wife. 'Be sure of what you say.'

Yrla nodded, dabbing at her eyes with the sleeve of her robe. 'Do you not see it now, Bethany? Hattim Sethiyan is now king.'

'Not while I live!' Jarl roared. 'Not by means so foul.'

'Be still,' Bedyr ordered, motioning the Keshi to silence. 'Hattim will be here in the moment – do we accuse him? Risk war?'

Jarl glared at him, turned to Corradon: 'When the murderer appears, arrest him.'

'My Lord?' Corradon stared in confusion, transferring his gaze to Bedyr.

'No!' Bedyr shook his head. 'We must be sure of this. Yrla, you say this proves the pattern you sensed – how so?'

'It is not a . . .' she hesitated to use the word, '. . . natural conclusion? Hattim swept Ashrivelle off her feet to become heir. Chadyn Hymet died most conveniently, leaving Hattim in command of the Galichian forces. Now poor Darr is dead and Hattim has rightful claim to the High Throne. Is that not a pattern?'

'How say you?' Bedyr asked Bethany.

'There is logic in it,' the white-haired Sister said slowly, 'but it assumes Ashar's hand, or rather that of his Messenger.'

'If you are right,' Bedyr stared at his wife, a fearful awe widening his eyes, 'then the Messenger is in the White Palace and Hattim Sethiyan has sold his soul.'

Yrla nodded tearfully.

'I do not believe Darr died of natural causes,' said Bethany into the silence that followed, 'and whilst I do believe I sense the taint of magic here, it might still be poison.'

'Poison or magic,' Jarl rasped, angry, 'what matter? It was Hattim's work and he must be brought to justice. If the Messenger works with him, then we must hunt down the foul creature and slay him, too.'

'Only Kedryn may do that,' said Yrla softly, 'and Kedryn is not here.'

The commotion beyond the door grew louder and Bedyr said quickly, 'If these suspicions are correct then we face a most formidable adversary. Say nothing – yet – to Hattim or any other. We must meet as soon as we may to talk of this and decide our battle plan. Do you understand, Corradon? Do you agree, Jarl?'

The captain nodded, the Lord of Kesh grunted furiously and sai⸱⸱
'Very well.'

The door opened then to admit Hattim and Ashrivelle, both dishevelled. The princess saw her father and threw herself, wailing, upon the bed. Yrla and Bethany moved to comfort her, Hattim stared at the dead king and turned to his fellow lords.

'What has happened here?'

Jarl made a sound like a snarl, deep in his throat, and Bedyr cast a cautionary glance in his direction.

'The king is dead, Hattim.'

'How?'

Bedyr studied the Galichian's face, trying to read the expression there, seeing eyes that widened, a mouth that slackened, wondering if the shock those movements suggested was genuine or if Hattim was merely an excellent actor. 'We are not yet certain,' he said.

'Sister Bethany?' Hattim looked to the blue-robed woman as Bedyr tried to judge the tone of his voice. 'What is your prognosis?'

'A burst heart,' the Sister replied, one arm about Ashrivelle's shoulders. 'Perhaps magic.'

'Magic?' Disbelief rang in the word. 'How magic? What do you say?'

'I am not sure yet,' Bethany answered. 'I require more time. There are touchstones to employ before I may be sure.'

Bedyr glanced at her, angry that she had let this slip, then dubious at Hattim's response.

'Touchstones?' said the Galichian. 'You would subject our late king's remains to such indignity?'

'Our king is dead and we would uncover the cause.' Jarl's voice was cold as unsheathed steel, his dark eyes burning as he glowered at the blond-haired southerner. 'Would you seek to obscure such revelation, Sethiyan?'

Hattim faced the dark-haired lord, something close to contempt in his eyes, his response more in keeping with his old arrogance than the newer, diplomatic man they had known of late.

'I find your tone offensive, Jarl of Kesh.'

Jarl's swarthy features suffused with rage, his eyes bulging. Bedyr made a small, cautionary gesture that went unnoticed or ignored, so furious was the Keshi.

'I care not how you find my tone, Hattim. Our king is dead and we shall discover the cause. And let those responsible beware.'

'You forget yourself,' said Hattim, his own responsive anger icing his words. 'You forget that you have a new king now.'

'You?' Jarl filled the single word with contempt, bringing a flush to the Galichian's face that matched his own.

'Aye,' Hattim snapped.

'My Lords,' Bedyr said quickly, moving between them as he saw that Jarl must soon spring at the Galichian, 'calm yourselves. King Darr is dead and we are distraught. I would suggest we discuss the matter of investigation when we are more calm, but meanwhile, Hattim, your wife grieves and has need of you.'

'Ever the moderator,' Hattim nodded, 'but you are right – Ashrivelle needs me. I shall summon you later; perhaps by then you may have calmed our Lord of Kesh.'

He smiled tightly, crossing to the weeping Ashrivelle and putting hands to her shoulders. She rose at his touch, turning into his arms, her pretty face distorted, tears streaming from her blue eyes. 'Come,' he murmured into her hair, 'Sister Thera will provide some potion to calm you.'

Reluctantly, Ashrivelle allowed herself to be led from the chamber, Hattim casting a final, scornful glance at Jarl.

'Prepare your touchstones,' Bedyr told Bethany when he was gone. 'How long will it take?'

'I must return to the college,' the Sister replied, 'for the paraphernalia I need and Sisters to aid me. I can have answers by dusk.'

'Go,' said Bedyr. 'Jarl, Corradon, come with me. Corradon, leave guards on the king's chambers – no one is to enter.'

The young captain's pugnacious features creased in a frown. 'My Lord Bedyr,' he asked, 'what if Lord Hattim demands entry?'

'He cannot be denied,' Bedyr allowed.

Jarl snorted but said nothing and Bedyr asked, 'Where is Arlynn?'

'Waiting in our quarters,' said the Keshi.

'Then we go there,' said Bedyr.

Corradon issued orders to the men on the door and summoned a squad to clear a way as they hurried to the chambers set aside for the Lord and Lady of Kesh. Arlynn was dressed when they arrived, her plump, pretty features lined with concern. Her husband explained briefly what had transpired and she clapped beringed hands to her mouth in alarm, moaning, 'Poor Darr, poor Ashrivelle.'

'Poor Andurel,' snapped Jarl, 'Poor Kingdoms.'

Bedyr flung himself on to a pile of cushions, Yrla settling more decorously beside him. 'Hattim is king,' he said, 'there is no gainsaying it.'

'Unless we prove some gramarye slew Darr,' said Jarl. 'And that Hattim took a hand in the fell work.'

'If Hattim is the Messenger's creature,' Yrla said, 'then surely it is of greater importance that we discover his identity.'

'Aye,' Bedyr agreed, 'but how?'

'Will the one not stem from the other?' Arlynn asked. 'If Bethany's investigation proves the use of magic surely Hattim cannot assume the throne until the matter is resolved. And the Sisters will sniff out Ashar's minion.'

'They have not yet,' grunted Jarl.

'You are the one who foresaw this,' Bedyr said to Yrla. 'What is your prognostication?'

'The Messenger must be close to Hattim,' she said thoughtfully, 'though how he is disguised I cannot suggest. If I am right, he established this train of events and so has likely been with Hattim for some time.'

'He was not seen after the Horde's defeat,' said Bedyr, 'but might he have revealed himself to Hattim after the battle?'

Corradon coughed discreetly then, confusion and embarrassment in his eyes as attention focused on him. 'Are you convinced the Lord of Ust-Galich can fall so low?' he asked. 'Might King Darr not have died from natural causes?'

'No,' said Jarl firmly.

'It is possible,' Bedyr allowed doubtfully, 'but it seems unlikely. There was no reason to suspect Darr ill, and I have faith in both my wife's identification of a pattern and in Bethany's sensing of magic.'

'But the Paramount Sister was not absolutely sure,' said Corradon.

'Bethany is naturally cautious,' said Bedyr.

'Would that we had listened to Yrla,' said Jarl. 'We might have prevented this.'

'We did not,' said Bedyr, flatly, 'and it has happened. What we must do now is plan for a future that holds Hattim Sethiyan as our King.'

'Do you accept him then?' Jarl asked disbelievingly.

'I have no choice if he is lawfully come to the High Throne,' Bedyr answered. 'The White Palace is his by marriage right if Darr was not slain by magic.'

'And if he was?' Jarl demanded.

'If there was a glamour involved,' said Bedyr, choosing his words

309

carefully for he knew where they must lead, 'and if – as I believe must be the case in that event – Hattim Sethiyan has leagued himself with the Messenger, then we have no choice but to oppose him as an apostate and a murderer.'

'Civil war,' said Arlynn, her voice hushed.

'Aye,' nodded Bedyr, 'likely civil war, unless Ust-Galich denounces Hattim.'

'It must depend on Bethany's findings,' said Yrla. 'Hattim will waste no time in declaring himself king, but what if Bethany announces magic? How do we react then?'

'Kemm holds five squadrons of our finest cavalry on the Vortigen,' said Jarl fiercely. 'I summon them across the river to join with Corradon's Palace Guard and we denounce Hattim as traitor and apostate. Arrest him; try him; and execute him.'

'There remains the matter of the Galichian army,' said Bedyr. 'My own Tamurin are disbanded and Kedryn still not found – should the Galichians choose to support Hattim, Andurel will be hard to hold.'

'Do not forget Galen Sadreth,' Yrla reminded. 'He waits e'en now to carry us north on the *Vashti*.'

'Aye,' Bedyr nodded, 'but we cannot go north, not now. We must remain here until this affair is resolved.'

'But he could still take word,' said Yrla. 'If he could carry word to Kedryn, then Kedryn could raise our forces. And if Wynett is with him, her claim to the throne is stronger than Ashrivelle's.'

'If she renounces the Sisterhood,' Bedyr murmured.

'It would fit the pattern I discern,' said Yrla.

'Hattim Sethiyan bears little love for any of us,' Jarl interposed. 'Whatever the nature of his course to the throne, he will seek to hold it. I suggest we ward ourselves,'

'Aye,' agreed Bedyr. 'Let us be prepared for all eventualities and keep our swords loose.'

'I must dress,' said Yrla. 'I am hardly garbed for intrigue or battle.'

'To our chambers, then,' said Bedyr, 'and meet again, where?'

'The throne room?' Jarl suggested.

'Excellent,' Bedyr applauded. 'Any measures we announce must have the trappings of formality, and I suspect Hattim will find his way there soon enough.'

'Let me gird myself,' said Jarl, 'and I shall come to your quarters.'

'And I?' Corradon asked. 'What shall I do?'

'Gather those guards you consider the most reliable,' said Bedyr.

'Bring them to my chambers that we may present a unified front Hattim and his Galichians.'

'It is done,' said Corradon, rising to his feet and saluting.

The others rose, Jarl to dress while Bedyr and Yrla followed the captain from the chamber to make their way back to their own rooms. There Yrla hurried to exchange night attire for clothing more suitable to the business in hand, Bedyr to tug a stout leather jerkin over his shirt, hoping despite the weight of evidence that seemed to build against Hattim that their suspicions were wrong. If not, he thought, loosening his blade in its scabbard, there might well be sword work before the day was out.

Confusion still reigned as Corradon arrived with a squad of guardsmen, Jarl and Arlynn, accompanied by ten grim-faced Keshi warriors, close on his heels. He ordered his men into a wedge that drove remorselessly through the crowded corridors to the throne room, collecting a retinue of curious followers along the way. Once inside the stately chamber, Bedyr had the captain set watchmen on the doors with orders to allow entry only after permission was granted by himself or Jarl, regardless of the petitioner. It was, by now, mid-morning and none of them had eaten, and whilst they had scant appetite, hunger edged their tempers, rendering their debate increasingly irritable.

Jarl spoke for the immediate impeachment of Hattim, urging that they send for Kemm to bring the Keshi cavalry across the river to join with Corradon's men and hold the White Palace until the cause of Darr's death was uncovered, convinced that such revelation must condemn the Galichian. Bedyr was more circumspect, seeing that so precipitate a course must inevitably result in war with Ust-Galich, and wary of committing the Kingdoms to such turmoil. Although he was swayed by Yrla's conviction, and more and more convinced that Hattim was, indeed, leagued with the Messenger, he remained loath to follow so perilous a course until firm evidence should be provided by Sister Bethany.

Finally it was agreed that two of Jarl's men should ride to Kemm with word, alerting him to stand ready to cross the Vortigen into Andurel, whilst Corradon despatched guards to bring food and drink.

They were eating in a desultory fashion when Jarl's men returned with word that Galichian troops ringed the palace, denying exit and entry, placed there by Hattim, ostensibly that the murderer of King Darr should not escape.

311

'Proof!' raged the Lord of Kesh, wine spilling as he slammed down his hand to punctuate the single word. 'Do you need more, Bedyr? The upstart shows his hand.'

'There is some justification in his reason,' Bedyr said carefully, 'but, yes – I think you must be right.'

'Yrla,' Jarl turned to the raven-haired woman, modulating his anger, 'your husband was ever more cautious than I – and I respect him for his tact – but now the time to act has come. How say you? Am I right or wrong?'

'I believe Hattim must seek to pre-empt any measures we may take,' Yrla responded, 'and I am now convinced he does dance to the Messenger's tune, but I am not sure that open warfare is the answer. Let the battle flags be flown and all will be confusion. Do we seek to arrest Hattim and he will have the chance to cry treason against the king – for that, until he is proven guilty, he remains – and thus might confuse honest folk. I think we must wait on Bethany's findings. Let us have firm proof that we may openly impeach him, with none to claim betrayal on our part, and we have the chance to nip this heresy in the bud without risk of war.'

'Arlynn?' Jarl turned to his own wife. 'You have a say in this.'

'Yrla speaks sense as ever,' said the plump woman, dabbing with a silken kerchief at the spilled wine, 'and we none of us seek war, I think. But shall we have time to wait on Bethany's findings? If the Messenger is the eminence behind Hattim, will he allow us that evidence? Or that much time?'

Her eyes moved towards the windows as she spoke, the movement eloquent as they turned to see the light filtering through the tall panes of stained glass waning. Candles were already lit and they were shocked by the realisation that the afternoon shortened inexorably towards evening.

'Aye,' said Bedyr, 'both our wives speak sense, Jarl. Corradon? Will you send men to enquire of the Paramount Sister as to her investigation?'

Corradon nodded and barked orders that sent five guardsmen hurrying from the throne room.

'We wait on them,' said Bedyr. 'Mayhap they will return with confirmation of our fears. If so, we declare Hattim suspect, and consequently uncrowned.'

'And then?' asked Jarl. 'Do not forget he has the palace ringed with warriors.'

'Let them know Darr died by magic, by the Messenger's hand,'

said Bedyr, his voice grim as his stern features, 'and they will hop
fully take our side. If not – then we must endeavour to fight our wa_
out. Remember the *Vashti* awaits us, and Galen Sadreth is loyal.'

Jarl nodded, looking to Corradon. 'You have, what? Fifty men
here. Can you muster others?'

'Aye, my Lord Jarl,' promised the captain. 'These are the men of
my own troop, and were most convenient, but others will follow our
call if they believe Lord Hattim an apostate. I cannot answer for all
the Palace Guard, but I think we should have sufficient to cut our
way through the Galichians.'

'So be it,' murmured the Keshi, fingering the jewelled hilt of his
sabre. 'We may escape Hattim's plot, but what then?'

'You go into Kesh to raise your full army,' said Bedyr, 'and I to
Tamur. Galen sails north to High Fort in search of Kedryn.'

'And we leave Andurel in Hattim's hands?' Jarl barked. 'His and
the Messenger's?'

'What other choice do we have?' asked Bedyr evenly. 'The
Royal Guard, even augmented by Kemm's squadrons, will not be
enough to face the Galichian army. Remember, Jarl, this is
our last resort. If Bethany uncovers magic we may not need to
flee.'

'Hattim will not relinquish his dream easily,' grumbled the
bowlegged lord.

'He may have little other choice,' said Bedyr.

Corradon's men returned then, confusion writ large on their
faces. The sergeant saluted and said, 'We were denied entrance,
my Lords. Galichians – and men of the Royal Guard – hold the
king's chambers and allow no entry. They say it is on the order of
Lord Hattim.'

'And Sister Bethany?' demanded Bedyr. 'What of her?'

'It seems the Sister was similarly denied entry,' the sergeant
reported. 'She was not allowed to begin her investigation.'

'Heresy!' snarled Jarl. 'Now there can be no doubt.'

'No,' Bedyr agreed, sadness in his eyes although his tone remained
firm.

'There is more,' the sergeant offered, continuing when Bedyr
gestured. 'The college is under guard. Lord Hattim speaks openly
of murder and claims only a Sister might have slain our king.'

There was a silence at such heretical news, broken by Jarl's
furious curse.

'May Ashar take him! You were right, Arlynn.'

'We have no time to waste,' said Bedyr urgently. 'We must seek the *Vashti* now!'

'Aye!' Jarl slid his sabre from the scabbard, raising the blade high, candlelight glinting on the naked steel. 'Who stands with us? For the Lady and the Kingdoms!'

A roar of approval answered his call and Corradon shouted for his men to form a phalanx. Bedyr climbed the steps of the dais until he stood beside the High Throne, shouting over the tumult.

'Wait! We are outnumbered and the palace is full of servants, innocent folk. Sheath your blades until they are needed. We go out of here as warriors of the Kingdoms, with the right to go where we wish. If none oppose us, offer them no harm.'

'And if they do?' Jarl demanded.

'Then,' said Bedyr, a grim smile on his lips, 'we cut them down.'

'Let Hattim but present himself,' grunted Jarl, 'and he is dead.'

'My Lord,' asked Corradon, addressing himself to Bedyr, 'where do we go? What of the Sisters?'

'I cannot believe Hattim would risk so open a statement of heresy as to harm the Sorority,' Bedyr answered, 'and there is little we can do for them now. We go the harbour, to the *Vashti*.'

Corradon nodded, sheathing his blade as he gathered his men about him and flung the wide doors open.

Startled faces greeted the grim band. Bedyr and Jarl set themselves either side of Corradon, their wives behind, ringed with Keshi and guardsmen as they drove through the confusion. They reached the corridor leading to the banqueting hall before they saw Galichians, a squad of twenty-five armoured men with swords drawn, commanded by a cordor.

'Halt!' he cried. 'Where do you go?'

Bedyr shouldered past Corradon to answer, 'Do you not recognise the Lords of Tamur and Kesh? By what authority do you deny us passage.'

'I do,' answered the cordor without giving any way, 'and I have orders from the king that you are to be brought before him.'

'The king?' Jarl bellowed, furious. 'Hattim Sethiyan is an apostate! A creature of the Messenger!'

'I have my orders,' said the cordor doggedly. 'You will come with me.'

'You dare to order us?' Jarl's sabre left its sheath, levelling on the officer's chest. 'Stand aside!'

'My Lord,' said the man, 'I cannot.'

314

'I command you to give way,' said Bedyr.

'I am ordered to bring you to the king,' the cordor repeated. 'E
any means. Put down your blades.'

Jarl's rage could contain itself no longer. His sabre flickered out,
his wrist twisting as the point caught the startled cordor in the throat,
opening a crimson gap between chin and breastplate. The cordor
gasped and staggered back, dropping his sword as he pressed both
hands to the wound, blood spurting over his fingers. For an instant
there was silence, all present staring at the dying man. Then his
eyes rolled up and he fell to his knees, hands still clutching at his
throat as he toppled over. It was as though a signal was given:
the Galichians charged with drawn swords, seeking to press the
advantage of the corridor, where only a few guardsmen at a time
might confront them.

Bedyr brought his longsword out in a sweeping cut that gutted
the closest soldier, pushing him back against his fellows as Corradon
and Jarl applied their blades, the captain's men pressing in from
behind until half the Galichian contingent lay dead and the rest
retreated.

'Forwards!' Bedyr shouted, leading the way into the hall.

They crossed the great chamber, where the remnants of the previous night's feasting still lay on the tables, forgotten in the confusion
of Darr's death, and entered the salon beyond.

More Galichians appeared, summoned by the fleeing warriors,
and Bedyr led the refugees in a charge.

There was more space for swordplay here and the Galichians rapidly outnumbered Bedyr's group as reinforcements came running,
drawn by the din of battle. Bedyr hacked a man down, reversing
his stroke to drive his blade across another's face, then kicked him
aside to drive the longsword deep into a belly. He had no time
to look back, could only hope that Yrla remained safe behind the
defensive blades of Corradon's men as he struggled to cut a way
through to the hall beyond. He deflected a thrust, turning the
southerner's shortsword to ram his hilt against the jaw, feeling a
savage satisfaction at the dull cracking sound of breaking bone,
then grunted as a cut scored a bloody line through the leather of
his jerkin and he turned, stepping inside the man's guard to slice
an answering blow across the throat. Beside him, Jarl whirled and
spun, the speed of his sword work belying his greater years, the
curved blade of the Keshi sabre clashing on armour, carving wounds
from exposed flesh. Corradon, too, proved a worthy battle

315

mpanion, and his armour was a great advantage as he bellowed in
nger and drove steadily forwards through the Galichians.

The southerners had the advantage of greater numbers and full
war harness, but even so the refugees cut a swathe through them,
propelled by righteous fury at the blasphemy their opponents, albeit
likely unwittingly, supported and their own determination. Nonetheless, they lost men as they fought their way across the salon and
as they grouped in the hall beyond Bedyr saw that their numbers
were depleted, whilst their enemies' ranks were steadily swelling.
Yrla and Arlynn, he saw with a flood of relief were unharmed,
surrounded by a solid wall of blades, all bloodied now. The gash
on his arm throbbed, his sleeve darkened by the steady welling of
blood, and when he glanced at Jarl, he saw the Keshi was cut across
the cheek and favoured his right leg. Corradon's armour was dented,
but appeared to have protected the captain from any serious hurt,
though several of his remaining men, like Jarl's Keshi warriors, bore
the marks of battle. He wondered if they had sufficient numbers to
win through to the harbour, but knew even as he wondered that they
had no other choice.

More Galichians appeared between the doors opening on the
courtyard and Bedyr shouted for the guardsmen and Keshi to rally,
intent on cutting a way to the gates.

Then the southerners' ranks parted and Hattim Sethiyan
appeared, Ashrivelle at his side. The usurper wore the kingly
robes of purple and gold and about his neck hung the medallion
bearing the tripartite symbol of Andurel. Ashrivelle wore the dark
blue of mourning, her blonde tresses veiled with silk surmounted
by a coronet. Her eyes were dark and hollow, tears glistening on
her cheeks, and she clung to Hattim's arm as if she could not stand
unsupported.

'Put down your weapons!' Hattim shouted. 'Do you oppose your
rightful king?'

'Heretic!' spat Jarl.

'You betray yourself,' Bedyr answered, raising his voice that all
there might hear him. 'Darr was slain by magic and you have no right
to wear the regalia of kingship. You are not our monarch, Hattim!'

'Traitors!' Hattim's response was calculated, designed to play
upon the emotions of men accustomed to obedience, to respect of
the trappings of the monarch; to trust. 'They stand condemned out
of their own mouths! Darr proclaimed me his heir and Darr is
dead – I *am* your king!'

'Ashrivelle,' Bedyr called, 'you are Darr's daughter; do you support this heresy?'

'My Lord Hattim is king,' Ashrivelle responded, her voice slow and thick. 'My poor dead father ordered it so.'

'Your father was slain by magic,' Bedyr said, 'and the Sisters are forbidden to examine his corpse for evidence of glamours. Hattim locks them in their college – why? What does he have to hide? What does he fear they will uncover?'

'My Lord Hattim is the king,' the new queen declared, and Bedyr saw that she was either drugged or so stricken with grief that her responses were automatic, her sense lost. He felt his own hope wane then.

'You hear?' Hattim addressed the crowd as much as Bedyr. 'Darr's own daughter denies this foul charge. These traitors act from rank envy and ambition – they would deny me my right.'

'The king is dead,' cried a voice Bedyr recognised as belonging to Mejas Celeruna. 'Long live the king.'

'Long live the king!' echoed another, and someone else added, 'long live King Hattim!'

'We are lost,' Jarl muttered. 'Let us sell ourselves dearly.'

'I would not have you slain like common outlaws,' Hattim declared with transparently false magnanimity. 'Lay down your swords and surrender. I promise you justice.'

'With weighted scales,' Bedyr said softly. 'Try for the doors. If we reach them, we run for the gates. Yrla, stay close!'

Yrla nodded, gathering her skirts; beside her, the rainbow hues of her gown coloured further with splashes of crimson, Arlynn clutched a curved dagger, her face pale with fear.

'I offer you a final chance to surrender,' cried Hattim. 'What madness has prompted you to level these insane accusations we may discuss later, but if you refuse you stand condemned by your own actions.'

'He uses his own perfidy against us,' murmured Yrla, and Bedyr answered, 'Aye, he was ever cunning, though I had not suspected him capable of this deviousness.'

'He has a daemonically skilled adviser,' Yrla responded. 'If he takes us we have no hope.'

Corradon spoke then, seeing amongst the Galichians numerous guardsmen. 'You soldiers of the Royal Guard,' he shouted, 'you know me and you know our Lords of Tamur and of Kesh! Do you not know us for honest men? Do you believe us capable of treachery? Side with us that we may right the awful wrong done our lawful king. Until the Sisters examine his body there can be no rightful succession. Hattim Sethiyan is not your king! He has no right to give you orders!'

'Treason!' Hattim bellowed as he saw the guardsmen falter, swayed by Corradon's words. 'The traitors have suborned your captain. Kill him!'

'Halt!' roared Corradon as the warriors surged forwards, the force of his bellow stopping them in their tracks. 'Do you believe these lies? Is there a man amongst you can believe I would harm King Darr?'

Many of the guardsmen lowered their blades at this, and several shouted in Corradon's favour, others crossing the space between the opposed forces to join him.

'King Darr's daughter stands at my side,' Hattim raged, 'my bride! The High Throne is mine by right of marriage! I am your king and I order you to obey me – now take them!'

The Galichians charged at this, but sufficient of the Royal Guard remained doubtful that the numbers attacking the refugees were lessened and they were able to fight off that initial onslaught, moving steadily towards the doors. Furniture encumbered the swordsmen and the hall became littered with bodies that presented further obstacles to the attack, those of Bedyr's party who fell left where they lay as the survivors crossed the chamber. Then a group of guardsmen reached a decision and fell upon the Galichians from behind, allowing the refugees to reach the egress.

Bedyr found himself confronting a halbadier who stabbed his clumsy weapon at the Lord of Tamur. He sidestepped the thrust, fastening his left hand about the shaft as he plunged his sword into the man's groin, snatching the pike from him as he fell, screaming. He sheathed his sword and began to swing the long, heavy-bladed weapon in scything arcs, clearing sufficient space that the others might follow him out into the collonaded portico and the courtyard beyond. Here more guardsmen overcame their confusion and sided with the refugees, swelling their ranks until they were able to fight slowly across the yard towards the palace gates.

Here, though, the advantage returned to Hattim, for the open space allowed him to bring archers into play and as the refugees approached the gates, arrows rained upon them.

Men fell in profusion then, Galichians and loyalists both dropping to the whistling shafts as Hattim screamed orders and his bowmen

318

fired blindly, careless of their targets. There was no defence against that terrible storm and as the Galichians drew back, leaving the bloody work to the archers, Bedyr saw that his party must die there or surrender. A shaft plucked at his jerkin and he saw Yrla flinch as another tore at her gown. They had reached the gates, which offered temporary shelter beneath their arch, but beyond lay open ground and the avenue leading into the city, where they would prove easy pickings for the bowmen.

'We are lost,' he shouted.

'We can sell ourselves dearly,' roared Jarl.

'Against archers?' Bedyr shook his head. 'Would you sacrifice Arlynn?'

'What other choice do we have?' asked the Keshi.

'Surrender!' Bedyr's voice was bitter. 'Hattim promised us a trial – we can hope sense may prevail.'

Jarl ducked as a shaft fluttered his dark hair and snarled, 'So be it.'

'Surrender!' Bedyr raised his voice above the tumult. 'Lay down your arms!'

The hail of arrows eased and ceased as his shout carried and the warriors about him lowered their useless blades. Bedyr beckoned Corradon closer, lowering his voice to whisper urgently, 'Corradon, you have the best chance of going unrecognised – if such opportunity should present itself, slip away and go to the harbour. Find Galen Sadreth and the *Vashti* and tell him to sail north. Take word to High Fort. If Kedryn is there, tell him he is Lord of Tamur now and must act accordingly. If he is not, tell Rycol to raise the war banners and join with Kemm to oppose this cursed usurper.'

'I will, my Lord,' Corradon promised.

Bedyr nodded and shouted across the wide yard to Hattim.

'Do you accept our surrender, Hattim Sethiyan? Do you promise us justice before these present?'

'He will have us slaughtered,' Jarl muttered.

'I think not,' said Bedyr. 'Not with all Andurel watching.'

He sheathed his blade and put an arm about Yrla's shoulders, defeat lending stark lines to his handsome features as he awaited Hattim's response.

Hattim glanced about him as though assessing the merits of accepting their surrender or having them killed on the spot. He was about to order his bowmen to slay them when a hand plucked at his sleeve and a soft voice hissed in his ear.

'Alive,' said Sister Thera. 'I want them alive.'

319

'I accept,' Hattim called. 'Lay down your arms and you shall receive the judgement of the law.'

Bedyr glanced to the side and saw Corradon stooping to smear his fingers with the blood of a fallen guardsman, wiping the gory stain across his face, adding more to his battered armour. The captain smiled grimly and stretched out beneath the arch of the gates, dragging a body across his legs. Dusk had fallen and in the shadows he seemed merely one more bloody corpse. Bedyr nodded his approval.

Yrla whispered, 'Do you see the Sister with Hattim?'

'Thera?' Bedyr's eyes widened. 'Do you suggest she betrays her calling?'

'He heeds her,' Yrla replied. 'That is strange in itself.'

'Mayhap she pleads for mercy,' Bedyr said.

Yrla frowned. 'Mayhap. Or mayhap there is something else.'

'We shall doubtless find out soon enough,' grunted Bedyr, then, louder: 'We surrender to you, Hattim Sethiyan.'

Corradon lay beneath the arch, watching through slitted eyes as the diminished party set down their weapons and stepped reluctantly from the shelter of the gates. They were instantly surrounded by Galichians and escorted into the White Palace, the young captain cursing silently as he saw that men of the Royal Guard sided with the traitors. Then his cursing became a slow sigh of relief as no move was made to clear the bodies and the shadows of twilight merged into the obfuscation of night. He remained still until the last of the soldiers was gone and only the watchmen remained on the wall. Then he rose cautiously to his feet and moved to the postern, sword ready in his right hand.

Two Galichians stood watch there and as he approached they turned suspiciously, eyeing his silver breastplate.

'Hail, friends,' he said with false cheerfulness, 'the traitors are in chains by now.'

'Who are you?' demanded the closest man.

'One loyal to the king and the Kingdoms,' Corradon said, and drove his blade deep beneath the man's ribs. He twisted the steel as he dragged it loose, striking the second guard across the face before a cry could escape his gaping mouth. As he staggered back, Corradon stabbed him in the belly, stepping past him to drag the bolts free and dart through the narrow doorway.

He began to run across the sward beyond, praying to the Lady that no guards were posted on the outer wall, weaving as the horribly familiar hiss of arrows filled the air about him. He felt a blow against his back and faltered, almost pitching to his face, but righting himself and continuing his zig-zag path as shafts thudded into the frozen ground around him. A second blow caused him to cry out as fire lanced through his shoulder and he felt the grate of steel head against bone. He was hit twice more before he reached the perimeter wall and saw the outer gates standing wide, the lights of Andurel before him.

He plunged through the opening and ran a way down the avenue, realising that he lurched, aware of warm moisture on his back, a painful shortness of breath. His ribs seemed to clench against his lungs and the arrow protruding from his shoulder was a source of agony, but he was spurred by the shouting behind him and weaved to the side, lunging through shrubs as he entered the parkland that lay between the White Palace and the closest buildings.

He crossed the park and staggered down a narrow alley, moving unsteadily downhill, grateful for the darkness and the cold that shuttered most of the city behind closed doors. Farther on he encountered frightened citizens who stared and pointed, drawing back in deference to his guardsman's harness and the threat of the bloody blade he presented to them.

Then he was in the harbour area and staggering past warehouses, seeing pale starlight twinkle on the surface of the Idre. A riverman emerged from a tavern and Corradon seized his arm, gasping, 'The *Vashti*, Galen Sadreth, where are they?'

The mariner, bleary-eyed from drink, pointed to the left and Corradon let him go, continuing towards the river.

He reached the waterfront and began to lurch towards the vessels, realising that his vision blurred, ignoring the pain that filled his lungs with liquid flame as he shouted, 'Galen Sadreth! I seek Galen Sadreth!'

A vast figure stepped into his path and he raised his sword threateningly, no longer able to speak for the agony that throbbed in his chest.

'I am Galen Sadreth,' said the mountainous shape, 'and I think you are dying.'

Corradon fell into the massive arms and Galen lowered him gently to the ground, cradling his head, his eyes sympathetic as he studied the shafts protruding from the young man's back. One at least was lodged in a lung and two more had pierced the dented silver breastplate deep enough to be bleeding his life away into his belly.

'You had better tell me what you want quickly,' the riverman murmured. 'You do not have long.'

Corradon spat blood on to his chin and chuckled despite himself. 'You are blunt,' he gasped. 'Are you loyal to the Kingdoms?'

'I am,' said Galen.

'Then you must sail north,' said Corradon, summoning the last reserves of his waning strength to inform the giant of Bedyr's wishes.

'I will do it,' Galen promised as dark blood joined the frothy crimson on the captain's lips.

'The hope of the Kingdoms rests with you,' Corradon choked out, and died.

Galen lowered the bloody head and rose to his feet, crossing to the dark shape of the barque that bobbed on the evening swell.

'Cast off!' he bellowed, cocking his head at the hoofbeats he heard thundering from the direction of the White Palace. 'Make haste! We sail north for High Fort. For the Kingdoms and Kedryn Caitin!'

The cordor leading the pursuing Galichians found Corradon's body by the riverside, but of the *Vashti* there was no sign, for she was already pulling into the stream, running without lights, her oarsmen stroking as if their very lives depended on the speed of their escape; as, indeed, they did.

Chapter Fifteen

THE barque that slid wearily into the harbour below High Fort as the watery sun touched the western edges of the Lozins was a weather–beaten memory of the colourful *Vashti* that had earlier that season sailed south. Her sails were ragged and the brightwork of her gunnels dulled, her oarsmen lolled, close to exhaustion, in their places, and even bluff Galen Sadreth was subdued as he let go his tiller and moved towards the gangplank. Nonetheless, there was the gleam of pride in the eyes of the tired rivermen, for they had fought the wind and the winter spillage of the Idre to bring their craft swiftly northwards, and they congratulated themselves on a job well done.

Galen voiced a brief encomium and tossed gold enough for a keg of beer and warm beds to his mate before crossing the plank and starting the climb towards the citadel. There was little enough time to waste and he cursed with all the eloquence of his guild as he was required to halt before the gates and state his business, delaying further while a man was sent to bring word to Rycol, his impatience only slightly mollified by the rapid appearance of the chatelain.

'I bring alarming news from Andurel,' he declared without pre-amble. 'What word of Kedryn?'

'He lives.' Rycol studied the fat captain, seeing on his ruddy features an uncharacteristic nervousness. 'What news?'

Galen drew his cloak tighter about his massive frame and pursed his lips, glancing around in a conspiratorial manner before lowering his voice and saying, 'This is best told in private, I think.'

Rycol nodded and beckoned Galen to follow him across the court-yard to enter the labyrnthine bowels of the fortress, making their way to the chatelain's quarters, where Rycol produced evshan and Galen tossed back a cup as if the fierce liquor were water. He grunted his approval and extended the cup that Rycol might refill it, sipping more slowly as he lounged back in his chair, his bulk threatening to

323

overwhelm even that sturdy frame. Rycol sat before the fire, absently stroking the heads of the two brindle hounds that fretted at the nervousness they sensed in the riverman.

'What news?' the chatelain repeated.

'Darr is dead,' said Galen, 'and Hattim Sethiyan wed to Ashrivelle, declaring himself king. Bedyr, Yrla, Jarl of Kesh and his wife are, as best I know, imprisoned. Or dead. Andurel is held by the Galichian army.'

Rycol stared at the fat man, his lean face tense now. 'You are sure of this?' he demanded.

Galen nodded and explained how Corradon had come, dying, to the *Vashti* with word from Bedyr; how Darr had died so mysteriously; and how Hattim proclaimed himself monarch by marriage right. Rycol's features grew grim as he listened and when Galen was done, he rose to shout for Kedryn to be summoned.

'Bedyr feared him dead,' Galen said.

'No.' Rycol shook his head. 'With Wynett and Tepshen Lahl he escaped the downfall of the Fedyn Pass and succeeded in reaching the Drott. He has his sight again.'

'Praise the Lady,' Galen murmured fervently, 'that, at least, is a blessing.'

'He will need his eyes to lead Tamur against the usurper,' Rycol grunted. 'Are you sure Bedyr is taken?'

'The man who told me was a captain of the Royal Guard,' Galen said. 'He was dying – filled with Galichian arrows – and riders were on his heels: I believed him well enough to bring my craft north.'

Rycol nodded slowly, his eyes thoughtful now, assessing the strategy of a winter campaign. He turned as the door opened and Kedryn came in, Wynett at his side, no longer – to Galen's surprise – in the blue robe of a Sister, but dressed in a gown of soft pink. The riverman rose ponderously, his eyes troubled as he saw Kedryn's smile.

'Galen!' Kedryn crossed the room to clasp the big man's hand. 'You are well met, old friend. Are you come to bring us south?'

Galen swallowed and took more evshan as he braced himself to repeat his story, seeing Kedryn's smile disappear at the telling, Wynett's radiant features grow sombre. The pleasure he felt as he saw that Kedryn's eyes focused again, that love had blossomed and was acknowledged between them, dimmed by the sad nature of his information.

'Tepshen must hear this,' Kedryn said when the tale was done, and servants were despatched to find the kyo.

While they waited he turned to Wynett, taking her hands. 'I am sorry. Your father was a good man.'

Tears moistened her blue eyes, but she brushed them away, her face composed, the disciplines of Estrevan imposing a stoic calm. 'He was, indeed; but now he is dead and we must look to the future. I shall mourn him when the time comes – now we must think of the living.'

Kedryn nodded, grateful for her strength. Rycol said, 'My condolences, Wynett. I counted Darr a friend.'

Wynett smiled wanly, not speaking, a hand about the talisman she wore, as if that touch could lend her strength.

Tepshen Lahl appeared then with Brannoc at his side, both men flushed, in winter garb, the sweet smell of horseflesh lingering about them, their smiles fading as they saw the solemn features of those already gathered. Kedryn motioned them to sit and asked Galen to repeat his story a third time. As he spoke Tepshen's eyes grew cold, and when he was finished the easterner turned to Kedryn, direct as ever.

'You are – for the present – Lord of Tamur: do you send out the war banners?'

Kedryn, his own face pale, stared blindly at the kyo for long moments, the frown that lined his features ageing him so that he resembled more than ever his father.

'In such wolf weather?' He turned towards Galen. 'Was the Messenger's hand detected in this?'

'I do not know.' Galen shook his head, seeing in the young man a new maturity, a firming of character that prompted confidence. 'I know only what I have told you.'

Kedryn nodded, stern determination lending him an air of grim resolve even though dull fear gnawed at his mind, threatening to cloud his judgement. He reached unthinking to clasp the blue jewel hung about his neck and at its touch he felt a calm, the panic that menaced his thinking receding, a clarity possessing him so that he was able to foresee the options before him and weigh them one against another.

'If Hattim dares imprison my parents I doubt he would hesitate to hold their lives hostage against the approach of our army,' he said slowly. 'And if we do send out the banners, how long will it take to raise our forces? My parents might well be dead before we reached

325

Andurel. Or we might find them set betwixt us and Hattim. Swifter action is needed.'

'How?' Tepshen demanded. 'Hattim has his army before the city.'

'And Kemm of Kesh likely has his on the Vortigen,' nodded Kedryn. 'Knowing that if he crosses the river, Jarl's throat will be cut. I'd wager Hattim counts on that to stalemate our response and I'd not see my parents die as a result of precipitate action. Galen brought the *Vashti* out – can he not bring me in?'

He turned to the riverman, reaching for Wynett's hand as he heard her gasp. Galen ducked his head. 'I can bring you close, and whilst the Galichians would likely seize the *Vashti*, a boat could put you ashore unnoticed.'

'And then?' asked Tepshen, dubious. 'What do we do then?'

'We?' Kedryn smiled slightly.

'Do you think I shall let you die alone?' said the kyo.

'Or I?' said Wynett. 'If die we must.'

'You cannot come with me,' Kedryn said firmly. 'There is too much danger.'

'You forget something,' Wynett said gently, though iron resolution rang in her quiet words. 'I am my father's elder daughter.'

Kedryn frowned. 'I do not understand.'

'Do you not think,' said Wynett, taking both his hands in hers, 'that the time has come to make an honest woman of me?'

'By the Lady!' Rycol spoke for the first time, seeing the direction of her thoughts. 'Aye – that is it!'

Kedryn's frown grew more perplexed, confusion showing in his brown eyes.

'Ashrivelle is my younger sister,' Wynett explained, 'and now that I have renounced my Sisterhood my claim to the High Throne takes precedence. Were I wed, my husband should have prior claim to Hattim Sethiyan.'

'I?' Kedryn gasped.

'You,' Wynett nodded.

'King Kedryn,' said Brannoc, thoughtfully. 'It has a certain ring to it.'

'I had not thought to claim such rank,' Kedryn murmured.

'You had not thought to see your parents imprisoned,' said Wynett. 'Do you reject me?'

'No!' Kedryn shook his head quickly. 'You know that I would take you as my wife. But I had not thought to become king.'

'As Wynett's husband,' said Rycol, 'you become the legal cl.
ant. You would have rightful seniority over Hattim Sethiyan – .
the right to command his army.'

'Would the Galichian accept that?' demanded Tepshen
doubtfully.

'Likely not,' Rycol admitted, 'but others would have no choice, and any who opposed Kedryn would stand condemned of treason.'

'Hail the King,' said Brannoc. 'When is the wedding? When do we sail?'

'You, too?' Kedryn asked, his smile grateful.

Brannoc grinned. 'You will need a bodyguard, your Majesty. It seems hardly fitting that you present yourself to Andurel without suitable attendants.'

'It seems,' Kedryn said, almost ruefully, 'that it is decided for me.'

'I argue the wisdom of approaching Andurel without an army at your back,' said Tepshen. 'At the very least, take a force from Rycol's garrison.'

'There are no boats.' Kedryn shook his head. 'And I do not think this a matter for any army.'

They all stared at him then and he paused, marshalling his thoughts, clutching the talisman again as if communing with some power beyond the mortal. It seemed the jewel imbued him with a calm and a resolution that he had felt before, when he faced Niloc Yarrum and when he saw the way to making peace with the Beltrevan, though now it was stronger, as if the Lady herself spoke in some wordless way through the agency of the blue stone, ordering his mind, filling him with a power he did not understand, but accepted on faith for what it undoubtedly was.

'Time is against us,' he said, some indefinable quality in his voice lending him an authority they instinctively respected, 'and I suspect the Messenger has a hand in this. Wed to Wynett, I am – as you point out, my love – Darr's rightful heir and so able to command the warriors of the Kingdoms. If Alaria's Text is true, then I *am* the Chosen One – the only one capable of defeating the Messenger. I believe this is my fight. I believe the Lady saved us in the Fedyn Pass and aided us in the Beltrevan that I should stand ready for this struggle. I will go south alone.'

'With me,' Wynett said firmly. 'My presence lends authority to your claim. Andurel knows me for Darr's daughter. Ashrivelle knows my right is greater than hers. You shall not leave me behind.'

'Nor me,' said Tepshen Lahl, no less firmly.

'And I do not intend to miss so epic a confrontation,' said ɔrannoc.

'Very well,' Kedryn allowed, seeing that there was no deterring them. 'Will you give us passage, Galen?'

'The *Vashti* is yours to command,' said the riverman.

'Then,' Kedryn rose, only to drop to his knees before Wynett, 'if my lady consents to marry me, we sail as early as we may.'

Wynett took the hand he offered, smiling gravely. 'I do accept, my lord.'

Kedryn climbed to his feet and turned to Rycol. 'Will you arrange it, my friend? The sooner the better.'

'There are Sisters here and I have civic right,' nodded the chatelain. 'Do you but give me time to arrange a wedding feast, it shall be done this day.'

Kedryn nodded and High Fort's commander hurried from the room to begin the preparations. 'It will be a poor enough ceremony,' Kedryn murmured.

'It will be all the ceremony we need,' Wynett smiled. 'Now leave me to prepare myself.

It was not the wedding either of them had anticipated. There was none of the pomp that Ashrivelle and Hattim had enjoyed, nor time for much ceremony beyond the simple declaration of the vows, offered before Rycol and the Lady Marga, Wynett's nurses representative of Estrevan, Tepshen Lahl, Brannoc and Galen Sadreth the witnesses, but it was, nonetheless, a marriage, binding them in formal declaration of the love that had burgeoned through such hardship. The banquet that followed was marred by the absence of Bedyr and Yrla, by the sad news of Darr's death, but despite those absences there was a feeling of joy in High Fort's feasting hall, and when they retired Kedryn knew a sense of completeness, of rectitude, that filled him with delight.

He lay with his arms about Wynett in a chamber overlooking the dark sweep of the Idre canyon, the faint glow of the coals banked in the hearth washing the chamber with warm light, and felt a happiness that overcame all trepidation, all fear of the task that lay ahead.

'In Andurel, when all is done,' he promised, 'we shall marry again, if you like. A ceremony befitting the daughter of a king.'

Wynett stirred sleepily against him, brushing his shoulder with her lips. 'I am the wife of a king,' she murmured. 'I am your wife and I want nothing more than that.'

'I shall build a monument to Darr,' he said into her hair.

'There is no need,' she replied. 'I grieve for my father, but dea
a thing we must all accept and there is no point to shedding needle
tears. Let our life together be the monument.'

She turned then, presenting her mouth, and they spoke no more.

The next day Galen repaired to the dockside to supervise the
refitting of his vessel whilst Kedryn sat in conference with Rycol
and the others, delineating a plan of campaign that would, he hoped,
forestall outright war. Somehow he was certain the Messenger lay
behind these alarming events, and he sensed that when he sailed
south he would be moving towards a confrontation with Ashar's
minion that must determine the future of the Kingdoms. He felt
that he prepared to face a power greater than any he had known.
It was an awesome thought, one that would, had he allowed it, have
filled him with dread, but he fought that fear, strengthened by the
certainty that he fought in the Lady's cause.

The morning of their departure dawned steel grey, an icy wind
blowing skirls of snow down the river canyon, lashing white froth
from the surface of the Idre. The *Vashti* bobbed restlessly on her
mooring lines, as if anxious to be gone, and her crew, for all the
complaints they hurled at their captain, turned willingly enough to
their tasks as Kedryn and Wynett, with Tepshen Lahl and Brannoc
close behind, came on board. Rycol and the Lady Marga stood
on the harbourside as they had stood before to watch Bedyr and
Yrla depart, though now the chatelain had more to do than wait
for Brannoc to emerge from the Beltrevan, for Kedryn had left
him with clear orders. He was to alert Tamur, not to arm, but to
stand ready for war should word to the contrary fail to come out
of Andurel, and already the signal towers were flashing messages
to Low Fort, informing Fengrif of the events unfolding far to the
south so that Kesh, too, should stand ready to march against the
Galichian usurper.

'Shall we find peace some day?' Kedryn wondered as the barque
quit the harbour.

'Some day, surely,' said Wynett from the circle of his arm. 'Do
we not follow the path of the Lady?'

'Aye.' Kedryn watched the figures on the dockside diminish,
fading in the wintry grey light as the *Vashti* found the current and
the wind bellied her refurbished sails. 'But that path could lead to
our death.'

'We have no other choice,' Wynett said firmly, 'save to turn our
backs on all we hold dear, and that is no choice at all.'

'No,' Kedryn agreed.

For all the speed the steady wind lent them, the journey seemed interminable and Kedryn grew impatient as they scudded the roiling grey surface of the mighty river. Towns and villages swept past, Galen docking only when conditions rendered night sailing overly hazardous, and then their halts were brief as possible, their identities kept secret from their hosts. No word had yet escaped of Hattim's assumption of the High Throne, the unusually severe winter locking the hamlets of Tamur in isolation, and Kedryn began to wonder if he perceived a monstrous design behind the usurper's plan. By spring, when the roads opened again, the Galichian would be firmly ensconced in the White Palace, and if he held the Lords of Tamur and Kesh, and their Ladies, hostage he would hold a terrifying advantage over any counter action. It seemed too confident a stroke even for one so ambitious as Hattim Sethiyan, and Kedryn felt the certainty that the Messenger's hand lay behind it all mount apace. He longed to reach the island city and uncover the truth, no matter what the outcome.

The long winter stood at the commencement of its decline before they came within striking distance of Andurel. The north wind had softened and was bringing hail rather than snow, the hours of daylight longer, the sun appearing more frequently, and warmer when Galen announced that one more day's sailing would bring them to the city and Kedryn ordered him to bring the *Vashti* over to the east bank and find the mouth of the Vortigen.

They hugged the bank until nightfall and then moved cautiously into the tributary river, anchoring when the lights of Kemm's encampment showed. Accompanied by Wynett, Tepshen Lahl and Brannoc, Kedryn went ashore to find the Keshi prince.

Kemm was lounging on cushions, restlessly listening to a poet recite tales of his kingdom's past, when they were ushered in. He rose to his feet with surprise writ large on his fleshy features, staring at them as if they were the last folk in the Kingdoms he had expected to see.

'Kedryn?' His dark eyes were doubtful as he studied the prince of Tamur, dredging old memories for recognition.

'Aye,' Kedryn nodded, 'we were boys when last we met, Kemm.'

'And likely orphans soon,' the Keshi announced dramatically. 'Do you come with an army? It will do us little good, unless we agree to see our parents butchered by that Galichian upstart.'

330

'I have no army,' Kedryn replied. 'Tell me what transpires.'

The same confidence that had gripped him in High Fort showee now, prompting Kemm to submit to his authority even before he learnt that marriage had raised Kedryn. He called for food and wine, dismissing the poet as he explained the events of the past months.

There was, indeed, a stalemate, for when Kemm had learnt of Darr's death and found Galichian soldiery manning the approaches to Andurel he had sought formally to cross into the city and been turned back. Hattim himself had appeared to inform the Keshi that his parents were held prisoner, hostage against his conduct and likely to die should he engage in any attempt to free them or enter the city under arms.

'Yours, too,' he added mournfully. 'The Galichian holds them in the White Palace; and the Sisters are confined to their college. I have heard rumours that magic was employed against Darr.'

'Magic?' Wynett asked sharply.

'It is what I have heard,' Kemm nodded. 'Forgive me, Sister . . . Majesty! But that is what I hear.'

'It is what Galen suggested,' said Kedryn. 'Does the usurper employ advisers? Are there any close to him?'

Kemm shrugged, his black robe rustling. 'News is a commodity in short supply these days. I have seen nine of my spies hanged from the Vortigen bridges, but what little word there is has it that a Sister stands close to Hattim.'

'You said the Sisters were confined,' Kedryn said.

'All, it seems, save the one,' Kemm nodded. 'I do not know her name, or even if what I hear is true.'

Kedryn turned to Wynett, his expression doubtful. 'Is it likely a Sister would accept him as king?'

'No,' she replied confidently, 'not if these rumours of magic are true; not with her fellows held under guard.'

'There is more,' said Kemm. 'Many of the Royal Guard opposed Hattim and were slaughtered on the spot. Those who surrendered were executed. Their bodies rot on the palace walls. Sister Bethany demanded the usurper remove the sentries from the college and was declared traitor for her presumption.'

'No!' Wynett gasped. 'I cannot believe even Hattim would dare so open a declaration of heresy.'

Kedryn's eyes were angry as he faced her, his visage grim. 'Does it not give proof of our suspicions?' he asked, his voice harsh. 'The Messenger would not baulk at such measures.'

'No,' she agreed, 'he would not.'

'This must change our plan,' said Tepshen. 'Gone thus far Hattim will not hesitate to kill you if you enter Andurel.'

Kedryn studied his friend's face, recognising the truth in his words. Did Hattim thwart him so adroitly? He touched the talisman, seeking again that inspiration the jewel seemed to bestow, and felt its power fill him, calming the rage that threatened to erupt, opening avenues of thought that revealed ways around the Galichian's – or the Messenger's? – design. He looked to Wynett, and saw that she, too, sought the unspoken advice of the strange stones.

'It changes nothing,' he said slowly, not sure the words were his, for they seemed to come not from his own mind but from something greater, something that lay beyond the mortal plane. 'Hattim can slay me only at risk of announcing himself a regicide. Whatever fell glamours were used against Darr he has succeeded in concealing. Should he seek to employ those same gramaryes on me, he must stand openly condemned of heresy. Should he seek to slay me by more mundane means, he rebels against the king-elect.'

'Do you think that will stay his hand?' demanded the kyo, concern making his voice angry.

'Aye, if he knows such measure must bring all Tamur and Kesh against him,' Kedryn answered grimly, 'and mayhap sway Ust-Galich, too. To seize the High Throne in the confusion of Darr's death is one thing; to openly slay the rightful heir, another.'

'So what do you propose?' asked Tepshen.

'I shall enter the city and confront Hattim,' Kedryn said. 'Before all the people of Andurel I shall announce my right to the High Throne and demand that Hattim stand down.'

'There is another consideration,' Brannoc suggested. 'You believe the Messenger stands with Hattim – do you believe he will stand idly by whilst you depose the Galichian?'

'No,' Kedryn answered, 'I believe he will reveal himself, and when he does he will show Hattim's followers the anathema they support.'

'He will destroy you,' rasped Tepshen.

'Or I him,' said Kedryn, his voice calm. 'Is that not what the Text foretells? Listen, my friends, I wanted no part of this – I did not believe I was the Chosen One, did not believe I *could* be, but do all these paths we have trod together not lead to this one thing? It seems my destiny is inexorable – it leads me inevitably to the Messenger. I *must* face him. Or grant him sway over the Kingdoms.'

'He is right.' Wynett's voice was hushed, though it carried clearly

enough through the silence that followed Kedryn's declaration. '
Lady chose Kedryn as her champion and he must follow his destiny

'I thought,' grunted Tepshen, 'that your Lady gave you free
choice.'

'To see the Kingdoms trod down beneath the heel of a usurper?
To see Ashar rule our lands?' Kedryn shook his head, his voice
gentle as if he delivered a lesson to a child. 'To leave my parents
hostage? Or drag the Kingdoms into civil war? Those are my choices,
Tepshen, and I reject them all.'

For long moments the kyo stared at the younger man, realising
that familiarity had blinded him to the changes taking place. This
was not the boy he had trained in swordplay, the youth he had
escorted into the Beltrevan. This was a king who spoke, a full-grown
warrior who faced his destiny as must all men, unafraid, resolved to
take the only course he perceived as honest, unable to relinquish his
integrity for the safer way. He nodded.

'So be it.'

'We cross the river on the morrow,' Kedryn said.

'And I?' Kemm asked. 'What would you have me do?'

'The hardest thing,' Kedryn told him, 'maintain your vigil. If the
bridges open, you will know Hattim is deposed and the Messenger
slain. If not – Rycol of High Fort raises Tamur and will join you
in war.'

'May the Lady go with you,' said the Keshi.

'She does,' Kedryn replied confidently.

The changing weather, or perhaps the good offices of a benign deity,
cloaked the lower reaches of the Idre in fog that dawn as a boat put
out from the shore above Andurel. At the tiller, his weight settling
the small craft low in the water, sat Galen Sadreth. Amidships sat
Kedryn, Wynett, Tepshen Lahl and Brannoc, cloaked and hooded,
though beneath those shrouding garments each man was dressed in
battle harness, their surcoats emblazoned with the clenched fist of
Tamur, their blades honed, the sheaths fresh-oiled. Wynett wore
the blue robe of the Sisterhood, though now, thanks to Kemm,
the tripartite crown of Andurel was sewn over her breast, and like
Kedryn, the blue stone that was her half of the talisman hung beside
that emblem. They said nothing as the boatmen dipped their oars,
driving the fragile vessel swiftly through the concealing mist, each
wrapped in their own thoughts as they drew steadily closer to the
fog-veiled city.

Lights showed as they approached and to the east the rising sun began to dispel the grey vapour, the sounds of the awakening harbourage coming muffled through the obfuscation. Galen brought the longboat in against a pier and the crew made fast as the quartet disembarked.

'I will do as you bid,' he promised. 'That tavern is as good a place as any to start.'

Kedryn looked to where the riverman pointed and nodded, clasping the ham-like hand.

'You have my thanks, Galen. For all you have done.'

Galen smiled briefly. 'The Lady be with you, Kedryn.'

He watched as they strode into the receding mist, wondering if he would see them again, then beckoned his men to follow him and went inside the inn.

'Praise the Lady,' he declared, using the full force of his impressive voice to attract attention, 'we have a new king and I propose to stand a glass for every man ready to drink his health.'

The tavern was already well populated with longshoremen and sailors and all their faces turned at this announcement. The bulk of the early morning drinkers were daunted by Galen's size, but one found the courage to spit noisily into the brass bucket provided and say, 'A toast to Hattim Sethiyan? I'd sooner go thirsty.'

'The Galichian usurper?' Galen affected surprise. 'Why, my friend, the only toast to him I'd drink would be in his blood. No, I toast Kedryn Caitin, newly wed to good king Darr's daughter, Wynett, and so our rightful monarch.'

'Prince Kedryn?' The dissenter fixed narrow eyes on Galen. 'Kedryn is lost in the Beltrevan.'

'Kedryn goes e'en now to make his presence known to the upstart Hattim,' beamed Galen. 'With Wynett at his side. I witnessed their wedding myself. Now – who joins me in a toast to Kedryn, our king?'

'Evshan,' said the man. 'And may the Lady bless Kedryn. And you, captain, for bringing us this news.'

Galen dispensed coins as cups were rapidly emptied, quaffing a brimming glass himself before departing to the next tavern to repeat his performance.

He had visited three before a squad of Galichian soldiers under the command of a sergeant appeared to demand what treason he disseminated.

'Why, is it treason to toast the king?' beamed Galen.

'The docks are alive with scurrilous rumour,' snapped the

sergeant. 'You spread word that Kedryn Caitin claims the H
Throne.'

'As, indeed, he does,' the riverman retorted loudly. 'He has mar
ried Wynett and so claims precedence over Hattim.'

'You had best come with me,' the sergeant decided.

'Why?' asked Galen.

'You sow the seeds of rebellion,' the sergeant barked. 'You mouth
treason.'

Galen spread his arms, looking down at the smaller man. 'What
rebellion in hailing our rightful king?' he smiled. 'Do you deny
Kedryn's lawful claim?'

'Damn you!' The sergeant put a hand on his sword. 'Hattim
Sethiyan is our king.'

'No more,' said Galen, and clapped his massive hands together,
the sergeant's head between them.

The soldier gasped, his eyes rolling, and Galen took hold of his
belt and the neck of his breastplate, lifting him high. For an instant
the sergeant hung suspended above the giant's head. Then he was
flying into the men behind him, propelled by all the strength of
the riverman's arms. Galen's crew fell upon them as they toppled,
belaying pins appearing from their belts to clatter against helmets
and more yielding flesh.

'A round to celebrate the downfall of Hattim,' Galen roared, and
all the tavern joined him in the toast.

Before the sun had burned off the last of the fog the entire harbour area was alive with the news. Word spread like wildfire, from
tavern to tavern, to the warehouses and the merchants, through
the boatyards, inland to the emporiums lining the avenues and on
amongst the citizens, to the schools, the stables, to the servants of the
private houses and from them to their master; everywhere it went:
'Kedryn Caitin is come to claim the throne. Hail, Kedryn!'

A squad of Galichian infantry led by a cordor declared the
entire clientele of one tavern under arrest and was promptly set
upon. Five of the soldiers were killed and their officer hanged,
the rest forced to retreat in disarray under a bombardment of
impromptu missiles. Five cavalrymen were dragged from their
horses and slain. Nine more were unmounted and tossed into the
Idre, where three drowned as laughing sailors watched them try to
swim in heavy armour. Throughout the city folk stood up against
the oppressors. Galichians who had arrogantly assumed superiority
were insulted, and those who protested or threatened retribution

nmarily dismissed. Swords were brought from concealment nd turned against the southerners, their own snatched from them and used against them. The fighting spread, sporadic at first, but growing steadily into a concerted rebellion as the word passed from mouth to mouth: 'Kedryn Caitin is come to claim the throne. Hail, Kedryn!'

While this went on Kedryn approached the outer gates of the White Palace.

Behind him he could hear the clamour of insurrection, and several times his little band sheltered in doorways as troops of Galichian soldiers came hurrying from the walled building atop the hill. The mist was clearing more rapidly now, pale sun showing against a blue sky striped with white, wind-driven clouds, revealing the walls of the palace hung with the grisly reminders of Hattim's supremacy. Wynett gasped, horrified, as the rotting corpses in the silver armour of the Royal Guard became visible, but Kedryn made no sound, though his mouth settled in a tight, angry line. The tumult grew louder and Brannoc touched his arm, pointing back down the hill. Kedryn turned to see a crowd filling the avenue behind, swelling as rivulets of people flowed in from the the sidestreets, moving like some human flood, coming up the avenue, many bearing swords, others with halberds and axes taken from the Galichians, more with makeshift weapons, butcher's cleavers, rakes, even brooms. He paused, cocking his head to hear what it was they shouted, and smiled grimly as he caught the words that roared defiantly from a myriad throats.

'Hail Kedryn! Hail the king!'

'You have an army,' Tepshen remarked.

Kedryn nodded and continued towards the gates.

Bowmen manned the wall and a telleman appeared on the arch. Kedryn shed his cloak and his companions followed suit, revealing the insignia decorating their surcoats.

'I am Kedryn Caitin, Prince of Tamur, and husband of Wynett, elder daughter of King Darr,' he shouted. 'I demand entrance.'

The telleman stared at him, frowning, his eyes lifting to the mass drawing steadily closer, its proclamatory shout clear. Tepshen Lahl moved a few paces forward, his body tensed to fling himself between Kedryn and the threatening shafts. The telleman's gaze shifted to his archers, then back to the quartet confronting him.

'How do I know you?' he called doubtfully.

'Bring out my parents,' Kedryn replied, 'Bedyr Caitin, the Lord

of Tamur, and the Lady Yrla. Bring out Jarl of Kesh. They kno
me. As does Hattim Sethiyan!'

The authority in his voice put further doubt in the telleman's eyes
and he called, 'What do you want?'

'I demand entrance,' Kedryn shouted back. 'Open the gates or
you answer to me!'

'I serve Hattim Sethiyan,' said the officer, though somewhat nervously. 'Lord of Ust-Galich and the Kingdoms.'

Wynett spoke then, her voice firm as Kedryn's, her blue eyes
defiant as she stared at the telleman. 'I am Wynett, the elder
daughter of King Darr, and wife of Kedryn Caitin. Do you deny
the High Blood? Do you deny my husband's rightful claim?'

The man studied her, confusion growing on his bearded face,
something like fear showing as he looked towards the shouting mob
that soon would reach the wall. Then he nodded and ordered the
gates opened.

'I will bring you before King Hattim.'

'You are wise,' said Kedryn calmly, marching between the portals.

The telleman ordered off a squad of soldiers and led the way
to the inner gates. On his command they, too, parted and the four
companions entered the White Palace. Behind them the mob had
halted at the walls, defying the archers who stood nervously, no
longer certain of their commander's authority, unpleasantly aware
that so large a mass of folk might overwhelm them.

Inside the palace there could be no doubting the identities of
the visitors, for the Galichian nobles recognised Kedryn from the
battle of the Lozin Gate and palace servants paused in their tasks,
staring at the young woman they recalled from childhood, regal now
as she walked beside her husband, her wheat-blonde hair so like her
sister's.

The telleman halted before the doors to the throne room, wary
now, for he found himself caught between loyalty to Hattim and
the growing conviction that Kedryn did, indeed, lay rightful claim
to the High Throne. His dilemma was taken from him by the
appearance of a plump man, his oiled hair curled in artful ringlets,
earrings glittering at both lobes, a disdainful expression on his fleshy,
rouged face.

'What is it?' he lisped irritably. 'King Hattim demands the cause
of this disturbance.'

'Lord Celeruna,' the telleman began, then broke off as Kedryn
stepped towards the portly courtier.

'You know me, Mejas Celeruna,' he said sternly, 'now stand aside.'

Without further ado he brushed past the fat man and strode into the throne room.

'Kedryn?'

Surprise and anticipation mingled in Hattim's voice. Kedryn stared at him, loathing in his eyes, but also sadness, for he saw a man consumed by ambition, risen higher than he had any right to hope only to fall lower than a human should. Hattim was become dissipated, excess flesh swelling his cheeks and bulging above the belt of his splendid golden tunic, his lips pursed in a grimace of displeasure, as if power magnified his decadence and left physical mark. He lounged on the throne, a dropped goblet bleeding wine red as blood slowly down the marble steps. A servant stooped to retrieve it and Hattim glanced at the man, then turned swiftly to the blue-robed woman standing at his right elbow.

To his left, starting from her throne, Ashrivelle stared in disbelief at Wynett, a hand pressed to her lovely mouth.

'Do you know me, sister?' Wynett asked.

Ashrivelle nodded, the hand that had covered her lips moving to toy with a strand of blonde hair fallen loose from her elaborate coiffeur, doubt and embarrassment in her eyes.

'Then say it,' Wynett demanded. 'Say it that all here may know it.'

'You are my sister,' Ashrivelle said, and looked nervously to Hattim.

He no longer lounged, but was sitting forwards, hands resting on pale green satin breeks, his eyes narrowed.

'What do you want?' he cried, his voice shrill.

Kedryn moved to the centre of the room, Wynett beside him. Tepshen and Brannoc positioned themselves slightly behind and to the sides, their eyes roving, deceptively casual, over the watching throng of courtiers.

'By what right do you claim the throne?' Kedryn demanded, his voice cold.

'By marriage,' said Hattim. 'And Darr's proclamation.'

'I am wed to Wynett,' Kedryn retorted, 'and she is the elder sister.'

Hattim gasped, turning again to the Sister now glaring avidly at Kedryn. It was she who spoke: 'Wynett is of the Sorority. She cannot marry.'

'I chose to relinquish my vows,' said Wynett. 'I am wed to Kedryn.'

338

'Words,' said the Sister. 'What proof have you?'

Kedryn stared at the woman, ugly realisation stirring. He becam[e] aware of a tingling sensation against his chest, a strange, cool warmth. His nerve ends prickled, but simultaneously calm gripped him, dispelling rage and fear, leaving behind only certainty.

'You have my word,' he said coldly. 'But should any here require more, bring Sister Bethany before us and let the ceremony be performed again.'

A buzz of conversation erupted, stilled by an angry slash of Hattim's hand.

'The Paramount Sister stands accused,' he muttered.

Now Kedryn's voice rose angry, ringing over the throng, commanding. '*You* stand accused, Sethiyan! Of the unlawful imprisonment of my parents! Of the murder of King Darr! Of heresy!'

The silence that fell then was palpable. Into it Kedryn roared, 'Come down from that throne you befoul traitor! Or do I drag you from it?'

Hattim gasped, his face paling. Beside him Ashrivelle stared dumbstruck. To his right the Sister cried, 'Kill him!'

'Does any dare attack their rightful king?' Wynett cried.

Only one did. Mejas Celeruna shouted, 'For Hattim!' and sprang forward with a slender dagger upraised. For so effete a man it was a valiant effort, albeit misguided and quite useless. Tepshen Lahl spun round, right hand fastening about the hilt of his eastern sword, draw and cut so swift they were a single blur of movement, the long blade slashing sideways to strike the courtier's belly. To strike and progress through the robe he wore and the flesh beneath. To emerge bloody as Celeruna screamed and collapsed forwards, his blade striking sparks from the flagstones as he pitched on to his face, crimson spreading beneath his corpse.

The kyo turned in a half circle, blade extended in readiness for further attack. Beyond, Brannoc's Keshi sabre was out, menacing the gape-mouthed court. Those who had thought to lend support to Celeruna halted with hands on sword hilts, stilled by the menace of the two warriors and the authority that radiated from Kedryn. Hattim was on his feet, his eyes wide with horror, looking, as though he sought her help or approval, to the Sister.

Kedryn stood watching her, aware of the steady pulsing of the talisman beneath his surcoat, hardly daring to believe what, rapidly, he knew he must.

'The Messenger!' he said softly.

'Aye,' Wynett confirmed. 'I feel it, too.'

Beside Hattim, Taws saw that all his plans stood in jeopardy. He had not anticipated his prey walking so openly into the trap he had set, nor thought that Kedryn might outwit him, that he would come not as some adventurer seeking only to free his parents, but as the husband of Wynett, with lawful claim to the High Throne. It was that, he saw, that stilled the hands of the Galichian's sycophants, for whilst they were fully prepared to support Hattim in his regal claims, they still adhered to the customs of the Kingdoms and must therefore acknowledge the Tamurin's prior right. Frustrated rage burned within his borrowed body, and a mighty fear of his master's fury should he fail Ashar now, so close to the successful culmination of his design. Desperately, he sought to retrieve the initiative and whispered in Hattim's ear, 'Challenge him!'

'How?' moaned Hattim. 'He has the right. Wed to Wynett, I cannot gainsay him.'

'With swords, you fool!' cursed Taws. 'Take the throne by sword right! Hold it, lest we lose everything!'

Hattim swallowed, licked fleshy lips, remembering how Kedryn had defeated him before, remembering how Kedryn had slain Niloc Yarrum, a youth then, a man now, confident of himself; frightening in that confidence.

'I cannot,' he groaned. 'He will slay me.'

'Ashar curse you,' snarled Taws, anger getting the better of him.

'Heresy!' Kedryn's voice thundered through the silence, an accusing finger levelled at the body of Sister Thera. 'The Messenger walks among you and Hattim Sethiyan is his acolyte.'

The gaze of all present fastened on the trio now standing before the two thrones. Mouths gaped wide in horror as Sister Thera's eyes burned an unholy red, like coals blazing in some hellish furnace. A woman screamed; a man shouted, echoing Kedryn's accusation. Hattim felt himself hurled forwards, staggering from the throne to stumble on the steps and topple face down to the floor. He raised his head to find Ashrivelle at his side, stooping to aid him, her hands clutching with painful force on his arm as she froze, her face horrorstruck as she looked towards the throne.

At Kedryn's side Wynett cried out in disgust. Tepshen mouthed a curse. Brannoc shaped the warding gesture with his free hand. Kedryn himself stared with an awful fascination as Taws, his fury incandescent, finally revealed himself.

The blue-robed body that had once belonged to a woman co
torted. It stretched upwards, rising to the tips of its toes as its arn
flung out, the fingers clawed. Red eyes bulged above flaring nostrils,
the mouth wide, the lips curling back from parted teeth as a weird,
high-pitched shrieking filled the throne room with ear-piercing
sound. The body shuddered, blood erupting from the mouth and
nostrils and ears, from the eyes, staining the gown of Estrevan blue
about the loins. It thickened where it came from the gaping lips,
oozing over the chest, coagulating. The body fell back against the
throne, fouling the stone with its outpourings, and the blood pooled
dense in the lap. Then, though after none there could describe it
precisely, unsure whether what they saw came from the blood or
from thin air, a shape formed, hovering about the writhing body,
becoming solid.

Kedryn gazed at the wraith. Saw it become flesh, if flesh it was that
clad that awful shape, and knew that he faced his destiny. Taws stood
before him, ghastly in his nakedness, though even the malformed
contortion of his unhuman lineaments could not surpass the sheer
horror of his rage. Red eyes burned in sunken sockets, narrow lips
drawn back in a snarl from pointed teeth, the mantis face framed by
a mane of corpse-white hair. An arm that hinged unlike any human
limb extended taloned fingers towards Kedryn, and from them came
a wash of flame.

'No!' Wynett's shout was a denial of Taws' power, of his intent,
and at the same time a declaration of her love.

She flung herself before Kedryn, one hand about her talisman,
holding it out so that the flame of the mage's gramarye burst
against it, filling the air with a charnel stink. She was thrown back
against Kedryn, and he held her, believing her burned until she cried
again, 'No!'

That shout broke the hypnotic fascination Taws exerted and he
set a hand to his own talisman, knowing instinctively that only the
blue stones could offer salvation from the destruction that threatened. It seemed then that he stepped aside from time, that with
Wynett he entered some limbo existing contemporaneously with the
chronology that governed life, facing the Messenger on a plane that
transcended the existence of human flesh. He saw Brannoc hurl a
knife, and witnessed the blade burst into flame, falling in molten
droplets to the floor. He saw Taws laugh and turn both taloned
hands, palms outwards, towards him, a great flood of fire, a tidal
wave of flame, roar towards him. Not knowing how he knew, he

thrust out his own free hand – saw Wynett do the same – and saw Taws' fire again repulsed. He saw Tepshen raise his blade high and charge the mage, and turned his hand to send a wash of blue light out to the kyo, bathing the yelling warrior in its radiance. He saw Taws turn, sending tongues of flame licking at Tepshen, and the tongues die as they touched the pulsing blue effulgence, Tepshen's blade descending in a lethal arc that ended and rebounded as it met the grey-white hide of the Messenger, Taws hand lash out to send Tepshen staggering back as if his blow had struck a wall of rock.

'Stay back!' he roared, and felt Wynett take his hand, her touch enhancing the power he could feel within himself, the glow of their two talismans increasing with the contact, pulsing fiercer, surrounding them until they moved within the shield of its radiance.

That sense of purpose that had gripped him before, that surety, was on him now, stronger than when he first fought Hattim or Niloc Yarrum, stronger than ever, and with Wynett at his side he moved towards the insectile figure that roared and bellowed beside the High Throne. Waves of furious red fire burst from Taws outthrust hands and were repulsed by the blue light. Tapestries burst into flame and stone melted, lava seething across the chamber's floor. Tepshen Lahl rose unsteadily to his feet and retreated from the capering figure of the mage, Brannoc moving to support the kyo, the two drawing back from a duel they recognised as Kedryn's and Wynett's alone, knowing it utilised powers far greater than sword blades. The Galichians and those incumbents of the White Palace still remaining ran in screaming panic from the holocaust.

Kedryn shouted, 'Get out! Clear the chamber!' and advanced on the ghastly shape of Taws.

Flame crackled about the Messenger now, fire escaping his lipless mouth, tendrils of smoke oozing oily from his nostrils and ears. It seemed he had become the very embodiment of his frightful master, less flesh than some combustible thing, a reeking fire demon that howled and pranced, hurling bolts of random energy carelessly. The throne itself cracked and burned, becoming molten, the deserted corpse of Sister Thera withering, the flesh blackening, melding with the liquefying stone of the regal chair. Windows shattered, exploding glassy shrapnel in a whistling rain throughout the chamber; candles melted in sconces that themselves glowed white hot, dripping metal tears over blackened walls; wood flamed, pungent smoke miasmic in the thickened, stinking air.

'You cannot slay me,' Taws rasped, and directed a bolt of glowing energy at the vaulted roof.

Stone fell in a murderous rain about his opponents, but though blocks the size of a full grown man crashed down, none touched them, for it seemed the azure radiance held them within a cone of force through which nothing might penetrate. Guided by that power that was in him and beyond him, Kedryn raised a hand that unleashed blue light at the Messenger, hurling Taws backwards as if a great wind tossed him wilfully as a storm-driven leaf. He flew from the dais, tumbling to the floor behind, and when he rose Kedryn saw fear in his stance, a hesitation born of doubt. He raised his hand again, and now Wynett joined him, the lances of light that erupted from both their hands joining, sending Taws rolling over the flags.

They climbed the steps of the dais, ignoring the molten stone that ran beneath their feet, ignoring the almost consumed corpse, their eyes fixed on the hunched figure beyond, their features grim as they raised their hands again.

Taws met the bolt of blue with a spear of red, and the convergence of those twin sources of power erupted in a thunderclap that shook the rotunda, spilling more stone from the fractured roof, the flash of the explosion blinding them momentarily.

When their vision cleared they saw the Messenger scuttling crab-like along the wall, reminiscent of some obscene spider, each step he took imprinting a smoking mark upon the flags. Again they raised their hands and sent the purity of the blue energy lashing over him, and now the Messenger screamed in pain and terror writhing back with uplifted hands, his ghastly features contorted as he sought to ward off the potency of that cleansing puissance. It was a power greater than his, for it was born of compassion and affection, honest in its intent, stemming from the Lady's benign concern and the love shared by Kedryn and Wynett, and for all his rage Taws knew that and felt its greatness. Felt it as it drove him back, remorselessly, his own weakening as he fought it, draining from him until he crouched, cornered like a rat, in the angle of the walls.

Wynett's right hand held firmly in his left, Kedryn maintained the flow of energy, joining it with the light that blasted from his wife's outthrust left hand. It mingled with the fire glow emanating from Taws, darkening to violet, becoming a midnight black tinged deep within with red. The Messenger became invisible, wrapped in the weird light as they descended the far side of the dais and moved inexorably towards him. As they drew closer the talismans they wore pulsed brighter and the black began to fade, assuming again the azure effulgence, a core of crimson at its centre.

From within that core came a wailing scream. 'Master, save me! Ashar, I beg you!'

And a booming voice filled the rotunda with its thunder, so loud the words were indistinct, contempt dripping from each syllable, implacable in its unhuman severity.

'*You have failed me.*'

'Ashar!' Taws screamed. 'Ashar, I am yours. Master, save me!'

His cry was despairing as the two continued their advance, the shimmering force they sent out becoming brighter, stronger with each step.

Suddenly fire flared bright within the veiling blue. A stink as of scorching flesh gusted mephitic through the chamber and the reverberant voice rang out again.

'*He is mine.*'

The fire burned fiercer, swelling within the encompassing azure, transcending colour to become pure light, a core of blinding intensity that then dwindled to a pinprick and flashed out.

Kedryn blinked, realising that the blue radiance was faded, slowly aware that the talisman no longer pulsed in his grip. The afterimage of that incredible brilliance still burned against his retinas and as his sight returned he saw that where Taws had crouched there was now only a blackened stain, the great blocks of the wall and the stones of the floor bubbling liquid, oily smoke rising to mingle with the stench of smouldering tapestries and burning wood. He turned, still holding Wynett's hand, letting it go only when she stood close against him and he could put his arms around her and reassure himself of the physical presence, her arms about his waist, her eyes intent on his.

'We defeated him,' she whispered, scarce believing what they had done.

'We have saved the Kingdoms,' he murmured.

'Is he dead?' she asked.

'I do not know,' he said, feeling weary now, 'I do not know if such as the Messenger *can* die.'

'But he is gone.'

'Aye, he is gone.' Kedryn held her close, glorying in the pressure of her body against his, content in their victory. 'Dead or not, he is gone and we have won.'

They turned, seeing clearly for the first time the wreckage that lay about them. The chamber lay in ruins. The king's throne was melted down to misshapen slag, Sister Thera's body part of it; great streaks of glass-like magma cooled across the floor; chunks of masonry lay all around, a cool breeze from the jagged gap in the roof swirling the smoke that drifted from wood and cloth; the glass of the windows was run away, indeed, anything burnable was consumed. It was a scene of chaos and they left it swiftly, seeking the fresher air of the chambers beyond.

The great wooden doors existed no longer, only a pile of white ash that was warm beneath their feet as they stepped through the smoke to see the corridor filled with frightened faces, unsure who – or what – might emerge victorious from that epic combat. The folk of Andurel had broached the walls, or been granted passage by Hattim's soldiers, for now they stood shoulder to shoulder with the Galichians, nobles and servants mingled, soldiery and city folk, differences forgotten in the frightful recognition of Hattim's apostasy. They cheered as they saw Kedryn and Wynett, the Galichians no less forcefully than those who had remained loyal. Galen was there, beaming hugely, and Brannoc, a grin on his dark features, and Ashrivelle, her face unnaturally pale, tears flooding from her eyes.

At her feet lay Hattim Sethiyan, a knife protruding from his back. Brannoc stooped to retrieve it. Wiped the blade casually on the usurper's finery and shrugged innocently as he held out the king's medallion to Kedryn.

'He sought to flee. I stopped him.'

Kedryn nodded. For now he could not find it in himself to pity the Galichian, for Hattim had chosen the path he trod and in so doing brought terror down on Andurel and the threat of war to the Kingdoms.

'Where are my parents?' he asked. 'Where is Tepshen?'

'Gone to find them,' said Brannoc. 'It seems Hattim at least accorded them the privilege of imprisonment in their own quarters.'

Again Kedryn nodded, turning to Ashrievelle now.

He was about to speak but she halted him with a shake of her head, drawing herself up with obvious effort. 'I did not know,' she said softly, her voice frightened. 'I loved him, but I did not know what he did. It was as though some spell was laid on me.'

'Sister,' Wynett said gently, and left the circle of Kedryn's arm to hug her sibling.

Ashrivelle burst into fresh tears, clutching Wynett as might a drowning man clutch a floating spar. 'I will make amends,' she wailed. 'If such is possible. I will go to Estreavan and devote my life to making good the ill I supported.'

'You did not know,' Wynett comforted. 'The Messenger held thrall here and you cannot be blamed.'

Kedryn put a hand upon her shoulder and said, 'His power was great, Princess, no blame rests on you.'

Ashrivelle turned grateful eyes towards him and he smiled gently. Then his expression became one of pure pleasure as the crowd parted on Tepshen's shout to allow Bedyr and Yrla passage through, Jarl and Arlynn close behind.

'Praise the Lady,' said Yrla, throwing her arms about him. 'You are safe.'

Bedyr put his arms about them both, his smile jubilant. 'You slew the creature?'

'He is gone,' said Kedryn quietly.

'And you are risen,' said Bedyr, solemnly. 'Tepshen has told us of your marriage.'

Kedryn nodded, extending a hand to Wynett, who moved to join them, her face radiant.

'Welcome, daughter,' smile Bedyr.

'Oh, Wynett!' Yrla kissed the younger woman. 'How happy you make me.'

They stood for long moments, oblivious of the crowd, content with the closeness, happy in the ending of a nightmare, then they turned away and Kedryn drew Wynett close again as they walked together towards their shared future.